O o O o O o O o O o Q

"The supreme irony of the universe has got to be that a planet of raving maniacs, hidebound traditionalists of the worst sort, haters —no, despisers of all outsiders, is able to ferment the one thing the rest of us need absolutely, the longlife drug.

"To our credit, they have never been subjugated, but we don't permit them modern weapons, either. They have tried—give them credit for that, and they're plenty inventive, but since they have to endure us, they don't object to making a profit at it.

"Now if they had the device that Speculations is trying to perfect here on Mulcahen, a means of tracking and targetting spaceships without a visible artifact at cosmic distances, then the drug supply would be cut off. . . ."

WAVES

M. A. Foster

DAW BOOKS, INC.
DONALD A. WOLLHEIM, PUBLISHER
1633 Broadway, New York, N.Y. 10019

FIRST PRINTING, OCTOBER 1980

1 2 3 4 5 6 7 8 9

 DAW TRADEMARK REGISTERED
U.S. PAT. OFF. MARCA
REGISTRADA. HECHO EN U.S.A.

PRINTED IN U.S.A.

1

Fraesch had been dozing through planetfall. He woke up now, suddenly. Gravity, real gravity, was different, he thought. Our bodies betray us—they still sense one G and nothing else feels quite right. Ship gravity, being generated from an arbitrary plane surface, lacks the mass centeredness of real gravity. Now they were beginning to return to real-body referents. The windows: Fraesch tried his cabin window, and the safety catch released and he slid the visor up.

An outside! By God, there *was* an outside, instead of a hyperspace nothing, an absence, a furry emptiness that looked like a hangover felt, or the static of an empty wave band sounded. An outside: a black sky full of stars, piercing naked sunlight, and then below, where his eye fell, brown-golden earth, writhing courses where water had been, or was, all dimmed and made subtle and mysterious by the haze layer; patches of rust, pale blue, purple. Imbedded in the haze layer, to the shrinking horizon were cumulonimbus clouds, still small and faraway, but the scale of how much of the planet he was seeing told him how large they really were; enormous, by any measure. Over water and land, so it seemed, about equally.

There were about ten of them in view, scattered without plan or system, so it seemed; blinding white in body, but also stippled, freckled, delicately laced with a tracery of colors diminished by distance—red, brown, venomous green. Thunderstorms! Fraesch watched the perspective change as the liner *Severo-Pelengator* dropped into the atmosphere of the planet Mulcahen, streaming its braking drogue parachutes forty kilometers behind it.

There was a faint whistling sound from outside, and the ship began to enter the atmosphere proper. The storms were still below, but now not so far. How high were they in the air? He wondered how they looked from the ground. They looked unreal: swelling bulbs of what unknown flower,

5

sprung from the leaf mold and moss of the forest floor. Twenty kilometers? He couldn't tell. But as he watched, he could sense that there was activity in them, subtle movements just barely too slow to be seen directly. Flashes inside. . . . There! A fretwork of golden electricity crawled groundwards over the surface of one, like raw nerves, like . . . what? The current fell cascading out of the filmy hailstone top, extended to the spread skirts buried in the ground haze layer and held for an impossible moment, writhing; then faded out, last along the lower parts, indescribably beautiful and bizarre.

The *Severo-Pelengator* began to bump and sway a little. The *G* warning light illuminated and a soft, unemotional voice whispered, directly in his mind, so it seemed (though he knew very well that it was direct stimulation of the aural nerves), "For our descent, deceleration is imminent. With your safety in mind, we ask that you now attempt no sudden movements, as you are being restrained by protective fields."

Fraesch's eyes felt heavy, leaden, and along the edges of his field of vision he saw fire. . . . The ship gave a sudden, solid bump, and then felt floaty, disconnected. He felt the field relax and looked out again, *up* at the hailstone veil tops of the nearer storms. The sky around the storm tops was a peculiar neon-aqua color, deep and electric in its intensity; blue, yes, it was blue, but also with a green overtone.

Now they were a part of the planet, disengaged from the free flight of space. The remainder of the grounding of the huge mass of the *Severo-Pelengator* would take considerable time, perhaps an hour, perhaps more, towed to the ground by tugs. Fraesch decided to review the handout they had given him about Mulcahen once more, to pass the time well.

Fraesch retrieved his briefcase and withdrew a package from it. He glanced out the window, looking for evidence of continued descent; yes, they were well within the atmosphere now. The storms seemed farther away, their tops reddened by distance into dirty orange. Only the nearer ones showed. There was more ground detail visible, though. He could make out highlands, drainage basins, broad flats. . . . The land looked dry, but not desert. It was mostly gold and brown, with scattered spots of blue and purple, and a very dark greenish black, which he presumed to mark vegetation. He turned his attention to the papers in the package.

The first was a letter from an old colleague, Ramo Pergales. It was on company letterhead, the logo displaying a stylized image of a pleasant, competent man of no discernible age rising from behind a simple desk in greeting. The address read: INTERCORD, S.A., Contractural Administrative Services, 440 Yeni Harman Caddesi, 18 Erzerum 1485, Turan, on Yagmur. The letter ran:

To: Fraesch, Joachim, L9a/44-14643343-3152947-F
Re: Your Reassignment
Fm: Pergales

Dear Jake:

1. Was informed of this transfer so I send you best wishes and good luck. This is a routine Tempo-Replacement, of course, until later, as you know. Should be about a year or so, judging from the contract parameters.

2. There's been some loose talk about concerning this one, all unconfirmed and unsupported. But there well may be some curious circumstances there; or perhaps not. At any rate, I should advise some alertness and use of the skill. We'd like to have you back here in the "schoolhouse."

3. Atch is a report on the planet. A bit raw for my taste, a recently opened developing world and all that; but you field men always did seem fond of roughing it. Advise.

Regards,
R.

Fraesch had just glanced at the letter before he left, and he had not perused it intently during the trip. But one phrase caught his attention, out of context: ". . . curious circumstances . . . like to have you back. . . ." Were circumstances such that he might not come back? There had been no mention of danger, or indeed, of any but the most routine sort of hazards in this situation.

Fraesch reviewed what he knew: that Mulcahen was a world owned by KOSTORG, which was an acronym for Kosmicheskaya Torgovlya, Ltd—typical frontier exploitation outfit. They had bought it on a speculation from Yildizlar Maddesi, who in turn bought out its discoverer, one Patrice Mulcahen. He had retired, and well he could afford to.

A research and development company, Speculations, Inc.,

had leased a small landholding on the coast for the purpose
of doing long-term data collection research, using ocean
waves as the presumed data source. Fraesch did not know
what they were looking for, nor was he especially interested.

It seemed that the station director needed replacing, and so
Speculations, Inc. had contracted with Intercord for a temporary station administrator until a qualified replacement
could be recruited for the original director, one Leonid Moricle. Fraesch did not know what had happened to Moricle. He
hoped, with some general charity, that it had been nothing
bad. Still, people were replaced and pulled out of operations
for cause; otherwise, how would Fraesch have had a profession all these years? And, apparently, Moricle had been fairly
highly specialized for whatever they were doing at the station,
which Fraesch recalled had been named with some flair—
"Halcyon." A place on the northwest coast.

Mulcahen had been discovered by Patrice Mulcahen almost fifty standard years ago; he had sold it to Yildizlar
Maddesi, who had promptly sent an exploration team in. But
YM was oriented toward agricultural products and natural
organics, and the reports on Mulcahen had not been encour-
aging. They had kept a claim party there, but done almost
nothing with it. Some of the party had wandered off into the
wilds and apparently gone native. There were no intelligent
life forms.

YM was a small company, and they had more promising
planets to develop, so Mulcahen had languished, almost forgotten—except by YM's comptroller, who had still been sending royalties to Patrice Mulcahen for discoverer's rights. They
had put it up for sale, and KOSTORG had picked it up with
a minimum of haggling. The reason was that KOSTORG was
a metals specialist, and Mulcahen was apparently rich in
metals. They occupied the planet immediately, paying fantastic bonuses to those who would go there and rough it and
who would become the founders of a world in the future.

Mulcahen was a small world with a single continent which
occupied 22 percent of the planetary surface. The continent,
named Pangaea by the YM explorers, was roughly pear-
shaped, with the stem of the pear aligned over the north pole.
This region was also mountainous, and was permanently gla-
ciated. The single continent was elevated and flattish in the
interior, slightly mountainous along the west coast, and rather
nondescript along the east. Along the foot of the great glacier

of the north a belt of tundra separated the icelands from more temperate lands; a zone of humid continental which gave way to Mediterranean in the west and subtropical in the east. Below that was a desert area north of the equator, open to the west, and tropical rain forest along the equator itself. South of the equator, below the forest zone, where the continent ended in the southern ocean, forest gave way to savanna, which in turn became desert, which through oxidation of iron compounds had taken on a ruddy hue. Out in the vast ocean, which the YM explorers had named the Empyrean Sea, orbital imaging systems had spotted several small islands and atolls, but these had never been explored.

Mulcahen had a 30 degree axial tilt; accordingly, seasons were notable and the seasonal changes were abrupt to a ground observer. The native vegetation, although somewhat deciduous in the north temperate latitudes, was apparently exclusively gymnospermous, the entire planet being covered with conifer analogues and fernlike low plants. The predominant colors of the vegetation were blue and purple, with some reddish types. A very few were dark green.

KOSTORG had built their administrative center near the center of the continent, and with singular lack of imagination named it Gorod.[1] A complex in the northeastern hill country had been set aside for heavy industry and metallurgy and had been called, with equal candor, Promysel.[2] This latter was popularly called Zavody[3], meaning the general area, or virtually a province, although the term had no official sanction.

The KOSTORG operation had been in effect long enough to show some results: some mines were in operation, some mills were producing; basic heavy industries making heavy capital goods were beginning to make some inroads on the imported goods, and in the settled areas, chiefly around Gorod, and in Zavody, there was an air of raffish self-sufficiency, despite the fact that almost all consumer articles were still being imported, at enormous cost, from most finished worlds closer to the center.[4]

[1] Russian, city
[2] Russian, trade, or industry, or both, considered as a whole.
[3] Russian, factories.
[4] Human space in this space-time may be viewed as an expanding sphere, whose leading edge or surface is entirely controlled and operated by private enterprise organizations financed by investments from the interior. Only the older planets have governments in the strictest sense of the term, and none of these extends out

Fraesch surmised as he read. At a point, he put the report back in the envelope, and that back in the case. That it said little was plain enough; what it hadn't said was worth volumes more; there had been nothing in the report—an ordinary commercial intelligence report—about transportation, entertainment, tourist amenities, sights to see, notable accomplishments. Nothing! And the reason was simple—there were none! He favored the mottled landscape outside the window a suspicious glance and imagined the surface of Mulcahen: dust, insects and tent cities with ditch sanitary systems. They probably ran convoys of crawlers between settlements, when there was travel at all. A raw, untamed world full of mining engineers, eating spam from a tin and using a packing case for a table. And where he was going was considered remote, for this planet! He sighed once, deeply, and thought wryly that at least he wouldn't be squandering his bonuses.

Fraesch keyed the call switch, and when the amber light illuminated, asked the ship's computer for a ground-weather summary. There was a slight pause while the data center deep in the ship extracted information, and vocoded it in a voice it judged would be pleasantly neutral and reassuring to Fraesch.

It said, in a soft alto that was unmistakably female, "Current time, Mulcahen Standard for this longitude, is 1630 hours. Sunset will occur in less than two hours. Bear in mind that due to the day here being shorter than the standard day, because of more rapid rotation, it will seem even shorter. In words, it is late afternoon, evolving to dusk.

"The temperature is 18 degrees centigrade, and surface winds in the Gorod vicinity are calm to light and variable, which is unusual for the season. The season is autumn. The provisional Mulcahen calendar consists of a year of 372 days, divided into twelve months of 31 days each, with provision for an adjustment year every ten years. The date is day nine, month ten."

Fraesch substituted in his mind. *October ninth!*

It continued, "Conditions are expected to remain stable

---

of its own planetary system, although certain "customsunions" exist. This is a consequence of governments deciding space had no value. The system is not without abuses, but on the whole, its effect has been beneficial. One immediate by-product of great value has been the lack of interstellar war, for megalomania has proved to be, to date, unprofitable. Conflict continues to exist; however, it is on a very small scale.

over central Pangaea for at least four more days, with a
slight warming trend being in effect. During this period no
precipitation is anticipated, although haze conditions will be
more noticeable, and ground condensation will be heavy in
low elevations. Frost cannot be ruled out."

Again the voice paused, and then said, with slightly more
authority, "PPZ wishes to appreciate your patronage, and to
remind you that we offer monthly service to and from Mulcahen with suitable accommodations for all classes, as well as a
complete schedule of both chordic and radial connections.
We trust your visit will be an enjoyable experience."

Fraesch chuckled to himself. ". . . complete schedule . . .
PPZ wishes" . . . *Putesheshtviya Po Zvezdam*[1] was a jack-
leg tramp freighter outfit specializing in near-monopoly service to obscure worlds. As soon as other lines started landing
on those worlds, PPZ found reasons to terminate that service.
They were well to do so, for almost any line was better.
However, the company had remained solvent for a remarkable span of time and showed new vigor with each new year.
It was, after all, Fraesch thought, just the kind of thing he'd
expect. Or should have expected.

And now he was on Mulcahen. The port had been flung
open, and there had been a confusion of late-afternoon slant-
ing sunlight lying across amber-gold tawny plains and sweep-
ing rises, not quite hills. There had also been a babble of
voices, odd fragments of obscure languages, unfamiliar signals and opaque idioms from the ground crewmen, voices
from those tossing his scanty baggage out of the hold, others
directing him to a surface transporter which would convey
them to Gorod, which was some distance over the hill to the
east. He had time for nothing more than impressions.

These impressions: open country, rather level but not especially flat, for there were sweeps and rises all about, some
peaking in stony outcrops of a brown, flaky rock. In the distances there were higher ridges, none quite the height of real
hills. Open distances, and nowhere could he see any sign of
habitation. The spaceport was nothing more than an unoccu-
pied tract of land marred by the pad marks of the landing
feet of the spaceships. Around the edges rested hastily erected
shantylike buildings, made apparently of native woods—

[1] Russian, Travels among the stars.

machine shops, warehouses, a communications hut. It was desolation and crudity.

The transporter, a hovercraft of trashy appearance and noisy operation, obviously a local product, had waited for them, motors idling, Fraesch thought it looked like an omnibus built by small boys to model a streamlined battle cruiser. It had six fans; four large ones about a third of the way from the stern, protected by decorative fenders which were much dented and abused. Two smaller fans at the front, protruding in chinlike housings, steered the craft. Squatting in the dirt on its landing brace bars, the fan skirts crumpled, it had the appearance of a bored dog.

Now they were underway. The shuttle slewed and lurched along a wide dirt trail winding eastward into the growing darkness. The seats were wooden benches with low backs, and all the visible metalwork showed the marks of hasty and ill conceived assembly: dents and overlaps where pieces had been hammered to fit, bolts too small for the hole, fitted in with assorted washers from the junk box, suspicious-looking welds that looked burned in with coat hangers melted by landing flares. The fans, housings, bearings and motors all emitted a catalog of the sounds of mechanical distress. The skirts, dirty canvas, lead-weighted along the hems, rolled and flapped as clouds of yellow dust billowed about the careening shuttle. Fraesch could catch a glimpse of the pilot from time to time, as the lurching, alarming motions presented him a short view across the other passengers; he saw a man striving mightily with the steering bars and lift levers. It seemed the controls were direct mechanical linkages, a thing Fraesch could not recall seeing outside museums.

Through breaks in the curtain of dust thrown up by the fans, Fraesch could make out an occasional passing transporter or lorry, skidding on hoverfans, or pounding madly on oversize pneumatic tires and ruberoid bladders, the drivers all making ferocious gestures at the lunging shuttle. Some of them bore heraldic badges and legends; others, personal designs and logos. Still others had only plain paint over dented and scarred surfaces. One he saw particularly well had carried a load of sand, and had been emblazoned by an enormous drawing of a grimacing insect holding a tool in each of its six claws as it flew, and whose rear end glowed and emitted stylized lightning bolts. A flowery script below it said "Lightning bug," but Fraesch couldn't determine if the name pertained to some company or to the driver, or perhaps the

vehicle. It vanished into the dust, westbound, engine pro-
testing.

Their own laboring engines shifted tone to a deeper throbbing, indicating a greater strain; they were climbing a gentle
grade now.

Half fearing a probable collision, Fraesch had paid little
attention to the rest of the passengers; they had all come with
the liner *Severo-Pelengator*, save a handful of what appeared
to be locals, probably sneak thieves and barroom bums
hoping to cadge some off-world currency in return for a
guidance to the pleasure spots of Gorod. He thought, half-
hoping, that Gorod wasn't as rough as Magnitogorsk-Mars,
where the whores plied their trade in the access alleys between the iron extractors. Veritable thruppenny uprights!
Aheu! Magnitogorsk-Mars had been ghastly, sure enough.

Seeing that the driver seemed to have the shuttle well in
hand, Fraesch looked about. All of those he saw bore expressions of apprehension, or numbness. The voyage was
over, and now the reality of a rude world intruded. There
would be dust, inconvenience, a line to the public baths.
Beside him sat a woman whom Fraesch recalled seeing once
or twice aboard the ship, in the lounge, but she had been as
unremarkable then as she was now. Except. . . . She was not
attractive in the popular sense. She used no skin toning, nor
did she draw accents on the contours of her face. A professional type, obviously—medic, perhaps a metallurgist or computer technician. Clipboards and hard hats! But she was also
one of a rare type who revealed an extraordinary beauty . . .
on a second look. There was nothing about her face which
Fraesch would have written in his journal to key a memory
with the subtle alchemy of words. Except that she had very
pale, clear skin, luminous dark eyes of a brown so dark it
seemed black in the failing evening light, black, short hair cut
short and severely, which highlighted her face rather than
diminishing it, and the delicate structure of one born and
trained to the intense study of the arts. The hands, tightly
clenching her attaché case in her lap, echoed the face: pale,
slender, aesthetic and delicate. He could see her painting, or
playing a musical instrument (a violin rather than some
grunting saxophone, which had recently come back into favor) or doing something which required fine touch. Fraesch
felt a little sorry for her, whoever she was; Mulcahen was by
no means an art colony!

Noting his regard, the woman leaned over so as to be heard above the clangor of the roaring shuttle, and said, "Excuse me. I quite forgot to ask what the season was as we were landing. It seems cold."

She was wearing a blue blazer, a rather chestless loose blouse, tan culottes which fell well below the knee and dark boots. She looked like a cross between a storm trooper and a gypsy, with her true sympathies at odds with both appearances. The clothing was light and airy.

He answered, "It's autumn, so I believe. It said that it had been a bit warm for the season. Mulcahen has strong axial tilt, so I expect a hard, sharp winter. I hope you brought adequate clothing."

She looked off at the violet landscape. They were still laboring up the low rise, hovercraft performance falling off on inclines. She said, "I had little enough time to pack; one always thinks it won't be so different from where you were."

"You were on a pleasant world?"

"Aegaea."

"Indeed? I heard that is where the discoverer of Mulcahen retired. One of those islands."[1]

"The whole planet is islands."

Fraesch said, politely, "I've never been there. Always wanted to go, but somehow. . . ."

"Most people think they added the islands to what was already there, but it's more than that. Before the islands were dropped, there was nothing but water. A shallow sea covers the whole world."

Fraesch commented, "I would have imagined that a native of Aegaea would have been more . . . something more of a suntanned amazon."

"I was working on one of the northern islands, and besides I don't tan well." She waved one hand in a delicate gesture of

[1] Aegaea had originally been covered with water. A land sales company, irritated with such insipid waste of potentially valuable real estate, had combed the local stellar system for stony asteroids, and then, with clusters of rocket motors braking their fall, had dropped thousands onto the surface, to invent rocky islands in the shallow seas. These they had sold off at enormous profit, despite the fact that there was no fresh water on the whole planet except that which fell as rain, and no soil, and no vegetation. Today, Aegaea is a noted tourist world whose permanent inhabitants and paid workers are noted for their thrift and reclusiveness.

self-deprecation. "Nothing seems to work." But she smiled as she said it.

Fraesch inquired, "May I ask your name?"

She paused a fractional bit of time and answered, as if slightly reluctant, "Techist Vicinczin." She retained some formality, giving title and surname only, not a personal name or lineage name. But Fraesch's first impression had been correct: she was a technician. He wondered, of what?

He introduced himself, "Clericist Joachim Fraesch. I work for Intercord." That alone would tell her a lot, for Intercord was well known.

It was now almost dark outside. She looked away, shyly, and then said, softly, "My first name is Tula. Are you . . ." And then she stopped, for two things happened in close succession.

The first was that they topped the rise separating Gorod from the landing field. Gorod, it seemed, had been situated in the center of a vast depression, an enlarged rift valley. They could not see much of the road, but out there on the open plains spread a large city of glistening lights. There was still the softest hint of deep violet in the sky, and the brightest stars were visible, but Gorod dimmed them. There seemed to be no tall buildings, at least not tall enough to stand out of the background. It was a magic carpet of multicolored, rippling pastels, with points of harder light among them. It was both beautiful and incongruous.

As they gaped like tourists, the second thing happened. Someone abruptly sat on the bench on the other side of Fraesch. When Fraesch turned to see who it was, the person began talking to him.

He said, "Sir, your pardon. I look for a passenger from the great ship. I hold a commission for the finding of such a person as would be known as J. Fraesch."

Fraesch looked at the man critically. He was of indeterminable age, but whatever it might have been, it was his own; from his appearance it was obvious that this man had never had access to the drugs that lengthened life and retained, if not the suppleness of youth, at least the hard competence of maturity. This one was bearded and ragged, dressed, despite the chill in the air, in a cast-off jacket, torn trousers tied with rope at the waist and sandals made from a section of truck tire. His skin was weathered and tanned and around the watery eyes were deep squint lines.

Fraesch said, coolly, "I know of Fraesch. Who is it that wants him?"

"The guide, the fixer, the arranger of deals by night. Also orphan of the streets and the serf of none, a freeman, myself, Malo Pomalu," the man declaimed, striking a dramatic pose. He said, "See yonder city gleaming in the autumn dusk? Beautiful, is it not? There the strivers strive in constant strife. Held on the old but made on the new, as they say of money and the planets. And truly advantage is to be had here on poor empty Mulcahen, Mulcahen whose people are immigrants, starfish on the beach, stranded far from home, which is not a place but a way to do things and biscuits that taste correct." He had accented his last name on the penultimate, which gave the name an odd rhythmic canter.

His speech made little sense, Fraesch thought. Here, indeed, was a fool, one of the derelicts from the underside of the city, come out to try a cheap little swindle, a little confidence game. Fraesch thought that with chilly contempt, but he also noted that the man was shivering from the cold, or infection, and recalled that on a planet like Mulcahen, there would be little protection from foot pads and highwaymen.

He said, "You are Pomalu?"

"Yes. Malo Pomalu. And you are Fraesch. Who else would be so careful."

Fraesch sat back. Indeed. A fool, but a shrewd one. And one whose name was not a name but a phrase in Old Russian, that meant, "little by little." Fraesch felt a momentary panic. Had they spotted him so fast? And how had it gotten to Mulcahen, to the street, that he was doing a little contract intelligence gathering on the side for a rival of KOSTORG. He couldn't test him, either, here on the shuttle. And even then, he couldn't be sure of the answers he'd get.

He said, reluctantly, "I am Fraesch. What do you need of me?"

The hooligan answered, "Blyadu Budu![1] Luck on the first try! I ask to serve as your guide through the maze you are about to enter."

"How do you know of J. Fraesch? Is he so renowned?"

"Tsk. *Ehrundah and Ehrenburg!*[2] Is it such a mystery? Passenger lists may be seen at the port. Communications flow

---

[1] Russian, profane euphemism.
[2] Literally, "Nonsense and Ehrenburg." Ehrenburg was a 20th-century writer and critic.

across the void to facilitate exits and entries. *Buyurun!*[3] My patron is an ordinary sort, a person of mostly local concerns, who will wish your aid without the interference which other concerns might place in the way. He has, as you might say, a mystery he cannot unravel."

"Be that as it may, how does he know of me?"

"On another ship, the passengers leave the newspapers they brought with them—it's old news when they get here. But not to us! And so I clean the cabins and cart off the trash, and trade it off. We can't read some of it, we can't, but some of it we can. And he reads about the contract admin man who uncovered the gentlemen swindlers on Bedistlisle, and there's a letter which he reads that says you're coming here. *Tamam!* And he says, he does, 'There's one I can't suspect,' and he'll get to the bottom of it."

"A simple, plausible reason."

He agreed. Pomalu said, "Simple people, most of us."

"You will take me to your man for an honorarium?"

Pomalu raised a callused hand. "A moment! Not in the least! Not a crust, not a grosh, not a den'ga! I have already been paid."

"What's grosh and den'ga?"

"Den'gi are monies here—that's what they call it. Money is 'money,' after the motherland. And 72 grosh make one den'ga; no decimal abstractions for us! Here, now, I've done my job."

"You've done nothing! Who am I looking for?"

"You'll find him, he'll find you; where two look so hard, they can't fail. As a fact, he's come to town to take you there, and the others will take you to him. But don't believe what they say."

"What do they say?"

"That which you must ignore, a distraction. Noise." Here Pomalu paused, to give emphasis to the word noise.

Fraesch asked, "Why is this important . . .?" He let the end trail off ambiguously.

Pomalu gestured at the city lights, now much closer. He said, "Do you think they would shut that off like throwing trash in a bin? But men came here and found an Eden, a Cretaceous Eden, and they'll clean it out like a slug works an apple. But now, and now it's still costing them to set it up,

---

[3] Turkish, "If you please . . ." Used to one entering a house or business.

and if they were to lose it, a lot of den'gi would float away. Make no mistake about that, they'll kill to keep it. And now . . . good evening!"

And with that, he stood up, slipped acrobatically to a hatch just behind one of the aft fan housings and deftly stepped out of the hovercraft, rolling as he landed to soften his contact with the ground. Fraesch looked for him behind them, but he was lost in the dusty darkness.

Now Fraesch sat still for a time, as much as he could, allowing for the motions of the shuttle. He tried to sort out what he had heard from a ragged derelict who very obviously knew much, much more than he was telling. Fraesch felt as if he had been subjected to a bombardment of ideas, if he could only sort them out. And Pomalu—whatever his real name was—was neither retarded nor shy, but might have been abnormally sensitive to . . . what? A listener who didn't have some key piece that he would have given away by speaking too directly. Now. What was it? Someone was looking for him. . . . No. Someone was waiting for him. A person who . . . had no conspirator's part, but was acting on his/her own; and who . . . was tampering with a puzzle which might be extremely dangerous to try to open. Another thought occurred to him as well; was there any connection between the warning implicit in Pergales' letter, and this "little-by-little"? Fraesch sighed. Things were not going to be simple here, not at all. But—and he brightened at this a little—he had, as Pomalu had known, run them to earth on Bedistlisle. And that had been a murky environment, indeed.

Tula Vicinczin interrupted his musings: "Who was that man? Do you know him?"

Fraesch started to answer, but stopped. He substituted, "He was a panhandler, a tout, a . . . a factotum of sorts."

"A *maquereau*? Here? Already?" She looked at the ceiling briefly. "I had hoped they would not have appeared until later." There was not so much condemnation in her tone as there was a flavor of distaste. And there was also the flavor of an accent Fraesch had not heard for many a year, in the word "*maquereau*," in the "r" of it, a gargling, rolling uvular "r" one heard in few places . . . one of those places was Paris, on Earth. Perhaps he was abnormally sensitized after Pomalu, but he thought that discretion might be the better course for now where Techist Vicinczin was concerned. A pity. . . .

Fraesch commented, "Man seems to transport his ancient

vices as well as his ancient virtues. Even though I do not associate with such men, I can understand that the pressures of
society sometimes push uncommon types to the fringes. . . .
I passed him a small gratuity and advised him to seek elsewhere, which he apparently decided to do. . . . And what
are you to do on Mulcahen?"

"Lab work," she said shortly. "Nothing exciting. Or at the
least, so I hope." And she said no more.

"I trust you have made arrangements for a place to live."

"My sponsor has me traveling to the place where I am to
work tomorrow. For tonight, I have a reservation at The Export House."

Fraesch did not recognize the name. It was probably a
smaller hotel, often used by traveling representatives and professional people. Small, neat, off the main thoroughfares and
discreet. He said, "Fortunate. Intercord tells me I have a
small apartment, which they lease for such purposes, off
Cavafy Alley, number three. I have no idea how to locate it. I
don't have a map of Gorod. As a fact, I don't think one
exists."

"Perhaps the shuttle driver would know and let you off
near there. That would be useful."

"An excellent idea, for which I thank you, Techist Vicinczin. I'll just go and ask him before he gets any closer to
the city."

It had been a good place to break it off, he thought. As
he left the bench and made his way forward to the driver, he
could see that now they were very close to the city, and
he could make out the words of the signs that illuminated
the night darkness.

In the pastel light of the advertising signs he could see that
Gorod was not at all a mining camp of shanties, but a contemporary city with well-planned streets and modern buildings, most plain, but apparently well-built. Tasteful plantings
of native evergreens ornamented the courtyards of office
buildings and apartment towers, none particularly high. He
read some of the signs, looking for familiar brands and logos.
He saw Horbert Hever Engineering. Mine engineering consul-
tants. Reliable Mingo. That was a new one. One sign is soft,
deep indigo, said, Puteshestviya. As if they had any competition to advertise against. Osman Gul Elektrik. Another local.
Memoroid. Computer outfit. Empyrean Import in dusty
orange. Gastogne Beer. Underneath that one, a smaller section repeatedly spelled out, "No Artificial Bubbles," in a dart-

ing, swooping script that skillfully suggested bubbles. All of
the illuminated signs were done on soft, even colors. Nothing
garish or feverish. Amazing! KOSTORG had brought good
taste with them. And now they were quite in the city.

Fraesch had now gotten close enough to the driver to
speak to him. He said, in a relative lull in the driver's wres-
tling with the control bars, "Do you know Cavafy Alley and
can you drop me there?"

For a time, it seemed that the man had not heard him. He
continued to mind his machine, now with exaggerated care in
the clean streets of the city, as if he were carrying a load of
eggs in cement cartons. Fraesch was about to repeat his questions when the driver answered, over his shoulder, not looking back, "A tenner."

Fraesch hesitated a moment, not sure he had heard correctly. Then he said, tentatively, "I didn't change my money.
All I have are Interworld Credits."

The driver said tersely, "Twenty of those."

Fraesch thought it too much, but he agreed. "Done."

The driver freed his right hand and opened it. Fraesch
withdrew a twenty and placed it. The driver retrieved the bill,
glanced at it contemptuously, and said, "Last stop, after the
swells. Go back and sit down."

The disreputable shuttle stopped often to let the passengers
off, a time-consuming project. It seemed to follow a roundabout course, through the built up central section of Gorod,
pausing at all the major hotels, and there were a considerable
number of them. Oddly enough, none of the well-known
chains was represented; these circumstances suggested several
explanations, but the most plausible one was that there was a
shortage of other residence housing. Naturally enough—all
the leftover capital was going immediately back into the
formation of more of the same. KOSTORG was apparently
going to make Mulcahen a paying proposition as fast as hu-
manly possible. Come to think of it, he could not recall
seeing even one private residence, although they had passed
through several areas which were obviously residential. Ha!
Luxury on Mulcahen, in Gorod, consisted of a block of flats
with only ten units!

The Export House was rather large, but somewhat plain.
There had been no dramatic entry concourse, and the lobby
had resembled a back-country library—back-issue periodicals
from settled planets and company flyers from the local area.

He had offered to help Tula Vicinczin with her baggage, but she had politely refused, saying that she could manage. And she had, carrying it all in with slight struggle and no loss of composure. Fraesch had caught himself admiring the effort. What he had found somewhat out of phase with the general flow of events as suggested by Tula's remarks were the shipping tags on the valises, which naturally listed the beginning and ending of her journey. The terminal point was of course Mulcahen—coded MU/GS VIA PPZ. It was the beginning that didn't fit. It was coded ER/PL VIA REX. Which meant that she had begun her trip to Mulcahen from Earth, out of the Plesetsk Launch complex in the northwest of the Russian sector, and traveled on Radial Express most of the way. If he recalled his spatial orientation correctly, Aegaea was almost 180 degrees the other way, and at that, a long way off toward Galactic South.

He thought that there was a reasonable explanation for the discrepancy . . . but the most obvious explanation was that she had not been completely candid. Now he was curious as to why. A pity that he would never know the answer, as Fraesch imagined that he would not see the woman again. He to his assignment, she to hers, whatever it was. An interesting problem, but not an obsessive one.

Much later, with Fraesch the only passenger aboard the shuttle, they followed a roundabout course diagonally across the north-south and east-west street patterns to a quiet, tasteful neighborhood a walk away from one of the major boulevards. The buildings here were quite small, some of them suggesting only four dwellings. By the glow of amber streetlights Fraesch could see that considerable effort had been expended to plant lanes of one of the native conifers, these narrowly columnar, suggesting cypresses.

The shuttle stopped, and the driver, without looking around, announced, "This street is Cavafy Alley, to your right. I can't go into it in this thing. Number three is the second place on your left. Ask at unit one of the building—they'll have a palm-print insert and any messages, if you're expected."

Fraesch thanked the driver, collected his scanty baggage and left the shuttle. He smelled the night air, trying to feel some of the strangeness he knew had to be here, on a new world. There was nothing distinctive; only the odors he was familiar with: city odors and a pungency from the conifers not sufficiently alien to excite him. There *was* something there, but it was too subtle for him to sense enough to identify. A tingle, an ozonish sharpness? And out of the corner of his eye, he caught the flickering of a distant thunderstorm. He couldn't see *that* directly, either.

Fraesch retrieved the palm-lock for his unit from the super, whom he had interrupted smoking a narcotic herb and listening to tapes of subtle, complex music at low volume. The super had not seemed disoriented by the drug or the music, but had proceeded with efficiency and courtesy. He had identified the music as jazz of the forgotten "Third Stream Music" type, played, of course, by computers programmed to reproduce the exact flavor of the original. The originals would have been priceless, even had they existed, which both the super and Fraesch doubted. He even invited Fraesch down some evening to listen to some of his prize tapes.

There was no mail of any consequence, save a note from the local forwarding office for him to arrange to meet with a certain Shartason Aalet at the KOSTORG Building upon his arrival. That was all.

2

 ——•◆•————

Fraesch slept late, according to the rapid dawn of Mulcahen, but when he arose, he felt as if he'd gotten up too soon. The change was just enough to irritate, but not quite large enough to ignore so that one could live on arbitrary time.

His place had been on the east; the slats of louvered, narrow, double doors, in place of windows, were brightly illuminated in dappled patches from behind, but the flat was cool and dim. He opened the doors and looked out. A tiny courtyard separating his block of flats from the next seemed to be entirely filled by an enormous evergreen something like a hemlock, except that it was more delicate, stirring with every vagrant breeze, and was colored an astonishing dark blue, almost the color of blued steel, and the tiny, almost invisible needles of the foliage reflected infinitesimal sparklets of sunlight from glossy surfaces. The patterns of cool, dense shade and bright sunlight, combined with an almost alpine clarity to the air, made him feel good; fresh and confident, despite his misgivings of the evening and night before.

Breakfasting with the super, Fraesch was surprised to learn that he was not especially distant from the center of Gorod, and expressed surprise that it could be so quiet in the midst of the city.

"Not at all," commented the super from the back of the pantry. "They didn't want a real center to it in the first place, and so it got built that way. Not so difficult to find a place near work. And also, a lot of the people are out in the field somewhere. The only time it's noisy is when they're building something nearby."

Another cause for Gorod's quiet was that there were very few private vehicles which were powered, and the majority of public vehicles were electric, rolling on soft rubber tires and connected by catenaries to overhead DC lines. The electricity came from a breeder reactor located out of town to the south. They had been driven to this system because of the

23

unique distribution of energy sources on the planet—there was an overabundance of coal, but virtually no petroleum. Vehicles which needed to be free of the electrical connection burned acetylene.

The super seemed knowledgeable enough, but Fraesch felt that they could talk another time. At the least, he wanted to go and speak with this Shartason Aalet, and find out what, if any, arrangements had been made. At the least, of these the super knew nothing. He was a paroled convict and had been set to a job of limited responsibilities. He maintained the company apartments for Intercord. Folk would have to fend for themselves beyond number three Cavafy Alley.

He did, however, provide excellent directions for Fraesch to get to the KOSTORG building, and also to change his currency from ICs to Mulcahen den'gi, for the sake of convenience and economy. Unlike the inside worlds, Mulcahen, like most of the outer worlds, insisted on its own currency, printed and backed by one of the major local banks, in this case, the Yapi ve Kredi Bankasi, the Turkish title harking back to the old days when Yildizlar Maddesi SA[1] had owned the planet. The name meant "Building and Loan Bank," a singularly inconspicuous title.

The KOSTORG building was remarkably close to Cavafy Alley, close enough so that Fraesch hardly had enough time to collect his thoughts, which were confused by the discrepancy between what he had expected and the reality of Gorod, an airy, clean, modern city. On the trolley, he said as much to a fellow passenger, a young man wearing one of the ubiquitous coveralls which seemed to be the most popular type of clothing.

The fellow answered, pleasantly enough, "That's true, of course, here in Gorod; we don't notice it so much—I was born here, by the way—but outside the city it's probably more like you expect. All the settled areas are either here in the central highlands, or over eastward in Zavody. Elsewhere it's the camps, where there are people at all."

"Mulcahen's a pleasant world with no great dangers I've heard of . . . they could easily accommodate tourists as well. What about the coastal country?"

"The way I heard it, they want to do the major mining first, so they don't get tangled up with people who want to lock up private preserves. . . . There's den'gi in that, of

1 Yildizlar Maddesi: Star stuff, Turkish.

course, but much more in getting some production out of the same tract of land. . . . The coasts? There's little enough there. With only one continent, there are no ports, because there's nobody on the other side to ship to. A few depots, scattered fishing villages. You haven't seen the local animals around here, of course. Some are quite dangerous. Although they may look familiar to you, Mulcahen has some odd twists to the way its life forms filled the available spaces. You've seen things flying around?"

Fraesch said, "Yes. I assumed they were birds; I didn't pay much attention."

"Right. Things are so familiar you fit it right in. Something flew, so it's a bird. But there are no birds on Mulcahen. They never happened. The flying niche has been preempted by bats."

"Bats?"

"Bats." The local term is *kryloruki*. They do everything birds do, or things like birds, except sing. If ours sing, we can't hear them. . . . They avoid the brightest part of the day, but you'll see them everywhere. Some of the larger predatory kinds are fearless and vicious, and dangerous antagonists, despite their general fragility. I mention this as an example, because if you're going out in the field, you're going to see some wildlife; you have some new patterns to learn. . . . Here's my stop. Enjoy your visit."

A block or two later, Fraesch came to a large plaza centered on a park landscaped with more of the local evergreens, these all in shades of red. Around the borders of the plaza, small import shops alternated with low office buildings. At one end was the KOSTORG building, which was a concrete cube fifty meters on a side, a delicate pastel-brick color, its stark plainness broken by randomly placed small windows inset into small protruding pyramidal turrets, and an inlaid company logo in the upper left corner of every face, a red star with gold letters inside, BKT in Old Cyrillic—Buro Kosmicheskoi Torgovli. Underneath the logo, in modern letters was a small word: KOSTORG. The understatement of it suggested both great confidence and immense sophistication.

The trolley stopped of its own—apparently this was one of its major junctions—and Fraesch debarked, cutting across the cool shaded patterns of the plaza and going directly to the KOSTORG building. As he passed under the trees he felt a lingering coolness from the night before, although in direct sunlight it was distinctly warm. The sun was well up, late morning by the altitude of it, but it hardly seemed time enough.

Fraesch paused before entering the building, and looked back, across the plaza. One of the trolleys was approaching the stop he had just left; it was plain and functional, a rectangular box with four large, soft tires and an articulated pantograph on the roof to connect it to the power lines. Nothing at all like the disreputable hovercraft, it was finished and well-made, but also carrying with it an air of the far past reiterated. It seemed an excellent emblem for the city, as the hovercraft had been for the countryside; Mulcahen would have a planet full of these odd recapitulations.

Inside the building, he began negotiating a slow and frustrating course through a series of referrals, coordinations and receptionist flunkies, although they all behaved with extreme courtesy, so much so that his aggravation at the delays faded. At the last, as he was beginning to get the rhythm of it, he was conveyed to a cubicle walled off from a working area filled with people and presented to a youngish man who was working madly at a drawing table covered with architectural drawings, booklets, advertising flyers, blueprints and even a badly done scale model of some unknown industry.

After a moment, he looked up. "You're Fraesch? They said you were coming, although I didn't expect you so soon. Sorry about the delays in the building, if you're not used to that sort of thing. We reinvented red tape here because we are all from so many places. . . . No culture seems to dominate, and as a result, we live in a stressed environment, so we have to make time work for us."

Fraesch said he understood.

"Good! I'm Aalet, by the way. I'm what passes for a governor here when I can find the time. Actually, I'm a low-management flunky from the Engineering Department. They elected me to come out here and pay my own dues."

Fraesch said, "Of all the things I could have said about Mulcahen, the last one would have been that it's high stress."

Aalet was not offended. "Oh, but it is, it is. You see, we are all together down here, but we don't know how to act, or interpret how others act. A gesture of greeting I know of on Artemus 4, is a gesture of deadly insult on Hegira. All the things we've learned somewhere else don't translate when we're all thrown together. So, even if we accomplish nothing, we create stress just by existing. And so we try to make things pleasant and time-consuming, and generally nonthreatening, so some of us can concentrate on the real stress—getting it together out here at the end of the line."

"You've accomplished something. Gorod might be the envy of many a planet."

Aalet made a gesture of disclaimer. "Not at all! When you only have one city to worry over, you can concentrate on doing it right. But we have to use so many things from the past—because they are relatively easy, at first . . . I suppose in the end it'll be all the same—criminals in the streets, slums, urban decay, budgets that won't and can't balance, taxes to support marginal achievers and safety-firsters and outright losers . . . But all the same you'd feel like an idiot if you didn't try at the first."

"An excellent sentiment, Governor Aalet. May I wish you success in your efforts!"

". . . Efforts. Fraesch, you don't know the half of it. Why . . . yes, I suppose I could tell you. Mulcahen's been open fifty years, and under development for the last twenty-odd, and we're now rated by the KOSTORG Examiners at Level 20/4 overall—we've attained the 20th century, fourth decade."

Fraesch observed, "Only twenty more to go."

"The first one's the hardest when you have to live here and be self-sufficient, and catch up by your own efforts with the absolute minimum of outside capital. These things don't happen overnight. The lack of sapient natives makes it easy and makes it hard—we don't have to pacify them or accommodate them, but by the same token we can't use them as an excuse, either."

Fraesch had the feeling that Aalet would go on indefinitely, and that he was used to doing so; part of the adaptation of the planet to a world full of strangers, he supposed. He gently reminded the governor of why he was here. "When I arrived last night, there was a note for me to come see you; I didn't know the name, of course, but it is odd that a planetary governor would want to see a journeyman administrator on tempassign to a leased project."

Aalet leaned back in his chair, which was plain and functional. He placed his hands together, fingers extended and touching only at the tips, as if thinking. After a moment he said, "Well, yes, I did have one of the girls drop a note off to Intercord to that effect. I know they never tell you what you are going into—it's supposed to keep you from forming prejudgments. I had a friend who went into Intercord after college. But Halcyon has been strange, a strange case. . . . I was hoping that you could . . . ah, look into things there, say, for me."

"For KOSTORG."

Aalet fiddled with his fingers. "Yes, of course; it'd have to be that way . . . the usual informer retainer?"

Fraesch felt a sudden urge of charity, something he rarely got. "I'll do it for half if you'll tell me why."

"No—all or nothing. The accountants will suspect me of squirreling the other half away somewhere and will ransack the files and be general pains in the arse to do so. And I was going to tell you anyway."

Aalet paused and called to one of the workers outside to bring him the Halcyon file. Presently a matronly woman appeared with an old-fashioned paper file, and an envelope of microfiche. Aalet opened the file and inserted a fiche in a minireader console built into the desk. These he looked at intently for another moment, as if he wanted to refresh himself, or find some particular point.

Then he leaned back forward and looked at Fraesch directly. "At the beginning of summer, there was an accident at Halcyon. An explosion and fire. The project director and his chief technician were killed in it."

Fraesch expressed surprise. On a leased project, everything would be modern, complete with the latest in safeguards. "In what sort of installation?"

"The Computer Room."

"An odd circumstance."

"Indeed, odd. Odd enough that the safety reports on it caught their attention at KOSTORG. Not to mention mine. We sent a team of accident investigators out there—the best, so I hear."

"What did they conclude?"

"Cause unknown. Machine malfunction probable."

"Still odd."

Aalet said, "Yes . . . The computer was a Memoroid Model 3000."

Fraesch whistled in surprise. "What were they doing that they needed a 3000?"

Aalet handed Fraesch an inforsheet from Speculations, Inc. "What they say here . . . is that they were trying to determine the information content of ocean waves. It doesn't say to what purpose. I found out through another source, ah, that it's part of a feasibility study for the electors of Klatzana; an ultrasensitive target-tracking system."

"Klatzana is a planet of xenophobes. . . ."

"Who have not been permitted to possess weapons. Any tracking system has highly visible artifacts."

"If they could do it, then all they'd need would be a computer strong enough to get information out of the noise . . . tidal perturbations. . . ."

"My source said that Speculations had refined a system good enough in the past to detect bodies 1000 kilometers in diameter at a distance of a tenth-light."

Fraesch said, "A spaceship is considerably smaller."

"It goes without saying. . . . But we also found out that the Mulcahen system is dynamically equivalent to the Klatzana system, and that the position of land and water is similar."

"So they brought it here to refine it."

"We think so."

"How did they deal with Klatzanans? They hate all off-world traders."

"One needs to buy, another needs to sell. . . . I suppose a way can be found to overcome the ideological difficulties. It also goes without saying that Speculations would charge them something for the service."

"Enough so that Speculations could work for fun and live on the interest."

Fraesch asked, "So much?"

Aalet shrugged. "They are supposed to have it . . . you know that's where all the Longlife comes from. The whole family of those drugs. And they can't be synthesized—only fermented in those jungles by a gang of ill-smelling natives, nonhumans to boot."

Fraesch laughed and said, "Bloody Wogs," with an elaborate British accent.

Aalet said, "Well, there it is, nonetheless. The supreme irony of the universe has got to be that a planet of raving maniacs, hidebound traditionalists of the worst sort, haters—no, despisers of all non-klatzanans, is able to ferment the one thing the rest of us need absolutely. To our credit, they have never been subjugated, but we don't permit them modern weapons, either. They have tried—give them credit for that, and they're damn inventive, and since they have to endure us, they don't object to making a profit at it."

Fraesch politely interrupted, "If they could track and target ships without a visible artifact at those distances, then the drug supply would be cut off . . . surely Speculations knows this."

"Well, yes. The whole idea is insane. If it worked, Speculations would sell them the means to keep spacefaring races out of the Klatzan system, therefore no drugs, therefore. . . ."

Fraesch said, "Reduction *ad absurdam*. There's something else."

"Yes."

"That . . . does Speculations have a project on Longlife?"

"I understand they're within reach of a product that compares to the natural drug. They are deep into it—in fact, they are in considerable debt over the project. . . . It kept staying just out of reach, just a little more . . . Apparently, they're making the final push on it. They bought a planet—I don't know where—and have units in production. I have been able to find out little about this, except that instead of a gang of sweaty natives, a clearing in the jungle and a longhouse full of stone crocks, they have a chemical factory whose area is greater than the arable land in hectares of Pangaea, here. Needless to say, they're on the edge of going broke. That's a big gamble in the biggest game of all. I think the situation would suggest itself to them—for if they allowed the Klatzanans to continue to export Longlife, they'd be ruined by price wars, even if they managed to synthesize it; the Klatzanans would halve any price Speculations could make."

"And the end result of the whole project is that Speculations would have the corner on Longlife, they'd allow the Klatzanans to shut themselves off, and. . . ."

Aalet finished it, ". . . And they'd have the best target tracking system in the known universe, and could protect their own place. The possibilities are frightening."

Fraesch sat back, his head swimming. Longlife! "What you are saying is that they are going to reach for a government."

"Such are the predictions."

"Who knows about this? How did you find it out?"

"Well, I have good people here . . . and I also have a Memoroid Model 3000 in the basement, and Mulcahen attracts people from all over—you know how a new planet is—you can't keep them off it. I had some informers paid. . . . Trouble is, with something like this the profit potential is so great that others may be subverted into getting into it. . . . A Speculations, Inc. directorship is powerful motivation; even to become a major stockholder would be interesting, so there's a problem with knowing whom you can trust. This issue, you see, has the potential to cross any loyalty line anyone could set up. I have reason to believe that there may be some KOSTORG people in it, so since then I have been careful. There have been some bad slips here; that is how I got into it in the first place."

"How do you know you can trust me?"

"I have an informer at Intercord. Never mind who. I found out the reason you were picked . . . You're relatively straightaway, honest and all that, and you have had no previous connection with anything that could touch on any of these things. They have to have an administrator—it's in the lease agreement, so they picked what they thought was a double-blind. You'd come in, hold the thing together, replace the equipment, and by then they'd have their own man back in here—you can guess they wouldn't have just anybody working on this thing out in the field—they'd have one of their key people here to ram it through."

Aalet paused, and glanced at his hard hat, hanging conveniently nearby on the wall. "I know I can trust you because Speculations cleared you as knowing nothing about them. The problem is now that my informer is no longer informing me . . . and the only input I have is through Halcyon, here."

Fraesch said, "You've been candid with me, Governor. I will be candid in return. I'm on informer contract. . . ."

Aalet was not surprised. He said, "Most of the new arrivals are. Everyone likes to keep an eye on the competition. What company?"

"Novaya Ekonomicheskaya Politika."

An oath escaped Aalet, "*Vo istinye Khristos Voskresen!* NEP, Incorporated. I thought that outfit had gone under long ago. . . ." A troubled expression passed across Aalet's dark, handsome face.

Fraesch had imagined Aalet young until he saw that expression. It was the visible sign of someone who had been exposed to a lot, a long life. . . . Aalet must have started on Longlife at an early age.

Aalet said, "As a fact, I know they went under." He rummaged about absentmindedly and finally produced a communicator. On this device he punched several numbers, talked with some intermediate party, punched some more numbers, and finally reached someone. Or their office. Aside, to Fraesch, he said, "Gorod Stock Exchange. I have a friend over there. . . ." Now he turned back to the commset.

"Hello, Delmo? This is Aalet."

"Fine, fine, buried in work, as the usual. Say, can you give me a quote on NEP?"

"Why? I heard they'd been picked up by someone, and were back in business . . . Fine, yes, I'll wait."

He nodded to Fraesch, who had been hearing only one side of the conversation. He said, "Delmo Arbridge. Broker. Good sort. He may be able to tell us a few things. . . ." He returned his attention to the unit.

"27½ . . . ? Who bought them out?"

Aalet wrote rapidly on a pad on his desk.

"That's good news, Del, yes, very good news. Yes, I may be calling you in a few days. . . . I'm waiting for some news to break, and I may be seeing you on this one, looks like a real sleeper. . . . Right. Yes, I'll call you first, I promise. See you."

Aalet turned back to Fraesch, and said, consulting the notes he had written, "A consortium headed by one Tyrone Ractol purchased all assets, sold off a bunch of stuff and is putting the company back on its feet, at a reduced scale of operations. Ractal is known to be a major stockholder of Speculations, Inc. although he is not listed anywhere as an official of the company. . . . It would seem that they've built a control on you, Fraesch."

"They hired me to run the place, and then had another outfit contract me in an infotrieve targeted against KOS-TORG so they'd know if I spotted anything? They must take me for a complete goose!"

"I wouldn't say that they had it done . . . but that they did it themselves. Ractal will be deep in this operation. By the way, I hope you will furnish them with detailed reports on the goings on here."

"The *Karachkini*![1] I'll send them reports!"

Aalet held up a hand, broadly smiling. "No, no, not so fast, not so hasty! I'm quite serious; I want you to send them reports, regularly, as if you were an idiot on your first commercial espionage mission. Send them everything! I will arrange for you to have a contact in the Bureau of Statistics who will send you stuff. It will be certified capable of putting a methamphetamine addict soundly to sleep in the midst of a boiler factory. Who knows? You may even get a bonus for

---

[1] Russian vulgarism: One who goes on all fours; passive beastialist.

zeal. And in case you're tempted by the corner they might have. . . ." Here the humor left his voice entirely, although the smile remained. "KOSTORG will pay ten times what they have you on at the conclusion of this."

Fraesch said, "There's nothing personal in it; I agree with you entirely that they must not succeed in this. It will be as you suggest."

"Good. I'm glad you understand. We simply cannot permit this to occur."

Fraesch asked, "What is being done to delay, obstruct, or stop this?"

"You are doubtless thinking of lawsuits, boycotts, catastrophic depricing. . . . All these things are moving along, but they are slow to set in motion and slow to act. KOSTORG, for example, does not have any kind of operation in the think-tank free-research business, so direct competition is out of the question. And as I said . . . I'm not entirely certain I want to involve KOSTORG until we can verify that the company is free of sleepers. There are clever tests for this kind of thing, you know; their disadvantage is that they take time. No! Their worst enemy appears to be their own motivation."

"How so?"

"They have promised to deliver goods they didn't have at the time of the offer. . . . That they don't have now . . . and that they seem to be having trouble getting."

"You've lost me."

"The whole plan depends upon delivery of the detection system. They already had a crude model in operation, to demonstrate. But increasing the capability as they promised, as they *contracted* to do within time limits; it's proven more difficult than they imagined. In fact, I know from intercepted reports that about a year ago they came to a complete standstill on further refinement of the detection system."

Aalet paused to let that sink it, then continued, "Moreover, the station up there got deeply involved with some kind of side effect that is not discussed on any medium we can monitor. All we know is that the director of Halcyon turned the whole power of a Model 3000 onto it and ignored orders. That's why they had to have someone like you—the right person for that station is critical to the execution of the entire plan."

"Why didn't they replace the director, then?"

"He told them they had stumbled onto something they could not ignore, something they had to pursue for the success of the operation. He never said what it was. Apparently there was an inner circle only at Halcyon who were in on it—I should imagine people who were in the heart of the research end of it."

"They must have let him have a long tether to accept excuses for a year, where something like this is involved."

"It had to be thus: the director, Leonid Moricle, had been the originator of the whole plan. If he told them he had found something they couldn't pass, then they'd have to take his word for it. He was their expert in that area. Him, and his assistant, a woman named Jenserico Nachitose."

"They were the ones who died in the fire."

"Yes. Presumably; no bodies were found. It was, I hear, bad."

"I suppose it's occurred to you, Governor, that Speculations decided to take drastic action."

"That was my thought also, as well as, for other reasons, those of the local constable who has done most of the investigating in the field. But those kinds of things leave traces. So far, we've found none. Also, we could expect certain patterns of behavior on the part of Speculations, and we don't see them. Quite to the contrary: they are extremely agitated over this. Losing Moricle and Nachitose was a profound loss to them—imagine, two of the best users of the Model 3000 in the inhabited universe, and they allow it to malfunction and then through a series of coincidences, explode and burn—at least, that is what it looks like."

Aalet added, "We know requisitions and invoices we've seen or had mention of, that whatever they were doing *was* giving them something. Moricle had the sensor array rebuilt, doubling it from its original size, and added another duplicate sensor array. They added a wing to the lab to house recordings they had made of something. The mag tape requisitions alone for the past year would strain KOSTORG's patience. Moricle *was* on to something, make no mistake."

"What's on the tapes?"

"There are none. The fire destroyed everything—memory units, tapes, files, journals, logs. Not so long before the fire, Moricle had moved everything to do with the work into the data wing of the lab—said it was more secure, that he suspected an attempted burglary, and so forth."

Fraesch asked, "So there's no operation now, as such?"

"On, no. Speculations immediately ordered the whole thing rebuilt and bought another five years' worth of lease. In fact, it has been rebuilt. They hired a fastruct team from Red Ball, Limited, and they came in here and rebuilt it. Just like that! Complete with a brand-new Memoroid Model 3000. You won't be operating the thing, of course—Moricle and Nachitose did all that themselves, and the new stuff will be run by the permanent director that Speculations sends in. All indications are that they are going to keep after it."

Fraesch said, "Red Ball fastruct teams don't come cheap; and they only work for cash, in advance, 100 percent. Speculations must be strained to bursting over this."

Aalet's face took on a perfectly villainous expression. "That is so, exactly the case. Now we don't have the exact figures from which to predict, but . . . I believe the expression is, 'The wolf is at the door.' If you can stall them, somehow, while finding out how close they really are. . . ."

"How much power do you have as governor?"

"As governor, virtually none. This is the Edge, Fraesch, out here. We don't have governments—everything is done on a cost competitive basis—police, courts, currency, prisons, the mails. What I am is simply the company rep for KOSTORG, who is the owner and seller. . . . I can get things done because of who I represent, and the financial resources I control, but I'm on a short tether—everything has to stand up to the accountants K. brings in. Mind, I'm not asking you to take any risks—just keep me informed as to what you can find out. And slow things down if you can."

Fraesch saw Aalet's point, even though the governmentlessness which was practiced in the worlds of the Edge of settled space was difficult to live with. Mulcahen would be an extreme example of this, and it would require some adjustments. Back in the center, everything people did was filtered through an idea that they had to have a government—politics. Here, and along the Edge, it was that they had to have an economic base. Fraesch himself accepted without too deep a questioning that some level of government was necessary. He would, he knew, perceive Aalet and indeed the whole planet as things they were not. This trip was in fact the first time he had been so far out.

Fraesch said, "I've told you where I stand on this. I'll do what I can."

"Fine. I wouldn't ask more. Are you ready to leave for Halcyon?"

"I hadn't made any plans to the contrary."

"Then you won't object to some arrangements I've taken

the liberty of making; you don't have to worry about travel expenses—Speculations pays that. But I made some reservations, and there is a man I would like you to meet."

Fraesch thought, *and now comes the things I must do*. He said, "Please continue."

"The Constable, Anselm Urbifrage. He's come to town to ride back with you."

"What's he like?"

"Well . . . a lot of things. He's a native; born here, and not on Longlife—there's a streak of that in the native-born. Still, for all the shortness of the natural life, he's managed to do and be a lot of things—I haven't exhausted his repertoire of tales and adventures yet. He's been a sailor, a machinist over in Zavody, a welder, a farmer; also a wandering hobo, and the Storm Cult holds him to be what their religion calls a Magus, although I've not yet determined what a Magus *does*. He seems to ignore them."

"You have a native religion here?"

"Well, you know how Yildizlar Maddesi is; most of the people they brought in here to establish their claim just wandered around. Most of them were here when we came, still wandering. YM had forgotten about them and let them fend for themselves. Some of them had some odd adventures—you know how the imagination goes wild on a wild planet, however familiar it seems—chemical fractions in the air, the water. There was no resistance to us at all—in fact, they seemed to be grateful for it—they wouldn't have to pretend anymore, they could do what they really wanted, which was to go off in the wild. We ignore them, they ignore us. Sometimes they work for us, more often not. Urbifrage is intelligent, capable and very adaptable—but he is also very uneducated, and I don't pretend to understand his motivations at all. At any rate, he is completely trustworthy—he'll tell you exactly what his loyalties are."

"What does he do?"

"There is a loose community in the area surrounding the site Halcyon leased. Some are squatters—people from the YM days and their descendants, and some are landholders who bought tracts from KOSTORG Mulcahen. They are not completely dissimilar, in fact. They asked Urbifrage to serve, at a modest stipend, as the local constable—that's what they call it—who settles disputes, chases strays, pursues criminals. Someday far away people like him will be making the decisions here . . . but when the fire happened, we had some problem dealing with the local security companies. They just didn't want to work that far in the field. So I hired Urbifrage to conduct an investigation."

"And . . .?"

"Well, he did a hell of a job. Thorough. The only problem is that he's convinced the fire wasn't accidental, only he can't find any trail of evidence to substantiate that. He'll drive you crazy, because everyone in the general neighborhood is a suspect. But endure that—he knows the area and he knows Mulcahen, and I know he's definitely not working with Speculations—in fact, although he won't say so directly, I think he objected to them."

"Being there. . . .?"

"No. The natives are completely passive there. They don't care who comes, or what they do. . . . I have noticed that, though, about Urbifrage—he suspected something."

"Does he know about Speculations?"

"If he does, it's not because I've told him."

"You think he knows?"

"I tried to tell him. It wouldn't take. The whole concept is like something he can't focus on, as if it has no meaning to him. Perhaps I tried to be too simple; Urbifrage is a complex person, as are most of the native-born."

"I know. I've met one."

Aalet grew attentive. "Who? Where?"

"On the shuttle from the 'port. A wild man, called himself 'Malo Pomalu'; babbled incoherently, more or less. Who is Pomalu?"

Aalet relaxed. "Pomalu! Is he still alive? Now there's a story. The way I hear it, Pomalu is not his real name—I think he's forgotten it. But it seems that he was a mad poet somewhere, I don't know where, and he decided to go find some wild world and go live on it, be an explorer. Signed on with YM in the Initial Survey Team, and acted responsibly for awhile. When the YM thing started drifting, he held it together for awhile . . . then he wandered off into the bush with a couple of women, and since then, he appears from time to time. A wild man. Nobody listens to him, of course, but did they ever? He must be ancient, now—he was a mature man when he came here—hell, he was here when they went around wearing spacesuits and carrying combat arms, when they didn't know anything."

Fraesch decided that he would say no more about Pomalu, at least for the time. Aalet said, "Where was I . . .? Yes, Urbifrage. Well, meet him, if you will, with your baggage, at a place called Sherst Sobaki. It's a bar and restaurant, a place Urbifrage frequents when he's in town. The name means. . . ."

Fraesch said, "I know. Hair of the dog."

"Very good! About sundown. Go there and ask for him. They know him well enough. And at least until you get to Halcyon, he'll be your guide. And now. . . ."

"I understand. You have been kind to spend the time." Fraesch arose, and left the informal office of Shartason Aalet.

Fraesch threaded his way back through the rows of cubicles, of functionary rooms, of deskside conferences, halls, stairwells; he walked out of the plain KOSTORG building and back to the park. There he stopped, slightly dazed, although he was not sure it was from what he had heard, or the distinct afternoon—late afternoon—slant to the sunlight. Afternoon? It seemed hardly lunchtime. Fraesch looked about, trying to orient himself to the fast time of Mulcahen. Over the tops of the low buildings around the plaza he could make out the bulging top of one of the thunderstorms, lit from the side by the sun, blinding white, soaring, drifting to the east, muttering with distant thunder.

Fraesch sat on a nearby bench. From his pocket, he removed a small notebook, and his pen. In it, he thoughtfully and methodically wrote three names:

> Leonid Moricle (D)
> Jenserico Nachitose (D)
> Anselm Urbifrage

Something was still bothering him. He looked about again, as if the soft shaded streets might give him some clue. Then it occurred to him, a process similar to the turning of an intricate geometrical prism: Aalet had smoothly avoided his question about the Storm Cult. He shook his head and added that title to his list of names.

> Storm Cult (cf A. U. and M. P. if available)

3

Fraesch uncovered directions to the night-spot Sherst' Sobaki without great difficulty, finding out several things about it at the same time. It was, so it seemed, beer hall and restaurant both, and was highly esteemed in both capacities; but it was more yet, and the limits of that "more" seemed a little vague. In fact, all the bars and restaurants of Gorod seemed to be, in varying degree, a sort of floating town meeting. People sat in their offices or stood in their shops and gave the official reasons by day; but at night they drifted to places they felt appropriate in and discussed real reasons. All of these places seemed to possess odd, incongruous, or vulgar names: others he heard mentioned were Glavny Shtab (which name meant, General Headquarters, this on a planet with virtually no military nor any tradition of one); there was a Zadny Khvostik (Hindmost tail-stub), and a Steel Breeze.

He also found out that Sherst' Sobaki was used extensively by travelers, and maintained a locker room for baggage. With that in mind, he went back to Cavafy Alley and retrieved his baggage before going there. Along the way, he noticed that nobody seemed to mind, or even take notice of it. He had timed it right; he arrived just after sundown, when the light was still in the west.

Fraesch had expected either a dive or a palace; what he saw was neither. The Hair of the Dog was a large establishment of modest decor, whose customers seemed to be trying to outdo one another solely in informality. Inside, it was divided up into several areas according to activity—eating, drinking, serious drinking or socializing. There was also a section given over to gambling, although KOSTORG had prohibited house-run games of chance. By asking several people he encountered as he progressed farther into the place, he was at last able to find a section where Urbifrage was most likely to be found, a subsection of the socializing area.

This room had a fireplace, rustic tables, homely hooked rugs. It was not filled but there were several groups already there—couples beginning a night on the town, small groups. Fraesch looked about and found the clientele to be mostly young and nostalgic. One man alone immediately suggested himself as either being Urbifrage or someone who would know him. The man was seated, but even so, Fraesch could see he would be described as short and stocky. Fraesch estimated his age at around fifty standard, unaltered. He had iron-gray hair, cut unfashionably short, and a heavy, broad face. The man wore a workman's coverall and a light jacket, but the clothes were clean and neat.

Fraesch approached the man and asked if he knew of a man named Urbifrage.

The man turned an uncomfortable direct look to Fraesch and regarded him momentarily from small, watery blue eyes. He said, "I am Urbifrage." The voice was gruff and precise.

Fraesch introduced himself, to which Urbifrage replied, somewhat more warmly, "Please sit. A waiter will be along presently." After Fraesch had gotten settled, Urbifrage added, "Pleased to meet you, of course. I heard you were about, and headed here. I've taken a passage for us tonight, but we've got some time."

"Tonight?"

"Did you have anything else in mind?"

"No, but. . . ."

. . "Gorod's a fine place, but it misleads one into believing that the action's here because they know about it. Actually, it's all happening out there. I took the liberty to assume. . . ." He let his words trail off.

Fraesch said, "You were right to do so; I was just a little surprised by the swiftness of things. You see, in most places they want to drag you all over the place first."

Urbifrage said, "I know."

"I imagine there's a lot to be done there, at Halcyon."

Urbifrage grunted, and said, "Too much, and too little. Most city people get bored out there . . . even native-borns think the northwest coast is remote. You'll have some work to do, at first, I'm sure. There's nobody there except technicians—all of them off-world, of course, and little's been done outside the necessities since the killing. . . . They've patched up a committee to sign for things and issue the payroll, but it's clear they're waiting to turn it over to you."

A waiter appeared and handed Fraesch a hand-printed

menu. Urbifrage looked up and said, "The usual for me."
Fraesch looked over the list, which was short and plain. He
asked Urbifrage, "What's 'Plainsman Goulash'?"

"A stew . . . made of a local animal native to the great
plains west and north of the central highlands, the bol'shoy;
you'll probably see one tomorrow. It's quite good. . . ."

Fraesch ordered, along with some local beer which Urbifrage recommended, and after a short wait, was served a
steaming bowl of stew, that from the aroma of it was highly
seasoned. Fraesch had taken his anti-upset injections before
debarking, but nevertheless he started on the stew with misgivings. Urbifrage glanced his way, to insure he was enjoying
himself, and dug into a platter of what looked like a very
tough broiled steak, garnished by something that looked like a
boiled pinecone.

During supper, Urbifrage said nothing, save an occasional
comment on the quality of food and drink in several places
in and around Gorod. Fraesch politely refrained from men-
tioning some of the more refined diets he had enjoyed on
more civilized worlds for fear Urbifrage would think that he
was trying to impress him.

Fraesch felt a little ill at ease in the presence of the re-
doubtable Anselm Urbifrage. "Native-born and not on Longlife." That was what Aalet had said. That would mean that
he, Joachim Fraesch, was chronologically older than the man
sharing the table with him; that he had been working on assignments for Intercord before this Urbifrage had been born
. . . that Urbifrage would have returned to the wide earth of
Mulcahen before Fraesch showed a clearly visible sign of aging. Those things Fraesch knew. But he still felt odd—somehow inexperienced, somehow subordinate. Not inferior,
but. . . . He couldn't put his finger on it.

Urbifrage interrupted Fraesch's musing on the fire. "You
met with the *Dunyamuduru* today?"

The term caught Fraesch by surprise. He had to reflect on
it. It was Turkish, of course . . . "world" . . . "its-ruler."
Something like that. The old word for a planetary governor.
He replied, "Yes. This morning."

"I suppose he told you what they know of events at Halcyon?"

"As much as he knew. . . . He says 'accident,' but you
said 'killed.' "

Urbifrage looked unperturbed. "Aalet's a good sort, but he

must needs conduct his affairs through reports and the con-
clusions of others, whereas I've had to deal with the hot
wreckage, the bodies, or what was left of them. I also have
spent a great deal of time with some local technical reps
from Memoroid, as well as Kay Electronics, the supplier of
the rest of the equipment; it's as if . . . someone told you a
bicycle blew up. The only reasonable conclusion would be
that someone stuffed the frame with blasting caps. The stuff
in that lab would have had to have been rigged to burn and
all the failsafes disconnected. My conclusion is that it was
done."

Fraesch said, "We have weapon and method. Now we need
suspects and a motive."

Urbifrage said, in a reduced voice, "Judging from the types
that were assigned there, I should say sexual jealousy was the
motive; we've got no shortage of suspects. The trouble with
Halcyon . . . was that most of the time, no one seemed to
know who was doing what, with which, and to whom."

Fraesch was amused at this mild prudery. He said, "Off-
world manners surprise you?"

Urbifrage favored Fraesch with another of those pointed
stares. "Only when they are inconsistent."

"Inconsistent?"

"Promiscuity neither surprises nor shocks me; we have a
form of it practiced locally . . . but free-love cults have to
accept non-possessiveness, or the members shortly proceed to
murder one another."

An idea struck Fraesch. He asked, "Are all the project
people from the same place?"

"No."

"Do you know the planets and the locations?"

"Not that I recall . . . we can look that up, if you want.
It's all in the files."

"I think of a way it could be as you suspect . . . a circumstance. Were Moricle and Nachitose involved with others?"

"In the past, yes, to varying degrees. Of late, they were
not. This was a change in the pattern I detected through ex-
amination of the people's testimonies at the accident board."

"I want to pursue another angle. . . . Aalet is satisfied to
let things remain as they are; why . . . ?"

"Why do I pursue it?" Urbifrage shrugged his heavy shoulders. "Call it a sense of justice derived from personal values.
Things are unfinished."

"Aalet told me some things, some disturbing things about

them. It is possible. . . ." Fraesch looked around to see if anyone were within earshot.

Urbifrage said, "He spoke of the off-world plot to me. Certainly the owners are suspect. But that seems like a long shot to me; the time element is all wrong. Besides, the accident or killing occurred after a prolonged period of isolation due to a transport breakdown. All people were accounted for. Nobody came or left, nor did they afterward until after the investigation."

Fraesch said, "On some worlds, they have vehicles which can land relatively silently direct from space; a commando party could land on the ocean, rig explosives and depart. It's been done before; and from what Aalet told me, there are people who would accept the expense of transporting such vehicles in secret, for none of them could fly here unaided from any other inhabited planet."

Urbifrage looked bland and self-assured. He said, "Nobody landed from off-world."

Fraesch objected, "The planetary detection system could have faked records. If it were official, this plot, they wouldn't tell you the truth anyway."

Urbifrage was not moved. "I know that. I also know that our local detection system, operated by KOSTORG, is a farce—it's only aimed one way. But I know that there was not a landing. . . . It's difficult to explain exactly how I know. . . ."

"I'm a good listener."

"Listening's not the point, but perception. . . ." There he stopped, as if he had said too much. "After a time there, you'll begin to see a little; then. . . ." He let it drop.

"So however it is, you know there was no landing and no infiltrators."

"Yes."

"Very well . . . how about planted people—who were brought in to be activated at a later time?"

Urbifrage brightened. He leaned forward, confidentially, as if he had just then made up his mind about Fraesch. "Excellent! You are as they said, even though not a detective . . . Sleepers would have been a good bet, but Aalet found out what he knew and put it together only recently. He hadn't had time to set a planted person."

"Someone else could have. A lot was at stake, I understand. It needn't be KOSTORG. . . ."

"That does suggest possibilities. But I have been told by

Speculations that they used a randomizing system for recruiting that had reduced that practice to the vanishing point. Also that they conducted a strenuous search, which, incidentally, turned up seven or eight such people . . . none of them here, or on any planet they were recruited from."

"Forgive me for rudeness, but I must ask—is Speculations retaining you as an investigator?"

Urbifrage answered candidly, "They have offered a reward for the murderer, and I can use the den'gi as well as the next . . . I hold no such commission. They are undoubtedly curious as to the circumstances. I understand Moricle was a person of some importance in his company, and that this project was of great interest to them. Still, they hired you and I hear a permanent replacement is forthcoming, so they are not waiting for the answer before moving on. . . . Practical people."

"Did you know Moricle personally?"

"I had met him once or twice . . . and the lady Nachitose."

"What kind of person did he seem to you?"

"When they first came to the northwest coast, he was an unpleasant person . . . driven by some inner knowledge of which he would not speak. The lady Nachitose was similar. They were demanding of the other employees. Later on, they became secretive and withdrawn, and then bemused. That was when they locked everything up. At the end, he ignored the station entirely, as much as he could, and either spent his time in the lab with Nachitose or writing excuses for lack of progress back to Speculations. He came here with the weight of great responsibility upon him, demanding expectations; but when his end came into its time, he had something different on his mind. When I saw him last, he was frightened and uncertain."

"And Nachitose?"

"An opaque woman no one fathomed; *suka vshla, suka vyshla.*"

Fraesch mentally translated, from the Russian, "A bitch she came, a bitch she left." He said, to Urbifrage, "Aalet says his spies told him they were getting unexpected results from their experiment."

"I have heard the same. The technicians profess to know nothing. They were there to maintain the equipment and make technical changes as directed. To my knowledge, none of them ever worked in the lab when the samples were being run. There has been some talk of overhearing voices speaking an unknown language, but mostly by drunkards or by notorious fantasists. The lab was inside a secured compound, and was soundproofed."

"Had you seen the equipment?"

"Only when it was being installed—carried in. I never saw it assembled, or operating. A lot of electronic gear . . . Moricle was, they say, quite specific about repairs or modifications."

"Then there were just two of them actually working on whatever they were working on."

"Never otherwise, so far as I know."

"And they kept it secured when they were out of it?"

"When in as well. It had a robotect guard system, which was said to be set in the 'kill' mode at all times. Moricle and Nachitose had the only known descramblers.

The robotect had gone beserk after the explosion and had been firing into the lab building—explosives, laser, microwave —it made a mess of what little was left. We disarmed it with great difficulty."

Fraesch said, after a minute's reflection, "It sounds like an accident to me as well. It sounds difficult to have been arranged, if it was arranged . . . more than passion would account for. That kind of motive would seek a dramatic confrontation, some public violence."

Urbifrage said, "Perhaps . . . but by and large, the lot there are sullen and secretive. Consider that Halcyon is a remote site, and that they are all working under severe pressure; yet there were no fistfights, and few open arguments, although the place seethes with repressed differences, and incidents of directed vandalism have been commonplace. Not enough to warrant accusations, but also not light enough to ignore."

Fraesch shuddered. "It must be a gruesome place to produce that. Where is it? In a gravel pit?"

"To the contrary, it's at the mouth of a river. Low mountains covered with trees, some cliffs along the ocean. A pleasant site, done, if I may say, in considerable good taste, if a bit plain. I attributed the behavior of the workers to circumstances off-world, not conditions on Mulcahen, or the North Coast Country. To myself, it's very desirable country, although the climate can be rough in winter. The growing season's short, and it's far from everything else. I wandered over that way from Zavody a long time ago. . . ." Urbifrage stopped and retrieved a large pocket watch from a breast pocket on his coveralls. It looked cheap and crude. Urbifrage consulted it, and announced, "It's a Mulcahen-made watch. A fellow made it for me over in Zavody. It doesn't keep accurate time, but it's time is our own; and it's time we were on our way."

Fraesch arose from the table with relief, anxious for action. He felt that he'd heard enough inconclusive talk, and wanted to get on with it, to arrive at the scene, and see what he could see.

Urbifrage paid for his meal with the money of Mulcahen, thin bills which looked like paper but weren't, and which the cashier passed through a narrow slot in the counter before accepting them. Urbifrage said, aside to Fraesch, "There's a passive computer sandwiched inside the bills, a verification circuit. Puts a curb on counterfeiters."

When Fraesch paid his, he told the cashier, as he had been told, that he was on an expense account to be tallied to Speculations, Inc., and handed him a Speculations ID slip, which was also passed through the same slot. The cashier manipulated his register without comment. Fraesch knew how that system worked; the register was probably connected to the nearest branch of whatever bank Speculations had chosen to set up its account with.

They exited through the homey foyer into the night streets of Gorod, now lit by the lights of stores, streetlights, passing vehicles. Fraesch had collected his baggage, and Urbifrage had offered to carry one of the cases. Now they set off down the sidewalk. Fraesch asked, "How far is it?"

"Not so far. . . . We'll go to the next trolley stop and ride a bit."

The trolley stop was only a block away. As they were on the way to it, Fraesch looked in the windows they were passing. Much as he expected, in a section of the city devoted to sales as this part was, there was considerable stuff offered for sale. What was characteristic of a frontier world such as Mulcahen was that in these windows there was little displayed of fashion or pleasure, but severely practical goods. Hardware stores and equipment dealers were dominant, with clothing stores coming in a modest third. Fraesch also noted the terminology—clothing stores called themselves "outfitters," or "personal environments."

After they had set the bags down at the stop, Fraesch looked at the establishment behind them, a showroom for what seemed to be exotic construction equipment. Apparently most of the shop was shut down, but inside, a solitary sales-man could be seen engaged in a strenuous conversation with a potential buyer of one of the devices. Like all strange, un-familiar machinery, at first glance it would not define its pur-pose or function. Fraesch could not recall seeing anything quite like it, although its component parts seemed recogniz-able enough: hydraulic cylinders and lines, heavy gauge sheet metal, steel legs which the thing stood on. There was an oper-ator's cab. The legs ended in bulbous, flexible, cleated pads.

Fraesch asked Urbifrage, "What is that? I've seen heavy equipment, but nothing like that."

Urbifrage looked around, glanced into the showroom, and said, "That's a strider . . . some folk call them spider-cars. You won't see many in the city or around the spaceport, al-though there are some larger ones there. They are common outside settled areas."

"What do they do?"

"Just vehicles, transportation. Instead of rolling on wheels or tracks, they walk. Don't need roads, or trails, or anything. Go anywhere—even climb. They don't tear up the ground so much. Anybody out in the country either walks or gets one of those. They have half a dozen on the project. Some of them have different kinds of manipulators for certain jobs—prospecting and assay, farming, exploring, what have you. Construction. A strider is the first powered vehicle on a site."

"Made here?"

"Not yet, though they tell me it won't be long. All import. That one, for example, a Pendrier Meretrix 11. Made on Lustrude, which is another outer world not so far away; a general-purpose lightweight. For this kind you have to buy specific manipulators at extra cost, but there are a lot of dif-ferent types, and it's thought versatile and rugged. Notice it has little room for passengers."

Fraesch now looked closely. Now he saw a machine that did resemble a spider in some ways; there were six legs, each one consisting of a vertical sliding post mounted in a heavy "foreleg" canted up at a slight angle, free to move only hori-zontally, back and forth. The body was a truncated wedge, narrow end to the rear, where a short exhaust pipe stood plainly erect. The wedge shape of it was oriented horizon-tally, and it was not thick. Fraesch imagined one could sit upright within it, but no more than that. The cab was placed in the very front, asymmetrically to one side, and was a

simple box with large glass windows. It overhung the front
slightly, and there was a window there, too, so the operator
could look down at the ground. In the bare space beside the
cab was a single large searchlight, and in the center of the
body in the front was what looked like a door. The bottom
was about a meter and a half off the floor. There were some
small windows, seemingly placed at random, at odd places in
the body, and there were several louvered intake screens. Inside the cab was a single plain seat, and a pedestal supporting
a small instrument panel and a rack of hand-levers, apparently used to guide it. It looked intricate, formidable and
expensive.

Fraesch said, "They have six of those at Halcyon?"

"Not Meretrix 11s. Those are utility models. Speculations
brought their own in. They tell me the ones there are older
models, but they seem to be very nice pieces. As acting director, of course, you'll have your own, a Fluxman Hunter."
Here Urbifrage allowed a slow, lazy smile to creep across his
face; a knowing semi-grin. "Ever drive one before? No, of
course not. I suppose they don't have them on the more civilized worlds."

"And I suppose I'll have to learn to drive it?"

"Yes. It's not difficult, and I advise it—you'll want to get
around in the country. Without it, you won't be immobilized,
but your range will be shortened a lot. Take it—you've
worked for it."

Fraesch could not tell if there was mockery in the voice or
expression or not. He said, "Do you have one of these
machines?"

"A strider? Yes. An older version of the one in the window. I visit some fairly remote places on my rounds. I have to
tinker with it now and again, but it still gets me there and
back, although not a lot faster than I could run when I was a
buck. Hah, I've had to walk plenty of times, too!"

Fraesch ruminated, "I wonder how I missed this . . .?"

Urbifrage commented, "You would only have seen them
on worlds that were poor in roads; once you get a road net,
the striders disappear. On a paved surface, almost anything is
faster—and easier to operate and maintain. Most of the control system is hydraulic, and there's a lot of high-pressure
pipe inside that thing. But they are uncommonly useful to a
new world. . . ." He looked around. "Here it comes, now,
our trolley."

As the trolley pulled to a slow stop in front of them,

Fraesch looked back into the showroom, just once, before the trolley took all their attention. He saw that the salesman and his customer had now retired to a small booth at the back of the building. The salesman was speaking into a commset, while the customer gazed out the window of the booth with a bland, glassy look to his face. Fraesch smiled to himself; here was a case where someone was just parting with a large sum of money. . . .

They boarded, and Urbifrage paid the fares. Fraesch settled himself by a window and looked back once more at the odd machine, which seemed more than ever an impossible combination of nightmare and farm implement, completely, absolutely immiscible, oil and water. He looked to Urbifrage and said, "Seeing that thing made me realize something about modern civilization."

"Yes?"

"That as we gain the eases that technology brings, we lose something; one person can no longer do it all, and we become a component population of specialists, and the whole man recedes further from us. I don't regret it, but there's a loss. . . ."

Urbifrage leaned back in his seat, glancing around once at the city scene passing them outside the windows of the silent trolley; he folded his hands in his lap and said, "That's why, I think, some of us walked away from it here a little ways: so we could be whole men again."

"Has any of you succeeded?"

Urbifrage shifted his position slightly, somehow changing his entire personality, chameleon-like, instantly. One minute he was Urbifrage the knowledgeable guide; the next, with no visible rate of change, he was Urbifrage the taciturn mechanic. "Who knows what people succeed at? You'd have to find someone who had done it, and then I don't know what they'd say."

The trolley glided along the street, and left behind the part of the city devoted to stores and shops, passing into an area of blocks of apartments and flats. The bars and beer halls grew smaller and more numerous, as well as more shabbily comfortable. People could be seen lounging on porches, in doorways, outlined by the brighter lights from within.

The trolley glided on, and the apartments became run-down. The bars ended entirely, and the strees were empty. Now there were establishments of a more functional sort—

wholesalers and warehouses, supply stations and depots. Loading docks fronted on the streets, which were now empty, save for a rare passer-by, or a watchman swinging a lantern. There were few bright signs: the places simply painted their names across the building-fronts: Nufuzlu Supply, Guvenlik Transport, Sokolsky Brothers, City Pipe and Tube. The trolley glided into a wide plaza, where it was to turn around and return to the city center, and stopped.

Urbifrage announced, "Here we are."

They gathered the baggage and left the trolley, crossing the plaza to a building not greatly different from those of the neighborhood. This one had a large entryway, and was well-lit inside. A plain sign across the front said "Transportation." Fraesch found himself wondering what passed for public transport on Mulcahen, but he refrained from asking.

Urbifrage led the way. Apparently he already had bought the tickets, or made what arrangements were to be made, for he passed the ticket windows without so much as a glance. A row of windows, some closed, ran along one side of the large interior. Opposite was a waiting room full of hard benches. In the middle was a stairway leading down, which they followed.

Urbifrage knew where he was going; Fraesch didn't. They went down the stairs and through a series of short tunnels and gateways, each lettered with incomprehensible abbreviations. After several of these, they passed along a long, damp gallery. Ahead, Fraesch began to hear noises, and he could smell odors of machinery—oil, tar, others he could not identify. They went through one last gate and emerged on a concrete platform inside a large tunnel. Before them was a line of metal cars, attached together at the ends, partly recessed in a large slot in the platform. Urbifrage paused briefly, selected one of the cars, and went aboard. Inside they found that the car consisted of a number of compartments on one side, and a corridor on the other. They selected an empty compartment, went in, and began stowing the baggage under the seats. There was a washstand in one corner, and a large window. It was well-made, but there was an archaic flavor to it Fraesch could not place.

He asked, stowing the last of the bags and settling into one of the seats, "Where's the operator?"

Urbifrage looked surprised. "The operator?"

"Yes. You know. The pilot, the driver. Where does he go?"

Urbifrage nodded. "I understand. There's not one to each

car. They're connected, and the engine goes at the front. It's a train."

"A train?"

"A railroad. *Zheleznaya Doroga. Demiryolu.* In a while you'll feel a bump—that's when they couple the engine; then we'll start. Make yourself comfortable; we'll be on this for two days. It's a nice trip—you'll get to see some fine country, in my mind, the best of Mulcahen.

4

There was nothing to do but be comfortable, and wait. At least this was close enough to civilization—one had to wait for a machine. Fraesch sat back in the cushions and allowed himself the luxury of apprehensions. He had not been one to wallow in introspection, but all the same he kept having a dizzy, giddy, vertiginous feeling that came and went, and that said, "everything's coming apart; everything you know is becoming progressively more worthless as you allow yourself to be drawn deeper into this mess on a colonial planet." Fraesch had just begun to have this intuition; it was easy to repress it. He rationalized it as a cultural disorienation.

It was like traveling backwards in time, except that at random intervals determined solely by fortune, chance, or the roll of random numbers, something from the future he had left, some artifact, came tumbling out of the air to surprise him. Electric trolleys! Railroads! Generating electricity, and that with a breeder reactor! Were they going to travel to a land where men fought with swords and lived in castles? No, not that far; Urbifrage had said they rode in powered surrealist contraptions called "striders," which were walking vehicles.

He focused on Urbifrage, who was sitting complacently in the opposite seat, looking aimlessly out the window at the dim platform. He said, "Urbifrage, why trains, of all things?"

Urbifrage scowled, as if Fraesch had interrupted some particular thought that had been entertaining him. "Why? Hm . . . I hadn't really thought too much about it, but I suppose it's because it's the easiest way to start."

"Why didn't they bring Maglines in here? Tubes? I could almost imagine KOSTORG was populated by a corps of Archaicists."

". . . I think that they had to start simple, because we are so far out. You can't bring much in here because of the transport cost. Inertia still costs den'gi to overcome. So you

52

have to use something you can build here—fast. The steel culture transplants easy. They had a mill going within two years after KOSTORG bought it out. But you can't make spacecraft out of steel, or airplanes. And consider this—there's plenty of coal on Mulcahen, but hardly any petroleum, any *nyeft'*. So we start with the steel culture—it's strong and easy enough to learn to work. And since we are going to be moving things around, ores to one place, basic products to another, finished stuff for export to get some money back, and the shortest way's overland, and there are no large rivers we can use . . . trains become the ideal solution. And let the people ride them as well. The most tonnage for the least investment. Or so I've heard."

"Electric, I suppose."

"No. Coal-fired steam power. It goes with the steel. And there's a lot of them, too. We've no roads, no draft animals. Later on. they'll replace it all with more modern stuff, more exotic stuff, stuff that only wizards would feel comfortable with, alloys that need a lot more care than we can supply . . . but for now what we have works well enough. There's a rail net all over Pangaea."

Fraesch sighed. "What sort of mechanical monster is going to pull this train?"

Urbifrage said, "No monster, I am sure, but this line is the Northwest Coast Line. They're known not to be fond of a lot of earthworks."

"They don't like spending money on straightening curves and leveling hills. They follow the terrain. That calls for agile engines. . . . Theirs were made here, but the original design was, I believe, intended for use in logging operations. Agile it is, if not very fast. Have no fears! NCL does not stint on engines. They make them good enough to sell to other lines on Mulcahen, and they tell me KOSTORG is going to buy some—disassembled of course—to ship to other developing worlds. The beauty is that they'll run on anything flammable—coal, oil, wood, trash, natural gas, sewer fumes, alcohol, acetylene, hydrogen . . . the list is long. KOSTORG claims that such primitive systems, tuned up to modern standards, cost far less than importing and maintaining modern systems."

At that moment, there was a bump from the front, which Fraesch assumed was behind him. It was not particularly a large bump; in fact it was barely noticeable. Urbifrage said, "That's the engine now. We'll be moving in a minute or so.

Get some sleep, that's my advice; there'll be plenty to see tomorrow." And suiting advice to action, Urbifrage rearranged
his position, propped his head back on a corner and closed
his eyes.

Fraesch, too, settled back, but he did not sleep. He looked
out onto the platform, where a few last-minute passengers
were hurrying to get aboard. Amazing, it was; they were the
only people he'd seen hurrying since he'd been here. Something caught his eye, and he looked again—a woman, her
baggage being carried by a ragged figure. It was the same one
he had seen on the hovercraft, he was sure, and the baggage
carrier, the wild man, Pomalu. What had she said her name
was? Sule? No. Tule—Tula. On this train? An astounding coincidence. He also noted that she had been wearing something more appropriate to the season and the planet—a plain
pantsuit, with a cape of matching material. Still, he smiled to
himself, she had managed to infuse the plain workaday clothing of Mulcahen with a certain style, a verve. And a lab technician, at that. Well, it wasn't impossible, he thought.
. . And he also thought about what she had seen today, what
facts she had gathered, about the place she was going, wherever it was. Was she as apprehensive as he was? She had vanished, passing out of sight, but she hadn't seemed dismayed
or worried.

Fraesch heard a sound. He looked from the window to Urbifrage. Urbifrage was snoring, a delicate little snore, a teapot
burble, not in the least a full-throated bullroar such as some
he had heard. When he looked at the platform again, he saw
that the platform was sliding backwards almost imperceptibly;
there was a motion to the train, something shorter than a
surge, longer than a jerk, and the motion became sensible,
direct. They were underway. Fraesch watched intently, savoring the experience; the forms of travel he was used to had no
such motion clues, nor did they have such an open view to
the outside.

For a time, the bare platform slid past the window, accel-
erating in bursts, rather than smoothly; then they were in the
tunnel, in which nothing could be seen except the bare walls
moving by, lit by the lights from the compartment. It went
like this for some long moments, until he felt their car making a motion underneath, as if traversing something uneven.
There were some odd side shifts, a roll or two, and a sensation of curving, and the tunnel ended, and outside the win-

dow he saw the city sliding past, quiet places covered with darkness and illuminated by puddles of light. There seemed to be nothing near the train, and he could not pick out any landmarks he knew. Below, he caught glimpses of the glint of lights shining on steel rails. There was no perceptible acceleration, but the train was picking up speed.

Fraesch leaned forward to look out the window. The stars were bright in the sky, but he did not know their patterns; there was no moon. And it was late enough so that there was no skyglow whatsoever. Northwest, they had said. Very well. The train was moving; Fraesch hoped it was northwest they wound up.

A thought crossed his mind here, like the constant flickering of distant lightning, that there was no way he could verify that what had occurred to him was in fact the real trip he was supposed to make. He had staked everything on the word of Aalet, done exactly as requested. In fact, he did not actually know if this snoring man across the compartment was actually Urbifrage or not, or whether the train was going northwest. . . . They could have sent him off to some desolate wilderness halt to waylay him. Enough was at stake. He dismissed it, with the counterthought: it would be simpler to eliminate him by almost any other means. Then how did Aalet know so much? Nobody expects his secrets to be undone by others . . . and there was something else as well; that Speculations seemed to be genuinely concerned about the failure of their project . . . that in part they probably wanted him to uncover why their best man had not only failed but turned an impressive array of sophisticated equipment to something he thought more important . . . and they could always keep him in place under open contract until it was time for them to move, and he couldn't release anything he learned there because he was under contract to them. One could take a chance, but with two already dead, he wanted to see more before leaping over a cliff of chance.

Fraesch looked long at Urbifrage, now snoring in great seriousness. No, he thought. That's the right man, and we are going in the right direction. That's my decision. And with that thought, he went to a dreamless sleep almost instantly.

What woke Fraesch up was sunlight directly in his face. He tried to cover his eyes, but his position was all wrong, and there was nowhere to prop his arm. The light slipped out of sight as they went into a sharp curve—he could feel it; but in a moment the track curved back, and with the motion, the sun was back, shining painfully bright in the window. Fraesch sat up. Urbifrage was already up, toweling his face off by the washbasin.

He looked outside. They were traversing a high, cold wasteland, from what he could see of it. Bare, tan-colored ground, dotted with low, sprawling blue bushes and a thin cover of something that looked like grass, but which Fraesch knew couldn't be, for true flowering plants hadn't yet appeared on Mulcahen. They were on the west side of a broad valley, moving north. He leaned forward, to look to the front of the train. The engine was hidden by the curves and the bulk of the cars between, and all he could see was a light smudge of smoke, which dissipated rapidly.

Urbifrage said, "Good day! A good eight hours out of Gorod, and no problems, so it seems—a light load, good weather and no unannounced stops. We'll be up on the plateau in an hour or two, and then we'll be heading west."

Fraesch said, "Looks cold out there."

Urbifrage nodded agreement. "Might be a little fresh at that, but it'll warm up."

Fraesch got up and walked, a bit unsteadily against the rolling motion of the train, to the washbasin. He had no beard to shave, having had it permanently depilated, but he thought a good scrub might clear his head. Urbifrage was putting away a primitive shaving kit—a bar of yellowish soap, a much-worn brush and a straight razor. He asked, "Do they have food on the train?"

"Up front. A restaurant car."

"What do they serve?"

Urbifrage laughed. "What else? All native stuff. Why worry—you haven't died yet; you won't now."

The restaurant car was like the rest, native woods and frosted glass inside, but it was different in that the dining room was elevated and the ceiling was a series of skylights that joined the windows. The view was incredible, and they seemed to be rushing along at a bewildering speed, although Fraesch knew on more serious inspection that their speed was probably no greater than about fifty or sixty kilometers per hour.

The service was pleasant, if a little slow, but the food was well worth waiting for; thin slivers of meat, a crisp, thin bread, enormous pine-nuts and a resinous, aromatic tea that had little color but which woke him up quickly.

Fraesch was mentally listing some of the questions he wanted to ask Urbifrage, when he happened to glance forward along the length of the train. They were now at the top of the western ridge of the great rift valley, and the restaurant car was just now following the curve of the tracks, to the left and west. His eyes automatically followed the diminishing lines of the cars to the front of the train, some twenty cars ahead, and across a great curve he saw the engine: it was like no machine he'd seen before. Long and heavy in comparison to the cars it was pulling, it seemed to be an enormous boiler bolted onto an assembly of wheels, rods, valves and levers, all in furious motion. The wheels were driven by rods, and the motion of the assembly was remarkably like that of the legs of some animal. It had a small set of guide wheels in the front, actually in front of the boiler, two sets of large driving wheels in the middle, and a trailing set behind. It looked naked and as mechanical as the interior of a geared timepiece, but in the bright yellow sunlight of morning and the neon-blue skylight from above, it also had a beautiful life to it that he had never seen before in the artifacts of civilized humankind.

Urbifrage, following Fraesch's gaze, said, "Nice, isn't it?"

"I wonder why we stopped using them."

"In most circumstances, they were less efficient, or so I've heard. Even on rails, linear induction's said to be better . . . but you couldn't have that in the wilderness areas we have to cross—L. I. needs constant cleaning. Barges will carry more, but they are slow and need a supporting fluid. They'll go out here, too, in time. That one is a lightweight, articulated engine—the frame is hinged in the middle and there's a set of valves for each set of driving wheels, so it will carry the weight but still go around curves. A sixteen-wheeler, arranged 2-6-6-2. The little wheels in the front and back only guide it and carry some of the weight."

For a time, the conversation continued on the subject of trains, about which Urbifrage seemed to be especially knowledgeable. Fraesch learned about the continent-wide two-meter gauge rail network, and about the various sizes and kinds of engines, and where they were made. Most, it seemed, came from two companies located somewhere in the confusion of Zavody: Workhorse Prime Mover and The Locomotive Trust. Others were assembled by hand in the maintenance shops of the lines that used them, and these were held to be the best, although their production rate was slow compared to the others.

This conversation might have continued indefinitely, because Fraesch found himself enjoying his excursion into a forgotten technology. But once he looked down the length of the car and saw that the woman he had met on the shuttle, Tula, had just entered and was now picking out an empty table. At a break in Urbifrage's exposition, he asked to be excused, that he might renew the acquaintance of someone he had met on the way to Mulcahen. The odd thing was that Urbifrage seemed to know, without turning and looking. Even odder was what he said, as they parted, simply, "Be careful."

She was looking at the menu with a slight puzzled expression when Fraesch arrived beside her table. He said, evenly, "On a strange world, it is a rare pleasure to see someone twice. May I join you, Miss Vicinczin?"

She looked up, as if startled, regained her composure and said, "Oh, yes, you are the fellow I met on that awful shuttle from the port. Forgive me, I am terrible with names, although I never forget faces . . . You are . . . Flask? Trask?"

"Fraesch. It rhymes with 'trash.' Joachim, although hardly anyone calls me that, except my father. Most people call me Jake."

She said, reflectively, "Tula is short for nothing. . . . Joachim is a fine old name, rich in tradition; I was named for a place on Earth, where my mother came from, a city in Russia, south of Moskva." She pronounced it as a native would have, two syllables, stressing the last strongly: Moh-*skvah*. However, she was not speaking in Old Russian, but in Interstellar Basic, and she had no discernible accent outside of occasional place names or borrowed phrases.

She motioned to Fraesch to sit, shyly, as if she did not quite wish to say it. He did, and said, "I would imagine you consider yourself fortunate that she was not from Verkhoyansk."

Tula's mouth curved in the slightest of smiles. "Indeed so! Or some other place equally dreary! But yes, please join me and tell me what is safe to eat. I am told they have no off-world foodstuff on this Mulcahen, that it costs too much, and so we must take our chances with a suppressed immune system. Come now! You seem well-fed; what is fit to eat? I am famished."

Fraesch suggested a breakfast similiar to what he had had, and summoned the waiter, also ordering an additional pot of tea for himself. When this had been accomplished, and they were assured that steaming trays would be delivered immediately, he asked, "It is odd to run into you again, on the Northwest Coat Line, of all the modes of travel I could have chosen. . . . To what place are you headed?"

She said, casually, "To an obscure research project sited by the endlessness of the Empyrean. They call it Halcyon Station. I am told, although I know little enough about it, beyond that one rides this train to get there; another odd coincidence for us."

"Coincidence?"

"Yes, just so. You told me that was where you were going, did you not? Halcyon Station. You are to be the temporary administrator."

"Yes, I am to be that. . . . I have been able to find out very little about what sort of an operation it is, although I understand that they were originally doing research on ocean waves with some very advanced computers. And you? You are a lab technician, but what kind? There are technicians and there are technicians."

"Actually . . ." Here she paused, for the waiter had returned with her breakfast and Fraesch's pot of tea. "Actually, I have had some question as to my utility. You see, I am an analytical linguist. The past director requisitioned a person of my sort, on emergency qualifications, but for the life of me I have been unable to fathom what use he might have had for one. I mean, on Mulcahen, one might run into scattered pockets of *russkovo yazyka* or *toorkcheh*, but those hardly qualify as unknown tongues; and there are no natives."

Fraesch made a noncommittal reply, but thought, *They sent for her presumably because of whatever it was that Moricle had uncovered. Most curious! Why would he ask for a linguist?*"

"I take it that you are not a translator, *oer se*?"

"Hardly. I am no more multilingual than anyone else, and I have never been able to do simultaneous translation, even with the languages I speak." She made a soft smile, as if apologizing for something she wished she could have been able to accomplish. "But no, I am the one who makes recordings, examines them, dissects them every possible way, and some ways that are not supposed to be possible. It's like mining, so I think—you have to feel a metric ton to recover a single nugget."

"You work with the spoken forms, then."

"Yes. I ignore the native scripts as a matter of course. I use my own system to notate written transcriptions. . . . I have to be careful in using it on stuff I send out; I occasionally forget in the throes of work that the universe does not use Tula's system."

"I would imagine that this line of work leads you into some difficult areas, at times."

"Is none of it easy. . . . Not all languages are done with words; some are whistled—there are some famous examples from Earth, but we have met others. Then there are the gesture languages, and the mixed forms."

"Are you expert in the analysis of all these forms?"

"No. I am a specialist of primarily spoken—if I may use the word loosely—forms."

"Did Moricle know that when he asked for you?"

She raised her eyebrows the slightest fraction. "What? Ah, yes, Moricle asked . . . for a specialist of my type."

"Then we might conjecture that he wanted something spoken investigated."

"Yes, spoken. Or heard somehow."

Fraesch noticed that she was becoming unaccountably tense, and so he steered the conversation away from the station. It was as if there were something bothering her about the assignment. Again, he avoided pressing her. There would, after all, be some time, and he did not wish to antagonize her at the start. She was a woman of subtle, but undeniable charm, but something nagged him there, too; he couldn't place her in any physical type he knew. The porcelain-white skin, delicate bone structure, were not particularly Russian, although the type was not unknown; but it normally went with light hair and eyes, and Tula's eyes were a startling deep chocolate brown, and her hair was flat black and very fine in texture. She had a suggestion of prominent cheekbones, but there was no epicanthic fold to her large eyes whatsoever.

There was something else he noted as well: her behavior. She moved confidently, without hesitation, however small and everyday the task, and used manners of refinement that spoke of a long life among people of similar behavior. Here was no ordinary lab technician. They were, by and large, a plain, direct lot of no great background. Her mannerisms would indicate either a high-class origin, or a long and successful life under Longlife, which no lab technician Fraesch knew of could afford. . . . There were curious circumstances, indeed. Although perhaps all things would fit into place harmlessly. He caught a shred of her scent—perfumed—as she reached for the teapot: it was very faint, almost unnoticeable. One of an herbal fragrance, tart and aromatic, slightly smokey, although he did not recognize it. It seemed to suit her well enough.

The train had increased its speed and was now pounding across the flat plains at a brisk rate. Fraesch could see no more of the engine, as the track was straight in this section, arrowing off into perspective across the empty plains. Looking that way, his attention was drawn by the sky in the west. The neon-blue depths were gone. A deck of high, thin but solid clouds was moving in, lending a touch of pearl to the light. Weather coming? He looked around, and found two of the ever-present thunderheads, both far to the west, seeming nowhere near the course of the train, and far ahead, on the western horizon, there was an irregularity, a wavering dark line—hills or mountains.

Tula finished her breakfast and called for another pot of tea. In the meantime, they passed the time trading anecdotes. The subjects were neutral, commonplaces, such as any man and woman might speak of before going on to a more immediate business. . . . Fraesch found himself hoping that she would continue that for a time; he enjoyed the game, regardless of the results in the end. They became so absorbed in this that they quite forgot the passage of time, and the sun of Mulcahen drifted across the sky with its usual rapidity.

Along the track ahead, Fraesch could see something, a huddle of buildings, perhaps, although certainly not a town out in this wasteland. The clouds moving in from the west had caught them and gone far to the east, and the light was now nacreous and sourceless, casting no shadows. The headlong pace of the train began to slacken, and Fraesch could see the wavering plume of smoke from the engine darken and thicken slightly. They were going to stop at this desolate location, for whatever purpose.

He said as much to Tula, who looked about for the first time. She agreed that it seemed a stop was likely. They were close enough now to make out the nature of the buildings. There was a cylindrical structure, elevated high up on sturdy legs, several sheds and a simple ramp. Out farther on the plains, an array of towers supported small windmills, each turning. Everything was made of wood, except the blades of the windmills and some projections on the tower. It was definitely not a town.

The train had now slowed noticeably and was coasting, emitting a trickle of gray smoke. The steward emerged from his cubby, which communicated with the kitchen below. As they were near the front, in fact the only passengers so close to the end of the restaurant car, he leaned over and spoke to them confidentially.

"Excuse me, esteemed customers, but ahead lies Battleground Waterstop. We advise that you go below, for your safety."

Tula turned to him. "Safety? Why? Are these bandits?"

The steward stroked his chin, as if explaining to a child. "They are not unknown in the empty places of Mulcahen."

Fraesch asked, "Then why do we slow, presumably to stop?"

The steward said, "The engine needs water—for the steam. We can't run without it. Battleground Waterstop is necessary. Have no fear, we are safe from most of the common sorts, and there have been no reports of stromads."

"What are stromads?"

"Wild men, mounted on war-striders they call Demons. They war with one another, and infest the open country. Have no fears! We have two gun cars, front and rear, and can shoot back. Still, the plastic is not unbreakable."

Fraesch and Tula both looked about the empty plains to either side of the train; there was no sign of movement or anything save the empty land covered with strands of something silvery, now that the light had changed. The windmills turned.

The steward suggested, "Perhaps not this time; after all, they don't raid every train that passes through."

The train slowed, drifted slowly to a stop with the engine opposite the windowless structure on legs. Fraesch could see movement; someone was climbing atop the engine, pulling down something from the building. An arm swung out of it, and water began flowing out. Several people, carrying what appeared to be weapons, moved nervously about near the engine. Fraesch looked at the dreary landscape again. On second glance, it was not totally featureless—although it certainly gave that impression. There were dry watercourses, some rockpiles, which looked haphazard and out of place. He asked the steward, who was also looking nervously about, "Those rocks, there. Left over from construction?"

"Yes, yes, of course, they've. . . ." He stopped and looked at the rockpiles intently as if something weren't quite right about them. Then he nodded and picked up an intercom handset, into which he said, excitedly, "The rocks, they've been moved, aim for the rocks. . . ." Then he stopped, because those at the other end could see for themselves what was wrong with the piles, they were moving; something was coming out of them.

There were two of them, striders of a distinctly warlike nature; bulbous-bodied, the legs attached to an operating mechanism along the upper surfaces. The fronts showed a two-piece windshield, swept sharply back, below which was a slit inside which something squat and menacing moved back and forth. Small guns or projectors overlooked the windshields, rather like antennae. The whole thing was suggestive of a cross between a bat and a spider, and they moved with sure deliberation, clearing their hideaways they had made under the rocks. Fraesch estimated that they might contain half a dozen men, if the power plant was small. One of them launched a blue flare, which arched high, bright enough to cast shadows. Fraesch did not look at it directly.

He asked the steward. "Why don't they shoot?"

The striders stalked closer to the train with chilling deliberation. Fraesch saw that one, from the first, had covered the passenger section, while the other menaced the gun on the train.

The steward said, "They'd only shoot up the train. Besides, this is Mehmet Karajaoglan, who only robs, neither does he molest, nor take slaves, from the train. I hear his relations with his fellow plainsmen are not so cordial."

"So we can be sure of being robbed."

"Oh, for sure, sir and madam. Remain quiet, and all will be well. Sometimes he's been known to take nothing, in which case we'll all have to go outside and listen to one of his vainglorious speeches."

"A speech?"

"In which Mehmet will describe his incomparable virtues and generosity, and urge degenerate city dwellers to join his band. I advise you to ignore such talk."

Fraesch said, "That I will." He turned to Tula. "Unreal! Molested by bandits, in the light of day!"

She said, with forced composure, "I can only set forth the wish that the steward is correct in his assessment of the character of Mehmet."

One of the striders crawled to a point from which it could conveniently oversee both train and the other strider. The second, changing its gait, broke into an odd motion rather like a canter, moving its eight legs in peculiarly, as if the full motion were being arrested. It quickly moved to make an inspection of the train, cantering from one end to the other, and then back again. It stopped opposite the dining car, and set its legs. Fraesch could sense movement within, although it seemed to lose none of its watchful air. A hatch opened on the underside, and several humans tumbled out, all men from their gestures and walks, carrying an odd assortment of weapons: one had an ancient laser, complete with a huge backpack housing the power supply, while another carried a double-barreled shotgun. Others had rifles of various sorts. These quickly fanned out, taking up strategic positions, while one other assisted a portly individual down out of the machine. Fraesch assumed this would be Mehmet. Mehmet and his assistant approached the dining car with gravity and circumspection. Fraesch continued to watch the rest of the party, for they seemed to retain an odd nervousness whose source he could not see. They had the train under control; what could they fear? There was nothing in sight.

Mehmet moved under the curve of the car and could not be seen. Presently, they could hear a door opening, and soft footfalls on the stairs, followed by the appearance of Mehmet himself. Fraesch saw nothing distinctive in the man, other than an erratic look to his eyes, as if he were keeping himself under strong control. Mehmet was portly, with brown-beige skin, a rather broad, flat face, a coarse, weathered complexion. For a long moment, he stood in the doorway, surveying the dining car, a frown flitting indistinctly around his brows and eyes, as if the population of the car had not been enough. He seemed like a man thwarted from making a speech which he had carefully rehearsed.

Suitable numbers or not, Mehmet drew in a deep breath, stepping farther into the car. Fraesch was close enough to him to smell him—an odor of onions and a light machine-oil.

There was a flurry at the door, and an excited subordinate clambered clumsily up the stairs. The assistant would not let him pass, so the subordinate hurriedly whispered something to the assistant, who immediately contacted Mehmet, who turned around impatiently. Another whispered conversation took place, of which Fraesch could catch nothing—it was in a tongue he did not know and was fast. Mehmet's reaction was immediate: He looked back over the car once, lingering once on Tula, and went back down the stairs hastily.

Fraesch looked at Tula incomprehendingly, a look she returned.

They both looked outside. Mehmet and his advisers were having an animated conversation, illustrated with elaborate gestures, between the dining car and Mehmet's strider. Some, those who had formed the original skirmishing party, were pointing excitedly at the ground, although Fraesch could not make out the source of their concern. Mehmet signaled his strider, or someone still within it, and from the vehicle an orange flare arced upwards and across the train. The train crew answered by causing the train to emit two piercing hoots from a whistle, and Mehmet's men began hurriedly piling back into their machines with what seemed to Fraesch to be evident fright and haste.

He asked the steward, "Why are they leaving?"

"They saw some sign, someone's been here; I couldn't catch much of it. They kept saying, 'Tuzun, Tuzun.' I don't know who or what it is. Never heard it before."

Down on the ground, the striders of Mehmet had almost completed their reloading, and were making preliminary moves to leave, nervous little jerks. The power-plants emitted a thin, bluish smoke and a high-pitched whine, and Mehmet's strider began to crawl off cautiously to the north, while the other strider covered his retreat. A puff of smoke from the engine and a jerk told Fraesch that the train was not waiting, but was getting underway.

Mehmet's machine crawled a respectable distance, and then the object in the slot below the windshields spit out a quick dazzle of purple radiance—short, random beams that caused a flickering of fire in whatever they touched. The other machine began firing as well—seemingly at random— here at the corner of a shed, there at a rock or juniper-like bush.

Without warning, one of the larger sheds, a depot-building, seemed to collapse and crumple from within, and from the wreakage crawled forth an even more astounding machine, somewhat larger than the oval, underslung machines of Mehmet's. This one was boxy and angular, and had four legs which terminated in mechanisms that looked like grippers. This device shook itself free of the wreckage of the building in which it had been hiding and began to stalk toward Mehmet, moving one leg at a time, methodically and chillingly.

Both Mehmet's machines turned their plasma guns on the new machine, spraying it with purple dazzle, which had little effect that they could see, other than scorching some of the paint, which was flat black. From the new machine, from a concealed orifice, a ball of burning material was ejected, to catch one of the legs of Mehmet's personal machine. The leg promptly melted and collapsed, whereupon Mehmet wheeled the machine about and began a hasty retreat, lurching where the missing leg fell due its turn. Then the black machine turned on the other strider, and fired several accurate shots which silenced the plasma gun. The orifice, or slot in which the plasma gun had been housed now emitted a thin trickle of greasy smoke, but the machine spun about, ordinary guns still firing.

The black machine gave cautious chase, stalking after the second strider. Cautiously an indistinct figure appeared on the roof of the black machine who manipulated a large, heavy gun which had been stowed in a concealed position. This the figure guided into place, where it made some adjustments, and then the gun emitted a bright white-yellow stream of fire and the sound of a prolonged scream, clearly audible, even offensively loud, inside the car. Where this beam touched the other vehicle, parts simply vanished, flew off, or melted. The other vehicle collapsed in a heap, legs moving disconnectedly, and presently burned. No one emerged from it. The black machine turned to give a last look at the fleeing Mehmet, and then stalked back to the train, which had prudently stopped.

The figure on the roof of the machine remained there, apparently guiding the machine through hand signals or telephone line. As it approached, they could see that it wore a helmet like a bucket, with stylized metal horns attached to the sides. The helmet completely covered the head, down to the shoulders, so they could make out nothing about it. The black machine, in its walking mode, was as tall as the highest part of the train, so they had to look upwards a bit to see the figure, gauntleted hands resting on the forward rail of the machine.

The machine stopped, and the figure restowed the gun, locking it into place, and then apparently reentered the interior. Shortly afterwards, a hatch opened in the forward part of the belly, and what appeared to be a child dropped with agility out of it, landing on booted feet effortlessly, like a cat. A child, or an adolescent. Probably a messenger, Fraesch thought.

The figure on the ground appeared to be a young girl, judging by the hair, proportions of hip and shoulder, motions as she moved. She cleared the underside of the black machine towering over her, stood and faced it, and made hand signals to someone within. The machine responded, turning around and setting out at an unhurried trot in the direction Mehmet and his surviving machine had gone. The girl ignored the machine and walked purposefully to the dining car, which she boarded without looking either left or right. Then came the familiar tug which signified that the train was underway again.

There were soft footsteps, a swishing of clothing and the girl appeared in the entryway. Fraesch looked closely. At first glance she was small and compact, the true contours of her figure hidden by the clothing, which seemed designed for both freedom of movement as well as warmth. She wore soft leather boots with the surface unsmoothed, something almost like moccasins. Loose black pantaloons were stuffed into their tops. For an overgarment, she wore a tunic-like, shirtlike wraparound reaching to the knees, which was made of some woven material and colored a most marvelously rich walnut color. It was trimmed with yellow along the borders, and was tied in place with a red sash of the same material. An ornamented slit on the side opposite the side to which it wrapped, outlined in the same yellow, and an erect but soft collar completed the garment. The effect was arresting and barbaric.

The girl herself was as attention-bound as her clothing: she had delicate, smooth skin of a pale beige tone, a round, rather childish face, small mouth, tiny nose which was slightly flattened and rounded, small eyes marked by pronounced epicanthic folds, which seemed all pupil beneath the lids. Her hair was dull black, the most of it tied into a single pigtail in the back, while straggling strands of it in front of her ears suggested sideburns.

Fraesch thought she had a strong look of Chinese ancestry, but her darker color and the sharpness with which her features had been drawn suggested something more northern, more hardy, perhaps Korean . . . no—she wasn't quite moon-faced enough. Her chin was small and delicate, and the nose had a subtle, but visible hook to it, giving her a slightly predatory look. Mongol? There were still pockets of pure types scattered about, who yet went by the names of old Earth, even though those place names were mostly meaningless now.

Fraesch found himself admiring her immediately. Here, he thought, was a creature who had taken Mulcahen in its own terms, who survived on the bare plains without benefit of the culture of the city; someone who would choose to be in the machine that defeated Mehmet in his own terms—incredible violence—and then step on the train as if she belonged there as well.

The girl glanced about the long compartment with some of the same impatience as had the unregretted Mehmet, as if she would have preferred an audience, However, she adjusted faster. The steward appeared, and without hesitation, she ordered a sumptuous meal for herself; and as an afterthought, ordered rounds of the same for Fraesch and Tula, who were currently the only inhabitants of the car. For payment, she retrieved a small ingot of something heavy and dull-silvery from a leather bag hidden under the folds of her wraparound tunic coat, which the steward took with bulging eyes. Silver? It never excited those kinds of looks, especially since the planet was full of it, and besides, it was too bright to match this. Platinum? Fraesch gestured to the table at which he and Tula were sitting, and the girl responded, settling herself with a graceful, whirling motion next to Tula, who had moved fastidiously over to give the barbarian girl room.

Fraesch took it upon himself to venture, "I am Jake Fraesch, and the lady is Tula Vicinczin. Tell us who you are."

"I am Tuzun," she said, as if it were the sole thing in the universe worth knowing, and looked at them blandly as if they were fixtures attached to the train.

Fraesch asked, politely, "You are a messenger from those who rebuked Mehmet and his friends?"

The girl broke into a broad smile, which revealed perfect teeth, and said, "Oh, no! I am the leader; that is my strider, and my friends will harry Mehmet now—that is a task they do not need a master of revenge for."

"Mehmet wronged you, then?"

She nodded, crisply, as if everyone knew the tale. "Just so. He visited a gathering of my people in the mountains, where he killed some, left some to starve, and took others for his slaves. When the Khan remonstrated with him, he caused slings to hurl severed heads back at us. This was judged a matter requiring redress, to which duty I addressed myself. . . . The results are plain enough."

"What will happen to Mehmet? Will they use the light beam on him when they catch him?"

"Light? Oh, you mean the gun. That is a. . . ." Here she stumbled, apparently at a loss for words. "That is a kind of rifle, except there are many barrels—the whole thing revolves. It shoots ten thousand rounds per minute, and every fifth shell is a tracer. A most holy weapon, and only I am permitted to use it. As Mehmet does not know I am no longer aboard, he will run forever. We will herd him into the northern wastes and mount vigil until his men elect to roast him over a spit, using the fuel of his own machine." She shrugged. "The matter is finished."

Tula commented, "The punishment seems excessive."

The girl, Tuzun, looked sidelong at Tula and said, "Only if you have not seen the vast miseries such a villain has caused. Indeed, there were some who wished to have him brought back alive, so that he could declaim to us of his innermost visions, that we might understand such evil; but I prevailed, for would not such words tempt us as well. To understand evil is to become party to it, and so we gave him the 'Scavenger's trap.' "

Fraesch said, "You mean some wanted to torture him."

"Yes. And his machines have the advantage of speed over ours, though ours are more agile and durable. So we waited for him, here, knowing how fond he was of teasing the civvies. . . . He will tease no more."

"Why did you get on the train? Did you wish to go somewhere else?"

Tuzun looked at Fraesch coyly, turning her head slightly to the side. He saw the soft, thick eyelashes and eyebrows, the loose dense hair falling over her ear. She said, shyly, "Oh, no, Ser Fraesch, off-worlder. . . . I came at the request of my father to guide you in some of the mysteries of our world which you must needs know."

Tula looked out the window and raised her eyebrows in a gesture of sardonic amusement. Befriended by a murderous barbarian!

Fraesch smiled politely, and asked, "Who is your father, that he should be so concerned of my welfare?"

"By now you should have met and spoken with him. We know him as the Mentor, and he interprets the word of the God to his people. You civvies would know him by his man-name: Anselm Urbifrage."

Fraesch stuttered, "You don't resemble him much."

"We are not a race, but comrades who call ourselves the Rainbow people. That you understand why is one of my tasks."

5

━━━━◦◦━◄◦►━◦◦━━━━

The train labored onward. Presently shadows on the western horizon expanded and enlarged to become mountains, and the dismal high plain came to an end. They began to see streams of clear running water and stands of native trees. The types with needlelike leaves were uniformly blue in color, while the broadleaved types were reddish or purple. These last kinds dropped their leaves, but without changing color, so that there was no brightness to autumn on Mulcahen.[1]

Settled places began to appear with increasing frequency, and the train stopped at most of them, save only the most isolated and wretched of them. The signboards along the track displayed their names, which were whimsical or frankly adventitious. They passed, in succession, Hope in the Wilderness, Without Thought, Men Wise Without Study, Three Thieves, My Illusions, this last being a major junction with a north-south line. Day had become night.

Another day passed without incident, or indeed anything for Fraesch to fix his mind on; he was growing bored with extended travel on a primitive world: all this trouble for a couple of thousand kilometers. At the evening, they passed through a wide land of flat valley bottoms, almost as if they had been graded that way, and harsh, blocky mountains, of no great height. Vast herds of nondescript large herbivores grazed, watched guardedly by men in the distances riding striders with long legs and small bodies. One moment they would be negotiating some tortuous passage, and the next, crossing an open area with a seemingly limitless vista to the dark north. Tuzun, who had borrowed another compartment,

[1] Trees on Mulcahen could be needle-leaved or broadleaved, evergreen or deciduous, of all four possibilities, and in turn, any of those could be predominantly colored blue (the majority), reddish or rarely, green. All were, without exception, gymnospermous, or, what could loosely be called conifers.

only referred to it as The Broken Land, and said that it appeared they would arrive sometime in the morning.

There was yet another mystery: Tuzun. After she had introduced herself, she had said little of consequence; indeed, little of anything, and after some short conversations with Urbifrage about people and events Fraesch knew nothing about, had retired to her own borrowed quarters. Urbifrage had also said little about her, and Fraesch had thought better of asking, at this point. What he had said had been terse and straightforward: that her mother had been one of a party of settlers who had come during the YM period, and that they had all been like her, and were from the same planet—which they only referred to with a phrase in Chinese he never could quite get the sense of—and that Tuzun strongly resembled her mother.

Something else was bothering Fraesch as well. Tula said she knew that he was to be temporary station administrator; that he had told her. But he hadn't. He had expected to arrive and have difficulties finding the place: instead, the first five people of six he had met seemed to be uncommonly well-informed. Well, he could explain Aalet easily enough, and through him, Urbifrage, and through him in turn, Tuzun and Pomalu. But not Tula. And bearing what Aalet had told him in mind, these anticipations did not reassure him. He felt strongly the presence of a trap. But what kind of trap? He could not imagine one that would benefit anyone, as long as it was focused on him; he certainly could not operate the data-recording system that had been reinstalled at Halcyon. Nor, he thought painfully, make any sense of what it recorded, even if he could operate it. He ate alone in the dining car and retired early.

It felt like all mornings on Mulcahen—as if he had just gone to bed. A soft, blurred outline was bending over him, Tuzun. She whispered, "Wake. Come with me. I will show you something." Urbifrage slept on, snoring lightly as was his habit. Tuzun slipped out of the compartment silently.

Fraesch dressed and stumbled to the corridor, where the girl was waiting. As soon as she saw him, she started off. Fraesch followed, hesitating only when he realized that she was going to the end of the train. Still, he followed her through several silent, dark cars, until he caught up with her at the last platform, out in the air.

The air was bone-chilling cold, but there was a cleanness to it he could not deny, and a tang as well, something he knew he should know, but couldn't quite place. It was dawn, and there was a cold blue light over everything. The train was lazily traversing some lovely country—broad, open, rolling swales covered with some grasslike plant that had long stems and waved gracefully as they passed, interspersed with patches of dense forest. There was a quiet, the silence of all dawns, and an expectancy in the air. He said, shivering, "What is it?"

"Watch on this side." She indicated the side opposite the one he had been sitting on. Fraesch moved to that side and watched. He only saw more rolling swale, more low hills, more patches of dark forest, alternating endlessly across the face of Mulcahen. But there was something odd about the scene. There seemed to be too short a horizon; there was nothing behind the first rank of low hills. They passed through a narrow cut, and he felt the train coasting, as if on a hill, and he looked out, and out, and down seemingly endless leagues to the silent blue emptiness of the ocean, the Empyrean Sea. He stood entranced, frozen in place, staring, unblinking. Another cut blocked his view for a moment, and then he could see it again—all the way to the horizon, a blue floor beneath an electric-ultramarine sky, streaked and whorled with the faintest tracery of cirrus.

Tuzun said, "It is worth it, is it not, the way it comes on you suddenly like that?"

Fraesch nodded, still struck by the empty grandeur of it. He said, "Perhaps now I understand a little of why they came and stayed. I see Mulcahen is not all high plateaus and dry wastelands. . . . Do you call this place we are going home?"

"Not Halcyon, of course, but the village back from the coast was the place where I was a child . . . more or less, although I have been with him much on his travels."

"Why did you come to meet me?"

"I told you."

"I still don't know."

"It's hard to say. . . . This looks like an easy world, but it's not, and it doesn't like being looked at closely. You can only endure it with a proper guide, someone to help you through the subtle parts; nothing is as it seems here."

Fraesch thought, *She hasn't seen some of the places I've been, neither she nor her father has been off-world, off this primitive backwater planet populated by disoriented immi-*

grants cut off from their proper roots, not knowing how to act.

She said, musing, but as if she were reading his mind, "You think I am a primitive barbarian girl, but that Moricle looked too closely at the face of Mulcahen, and his woman, too, and now they are not."

Fraesch's mind raced, unaccustomed to exercise so early in the morning. *Is she telling me Moricle trespassed on some native cult and was killed by them?* All he said was, "But why me?"

"You are from the old worlds, so you will have your vices—still, we know of you and know you are one we would spare. We hear of those worlds, but they do not know of us—words travel outwards easily. You have a repute for honesty and lack of plots. Still, one needs a proper guide to traverse difficult terrain."

"Well, what is it I must watch for? Aalet told me something. . . ."

"Aalet knows of one plot, and has spoken according to his station. Well enough—so much is true, as I understand truth. But of what is here, I will not speak openly. Believe me when I say that it is my intent to bring you through, whole and your own man. Afterwards, you may do as you will—or can."

"What about Tula?"

"If she can find the way, she will be welcome. I have no charge to guide her. She will find it difficult, for she shares much with Moricle and that one's woman."

"Do you know of her?"

"No. Only what I can see with my own eyes."

"I still don't understand why all of you would go to such trouble for me—say, in particular. What is it?"

"To say it now, which is forbidden, will preclude your passage later. You have not been set upon and murdered so far by us, so trust me in this. I will not follow you around, but only visit now and then, so that I understand your perception."

"And if I fail?"

"You will be like the rest; you will come and go and have seen nothing, or you will see too much, and be caught within a thing you cannot imagine."

Cryptic and mysterious, like a child playing a part she did not truly understand, Tuzun slipped in the door, back into the train silently. Fraesch remained on the bare platform, still shivering with the cold of morning, although he could sense that it had none of the bitter bite of the interior in it, but rather a tart freshness, as of the sea. He could smell it. Salt water, waves, a seacoast. He watched the morning erupt out of the east with the planet's disturbing swiftness and felt an odd, intangible joy rising, something he hadn't felt yet about this trip. It was a feeling he always looked for. Yes. This one would go right, somehow.

Tuzun reappeared, bearing mugs of steaming tea, which filled the blustering air of the platform with a resinous bloom. She handed him the mug and waited for him to taste it before she spoke. "I am going to leave at the junction. I have some things to take care of in the old town. . . ."

"Are we going to be there so soon?"

"Yes. Your trip by train is over. So I say: do now what you must do there. All will be well for a time. I only warn you about the woman who also came to Halcyon: Vicinczin. She is not what she seems, or suggests that she is."

"I hardly need a tribal hetwoman to tell me that. So what is she?"

Tuzun shook her head slowly. "I have tried to see, but it's something beyond my vision. I have only been able to see what she is not. But she did not come with malice to you, so therein is one less worry. Actually, I could almost say she doesn't really see you, properly, as if she were looking beyond you . . . at something."

"I should beware of night visitors in transparent nightgowns, no doubt."

Tuzun laughed out loud, saying, "Ha, ha, nightgowns indeed! At Halcyon, among the off-worlders, you will no doubt see things more plainly stated than nightgowns in the dark. They are a randy lot. They say it comes of the drug that prolongs life that you take." This last she said with an arch leer which Fraesch found most disquieting, as if she were seeing completely through him.

"I have undergone the treatment once and noticed nothing amiss. I do not accost strange women to excess; in fact, hardly at all."

"Perhaps we are wrong, then. After all, they are the only sample we've had to look at."

"There's always the settlers and the runaways."

"They act differently. The settlers are rigorous, as the runaways are loose, as you will see if you stroll along the shore. Perhaps these people at Halcyon suffer a tedium, being not of this world, but cut off from their own as well. However odd it seems, we need an engagement, a plunging in, to work properly."

"Well said, I will remember it."

"Apply it to yourself, and weigh carefully, for we become what we pretend to be."

"Tell me . . . before you leave, where did you learn your wisdom?"

"By being me, here and now, and doing what had to be done, without thoughts of might-have-beens." She said this with a shy smile playing around the corners of her small mouth. She added, "Make your identifications carefully, Joachim Fraesch. You are trying to see me as an unusual child, whereas in my own view I am an ordinary woman; I am not innocent, nor a fool, but sly and cautious. Be you so as well." And this time, when she slipped through the door, back into the train, Fraesch knew that she wouldn't be back. As he stood on the platform, he realized with a shock that he had been guided with exquisite care exactly to this conversation with Tuzun, all the time being prepared to hear what she had to say, and oriented so as to react to it with just the right amount of caution: neither skepticism, nor panicked acceptance—something between. Fraesch found himself hoping he negotiated the next set of exercises in the same manner, for somebody was going to a lot of trouble to see that he was . . . the only thing he could think of was "oriented in the correct direction." Or something close to that. It was the why that eluded him.

The northwest coast country was one of parallel coast ranges, none especially high or rugged, but in many places the mountain ridges would run out to the very edge of the ocean. There were many rivers and creeks, mostly small; one, of respectable size, came tumbling out of the soft, tree-covered hills, hit the more level valley bottom and made a winding drowned slough connecting its mountain section with the ocean. At the place where the river changed to slough, they had built a village, called, with the popular tradition of naming places with an odd phrase, On the Waves. It looked to Fraesch's civilized eyes like a living diorama out of a museum, or an old photograph suddenly brought to light.

Everything was made out of locally cut wood, and left unpainted. The newer buildings, and newly repaired sections of old ones, were a silvery-gray color. As the wood aged, it first developed tiny splinters along the grain, then became smooth, darkening in color to a streaked gray-brown, and finally, the color of burnt coffee.

Despite its antique air, it seemed a substantial place. There were docks of fishing boats and adjacent processing sheds. There were sawmills and piles of the same silvery timber. Along the railroad there were platforms and warehouses. The architecture of the town followed simple lines, and the majority of buildings were square or rectangular, with slightly sloping flat roofs, the owners living in lofts above their shops. Windows were narrow, with glass that had a distinct wavering to it. The odors of slough, ocean, sawmill and cannery mingled and complemented the shapes and colors; On the Waves was an elemental, earthy town. Surrounded by the blue forested hills on three sides, it was open to the west and the ocean along the slough, and illuminated from the open west with a marvelous, mutable light of the sea.

Fraesch had not found Urbifrage in the compartment, and imagined that he probably had debarked with Tuzun at a tiny village a bit back in the hills, called Laughter and Tears. It didn't completely dawn on him that he was on his own until he found himself standing on a rather muddy platform, with his baggage, listening to the echoes of the train puffing away up the river valley to the north. He looked about blankly, as if awakening, and noticed that Tula Vicinczin was standing, apparently in the same predicament, not too far away. She, too, looked slightly bewildered. Fraesch joined her.

Tula spoke first, and said, "I see that our guides have left us to our own devices."

"So it seems, for all the fine talk."

"Do you know where Halcyon is—or how to get there?"

"I know it's close to the ocean, in a secluded place not far away. There has to be a way there—they'd have to haul materials from the railroad."

"The natives seem most uninterested."

Fraesch looked carefully for some sort of suitable transportation; there wasn't much to be seen. Along the road which angled off from the railroad depot and ran along the docks there were a few vehicles in sight, but nothing that might be usable. There were a half-dozen of various kinds of striders, not in the best of repair, and none large enough to carry, apparently, more than one extra person. There were also two tracked vehicles, which Fraesch was later to learn were called "crawlers," but they, too, were small and seemed to have no extra room.

Fraesch said, sighing, "It seems nothing suggests itself. One of us could go about and see, while the other watched the baggage."

"Neither task appeals to me, but I especially do not wish to be touring door-to-door. I will volunteer to watch the baggage."

Fraesch answered, gallantly, "and I will start asking the idiotic questions of the stranger . . . 'where may I hire a convenience?' I will push if I can find a wheelbarrow."

"You will get muddy, I am sure."

"There may be no cure for it."

Fraesch moved his baggage beside Tula's, and started off the platform onto the street, which was paved with baulks of wood sunk into the soft ground with their butt ends exposed. It was pavement of a sort, but it was also slightly spongy to the step, wet and muddy. He managed to get across the first intersection without undue difficulty, when he stopped and motioned to Tula. Approaching them, quite silently, along the dock street, was a large strider in excellent repair, trotting briskly.

The machine proceeded along the docks smartly; bypassers looked at it carefully as it passed, and went on. It trotted up to the station platform and halted with a little flourish. It was only when it was right at them that they could hear the whine of the powerplant.[1] Fraesch returned from across the street, certain that this machine was one of Halcyon's, sent to pick them up.

This was an eight-legged machine, rather long in body, with a broad, buslike cab in front and a narrower section back of that. The leg mechanisms were attached to a deep keel beneath the body proper and was by far the most sophisticated strider Fraesch had seen yet.

A section of the front, at the chinline, detached and swung down: an extending stair. Down this stair stepped a slender young man wearing a leather variation of the local costume—sashed wraparound tunic, loose pantaloons and boots. The young man observed Tula critically for a moment, and then introduced himself.

[1] Strider powerplants were commonly small turbines burning a volatile hydrocarbon liquid fuel derived by distillation from coal. The turbines turned a generator and provided input power to the hydraulic pump system. Older units have diesels.

"Aha! You will be, I believe, the Techist Vicinczin; yes—you will be a welcome addition to our staff." He observed Fraesch. "You, ser, will be the Administrator Fraesch. You will doubtless be welcome as well. I am Nirod Pelletier, Mechanical Engineering Section; I repair striders and drive them, as bored with the tedium of Halcyon as the rest, and equally as adept at the exercises that banish ennui—at least until rotation, when I shall have to learn all over again to behave."

Fraesch observed the facile young man carefully. Here at last was a person from the station itself. This was not, to his mind, an especially good introduction. He was flippant and irrelevant, and much more interested in Tula than the situation would seem to warrant. Fraesch felt no jealousy, but he found Pelletier's ogling of Tula to be slightly disorderly. She seemed to be a little uncomfortable, as well.

Both Fraesch and Tula began picking up their bags. Fraesch said, "We were expected, then."

Pelletier answered, "Exactly so, although my timing was a little off. The Governor sent a 'gram ahead. . . . It's a bit of a walk, and few try it, although there are some who will do anything on break. Still, what's there to do when you get here. . . . Here, let me assist with that bag. . . ." He loaded Tula's bags into the strider. Afterwards, he helped her up the stairs into the cab. After that, he hastily lent Fraesch a hand.

There was a passenger compartment—back through the main section of the strider, but Pelletier would have none of their using it, insisting they sit up front with him, in the cab proper. The driver's seat was on the right, as one would sit in it, with the stair in the middle. On the left side was another seat, broader, and without operator's controls. The angular cab had a slightly sweptback windshield, and large windows on all sides, and large rear-view mirrors canted out on elaborate suspensions. Fraesch and Tula seated themselves, and sunk deep into soft cushions. Tula's face was brightened somewhat.

Pelletier arranged himself at the operator's console, seating himself with exaggerated care, and engaged levers and control rods. The machine responded smoothly and powerfully, pivoting about and starting off back the way it had come. Fraesch looked about in frank amazement. Except for a barely felt rippling vibration, there was little feel of the motions of the legs. The strider rippled along, with approximately the motion and speed of a beetle traversing a sand

pit, the body moving slightly as it adjusted to different ground
contours and power applications. The damp little town under
the shifting light of the seacoast rapidly passed before them,
thinned to shacks and junkyards and faded out. They had left
On the Waves and were on the way to Halcyon.

The time was late morning; the sky was deep blue, washed
clean by the pre-dawn shower which had made everything
muddy, not clear but streaked by a delicate tracery of high,
pearl-colored clouds. As they proceeded along a track running beside the slough, the vegetation changed, and the soil as
well. It became sandy, and the low ground cover became a
mixture of something that looked like dull-purple clumps of
long needles, and a low, feathery, creeping evergreen of a
pale blue that was almost gray. Instead of the forest of tall
conifers, the trees were shrubby and stunted and grew in
dense clumps, in which they could catch glimpses of contorted and histrionic branches.

Over the brackish waters of the slough they could see the
flitting, darting shapes of the *kryloruki*, gliding and plunging,
combining some of the qualities of the flight of sea birds, and
the erratic lunacy of bats. These, from what Fraesch could
see of them, did not look much like bats, but more like fer-
rets with slender wings, with streamlined, smoothly tapering
muzzles; they flew slowly and methodically in the upper parts
of their flight paths, but when they came down to the water's
surface, they allowed their speed to increase to an incredible
rate, and followed zany, dashing zigs and zags. Sometimes it
seemed their muzzles would tap the surface, but they caused
no turbulence, so it was difficult to be sure. Fraesch imagined
that they were feeding on something that lived on or near the
surface. He wanted to ask about them, but when he looked
across the cab of the strider at Pelletier, he saw that their
driver was looking out the other side of the cab with bored
disdain, and so he kept his question to himself.

The ground became sandier, but dunes hid the ocean from
sight. They could sense that it was there—a presence—by the
light, and an emptiness behind the hills. To the south were
hills covered with trees, and to the north, long ridgelines that
angled into the ocean from southeast to northwest, some of
them fairly lofty. The track, marked by the footprints of the
striders and strips where the crawlers had passed. Pelletier
guided the machine along this track as it turned to the north.

He said, aside to Fraesch and Tula, "Had to hold the speed

down while we're on sand; up ahead the ground's firmer, and
we'll let it pace out a bit."

The track became more uneven, pitching up and down, but
the strider followed the terrain without noticeable change.
They began to feel subtle changes in the motions it made,
and it did seem to be moving faster. Then the gait changed,
and the hum of the turbine dropped, but the speed increased,
and the motion inside assumed a floating, balancing quality.

Pelletier said, "We're in 'run' locomode now. All I have to
do is steer it and mind the power settings."

Fraesch sat back and stared through the enormous windshield as they raced along, following a curved and rough
track through a forest of the gnarled, twisted trees. They
were going much too fast now for details. Through gaps in
the dark forest they could see in tantalizing hints and flashes
the heaving emptiness of the Empyrean Sea.

The track turned sharply back inland, and began to climb
up the ridge. It became very rough. Here, the soil seemed
rocky, and tree roots crawled over the ground, the roots of
the gnarled trees being as wildly contorted as the branches.
Fraesch began to see why they favored striders and crawlers,
at least in country like this—the sand of the lowlands would
mire wheels, and the rough ground of the hills would require
massive engineering to make a passable road, but they simply
cut a path through the forest and let the crawlers and striders
widen it as they pleased.

They topped the ridge and began a precipitous descent, the
north face being steeper than the south. Pelletier did not re-
tard the speed of the strider, and it fairly fell down the slope,
plunging through a tunnel formed by the overarching
branches. In a moment, they were at the bottom: a sharp
turn, across a clear, gravelly creek with little water in it, and
then he slowed the machine to a crawl. Fraesch was certain
he had done so for effect, although they did have to traverse a
difficult open slope, covered with the feathery evergreen
vines. However it was, it was striking; they were there.

Whatever the motivations of Speculations had originally
been, they had spared nothing in creating an environment for
their people when they had contracted to have Halcyon Station built; this was no rude camp in the wilderness, but a
small community that had the flavor of a resort, an academic
retreat and an experimental commune for architects, all in
one. At first glance, Fraesch could not see a single straight

line in the entire site, and with all the visible structures being
painted or constructed of some insect's-eye view of a garden
of mushrooms. After he had looked at it, as they were climbing the hill to the site proper, he could begin to distinguish
different types of structures: there were the obligatory geodesic domes, but none were based on the sphere as the surface
of generation, but rather ellipsoids of various orientation. The
largest of these was apparently the computer lab. Shops and
storage buildings were tensile hyperboloids, saddle-shaped,
and held together by tension, not compression. There were
several sizes of these, some standing alone, some in small di-
agonal groups of odd numbers. Far up the ridge back of the
site, was a small white sphere with a hyperboloid structure attached to it: presumably a mobile power plant. But what
caught his eye most of all was what seemed to be the living
quarters. This was the largest building of all, and stood somewhat off by itself, if indeed "building" was the proper word
for it.

Fraesch could not quite categorize it as it rose into view as
they climbed higher; crystalline? Fungoid? It was apparently
a series of elliptical or ovoidal bubbles, placed together, in
the most random and unpredictable fashion. It looked *grown*,
not built. An irregular mass, the individual units always had
at least a major portion exposed to the outside, however
massed, although some were almost buried. The units had
one, two or three windows of distinctive shape: an equilateral
triangle with the corners softly rounded, slanted so that the
apex at the top leaned out. The whole window was recessed
within a molding which was part of the walls, and which
leaned outward even more—the effect was uncommonly eye-
like, despite the odd triangular shape. These units—rooms or
apartments—were connected by a fantastic network of balconies, catwalks, curved stairs, tubes, all curving, rising, falling
in apparent total entropic disorder. Porches and covered entries abounded, and some were dead ends. Many of the connecting ramps included little pockets offset to the side. Of
course, he could not see inside the structure, but he had a distinct feeling that it was equally complex inside as well as out;
that it was probably a labyrinth inside.

Pelletier commented, "And now you see we are approaching what we Halcyonites fondly call 'The Barracks,' although it does have its good points. There is an excess of room,
so no one need feel crowded. Most flats are suites of varying
numbers of cells. Ser Fraesch, we took the liberty of reserving

the old director's suite for you, so you need not tramp up and down the ramps like Hamlet's ghost. And Techist Vicinczin can have her choice of, I believe, about six different suites, each with its own ambience."

Tula asked, "Nachitose . . . has anyone taken her suite?"

Pelletier looked around, a little surprised. ". . . No, although it does have perhaps one of the better views. Why do you ask?"

"When they were telling me about the assignment, they said she had the most isolated suite. If they are open, I would like to have it."

"Certainly . . . I see you are not a believer in bad luck, or omens, or tragic destinies."

"Or similar poof and piffle. If I have to live in a dormitory, at least I want a room where I can be removed from the tumult. My work, once I get into it, is demanding of concentration and I will need a place in which I can relax."

Fraesch listened carefully to Tula's request, for it displayed an uncharacteristic degree of force and confidence, for a lab technician.

Pelletier assented without a moment's hesitation. "Easy enough to arrange! The suite is open; you shall have it. I may warn you that it is a bit remote in the structure and not a little difficult to get to—you will need some assistance with your baggage, and finding it."

"You know your way?"

"Assuredly. We old-timers are all like native grubs burrowed into an old log: never fear, I will show you the shortest way. It is a fine unit, by the way—there are two sleepers, two baths, a fine kitchen and eatery so you need not visit the taverna, a study, a company room, and a listening tower. And a fine view of both sea and mountains. A superb choice, although none of us would feel quite right taking it, after all. . . ."

"Understandable, Pelletier. But what is a listening tower?"

"Some suites have them. They are special company rooms in which clever acoustic chambers amplify the sounds of the outside—wind, rain, the waves on the beach, and the like—without interface. The sounds are not reproduced, but collected and carefully conducted through chambers. There is also a fire pit in the floor. They are places for . . . ha, ha, romantic musings and adventures."

Tula turned a warm smile on Pelletier, and also favored Fraesch with it. A secret, knowing smile. "Romance, is it? I

will be coy and shy, here; yet I would enjoy such a room, if
but for myself, alone."

Pelletier said, "Those that have them enjoy them greatly,
so it is said."

Pelletier concentrated on his maneuvering, now, frowning
slightly. They moved slowly now, circumspectly crawling between the buildings. Fraesch could see, close at hand, that
they were not the white he thought he had seen from a distance, but the subtlest off-white pastels, each structure different. It was so subtle that it took conscious effort to see the
difference. In the case of the dormitory, the sides and walks
were a wonderful soft matte oyster, while the rooflike parts
were a gray only slightly darker.

The strider halted before an arched entrance not greatly
different from any other of three or four more he could see.
Pelletier let the stairs down and helped them unload their
baggage. Pelletier disappeared into the structure for a moment to get someone to assist Fraesch. While they were waiting, Fraesch looked up at the structure before him, in which
he was going to be living for at least the next year, perhaps
more. Close, it was larger than it seemed from a distance, the
projecting bubbles and cupolas overhanging the entry court.
It was exquisitely beautiful, there was no doubt about it.
There was also no doubt whatsoever that it was intricate and
cryptic, to the point of self-indulgence and beyond. The odd
triangular windows looked more than ever like eyes . . . or
better put, like the eye-sockets of the skull of some odd creature. Fraesch knew he would be impressed by it, inside, but
he felt uncomfortable with it, none the less.

Presently Pelletier reappeared, with a thin, intense girl in
tow, whom he introduced as Ciare Dekadice. She wore her
brown hair in a mass of curls; the girl's face was thin and intense, with crisp features which were slightly blurred by some
internal state Fraesch could not describe. There was the faintest possible trace on her thin mouth of a pout; boredom or
lack of interest. But she helped Fraesch willingly enough, carrying some of his parcels, and found her way to his suite
without detours. She didn't say much, which at that moment,
Fraesch rather liked. She showed him where the key-plate
was, and left. Fraesch found himself in a small spherical
foyer. He saw that it led to a set of short stairs going down
abruptly. He sighed deeply, and said to himself, in the silent
room, "Now, it begins."

6

Fraesch knew what to do: find what passed for an office and start to work. He was certain, after meeting the oily Pelletier and the diffident Ciare Dekadice, if they were valid samples, that there would be plenty to do. To the two of them there had been an air of intense self-indulgence which Fraesch had found slightly disturbing, rather like being in the company of people who shared a very specific perversion, which was kept an absolute secret.

But first would come settling himself in these odd quarters, a process, he thought as he stood in the foyer, which would take the rest of the day.

The suite was dark. The foyer was illuminated by a translucent pane in the upper part, set in at what appeared to be a random and off-center manner until he recalled the erratic shape of the building, and remembered that because of its shape, the pane was probably in the only place it could be. He looked for, and found, touch-plates for the internal lighting system. One for the foyer he located and turned it back off. No need for that. Another turned on the lights in the room below. Fraesch peered into the room, located not quite directly ahead and down about a meter or slightly more, entered by an open stairs supported in the middle along its axis by a gracefully-curved beam, of the same off-white material as the rest of the building. It looked airy and insubstantial, but when he tentatively put his weight on it, it neither flexed nor vibrated, but felt solid and reassuring. He left the baggage in the foyer and went down.

The room was an arched ovoid in shape, deviating from a true ellipse at the top. Small panels at eye height cast a soft, shadowless illumination. The floor was carpeted, and around the perimeter were built-in platforms and cushions. Projections from the walls terminated in flattened, palmate fixtures—places to set drinks or ashtrays; at irregular intervals small bays were set into the wall. At first he could not divine

85

a purpose for the room, but it slowly occurred to him that this was a room used solely for greeting and entertaining visitors, more or less officially. It was private, reserved, almost austere, but it was not a place where one would remain if one were an inhabitant or a close associate. There was a slight staleness in the air. It had been unused for half a year, unvisited, except perhaps for cleaning robots, which he assumed would be in such a hypermodern structure.

A passageway, off-center now to the right, led elsewhere. Fraesch followed it, looking carefully along the walls for the light switch. The passage curved to the right, as if following the curve of the company room, and upward, terminating in a small circular chamber whose ceiling was very high up, the walls curving up to it. A small chandelier hung from a skylight of stained glass. Into this chamber opened several passages, some at floor level, some slightly higher and reached by short flights of steps. A junction, a nexus. Fraesch realized at this point that he had absolutely no reference system to conceptualize such a structure as seen from the inside; he had no idea where the passages, some reached only by ladders, might lead.

Proceeding with what he thought might be a system, he started with the first passage to the right of the entrance. This was a steep, narrow stair-tunnel down that curved left as well. The angle of descent was uncomfortably sharp. Fraesch guessed this would put him somewhat under the company room. The passage terminated in a landing facing a closed oval doorway. A small illuminated panel controlled it. He pushed a touch-plate labeled "open," and the door slid down into a recess. Inside was an area divided into two parts; the portion nearest the entry was a broad crescent, about three meters across its shortest dimension. Here, at least, some of the walls were vertical: cabinets and closets, a small built-in desk, several seats along the walls, counter space. A short slanted passage down broke the curve of the wall to his left. Probably a bathroom. Directly opposite the door was an elevated opening, rather like the windows, connected by an ornamental ladder. This resembled a bubble which had intruded into the space of the larger room-bubble. The opening was covered with a cloth drapery. Fraesch pushed aside the curtain, peered inside.

This space was much smaller than the room proper, and was the bedchamber. The bed was the floor of the chamber, and was an irregular oval shape. There were various vents, positionable lights, the usual small alcoves in the walls, a sky-light, a speaker grille. Cozy.

Fraesch looked about. It was clear that this was a guest bedroom. It had a specific air of tenantlessness to it, although it was spotlessly clean. Satisfied, and a little amazed, Fraesch returned to the nexus, feeling some satisfaction that it had remained at the top of the narrow stairs where he had left it: he had half expected it to move.

So far, he felt some confidence with his explorations. He tried the remaining passages in turn, feeling his way about the rest of the suite. He located, in turn, a homey kitchen, although small, a pantry and adjoining snack cubby, which he named the buttery; a dining room, which managed to be both frostily formal and tensely intimate, all in the same reference. An odd, ambiguous room. He also found a sitting room or parlor, with a window view of the land falling down to the ocean, and the water beyond; a study, a master bedroom, a gymnasium, a balconied living room of large dimensions, and at the very top of the suite, what they had called a listening tower, which had its own eerie ambience.

This was an ordinary, if somewhat lofty-ceilinged, sitting room; except for the fact that vents and grilles apparently connected it with the outside, but aurally and visually only. Fraesch paused, listening—it was like being outside, only more intensely so; every slightest sound was magnified, and he felt at the focus of elemental forces. He left, and began placing his things in the cabinets of the master bedroom and the study.

There were also innumerable short-cut passages, walks, ramps, balconies, connectives to other parts of the structure which he did not explore; time enough for that later, he supposed. At least, he found no secret passages in the walls; it would seem that there was hardly any room for them.

Fraesch was impressed with the suite, and thought that it was probably the most extensive of the living quarters. Still the rest were probably only slightly less intricate, judging by the apparent exterior size of the rambling, erratic structure. One thing bothered him: there were no decorations of any kind hanging on the walls. He laughed at himself at this. Of course not, when hardly any wall was vertical. Still, it was a lack. However, after he had gotten things somewhat arranged, he noted that the study, which contained extensive bookshelves with the previous tenant's books, possessed one odd fixture. He had seen it, but not really observed it, when he had first come in the room.

This was a panel, hanging on the wall, on a section which had the look of having been made especially for it. Rectangular-vertical, it was not a picture, but a framed blank, filled with some silvery-gray substance. The material in the frame had settled from long disuse, the heavy grains at the bottom, the finer ones at the top, which lent it a subtle layered look. But it was not a picture, not even an abstract one. Fraesch stared at it, puzzled. In a house with no pictures there was one frame hanging on a vertical wall made for it, and inside the frame was nothing—an entropy gradient. He looked more closely. On one side of the panel was what was obviously an off-on switch, and from its underside a cable led into a hole in the wall. Fraesch got down on his knees and looked at the wall.

Sure enough, there was a sliding panel below the frame. He slid it open; inside was an electronic instrument in an absolutely plain metal case. A small legend said: "S-5 Conceptualizer." A small red indicator glowed. The unit was active. There was no switch to it; apparently it was on all the time.

Fraesch straightened up and reclosed the panel. The instrument had been excessively large for a modern electronic device; accordingly, it must be extremely complex. It was as large as two large suitcases, and must weigh a substantial amount . . . and its only link seemed to be to the panel. Fraesch reached, and touched the on switch without hesitating.

He stood back and waited, for at first nothing happened. Then, when he was about to turn away, he noticed that a soft whispering came from the concealed master unit, the "conceptualizer." Like the passage of air . . . a cooling unit? Fraesch looked around, felt the air. There was no movement. Presumably it had its own vent to the outside. He looked at the frame again. It was now illuminated from behind and from the sides of the frame, a soft light that was both pleasant and reassuring . . . but the material inside the frame remained as before, layered in the exact sequence in which it had precipitated out of the solution in which it was suspended. He looked again more closely. Had there been a motion in the grainy layers? He saw nothing, shrugged and finished arranging things, leaving the enigmatic frame alone. Probably had developed a fault, and Moricle hadn't bothered to have it fixed. Probably there was no one on the planet who could repair it. He marked it down as mildly curious and promptly forgot about it.

Somewhat later, as he was preparing to go out, he thought of it again, but in an odd reference. He had not yet succeeded in uncovering any trace of Moricle—it was as if he had never been. Yet the mysterious frame and its master unit in the panel had not come with the room, or the suite, which was odd, considering that everything one could want was built in. The panel had been added later. Therefore, the frame was Moricle's, and not standard equipment. He made a mental note to ask someone about it.

The next few days went much more busily than Fraesch had imagined; it was simply incredible the amount of detail work which had to be done. Most of it was uncomplicated and straightforward—after all was said and done. Halcyon was a small site and despite its odd purpose, operated on a direct basis. Still, no one seemed to have made any decisions since the death of Moricle and Nachitose, save the rump payroll committee. Fraesch found out, to his surprise, that Urbifrage had been spending considerable time on the site, making suggestions here, hinting there, somehow holding the place together by indirection. The more he thought of it, the more it bothered him. It was as if everyone assigned to the site had simply lost any sense of initiative whatsoever.

It bothered him so much that he spent a whole day in the personnel office reading employee files to see if by chance Speculations had by mistake hired an entire busload of idlers. But there was no answer there, for to a person, their records all indicated high levels of competence and proficiency. Indeed, many had been cited for accomplishments, and in fact, he learned that the project had been manned with precisely that in mind. Nor was the answer money or creature comforts: they were all extremely well-paid, and the site was simply about the best that could be had.

As for the actual purpose of the site, Fraesch looked in on it—the lab, which was still operating under strict security, although not as severe as the regime set up by Moricle. It was impressive, even in its untried and rebuilt state. Basically, it started simple: the sensor arrays, located out in the water in a mouth of a bay to the north, received and transmitted the motions of the waves, to microscopic accuracy, back to the lab, where the fun started. The resultant signal was recorded and subjected to an extreme degree of in-depth analytical techniques, which Fraesch had not seen carried to such an extent outside of pure electronics, or perhaps astrophysics. There was nothing lacking that he could see. Bearing in mind what the real purpose of the project had been, he was not surprised. They were looking for a clear signal in the midst of what he imagined to be totally random noise, and not only that, but a signal with which they could track objects in space. It seemed a shame that the fine and expensive equipment would be essentially idle until Speculations could replace him with someone knowledgeable enough to use it for its intended purpose. He remembered the things Aslet had said, too. And he saw that things were at a standstill; perhaps he could keep them that way.

Several days passed in this manner. Fraesch set up a small office in the lab building. Apparently Moricle had run the place from his apartment. He concentrated on starting things moving again, and nudging the people back into line. They responded readily enough, as if relieved to have someone to tell them what to do, but it was also clear that without that someone, they would cheerfully revert to their old ways without much thought about it. This took long days, and Fraesch spent most of the first days working and sleeping, trying vainly to get accustomed to the short day of Mulcahen, which was growing shorter with the approach of winter. He got up in the dark, and it was dark when he got back. He acted as if he were just another employee, which was true in a sense, and pressured none; in turn, all he met were reasonably pleasant, but again, it was clear that their interests were elsewhere, although not obsessively so.

He had not explored the Barracks at all, but had limited himself to puzzling his own way in and out of the labyrinthine structure. He did learn that there were several common rooms somewhere on the far side of it—one, called the Taverna which was more or less a bar. There was another, called the Cabaret, in which there was dancing and socializing. He reminded himself to see if he could get someone to help him find them, as their location was not apparent to the casual visitor. There was hardly any real need for either, as the suites were completely self-contained, with well-stocked kitchens and pantries and all the equipment necessary to prepare so amazingly varied fare. And there hardly seemed to be a real need for a place to meet, for people visited one another as they felt the need, as he learned. A relaxed sort of casual promiscuity seemed to reign, although Fraesch suspected that they had long since exhausted any new combinations, which might explain why Pelletier had leered at Tula—she was an unknown face, a new, strange body.

Whatever went on at night, it made no noise; the suites were as silent as if each one had been buried individually within the heart of a mountain. There was no noise from the passageways whatsoever, nor could anything be heard through the walls, although he knew that at least some of the rooms must lie in close proximity to someone else's. He was thankful of that, but it induced a peculiar state of mind in him: it made for a sense of isolation, of increased selfness. So far, the effects of this had caused nothing more alarming than a mild restlessness, which he ignored.

Aside from some passing encounters, mostly in the lab building, Fraesch had actually had little contact with Tula since they had arrived. It was not that he didn't see her, but rather that both of them had plunged directly into their work, and that their paths coincided rarely. While Fraesch wandered all over the site, visiting the various support sections and working with them, Tula spent her time inside the lab, evaluating, testing components, tracing switching networks. Fraesch's "office" was little more than a place to have messages left, and he visited once or twice daily.

Tula intrigued him, but at the same time he felt a certain reserve about her; he did not wish to force things at such an early date. As for her, there seemed to be an interest, but for the present, it was being ignored in favor of other things. . . . Fraesch felt comfortable with this situation, which was common to those who had taken Longlife; they had time to let things ripen, knowing that the bodies which housed such emotions would not wither while they waited for the right moment. As a fact, Fraesch felt slightly uncomfortable among the station personnel, who seemed to live as if there would be no tomorrow.

Therefore it was a surprise to him when Tula approached him on a day just before a long four-day holiday, and suggested, shyly, that they might meet after work, to discuss in some detail a proposal she had to make about the lab. When he had asked her why not then, she had said that she was tired and wanted to rest before returning to the subject over which she had spent so much time. And that she was, frankly, a little tired of the lab and wished to get out of it, and "act like ordinary people."

Fraesch could appreciate that, and said as much. But when he suggested that they share dinner together, again she shyly demurred, claiming that would put too much involvement into what was, after all, to be a relaxing time.

Fraesch had said, "But it sounds so serious!"

And Tula had said, "Serious, yes, that it is, but I want to unwind some too—surely you have been pressing at it hard, too. And I do not feel at ease among the others, at least not yet; they are not like you and I."

Fraesch had agreed to that. They had played at a mock-argument over whose place would be used, but it was finally agreed upon that it should be Fraesch's, primarily because Tula knew how to get there, but Fraesch did not know how to find her suite.

Fraesch had returned to his suite, eaten, bathed and dressed, and had gone to the study to await Tula's arrival. It was the first time he had spent any time in the room since his first exploration, and to defuse an anticipation he felt, he went directly to the bookshelves to see in what detail Moricle had collected things. There were many tapes and cassettes, to be used in conjunction with a readerscreen also located in the room. There were also extensive collections of graphic art, which had seemed to be a hobby with Moricle; these Fraesch promised to examine in greater detail. There was a large section devoted to scientific periodicals, and extracts from them, which apparently Moricle had shipped to him, as some of the issues were fairly recent. And there was a well-stocked section of music tapes. Moricle gave all the evidence of being a cultured, intense personality.

One topic seemed to stand out somewhat more than others: sailing ships. Moricle seemed to have had an extensive library on vessels powered by sails, illustrated by highly detailed drawings and technical diagrams, as well as photographs and paintings, some of them haunting and beautiful according to any aesthetic. All types seemed to be represented, from the largest all the way down to small one-man sport types, hardly more than surfboards, but the majority of the material seemed to be concerned with rather smallish working sailboats—pilot boats, cutters, mail packets, cargo lighters and the like. Along with this, there was also a section of technical tables dealing with various physical and dynamic characteristics of wood, artificial materials, fibers and other engineering data. What was surprising was that there was a compilation on materials native to Mulcahen. Where he had gotten it would be anyone's guess.

As he browsed through the racks, Fraesch caught himself thinking that this was the only room in the suite which retained any flavor of a presence of someone having lived there, and that here, it seemed particularly strong. Fraesch felt this so intensely that he thought for a minute that he was being observed.

Yes, he thought. It was extremely odd; something he hadn't noticed before during his only previous visit to this room. He was sure of it: that the feeling of being observed had nothing to do with the diminishing sense of presence in the room. It was eerie, ghostlike. Fraesch was unaware that spy devices existed, but he had not imagined himself the target of them. Nor was he sensitive to them, any more than, he supposed, was an average person. But the feeling had come and gone. Something he perceived, but was not aware of. He replaced a book on its shelf.

There it was again. . . . it was as if someone was actually in the room with him. He felt a heat at the back of his neck, a tingling in his scalp. But there was no one in the suite except him, and he knew there were no such entities as ghosts, and even if there had been, they were not of the material universe and could make no overt acts. He laughed at himself for even going through the rationalization. It was while he was laughing nervously that he happened to glance at the frame hanging in its place on that section of the wall built for it. And in the silvery, slightly illuminated material inside the frame, he saw the face of a young girl of subtle, evanescent beauty.

Fraesch went to stand directly in front of the frame. It had changed. No longer were the grains in the device arranged according to a density gradient; the entire interior was now a homogenous surface, upon which, like a face emerging out of fog, a girl's face had formed by some incredible arrangement of the grains, and the interplay of light and shadow. As he watched, the face itself changed, with a mobility that suggested the fleeting expressions of life. When he had first seen it, the face had expressed intense curiosity, but that changed, as he watched, to a look of concentration. It also shifted its position slightly, so that he saw a different angle.

The changes were gradual and subtle; the face would take one aspect, hold it for a moment, and then shift to another. Even as he watched, he saw it turn to a profile of pensive watchfulness. Here was the source of the feeling that he had been watched. The representation was so realistic, so alive, that something about it made his skin crawl. But it was a flat picture! Whoever had designed this thing had not only had a profound knowledge of computers, optics, physics, but also of art, and human perceptions: the frame blended these in proportions with which Fraesch could find no flaw. As exact as a photograph, as suggestive as a Chinese watercolor. . . . Now the lovely young girl was fading out, as if retreating into a silvery-gray fog. The process was slow, but steady, and in another moment, the frame was blank. Fraesch whistled a low tone to himself.

Out of the nothingness, another face was forming, this one a face of a more mature woman, round and pleasant, with an animation and a lively sparkle to the eyes that completely lit up the whole face, which was rather plain and regular; the face had such a warm, engaging expression, as if of greeting, that Fraesch found himself smiling back at it. Then the face retreated slightly, not fading, for the picture was only increasing its field of view, to include the head and upper torso, which was nude. The body suggested a rounded contour that was not fat nor plumpness; the breasts were not large, but they were well-shaped; the woman looked off to her left, turning her shoulders slightly. . . . The image faded, became difficult to see; was gone.

Fraesch stood as if his feet had been nailed to the floor. Another face began forming in the material, another woman's face, this one rather harsh and determined. The view was as if one would see someone at a desk bending over some work; harsh and determined, yes, but also with a strong, demanding beauty as well. . . . The angle of view shifted a bit to the side, and the face turned, blurring slightly to look directly at him, a direct and interrogative expression which then shifted to a warmer aspect, as if she had been pleased by an interruption. This image continued for some time, passing through several more changes, until Fraesch felt as if he would know the woman instantly if he met her. Her hair was short and loosely curly; the face was long and slim, with a clear brow, very definite eyebrows, a thin but strongly drawn nose, a precise straight mouth with a rather full lower lip, a small, pointed chin. In many of the views of her she wore old-fashioned, large eyeglasses that lent her a slightly owlish look. The features were all very crisp, and all the expressions were direct and forceful. Her age was impossible to guess—it

could have been anything from an unaltered eighteen standard to perhaps thirty-five; but whatever age the owner of the
face had, straight or Longlife, it was a face that covered a
personality tuned to achievement and accomplishment, and a
complete lack of frivolity. The face changed once more, shifting so radically that Fraesch thought he was looking at a different woman. He couldn't identify the emotional content of
the image at first. The head was tilted back, the teeth were
bared and clenched tightly, the eyes were shut tightly, the
nostrils, delicate and perfect, were flared as with some great
physical exertion. Even as he watched, it began to fade out,
but this one changed as it did so, the tense, straining expression shifting subtly to one of intense pleasure. Fraesch realized what he had been seeing and looked away, slightly
embarrassed. He felt like a peeping tom.

Fraesch forced himself to walk away from the frame, which
was now beginning to show yet another face. It was intimate to
a degree that disturbed him. The faces were beautiful, each in
its own way, and so lifelike it was hard to maintain the
knowledge that it was just a picture—one reacted to the
faces! They were alive! Presumably they were generated by
the device in the case behind the wall, but to what purpose?
What was their source? And why would Moricle have had
such a device? Fraesch knew a lot about pleasures—some
simple and direct and instinctive, and others of Byzantine in-
tricacy and austere abstraction, but in all his travels and experiences he had never heard of such a machine, nor of the
uses to which such a thing might be put.

The intimacy of the faces reminded him of some of his
own appetites, now long unsatisfied by the press of events,
thoughts he lightly repressed for the sake of the moment. A
chime sounded from a concealed speaker far overhead in the
ceiling. Someone was at the front door.

Fraesch had dressed for an informal, possibly-intimate encounter: an ankle-length caftan with low-contrast vertical
stripes, rather broad. The color was a pale sand tint. It had a
hood, which was usually worn casually thrown back. As he
negotiated the passageways to the front door, he reflected on
this meeting. Tula had something she wanted to discuss—
away from work. Curious, but neither improbable nor impossible. He thought that there very well could be several
delicate questions she might have: one might be her continued presence at Halcyon, for she had been requested by Mor-

icle. But now, there was neither material for her to work on,
nor a Moricle to tell her what he was looking for. He could
understand that that would be a discussion she wouldn't care
to have casual clerks drop in on. Would he let her leave? It
would be a shame to let her go so easily—she was so far his
only link with the more settled, civilized worlds; yet Fraesch
felt himself no dictator, no tyrant. It was just a job, after all.
Were she to move onwards, who was he to say no.

Fraesch stopped at the foot of the stairs, releasing the front
door by operating a remote control panel. He had earlier set
the lights to a bright, shadowless diffuse illumination, to
properly set impressions: indeed, he was no pillar-saint, no
Simon Stylites, but at the same time, he was not roaming the
corridors searching for the gratification of blind urges.

The door slid aside, and Tula stepped into the foyer, as always, with a positive, determined motion, not ungraceful. She
wore a two-piece garment of soft white, with pearl over-
tones—a tunic top and plain, loosely-fitting pants of the same
material. The only concession to style to the garment was
that it flared at the sleeves and bottoms of the pants. Otherwise, there was neither seam nor line. With her height and
slender, graceful figure, it was extremely flattering. She wore
no jewelry.

She looked carefully about her, at the foyer, at Fraesch,
waiting at the foot of the stairs, a single motion, and exclaimed, with sincere admiration, "Oh, it is beautiful, really
nice—I can see that from here."

Fraesch said, "Are the others that different? Yours?"

"None are the same. Nachitose had her place done to suit
her—it's all burlap and weathered wood, knots and all. An
awful great mass of photographs of her from every conceivable angle and in every conceivable pose. . . . She must have
been a terrible egotist. . . ."

"Or unsure of herself?"

"Of course! Isn't that the way with all egotists? Actually, it
is not a little disturbing to be in there, so I am taking them
down, one by one, folding them carefully away—perhaps
somewhere there is someone who would want them."

"You are lucky. You have seen Nachitose in photographs. I
have not yet found any image of Moricle—not even in his
file, which was understandably sketchy—I shouldn't think
he'd need to have much for the people here."

"Moricle was . . . rather like a professor. Bushy hair, a
large nose, heavy in the face and shoulders, very hairy. There

is a picture of him with her, and the background is here, Hal-cyon."

"Well, enough of shadows and past people. We are present people. Please come in. It will be as if it were your own."

Tula descended the stairs, hesitating slightly. The stair did not look stable. But Fraesch had learned to trust it, and, after the first steps, so did Tula. She joined, standing close to him, easily within reach, close enough for the scent she used to be apparent, something tart and smokey. Her eyes were bright, animated. "This really is more to my liking. Will you trade with me? I think we have the same number of interior rooms. . . . But no, you wouldn't, nor could I blame you. Well . . . is it to be here?"

"I had hoped not. There are more comfortable areas, which I thought we might use—this is a bit bare for an earnest conversation."

"Oh, yes. Please let me see the rest of it . . . no, not all at once. Lead on!"

"I thought to suggest the listening room . . . I have taken up calling it the house of the winds. There is a charcoal fire in a pit, and some refreshment."

"You went to no trouble, please."

"None to amount. There is sthisk[1] and aurindt[2], if you are an enjoyer of such things."

"You have spied," she scolded Fraesch with mock serious-ness. "Or you have good taste. Yes, both, if you please, indeed! Our conversation need not be pressing our noses to the grindstone." Her enthusiasm seemed direct and genuine, almost schoolgirl-like, although Fraesch certainly knew Tula was no schoolgirl, by any means. Fraesch motioned, a beck-oning wave of the hand, and set out through the labyrinthine corridors. Tula followed, alternating between an exaggerated

[1] Sthisk: A mild alcoholic beverage, somewhat bitter and aro-matic, which is habitually drunk in tiny, thimblelike cups, norm-ally metal—silver or gold or platinum. It is extremely expensive.
[2] Aurindt: The shredded leaves of a mildly hallucinogenic plant, whose main effect is to heighten perception. The plant, a native of the single habitable plant of Bernard's Star, exhibits a re-markable similarity to the infamous Datura Stramonium of Old Earth, but the active principle, trans-methyl-daturinol-72, is not considered either dangerous or habit-forming, although like any-thing else, it has the potential for abuse. Heavy aurindt users tend to be excessively sensual, which is treated as a matter of abuse of custom or bad taste, rather than a problem.

conspiratorial sneaking and an infectious enthusiasm which
lightened Fraesch's mind.

Along the way, Fraesch touched light panels, briefly illuminating rooms, compartments, other ways within the suite. The
rest of the way they followed tiny step-lights set into a sill
along the floor, or the stairs. And at the last, at the very
highest point of the suite which was his, they came, by means
of a narrow ladder, and then an angled tube filled with
soundproofing material, to the listening room, or tower of the
winds, as Fraesch called it.

Now a smoke collector with a wire firescreen extended
down from the peak of the ceiling to hang over the firepit, in
which there was a glowing charcoal fire. There were artificial
lights, but tonight Fraesch had substituted candles, placed on
simple brackets, sconces and flat places. The light was red at
the center, and golden at the edges of the room. The ceiling
was in shadow, far away. To one side, the far side of the
room from the entry-tubeway, was a low, flat projection from
the substance of the wall. On this was a self-powered chiller,
in which sat ice and a small metal flask of sthisk. Beside it
was an old-fashioned water pipe of green glass, with something lazily smoking in the bowl.

Fraesch stood aside to let Tula enter, gestured. "Is this far
enough removed from the cares of the world?"

She looked about the room, slowly, reflectively, as if com-
mitting every aspect of it to memory. She was very quiet,
now, very still, and she answered in a small voice, "Here, I
could almost believe it didn't exist . . . Whereever did you
find candles? It's perfect."

"Moricle had a large store of them in a locker I found
. . . none of them had been used."

"That would be just like him."

"How so?"

"He looks like he would not use a room such as this . . .
this is a very intimate place."

Fraesch said, "Many of the suites have places like
this. . . . You have one; there are others somewhere in the
complex."

Tula shook her head, slowly, emphatically. "No. Others
have them, but this one has come to life . . . hsh." She
placed a finger over her lips, listening, her head tilted slightly.
"Can we hear the outside?"

Fraesch listened, too. Yes. There was wind, echoing softly
somewhere up in the vents in the ceiling. But the candle

flames were steady. Wind, and an irregular spatter of rain. He said, "There is a storm growing, I think."

"I could see by the last light of day that there would be one; the sea was not blue, but gray-green."

Fraesch said, "I have depolarized the windows. If there is lightning, we shall have that as well." He indicated that she should go first.

Tula went ahead, walking delicately around the firepit, slowly, seeing each candle, each flicker, each detail, savoring. Fraesch watched her and wondered how he could have ever thought her plain, or too wrapped up in her work; here, by subtle shifts, by a process of change in stages which had happened before his eyes, she had mutated into something more than a woman. He saw that the upper part of the garment she wore was only fastened by a clip at the back of her neck; between the overlapping sides of the tunic he could see in its shadows the smooth, pale curve of her bare back; if he had gone to some effort to make this a meaningful encounter, so had she.

Tula made her way to the cushioned platforms on each side of the table-like projection, picked one, and settled herself. Fraesch followed, took the one opposite, and poured two small thimbles of sthisk. She took one; they raised their thimbles and sipped. Tula found the mouthpiece of the water pipe, drew on it, inhaled deeply, and exhaled slowly. Fraesch did the same. As he expected, at first he felt nothing, save the slightly acrid bite of the aurindt; the active factor in it would take some time to make itself felt. As they each drew on the pipe in turn, it burbled softly, check valves preventing backdraw when the other was drawing on the other end. Tula tilted her head back, exposing the muscles and tendons of her throat, listening to the rising wind and the rain, the sounds softly filtering into the room.

She turned a direct gaze on Fraesch, across the pipe and the ice bucket. She began, "This is the best of all possible places to speak of things; there is a thing of which I must ask your leave, for you have the responsibility."

"You may speak if it, Tula."

"I have tried to discover what it was that caused Moricle to ask for a specialist of my type. As you know, all the records we might search were kept in the lab building, and so they were consumed with fire, and there is nothing. Yet I thought to go through Nachitose's effects within her house, to see if perchance there might have been some clue—after all, no one could have gone through everything. So thus I have done, night after night, and little have I found; but I have found something . . . I know that it was something they observed in the data they were processing."

"How did you find this?"

"Jenserico Nachitose kept a journal; she recorded everything. The problem is deciphering it, for it was a reference system, of use only to her. Without her, it is mostly useless: dates, initials, short little squibs. But this I read, and she said 'I doubted, but L. showed it to me today, and now there can be no doubt. We will have to see to it. To be more tests.' That is all. After that, the entries grow shorter, and die out. Toward the end, there were none at all. But from that I know that something they saw was . . . somehow, in the data they were receiving from the wave-motion sensor set. We need to operate that equipment, I believe, so that we may find what it was, and thus spare the next director similar embarrassment."

"You are certain that she was referring to the lab? And you must have run across the suspicion that someone killed them."

"The entry was coded so that it was a reference to the work they were doing in the lab; I have discerned that much. As to the rumors. . . . The talk I have heard cannot fix upon a perpetrator. I do not know what connection there may be from their problem to their termination or the destruction of the lab. . . . But I believe that we have a certain obligation to run the equipment. There was something there they saw that stopped their work, what they came to do."

"Do you know what they were doing?"

"I know they were looking for something in the waves. They sent for me to help them with what they found. I was not in the original makeup of the station personnel, so it was something unexpected. And an analytical linguist? I do not understand it: yet I would look into it, otherwise this will be a vacation. I enjoy leisure . . ." and here, she leaned back and let her body relax into a more supple posture. "Yet also do I enjoy my own work, else I would not do it."

"I must ask, can you run it without damage?"

"That I can. I have worked with similar equipment often, and have made myself familiar with the components here. Have no fears—I can operate it probably as well as Moricle or Nachitose . . . and we can also be building a data base for the director who will eventually replace you and restart the work in earnest."

Fraesch looked away from her for a moment, taking in the counsel of the winds, of the rain, of fire, of candlelight. And of the mingled scents of sthisk, aurindt, Tula's perfume. He said, "Of course. You have it. Go ahead and run it." Even as he said it, he knew that he had done the wrong thing, according to what Aalet had told him, that this would not slow the project down at all. Yet Tula's logic seemed clear, and it was useless to pay for sending her here across half the known universe, only to ship her back; he found himself as well wishing not to see her depart on her way, at least for a time.

Tula sighed, and said, "It's a shame, after all."

"What is a shame? I don't understand. I agreed. Is that so hard? It could only have been yes or no, and you are right—I could not think of a real reason to refuse you."

She smiled, and drew another long draw on the aurindt pipe, causing it to make its mellow burble. Again she listened to the sounds of the wind. ". . . A shame; of course it was. I had thought you would be difficult, and so for that I came prepared to seduce you if necessary; a pity it isn't. . . ." She reached across the low table between them and intimately stroked Fraesch's hand, as if they now shared something between them. Already.

Fraesch said, "Your work need not have been for nothing; I might yet require convincing."

Tula said, "You are thoughtful and sensitive to have done this for me, and sly as well; for what reason might you have thought it necessary to seduce me?"

"For the its own sake. We have a likeness. . . ."

"So we do." She slid out of the platform, to settle again on her knees before the low table, bringing the pipe mouthpiece with her, and a thimbleful of sthisk. Fraesch joined her, kneeling. Together they drained their thimbles. Tula handed him her pipe, and he passed his to her, intertwining the tubes. They drew deep draughts of the smoke, which now had no taste whatsoever. Fraesch thought the room was very bright, and the sounds of the outside very strong. And he could hear Tula's breathing. She touched his hands, and he leaned forward to lightly brush her lips. She slid her hands into his sleeves, and he felt her slender forearms. The skin was cool. Fraesch opened his arms, and she slid into them, burying her head in his shoulder, where he felt a wet nibbling at his throat. He withdrew his arms from her sleeves, and reached for the single clasp at the back of her slender neck.

7

There were homespun blankets with geometric designs stored in lockers cleverly concealed beneath the seats of the listening room; these they found and took out and wrapped around themselves and so clothed spent the rest of the night there. Fraesch, ever civilized, had offered Tula a proper bedroom in which to spend what of the night remained to them, but she had shaken her head, emphatic as a child. She had said, "No, and no again!" She wrapped her lean, pale body completely in the folds of her blanket, except her toes, which she presented to the firepit. "No. We change, we mutate, according to the place in which we act. You know that what we have just done is a simple exercise—it can be performed anywhere, but all the same you would say 'unthinkable' were I to suggest that it happen in the lab, yes? It could not be! We are different people, there. It is so wherever we might go. And so I will not budge, not tonight, not even to one of the comfortable beds of which there are so many in this place."

Fraesch said, "I had not thought of it so much, but I think I understand." But as he said it, he marveled at the change he had seen in Tula. Or was it his perception of her which had changed? He did not know. At the moment, he did not particularly care.

There was no more talk. They discovered that the pipe had gone out and Fraesch refilled and relighted it. They then smoked in a soft, reflective silence, while the fire in the pit reddened, dimmed, began settling into itself. Their eyes became heavy, Tula curled into a ball and put her head in Fraesch's lap, and he leaned over and pillowed his head on her hip, and they faded away into a sleep of dreamlessness.

When they awoke, it was well into a gray morning, judging by the dull light that came into the room through the high windows. The sounds transmitted by the pipes and chambers were cold and austere. The fire had gone out, leaving a faint scent of an old charcoal fire, and from sleeping as they had done, they were a little stiff. The room had cooled. They sat up, stretching and yawning and rubbing their faces. Tula's paleness looked bloodless in the gray light, which did not favor her. Yet Fraesch smiled at her, and said, "I know what you said last night—we were magicians as well as lovers. . . ."

She corrected, still half-asleep, "More magicians, if the truth be known."

"But it did not entirely leave us, either."

"A bad time for reflections, but even so, I would add to it—*because* of the way we moved with the wave instead of trying to impose upon it, it will never entirely leave us, and that is as it should be." She added, "Another thing that should be is that Tula requires a long steam in a hot shower, and something to eat." She stood, a little unsteadily, and rearranged the blanket about her.

Fraesch said, "I will arrange for something, and do the same. Will you stay for awhile?"

"You are moving with it; just so will I. Yes, for a time. . . . I will wish to change clothes, and would also like to walk outside. Will you come with me?"

"Where outside?"

"On the shore. Then we rest, apart, and tonight you will come to the place where I live."

"You can't use the firepit and the listening room: I have already done that."

Tula laughed in spite of herself. "No, not this. But Nachitose had some features of her suite which may serve as well. . . ." She looked at him meaningfully. "I should like to have you help me explore them."

"I will do so willingly."

"Good. Now let us go. We must make the most of the time that we have."

After they had showered and breakfasted and dressed, Tula insisting that Fraesch dress warmly and bring a heavy winter coat, they prepared to leave. First they would navigate the corridors to her place, where she could change, for what she had worn the night before was not suitable for an excursion. Fraesch asked her on the way, "I take you to be a civilized, reasonably sophisticated person—who may have had experiences different from mine."

Tula nodded.

Fraesch continued, "Have you ever heard of a device which consists of a picture-frame and a computer, and shows faces?"

For a second, a series of rapid expressions flickered across her face, none of which Fraesch could identify with certainty, so fast did they happen. After a moment, she said, with some difficulty, ". . . Yes. Have you not seen one before?"

"Never. I thought I was decently sophisticated, but this was new to me." Odd, but it was almost as if he had caught her at something. Still she proceeded directly, not evading an answer.

"It is a device developed not so very long ago. They are probably the most expensive entertainment artifact one could care to purchase, and so they are not widespread. Additionally, there are problems with their use. . . . Where did you see one?"

"Here." He gestured to the study. "Apparently Moricle had one. It was turned off, at least the frame part of it; I didn't know what it was, and turned it back on. I thought it was broken, but later I started seeing faces in it, faces that look very real, not at all like something a computer would generate. . . . There seems no way to turn the computer part of it off."

"Did you watch it?" Tula was tense as a drawn string.

"For a time . . . before you came, last night. Frankly, I stopped because I felt uneasy about it. I saw the faces of women in it, and the realism was incredible—it was as if they were real people. How does it generate the faces?"

"It doesn't generate them; it records them. Did you see anyone you knew?" She laughed, a little uneasily.

"The three faces I saw were strangers."

"It requires the implantation of a pickup unit in the visual center of the brain; they are preset to pick up certain images, or images of a certain intensity. These the pickup relays to the computer, where it processes the images, stabilizes them, and adds what it knows of human anatomy and various points of view, and then stores the images in memory. The part that directs the frame selects at random, and presents images. . . . You say it was here, turned off, but that it started playing when you turned it on?"

"Yes. I have assumed it belonged to Moricle. But he is dead. How does it continue to play?"

"It requires no pickup now. It probably picked up an image of every woman Moricle ever saw. They search out the memory, actively. They are diabolical machines—an absolute vice. With the changes of position and aspect it would apply, it could probably play a century without repeating itself. The only thing Moricle's death did for it was shut off the input . . . Joachim, if you are ever wealthy, I ask that you never buy one. Never."

"I'm not sure I'd want one. This one strikes me as . . . well, it's too private, in a way. I, too, am fond of women, and enjoy faces of beauty and animation, but I think I would feel a bit . . . well, uneasy, seeing those images from the past."

"Then I am reassured." She seemed to relax.

"Do you wish to see it?"

"No. I do not like them."

"Why?"

"They fixate one on the past. I should say they take one from the wave. Their use promotes a disturbing mental state in their users. On some planets where they have government, they have been outlawed. . . . Luckily, the cost of owning one will preclude their spread any further."

Fraesch laughed. "A vice. By God, a new vice! Rest assured, whatever vices come with the times, the leaders of the governments will have them!"

Tula was not amused. "Joachim, you must turn it off! I say this because of my concern for you. It is deadly to use one. Destroying it would not be a bad idea."

Fraesch said, a little mulishly, "If it was Moricle's, I would hate to destroy such an intimate record of his thoughts. Perhaps somewhere in it there is some clue as to what happened here, what it was he discovered. . . ."

"I doubt it would be in there, in a Conceptualizer. You say it displays the faces of women; then that was the way it was set—it would pick up nothing else, unless it fell within the target tolerances. Our knowledge of the brain is still inexact, and so the Conceptualizer is never exact, but they are close . . . I worry that if you spend too much time with it, you will change; that is a problem with them. You will see what Moricle saw, and included in that is why he remembered them. In time, you would fade, and something of Moricle would come to you. I enjoy you as you are."

"Warts and all?"

"You have no warts that I could discover." She looked coy, now, hinting, suggesting.

Fraesch said, "I will promise not to use it." But then they

left Fraesch's suite for Tula's, to get her warmer clothes, and
in their preparations to leave to walk along the beach, he
quite forgot to turn it off. In fact, just after their conversation
about the Conceptualizer, he rather let it slip from his mind.
But not for long.

Tula now led Fraesch through corridors, which, while the
public ways of the Halcyon dormitory complex, were not
much larger than the access corridors inside of the suites. They
curved, descended, ascended, passed through nodes and junctions, went up, and down short stairs which were also curved.
The walls were irregularly curved in cross section as well.
Small footlights illuminated their way, and an occasional
skylight. At random intervals, they passed landings which
gave way to suite entrances, or exits to outside catwalks and
balconies and overlooks, or to simple blind pockets furnished
with seats and brighter lighting. They met no one, and heard
nothing, a fact which Tula supposed was due to the day being
early and also the first day of a long break.

Eventually, they arrived at a landing not greatly different
from any of the rest. Tula presented her hand to the latch
sensor, and the door slid aside for her. Inside, the foyer was
not greatly different from his—a small, bare chamber, generally spherical in shape. But when Tula turned on the lighting
of the parlor, as Fraesch had come to think of it, he could
see immediately that things were quite different. Also in his
mind a concern was clamoring for attention: how was he to
find this place tonight? Or any other night? But that question
was overshadowed and silenced by the suite Tula inhabited.

The parlor was large, rather larger than the one in his
suite, and was conical in the upper parts, very high. The light
came from a chandelier suspended from the center, and the
chandelier itself drew the eye—a dandelion-puff of thousands
of crystal rods, each one terminating in a tiny starburst-light.
Looked at with eyes out of focus, it strongly resembled a
globular cluster of stars. The rest of the room was as Tula
had described it—burlap and wood, although in this room the
wood showed only as exposed, severe ribs which grew out of
the material of the floor, passed up the vertical walls, joined
the conical ceiling, and met at the peak, forming with a reverse curve a deep spike from which hung the chandelier.
Around the walls were an astonishing variety of photographs,
which he presumed to have been the artifacts of a hobby of
Nachitose's. Monochromatic prints in black and white, others

in color, still others in metal engravings which looked like photographs in lights. The only problem Fraesch had was determining what Nachitose's hobby had been; had it been photography, or herself? The photographs were all of the same person, a woman. The same woman he had seen in the third face of the Conceptualizer, the intense, severe face. They were all here, in an astonishing variety of poses and expressions, some as commonplace as the crudest of family mementoes, others the result of a sure and highly sophisticated aesthetic.

Fraesch looked around for a long time. At last he asked Tula, "Are all these Nachitose?"

"Jenserico Nachitose is the woman you see here displayed. I have taken them down from the other parts of the suite, but this room has been quite beyond me."

"I agree—she seems to have been an intimidating woman. It's as if she's still here, in a way, and would disapprove of being taken down."

Tula looked at Fraesch curiously. "You sound as if you almost think she's still alive."

Fraesch said, after a moment, very thoughtfully, "In a way, in a way. . . . Something lasts of us, the remains of the influences we had on the world. I am sure there is something left behind, fading, but real, nonetheless. I agree with you, Tula—you should take them down. He did not tell her he had seen this face in the Conceptualizer. But he thought long on it, and did not forget it.

Tula disappeared into the far parts of her suite, and reappeared in a few moments, dressed in very substantial clothing, and carrying a fur-trimmed parka. Fraesch thought that after the night she had spent, she looked remarkably vital and fresh.

She led him through the complex by another route, which shortly emerged outside at a plain entrance which did not seem much used; there was no landscaped path leading up to it, and the arch about it seemed hastily erected, as if the verve of the builders had begun to die out at this part. Tula said, "They tell me this entry sees more use in the summer, when it is warm, but at this latitude, even summer is cool, and the water is always cold, so few come this way then, and none now. This will be our secret, yes?"

And Fraesch remembered how surely and easily she had passed through the corridors, tubes, junctions, without any hesitation whatsoever, and he thought that she had been very

busy; Tula was beginning to show sides of herself he wouldn't
have imagined. The trouble was that it was as if she didn't
care that he saw them—she had shed her image of lab technician casually, as if it didn't make any difference anymore, almost before it had ceased to matter, an odd sense of timing
indeed. He knew she wasn't what she claimed to be; and he
found himself not caring. She was fascinating, and he felt
completely at ease with her. Not quite enough to reveal what
he knew; but he doubted if it made any difference to her. She
was directly engaged with him, and something beyond him,
and—here, an odd echo of the words of Tuzun—of no malice toward him. Strange and exotic she was, and he was sure
she would become even more so.

It was midday, and they walked along the beach, saying
little, watching the endless play of light over the Empyrean
sea, the changing cloudscapes, the wheel and turn and swoops
of the *Kryloruki*, who were out, scavenging and hunting in
the wake of the storm. They watched them, followed individuals, picked out ones who flew with particular style and
grace.

They listened to the churning of the waves, the hiss and
rumbles, and watched the endless play of light; Fraesch observed that despite all the tumult of the sky, it did not seem
to be clearing, to which Tula agreed, adding that another
storm was supposed to follow, this one a snowstorm. Fraesch
breathed the cold, windy air, and nodded.

They returned back along the shore of the muttering sea
the way they had come; except that when they reached a spot
near where they had arrived from the site, now clearly visible, Tula led them farther on southward, passing the living
complex and making their way down almost to the stream.
Here they turned back.

They stopped in the shelter of some windblown trees.
Tula's cheeks were rosy, and her breath was streaming wisps
of fog away in the wind; but cold as it was—and it was not
becoming bitter as only a cold wind off the ocean can be—
she seemed to be reveling in the discomfort.

She said, "You wonder that I come to you in thin, fashion-
able garments in the night, and in the day strive against the
wind. I have only one word for it: engagement. Everything
is rare, precious, a jewel! I admit to being a savorer of these
experiences, for it is sad to know that they will never be
again, no matter that we should come back. We are as fragile

and evanescent as the light, as the waves. Do you find that surprising?"

"Indeed I do, but your approach is one I admire, that I wish to share."

"That is why I wished you for my lover, for as long as this wave may last; I saw this! Not for me the glassy-eyed lust of reptiles, the mindless gratification of organs and glands, the fevered desire, the satiety, and then the disgust—stale bodies worn out and discarded. We must not become casual."

Fraesch felt surprise and amazement. Tula was an incredible romantic, but it was not a romance of youthful visions, but something ripe and ancient, and a little mysterious. He said, "You are rare and a wonder. . . . Were you referring to the site personnel?"

"Yes. I have seen them, as I explored, talked with them. They are not like us, do you see that?"

"I saw it at the first; Pelletier and Dekadice, and then others. They all seem to have an odd fixation, but I hadn't placed it."

"We are the only civilized people on the entire planet, you and I; we must ally, we must share for a time, that we are here, that we do not lose what is ours." She sounded both passionately concerned and completely sincere.

Fraesch said, "I feel as if you were . . . what's the word? Leading me, but that's not it. . . . That's odd—I should be leading you."

"You have unrealized potentials; if I may make you aware of them, that is a rare gift, is it not?"

Fraesch nodded, and looked along the coast hills to the south of them. Something caught his eye. He stood up, into the wind, and looked closer. Tula followed him. Together, they returned a little way toward the beach. Braving the wind, they looked—and saw, a bit farther on, near the top of the hill, facing the ocean, a shanty or shack fashioned of scraps and pieces, apparently left over from the construction days. It looked fragile, as if a puff of wind would blow it away, but the weathering of its irregular shape showed it had already survived several winters. From a crude chimney fashioned of beach rocks a thin trickle of smoke was drawn into the wind.

Fraesch said, "Someone lives there! Someone from the site?"

She said, "I think not. I have heard talk of a primitivist sect; perhaps it is one of theirs." And after another moment,

"Now I am truly chilled. Let us return. Remember, you will come to me tonight; now you know the way. Come early, I will fix something light and nourishing for us—I am something of a gourmet cook."

Fraesch smiled, "And afterwards?"

Tula smiled back, warmly, despite the chill. "And afterwards, something special, if you like."

They returned to the complex, walking up the hill holding hands like schoolchildren.

To say that Fraesch was completely enthralled, captivated and fascinated (all words whose roots have to do with capture, bonding, tying into bundles, and in general, bondage) would have been an understatement. He sighed to himself, once alone; in love like a schoolboy! Utterly ridiculous! Yet at least one part of him was enjoying the sensation, the little warm places of the beginnings which all had the potential of turning into dull and exquisitely painful dull aches later. Equally true, it could be said that another part of him was awake and wary and coldly aware of the undeniable fact that while he could discern no trace whatsoever that Tula was lying to him, it was also clear enough that she was not telling everything—not all the truth. The most obvious facet of this was that she was palpably too *finished* to be a lab technician of any sort; and that her expressed tastes were much too finely tuned to belong to a person of her apparent age—unmodified. Therefore, therefore. . . . There was a conclusion there, but what was it? That Tula Vicinczin was on Longlife? So? Many were. What of it? Good manners precluded him asking her directly, or indirectly so that an answer could be reasonably inferred. This was one social taboo which had survived everything. You did not ask, nor did you say, if asked. The stricture even had a name, so titled in honor of an ancient company of Old Earth, long since gone, and its employer, who forbade members of his company from asking one another what their salaries were: "to perrot" was not to ask embarrassing questions.

Fraesch concluded that Tula was correct in at least one thing: it was proper to take a nap. Last night had been demanding, especially so in light of the unbearable day of Mulcahen, and morning had come early; and tonight promised more of the same. But first he had something to attend to.

He went to the study, glancing at the frame, the Conceptualizer, still presenting faces, some beautiful, some plain, some even mildly homely, to an empty room, fragments of a disintegrated, vanished personality—the property of a man now dead. It had been cut off from its input: no matter—it now had enough data to extrapolate, to improvise, the project. Eerie and disturbing, those faces. No two were alike, it seemed. Moricle had not preferred blondes, nor brunettes, nor any particular shapes. Fat, thin, healthy, sallow, lazy, intense. Something had made him remember them all as remarkable in some way. Fraesch was certain that the unifying key was meaningless, as much as anyone's would be. The clue to what had happened to Moricle was not to be found in a gallery of what he considered were pretty faces.

Fraesch sat at the desk and removed from a drawer a pad of paper, on which he carefully composed a short message in a cipher of considerable complexity which he knew Pergales would recognize, and which he also knew would be reasonably secure from hobbyists and casual security officers. It involved first converting the alphabet into a binary code of "words" of five bites each, using strict binary standard progression to match against his standard alphabet. The resultant binary stream he carefully wrote out so that it would be encompassed in exactly five streams, one below the other, bites of all lines being aligned exactly. He then read back a cipher text by listing down the columns, across the lines, and transcribing a letter from the binary code. They had used the system before, and so far it had resisted, to their knowledge, attack from even professional security cryptanalysts; the reason was that they were looking too hard, in the wrong place.

In plaintext, the message said: "P fm F. Qy allpertfact conc one each Tula Vicinczin claimed resident Aegaea but also of Earth, Russian area also France. Addit urg req confidential resume Speculations, Inc. non-public data. Rush rush. End text."

This Fraesch folded up, placed in an envelope marked Mulcahen Public Message Center, and filled in the address space, "Ramo Pergales, Intercord, S. A., 440 Yeni Harman Caddesi, 18 Erzerum 1485, Turan, on Yagmur." He included his own address as a return. It would be sent transdata, and with luck, he would hear something back within a week.

As he was sealing the letter up, once again he felt the strange sensation of someone being in the study with him, which he resisted with determination; he knew no one was there, that it was that damned Conceptualizer again. He refused to look at it, in an exercise of will power. Fraesch put

the letter on the desk, and left the room, turning the lights
out and totally avoiding the Conceptualizer, even to the point
of turning his head away from it so he could not see it. And
he left.

And in the now empty room, the frame continued displaying the image of a woman's face, just another of its repertoire
of thousands, except for two pertinent aspects of the face.
The first was that the image of the person remained on for
several moments, displaying various views and expressions,
somewhat longer than the average display period. The second
was that the face in the frame was without question the face
of Tula Vicinczin.

Fraesch awoke from his nap, observed that it was somewhat later than he had expected, and rather hurriedly bathed
and dressed. He wore more formal clothes, since Tula had
mentioned a light dinner: dark pants of plain cut, and a
shirt-jacket of a lighter shade with a roman collar and a buttoned front which attached on the right side. Feeling that all
was as best as could be expected, he turned out the lights and
left, and he was a good ways up the corridor outside his suite
before he realized that he hadn't the foggiest idea how to get
there, even after Tula had taken him there. He was at a junction. He stopped, ruefully considering, trying to remember
how they had gone earlier in the day. *Damn this labyrinth,
anyway.*

Fraesch was sure that they had gone straight at this junction, and that Tula's suite seemed to be higher than his, so
that they went up more than down. Here, they had gone
mostly up. . . . He followed the passage, which indeed went
upward at a steep angle, shifting to stairs, which Fraesch did
not remember, and then it curved and descended, which was
not as he remembered it at all. He retraced his steps carefully, returning to the junction. Here was posed a problem.
(A problem, he recalled from his student days irrelevantly,
was not a problem but an opportunity to exhibit outstanding
performance.) It seemed that this junction did not have four
corridors, but five, two of which were opposite him. Which
had he come from? That would determine which way he
tried. Had they made a turn? Or had it been a sharp turn?
He decided to go back to his place and start from scratch. He
walked resolutely into the corridor he thought he had come
from, and found his steps not gradually descending, but following a hard, ascending curve to the right, which ended at

another junction. Fraesch returned to the first junction, and found that a peculiar sense of disorientation had set in, and he couldn't recall which tunnel he had come from; they were identical. No, not quite. But he had neglected to memorize the subtle differences in shape of the mouth of the tunnels and the lighting within them. He was not sure that it was the junction he had come from at all.

Now he was really perplexed, and a little embarrassed as well; he would certainly be late. He decided that some action was preferable to standing there, chewing his lip, so he set out along what seemed to be a reasonable choice, hoping that eventually he would arrive somewhere where he could at least ask directions, if not to the house of Tula, to Jenserico Nachitose's old place. After a time, Fraesch reconsidered, because he had become completely lost. He had passed several suite doors, but he had no idea whom they belonged to; there were no blazons or name tags, and the doors were also identical. He began to understand something of the psychology of the designers of this insane dormitory: they had known that in such a small, isolated site, unbearable tensions would accumulate, so they had built a maze house and deliberately designed in perfect anonymity. Inside, Fraesch suspected that the suites were all radically different. Outside, they were blank. The off-white material and the dim lighting gave no clues whatsoever. *How the hell had Tula navigated in this insane place?*

That thought rebounded like an echo. How could she have? She said she had been investigating, talking to people—the ease with which she had found his place, and led him back to hers, that could have been a clever memorization; or she could possibly know more about this place than she had told him. Fraesch suddenly felt a hot wash of paranoia, which receded quickly. After all, his problem was to find some way, now.

Fraesch thought he heard voices from somewhat farther along the section he was in, and decided that it was better to admit ignorance than remain in place. He set out along the corridor. But for a time, he did not catch up with the voices, which seemed to be engaged in a low conversation which he could not catch the sense of. If the suites were soundproof, the corridors transmitted sound in erratic and confusing ways. But Fraesch was beginning to feel a little desperation, and so he alternately walked fast, and stopped to listen, trying to follow the shifting, drifting bits of conversation.

He crossed several more junctions, and at last the voices seemed to be growing in volume and numbers. He was nearing something. They were not moving, were not receding from him. He ascended a tight spiral stairwell . . . and emerged into a broad, open area, roofed by a ⅜ triacontahedronal geodesic made of crystal. This room was occupied by about ten or twelve people in what he imagined could only be dress for a costume party whose theme might have been "The Whores of Babylon," or "Sodom and Gormorrah." The dome was ink-dark. It was night, and over it snow was blowing fitfully, lit by the soft light from the room, which was a bit dim, and flickers of lightning from somewhere far off, outside.

There were no chairs, as such, but there were a lot of cushions strewn about. A soft rug was underfoot; and to one side there was a small, self-service refreshment center. The people stood, or reclined casually among the cushions. A pungent odor was in the air, a scent he did not recognize, something apparently coming from an iron censer opposite the bar.

The people. . . . *These are my employees,* he thought, *ordinary people whose only apparent vice is that they seem a bit distracted at work. Mechanics, bookkeepers, clerks, managers.* But these were not his, in this place; they were figures out of a delirium induced by pernicious drugs. Faces were made up and painted in extreme designs, so as to obscure the lines of the plain face. Bodies were exposed, teased, highlighted, concealed, exaggerated. Sexuality was the most obvious characteristic, plainly stated. A girl wore nothing but shreds of animal skins (he was to learn later they were skins of *kryloruki*), like some jungle amazon, and had arranged her hair into a crown of evenly spaced tiny braids, each woven with white feathers. Her breasts were covered, but her genitals were bared, shaved, and surrounded with an abstract technicolor starburst that spread randomly along her thighs and belly. She was blonde, young in appearance, virtually adolescent, and exquisitely beautiful. A man passed, eyes heavily streaked with kohl like an Egyptian high priest, head shaven, wearing nothing but golden chains and bearing, for the edification of the party-goers, a colossal erection. There was a woman whose entire body was covered in black paint, except for luminous pale outlines about her bodily orifice. He looked again: yes, each. And he reflected that perhaps these three were actually among the more sober examples. Everyone seemed to be possessed of a nervous energy that made them pace like tigers, and which in turn lent a giddy, end-of-the-world atmosphere to the gathering.

The odd thing about it was that no one seemed to bother with him; they all knew he was there—each, in turn, turned and observed that someone had entered the room. Yet as they did, each one seemed to dismiss him from their minds, instantly. Fraesch felt like a ghost; he felt invisible—he did not have the proper . . . attire, if that was indeed the correct word for the bodily adornment and avertisement he saw before him. At least nudity, he thought, would permit me to talk with one of these bizarre people.

Fraesch stood, uncertain. He was suddenly thirsty, but he was unsure of the bar and what was being served; he did not wish to arrive at Tula's in some outlandish costume with his mind blown to the winds. Fraesch watched two satyrs, complete with hooves and goat horns, drag a maiden across the floor, while she struggled with music-hall theatricality.

A dark figure loomed before him, wearing a garment of dark strips of cloth, and whose body was painted with heat-sensitive paint; colors rippled over skin, broken up by the vertical strips. The eyes blinked rapidly, glassily. Fraesch thought the disguised face familiar. Pelletier?

A girl joined them, who distracted his attention: gold-bronze hair cascaded past her face in tight curls that gleamed oilily in the half-light. He had not seen her before. She wore the costume of a belly dancer, and moved, as if dancing to some unheard music, slow and sensuous. Her face was heavily lined and streaked with glittery colors, and her wide mouth was expanded with an even larger one painted on in bright blood-red. Her eyes were open and staring glassily; her eyelids moved abruptly, and Fraesch saw that she had approached them with her eyes closed; a pair of staring eyeballs had been painted on them, exactly the same color as her own. She half-circled about Fraesch, marveling at him, alternately opening and closing her eyes, which lent a lunatic quality to her face. She stared intently, either way. At last she came close, and presented her palms to Fraesch; each of these also had an eye painted on it.

As the girl marveled, the man said, "It's Fraesch, come to our party."

Fraesch tried to be rational, and asked, "Are you Pelletier? I'm trying to find Tula. . . ."

But Pelletier said, "I was Pelletier, tonight I am Lightning, the Lord, who will not strike twice in the same place."

Fraesch started to say, "I'm sure you will, but. . . ." But Pelletier had turned and flowed away, gliding like a dancer. The girl with the painted extra eyeballs remained, walking in a slow circle about Fraesch, opening and closing her remarkable eyes and presenting her palms to him with fingers fluttering exactly like eyelashes. She said nothing. Fraesch found the intense, lunatic scrutiny disturbing. He turned to follow her erratic motions, bobbing and weaving with her . . . he reached to touch her, and found that her skin was feverishly warm, and slippery. Fraesch touched her hair, and it was oily as well. Her body emitted a maddening fragrance of exotic spices.

At his touch, she stiffened, and then relaxed, smiling expectantly. She turned up her face and opened her mouth; there was a sharp, aromatic odor on her breath, pungent and metallic. Fraesch said, "Will you help me? I am lost."

The girl said, "We are all lost, but now we are found; I have found you and that is all I need to know."

"No, no, I have lost my way in this place, and I need to find the house of Tula Vicinczin. Please help me."

"Tula? Tula? I know no Tula. At any rate, she has not come to join us."

"Nachitose?"

"Ah, now, Jenserico, yes, but she is not here, either; she went away, I think, somehow . . . hm. She hasn't come at all lately, as I recall, no, not at all. It must have been because we were too timid for her—she was exacting, Jenserico, a stern teacher who always strode up the pinnacles we could only glimpse and urged us ever onwards, so much did Jenserico. And you to her place, and dressed as a minister of religion. Ah, now, a rare one. Will she accept more? Please take me!"

Fraesch seemed to catch some of the flavor of it. He said, "It is impossible, out of the question! I must now say no, for I was commanded to exactitude. But I have lost the way in the corridors, and must go onward as well. I am driven!"

"Oh, tragic destiny!" The girl leaned close, to whisper a secret. "She will use whips!"

"Nevertheless, still must I go to my certain fate."

She said, more logically, "You realize I will have to antidote to find my own way?"

"Yes, yes, how else could it be? How could I hope to arrive myself antidoted. It was specific!"

The girl rummaged through a pouch at her side, found a
capsule, and abruptly took it, without anything to wash it
down. She grimaced at its taste, but swallowed bravely. To
Fraesch's amazement, her expression cleared, like smoke
blowing away. In another minute she was sober and rational,
if a little shaky. She said, "Now I know you; the new director, at least for a while." Her new behavior was wildly
mismatched with her appearance, a fact which caused
Fraesch to feel an odd compassion for her; after all, she
was returning to sobriety, all to conduct him to a party
she was not invited to. In the space of less than a minute, she
had turned from a bizarre vision of the underside of the
world to a child in party clothes, the meaning of which she
hadn't the foggiest idea.

She turned and indicated he should follow her. As she
turned, Fraesch noticed that her nose was large and strong,
that it added character to her face. He decided that she might
have looked better dressed normally; no matter. She had
chosen her way.

She conducted Fraesch back down to the corridors, and
along them unerringly, never hesitating at turns and junctions of the ways. And in a short time, hardly worth asking directions for, she led him to a plain door which looked like
Tula's; and the corridor seemed familiar as well, the curve,
the lighting. The girl said, in a low voice, dispiritedly, "So we
are at the sanctum of the renown Nachitose; you may go
within to whatever awaits you." Then she added, thoughtfully, not looking directly at Fraesch, "But Jenserico is dead,
isn't she, and a stranger lives here . . . that is too bad—she
would have put you through your paces. But—yes, but!" She
brightened, and then she whispered, "But you would have
loved it! You would have been enlightened! You would have
known unimaginable things. She . . . I suppose all the
would-bes must be consigned to the methanizer."

Fraesch thought something was tugging at her, that the antidote had not been strong enough to pull her completely
back, to the here and now. He said, "You have done much to
bring me here; will you return to the party?"

'No . . . it is too late now. I am very tired, and shall return to my suite and sleep alone for a change. . . . If I go
back, what we have there to edify the senses will no longer
work against the antidote. I will become spectacularly sick,

and no one will love me. Better that I try again another
time."

"You are gracious to have ruined your evening to show me
the way; I am grateful—what I can do, I will, if you ask."

The girl straightened to go, and said, enigmatically, "It has
been a service worth performing, almost as good as staying
where I was; and now you will know our way, and soon we
will meet you at the gatherings in your secret soul; what will
you be, our hired administrator? What are you in the
darkness of your soul? Hsh! But tell me not, only ask for me
in Sodom." She turned and trudged back along the corridor
the way they had come.

Fraesch called after her, "Whom shall I ask for?"

She turned him a weak smile over a now-drooping shoulder, and she called back, "Lot's daughter!" and turned a corner and was lost from sight.

8

Fraesch rang, and the door slid back to reveal Tula, dressed in a manner he thought at first conservative. All black. Tula wore a long, loose skirt, a buttonless sheer blouse, and a velvet short jacket. It was at his second look that he noted that the skirt was a wraparound which opened at every step, the blouse transparent, and that she was barefooted.

She exclaimed, "Where have you been? Were you lost?"

"Yes, lost my way, I did, and also walked into a very strange party; one of them helped me." And he related a brief description of some of what he had seen.

Tula said, "I have seen them; that is why I said I thought that we were not of their kind. Practically the entire staff indulges themselves ... I am no puritan, yet I find such massgropes to lack taste, style and meaning, not to mention emotion. I am sure they are not completely aware of the identity of their partners."

"The girl who brought me here spoke of 'secret souls.'"

"Yes, that is how they call it ... they are young and so far have only one life, and they see it passing swiftly." She turned the full blaze of her attention on Fraesch, intense, now. "It was long ago that we thought those thoughts; and we have chosen rarity and that which is made valuable by scarcity, have we not? So now, to dinner. Come."

Dinner was light and subtle—a thin but delicious soup, wafers of a thin, dark bread, stalks of a reedy vegetable; Fraesch found himself enjoying it despite himself; it left no aftertaste and no sense of stuffing oneself at all, yet he felt alive, vigorous, full of energy for an unusual adventure.

Tula brought her own water pipe to the table after they had cleared the table settings, and over cups of a bitter chocolate liquor, and between draws on the pipe, which contained a flavor of aurindt Fraesch had never known, he said as much.

Tula nodded, and said, "I, too . . . are you of a mind for an adventure?"

Fraesch did not hesitate. "Yes."

She said, from under her eyelashes, "This is different." But she had the expression on her face of complete trust. A secret.

Fraesch asked, "What is it?"

"In this suite, there is a hidden room. When they were building this place, I have heard they let some of the key people design in what they wanted, for after all, it was to be an isolated place, and the work intense. You have seen what Moricle had built in for himself. Now I would like to show you Nachitose's specialty."

Fraesch allowed his eyebrows to rise. He said, "Nachitose seems to have had an unusual repute here; they spoke of her at the party with awe, at least the girl did."

"I have listened well to the tales, but I have not heard of this; I found it by accident, but when I did, I thought of you." She stood up, tossed down the remainder of the drink, and moved away from the table, extending her slender white hand to Fraesch. "Will you follow?"

Fraesch joined her, and she took his hand. "Then come with me." And she started out, back into the interior of the suite. Fraesch had not seen the far interior of Tula's suite, but while he had been there, he had had the strong impression that the bedrooms were "up" in relation to the part near the level on which one entered. The way her voice had carried. They started out along a bypass around the kitchen, and turned into a tiny alcove hardly big enough for both of them, which ended in a door with a conspicuous mechanical lock, which Tula manipulated, finally swinging it open.

It opened to a tiny landing which was the top of a tight, steep spiral which went down. Tula closed and locked the door. Fraesch asked, "Tula, what is it down here?"

She only smiled mischievously and placed a finger over her lips. Then she pointed down. Fraesch listened, and heard nothing. He looked. The light was not appreciably different from the rest of the house, save that it was fainter, and it seemed that there was a bluish tone to it welling up from the bottom. He sniffed the air. It was fresh, but there was a subtle scent on it, something musky, sexual.

He began descending. The spiral was longer than he thought, having seen it from the top—some trick of perspective. The stairs were narrow, so that only one could pass at a time. He went ahead, and Tula followed.

She whispered, "This place is not even on the site architectural plans: it was completely secret. I have found no one who will admit to having been down here—perhaps no one was."

They reached the bottom, which was a junction with corridors leading off into curtained alcoves. The light was definitely blue, now. All blue, and rather dim. Tula prompted, "Straight ahead. The rooms are interconnected. Go straight first."

Fraesch did as he had been asked, and entered the first room straight ahead.

What he saw and felt seemed to be a heated swimming pool with a domed roof, lit solely by underwater lighting. The room was dark and mysterious as a cave, and felt warm; almost uncomfortably warm. The pool must be quite warm. There was nothing but the pool, and cushions around it, and the entrance. And to one side, a tube that led elsewhere. Fraesch asked, turning to Tula, "This is special! Can we swim, tonight?" He saw Tula's eyes were wide with expectation.

She said, "It is what I brought you here to do . . . but I must tell you some things . . . that is not water."

"What is it?"

"A light, scented oil, heated and constantly filtered. It has also a large reserve tank, which has not been used. There is a steam room and shower through that tube, and the other room is a bedroom." Tula unfastened her skirt and let it fall away from her hips, holding it with one hand. "I do not know what kind of oil it is, except that is has a marvelous effect on you, and that it is lighter than water, so that you will not float, and it is shallow."

Fraesch removed his clothes as Tula finished with hers, and, they stored them in a small closet which she showed him. They clasped each other's hands, and she said, "It is body temperature. It will seem warm at first." They stepped in together.

Tula left him then and let her body settle into the pool, slowly. Fraesch did the same, slowly at first; it was warm, but the sensation soon faded. It was about waist-deep. Fraesch moved experimentally, feeling the slickness of it. The slight scent, the warmth, the slippery fluid all began to work powerfully on him. Tula let herself slide beneath the surface, a slender pale mermaid. Fraesch found a shelf built in, sat on it, feeling the warmth rise to his shoulders. He ducked his head under as she had done, and when his eyes cleared, slightly blurred from the oil, he saw Tula moving to the other side, where she stretched, reached for a portion of the wall, a switch it seemed, and the lights went out. It was totally dark.

Fraesch felt nothing, then waves in the pool, a current near him along his legs, and suddenly Tula slid around him like an eel, clasping him with her arms, her mouth searching for his, her legs sliding around him. He felt a rush of lust so intense he thought he was going insane, and in total darkness they found each other and slid together effortlessly. There were no concepts in his mind to measure it by. Time had stopped, marked only by their breathing and the light murmur of the waves they made. It was coming too fast, almost instantly, and Tula slid away from him gliding out of his grasp as easily as she had helped join herself to him. Fraesch groped for her. He felt neither frustration nor anger, but a swelling desire so intense it blocked everything else from his mind. He felt a light current and grasped at it, clutching madly, and his fingertips slid along a smooth thigh, and lost it. He moved toward where he thought she was, and felt current flow again. He leaped for her, caught a warm and slippery body, which squirmed away again, and she slipped out, onto the shelf which encircled the pool. Fraesch followed.

She was waiting for him, and let him catch her; half-sitting, they slid together again, their motions magnified, their minds blank. Again Tula slipped away from him, struggling and squirming. Fraesch felt as if he were being touched all over. He caught her again and pressed her roughly to the cushion, taking her violently, he thought rape, and as he did, he felt her grasp him with all her limbs with a strength he would not have imagined she had, and she began laughing and babbling madly in his ear, and then Fraesch felt his own desire suddenly peak up, up, into regions known only to the mad, and he also babbled nonsense, secret things he had never dreamed of saying before. It did not seem to stop, but seemed to continue for an unendurable time, and the intense lust only faded gradually, it did not subside rapidly after their shared orgasm. They continued moving slightly for a long time, as if they could keep it.

Now Tula let him gently disengage from her, although he did not leave her, but drew her back into the pool, where they sat on a ledge, together, moving their hands along the lines of each other.

Fraesch whispered, "Tula . . . this is insane."

"I know. You want the impossible here. You think that in this place it will never end; but we must let our bodies reset for a little. There is some property to this fluid, that we will want to do it again, soon . . . I know. And when we are exhausted, we must go and take hot and very soapy showers, steam ourselves, and we will sleep together." She slid off the ledge and half-swam out into the center of the pool, as if she wanted to be alone, briefly.

They did not stay apart very long. At the end of it, Fraesch could not truly remember precisely what they had done or how many times; it seemed to blur in his recollection. But a time came when they knew that their endurance was finally at its end, whatever the chemical message was in the fluid, and they climbed weakly out of the pool, and went to the showers for a long and soapy bath together, washing every trace of the oil from them, scrubbing each other wearily. Tula cautioned him, "You have to wash it all off, or the effects linger . . . you can't sleep, or anything." They went together to a tiny chamber where rushing hot air dried them, and then they went to the bedroom, a space not greatly different from the standard models in the suites above them.

Save that this one had a tiny night-light by the curtained door, and the ceiling, doming above them, was speckled with thousands of tiny points of light, like stars. The floor of the chamber, the bed, was soft, and there were soft blankets, which they pulled over them; Tula curled into his arms, and was breathing deeply almost before she had stopped moving, and Fraesch embraced her protectively, inhaling the wonderful clean scent of her hair, and fell into the dreamless sleep of total exhaustion. He had no reflective thoughts, no thoughts of any kind. There was in the universe only this fragrant, graceful woman and the bed they slept in.

Fraesch awoke, and had no idea what time it was, or even, for that matter, what day it was. The bed-cupola had no changes in lighting to signal the passage of time. Tula was gone; that he realized immediately.

He wondered, idly, how long he had slept. He felt cleaned, purged. His head was clear. Fraesch climbed out of the bed-chamber and retrieved his clothes from the locker by the lip

of the pool. For a time, he dressed in the entryway, looking
at the pool, seeing the slight current on the surface caused by
the filtration unit, the soft play of lights along the domed ceiling, the blue lights deep under the surface. There lingered a
hint of the scent of the oil, something vaguely attractive, although it had lost some of its potency after the time they had
spent in it. Fraesch marveled at it. High technology, indeed.
How had Tula referred to it, before he had known of it?
"Something special, if you like." Indeed it was special, an ut-
ter luxury.

Fraesch climbed the spiral back to the kitchen level, and
rather regretfully closed and dogged down the doorway to the
chamber of subterranean delights. But why, in a place obviously designed for such pleasures and the fulfillments of everyone's most basic longings, was such a place kept secret? It
seemed to him that the party goers should have had it, not
Nachitose, necessarily, although he suspected that Nachitose
might well have been able to afford it. He was glad it was not
public, however; Fraesch imagined that such an extreme of
intimacy would probably not cope so well with ten or twenty
squirming bodies, as it had with only two. And Tula! Who
would have imagined it? Yet her pale, lean body seemed to fit
the environment especially well, indeed, as if she fit it perfectly. Fraesch reflected that Nachitose must have been of
similar build, slender, muscular, wiry.

Tula had left a package of buns on the warmer, and over it
a folded note, which was very neat and precise. It said,
"Joachim—I awoke early and decided to go to the lab and
start the data collection, at least warm it up and do some test
runs, so that we can start looking into it in earnest come the
workdays. Do not wait for me, but proceed as you will; I will
come to you again—we have only just started. Love, Tula."

Fraesch heated the buns, made himself some coffee, and
afterwards, thoughtfully breakfasted in a tiny alcove off the
kitchen unit. He felt still bemused by the events of . . . how
long? Fraesch suddenly felt the need to return to the
rhythms of the world. He abruptly got up from the small
table and began looking about for a chronometer, or some
trace of time. The kitchen had no windows. Fraesch followed
another short corridor, and found himself in a dining room.
The entire room was paneled in a dark, waxy wood with
elaborate swirls and streaming patterns of grain in colors of
burnt umber, brown, gray-gold. Apparently the dining room
projected outward from the structure—in the ceiling was a

large elliptical skylight. At the far end, across a long, elliptical table sculptured out of the floor, were two of the triangular windows, leaning out at the apexes. The view was of the
ocean and a small strip of beach, and as he looked across the
length of the room, he looked into the setting sun of Mulcahen. A warm glow filled the room and evoked sympathetic
highlights from the polished and curved and sculptured
wooden surfaces. It was evening. He had slept through an entire day.

Fraesch did not rummage about through the suite, but
tidied up the kitchen and left, pausing only to look over the
images of Nachitose that filled the parlor. Yes, he was sure.
This woman was the same one he had seen in the Conceptualizer of Leonid Moricle.

Through the pictures of Nachitose, Fraesch was able to
identify Moricle, although he was not the only man displayed
in the collection of pictures. He was the only one who was
shown with Nachitose where the background was obviously
this site, Halcyon. Moricle appeared to have been somewhat
heavy-set in build, with a strong, Semitic face; he looked
competent and heavy-handed, and not at all a match for the
tense, vibrant Nachitose, who seemed . . . brittle, yes, that
was the word, beside him. But again, Moricle did not seem
the type to indulge in aesthetic vices, either. Many of the pictures had sailboat or yacht club backgrounds.

Fraesch left the suite, this time determined to find his own
way, however long it took; he knew he had to be nowhere on
time, so he proceeded with caution and deliberate throught-
fulness. Shortly he found himself at the party room, and he
felt as if he had now accomplished something. The room was
empty, and cleared of all traces of the bizarre events he had
seen in the room the night before. They had evaporated into
the air. Fraesch left, and carefully found his way back to the
spot where he had first heard the voices, and after a few false
starts, found himself back on familiar ground, near his own
place, and so returned home. As he entered, and closed the
panel behind him, he took a deep breath. The quiet and sense
of emptiness in his own suite was relaxing and secure after the
events of the last few days. He felt as if he had completed a
single revolution, and was now at a point in the wheel from
which he would embark upon a new phase.

Concerning Tula. . . . There as well, he felt secure, and a
warm glow began circulating as he thought of her. No doubt

there was much to be explained, but he felt certain that Tula
was probably harmless. Her account of things seemed plausible enough, even if what she had told was not the whole of it.
Everything fit together. An odd thought intruded, which he
dismissed. It hadn't seemed important at the time, nor could
he imagine why it had occurred to him, now. It was simply
this: that the access door to the underground pool had been
mechanical in operation, and the door had borne the mark of
a bare patch, where something had been removed—perhaps
an information plate, or sign. He tried to dismiss the thought,
but it would not go away.

Fraesch went to the study, where he stood, uncertain,
watching the Conceptualizer go through its endless changes,
its endless variations on a single theme. The frame was a
paradigm for what was happening to him: it was beautiful in
its own way, and to Fraesch's mind, completely empty of
Moricle in any sense that could affect him. It was distraction
from the reality of what had been going on here, was going
on now. He felt a sudden wavering of reality, a trembling.
He felt a need to get away from Halcyon, and its enclosed
environment, pleasurable though it was. Something was nag-
ging at him, just below the level of consciousness. Fraesch
could not dispell the feeling. He sat at the study desk, and removed pen and paper from the drawer, whereupon he began
to write.

a. Tula knew what I was doing at Halcyon, but I
had not told her.

b. I have been carefully seduced by the afore-
mentioned Tula, however much I have enjoyed it.
She has done the things I would respond to most
positively, which implies significant knowledge. This
may match with (a).

c. Urbifrage advised me, in an oracular manner
to "be careful," on the train. Tuzun also made observations. But how would they know? They had
never seen her before. One of two conditions per-
tains: either Urbifrage and daughter are paranor-
mally perceptive, or they have seen Tula before.
But how could they—Urbifrage has never been off-
planet, and Tula has ostensibly never been here before, although she has not said so—only implied it.
The reasonable conclusion is that she's been here
before.

d. Tula made her way through the corridors without help.

Fraesch looked at the sheet of paper and shook his head. Then he wrote:

The conclusion is that Tula has been here before. None of the station personnel seems to know her, so she was here before they came. Here on Mulcahen, here, in the northwest, and here, at Halcyon.

She knew who I was and why I was here. She has kept careful watch on me, and has gone to considerable trouble to "capture" my loyalty.

She has attained access to the lab and permission to operate the equipment.

Fraesch looked away from the paper and sighed deeply. This would go far to explain why she seemed to relax a little, and no longer insisted on her background as technician, but became more herself. It didn't matter any more. But an answer only provokes more questions, and for Fraesch, these were now obvious: why? For a moment, he started to say, "She's working for Speculations," but there was something about that which didn't quite feel correct. If for another group, who? And there was another thing, too; that it appeared she was working alone, without contacts, although he couldn't be so sure of that. He could be reasonably sure she had no close contact with anyone off-planet—she was prey to the same isolation as the rest of them. And if truly operating alone, she would have to be, by inference, either enormously self-confident or professionally experienced, or both. Preferably. He suspected it would be without contacts, then. That would fit. Then . . . whoever had sent her would depend upon her to get results, which would occur. Suddenly, he felt a sense of oppression. He was an amateur, not a practiced one at that, suddenly realizing that he was facing a seasoned pro. Yet the feeling persisted that it was just as Tuzun had said, that there "was no malice," that Tula was protecting him as well as getting him carefully out of the way. In some manner he was necessary to her. Fraesch had a cold chill, just then. He did not have the faintest idea how far he could push her, until he became unnecessary to Tula. He was not at all certain that he wanted to determine those limits without help.

He got up and began pacing around the study. Should he go now to the lab, look in on her, see if he could catch her at something? How would he know? Fraesch was no technician, but an administrator. No, he thought. That's the wrong way. He felt an odd and irrational burst of confidence. No, not that way at all. He smiled to himself. And thought: she'll tell me, I think; she doesn't lie—just doesn't tell the whole truth. And he added, as an afterthought, in a perverse sense, all this has made her more desirable than she was before, worth engaging, worth capturing, if only for a time.

He went to the frame and looked at it. As he stood before it, a face was fading from it, and the screen was assuming its silvery blankness of the between-pictures state. Yes. Another image was forming, now, out of the nothingness. But as the lines solidified they did not resolve into a face. Fraesch cocked his head and looked curiously at the frame. The lines came in clear, now, but they made no sense whatsoever. What the frame was displaying did not look like anything he could recognize—it seemed to be nothing but curved lines. These seemed to come in bunches, running more or less horizontally—six to ten or twelve lines would curve together for a bit, and then end, coming together in an odd, abrupt junction. There were some other lines, and also smudgelike marks, but these disconnected lines and marks occurred in places where the sets were not. The image began to fade.

Fraesch stood for a long time before the frame, puzzled. It was something utterly abstract, although it seemed to have definite order to it, in a device that had only shown faces, and rarely, upper bodies and faces together—busts, as it were. A malfunction? The machine's way of indicating mechanical/electronic distress? It seemed not to have malfunctioned, for it was displaying another face now as easily as it had the rest. Or it was something Moricle had seen which had somehow been picked up by the sensor unit, slipped through the gaps in its program. Something, then, significant to Moricle.

Fraesch returned to the desk, and set up his cryptogram for another message, which said:

"Urg req data on folw pers Leonid Moricle and Jenserico Nachitose both emp Speculations. Also data on device Conceptualizer. Stop."

Fraesch fixed himself something to eat, and afterwards took a short walk to drop his two letters in the message-center drop. He came straight back, found a thick volume of art prints and commentary from a planet he'd never heard of, and went to bed, reading and studying until he fell asleep. He turned out the light feeling irrationally pleased with himself.

9

For the first time, Fraesch woke up without prompting, early. His mind clear, he realized immediately that there was still a day left of break, and there was something he could do with the time. He breakfasted hurriedly and dressed in heavy clothing, insulated coveralls and an electric jacket with a winter hood, taking note of the light outside, which seemed watery and diffused, the tones of everything gray-blue.

Outside, it was the kind of weather he had learned to call bitter, on a humid planet on which he had once worked. They had known little snow, no glaciers except on the highest mountains; yet they had suffered under one of the worst types of winters imaginable; month after month of icy drizzle and freezing rain. This weather felt like that. There was a damp wind off the water which cut like a knife. Fraesch paused, halfway down the hill from the dormitory to the little creek. The woods covering the far ridge were dark and sighing mournfully in the cold wind, tossing their twisted branches covered with tiny scales. He thought of the distance to town, and the short daylight, and the worsening weather. He took a few uncertain steps, indecisively hesitating, and then changed his direction; not back to the living complex, but up into the site proper. Perhaps he could find someone about; the site did, after all, own its own fleet of striders.

As he might have expected, however, the work buildings seemed to be deserted. It was still break. Here and there, there was evidence of some activity, but none of it seemed to be useful—routine errands by clerks and checkers. Fraesch began to suspect that he would probably find the striders all locked up, and no one sober enough to drive one.

At the large hyperboloid in which the striders were housed, however, one of the bay doors was open a crack, and there was light inside. As he drew near, he could hear voices, and low mechanical sounds, as of hand tools on metal. Someone was working.

He pulled the door open a bit farther, peered inside. There was a red strider there, under light repairs, judging from the fact that it seemed yet to be assembled, with two parts of people protruding from its rear section; one was standing, with head and upper torso inside the machine, while a pair of boots protruded ungracefully out into bare space from a horizontal access panel.

A voice issued from the interior of the machine, distorted and muffled, and reresonated by the metal. "Close the door, will you! You're letting a draft blow up my arse." And another voice, somewhat shrill, added, "Born in a barn?"

Fraesch, somewhat chastened, turned and slid the door closed.

One of the voices said, "Have you got that connector B-2 torqued?"

"Right; just to specs. It's tight."

"Does it test?"

"Right."

"It's a wonder; damn replacement parts never fit right—this end or the other, one will be out of tolerance. I'll say it, it's a damn good thing we thought to check it before we tried to install it. I hate to think what it would look like in here if I hadn't remachined that male hookup on this end. . . ." There was a rattle, as of something small and metallic being dropped, followed by some interesting, if low volume, methodical swearing. Finally, the boots began waving about and emerging from the bowels of the machine, attached to the legs, and a body, clothed in winter coveralls. The other, who had been standing, ducked out of the underside of the machine, gathered the tools he had used in one hand, and closed a hinged panel with the other, tightening it down with his free hand. This was a smallish man of no great strength, seeming slight in build, with a balding head and a fringe of brown hair. He had a long nose, red with cold, and watery blue eyes. Young, but homely enough for only a mother to love.

The other one was more robust, and wriggled out of the compartment without attempt at grace, landing squarely on the floor. The mechanic dragged a small stool over, totally oblivious to Fraesch, and stood on it to close the access panel it had been in. This one wore a protective leather cap, rather like that of some aviator from the most primitive of times.

Stepping down, the larger said to the smaller, who was putting tools back into a large, upright chest, "Elester, I guess you can go on back, now. We're done and I'll take it out and test it . . . I'll call you if I need you when I get back."

Elester finished putting the tools up, and sauntered off towards the door. He replied, "Good enough. See you tomorrow."

"Be early if you can—we have to start on the winterization of all the units tomorrow—starting with number four."

Elester paused in the door. "The hangar queen? Why don't you just give in and start cannibalizing it for spares? You can't keep the damn thing in service more than a week at a time."

"See you tomorrow, Elester."

"See you, Chim'." Elester slithered through the crack in the door, and pushed it shut behind him.

The mechanic now put his own tools up in the chest, and came back around the corner of the strider, ducking under its rear part, when he saw Fraesch.

Fraesch thought the face under the cap was familiar, but he couldn't place it precisely. Someone he had seen before: deep-set large eyes, large nose, broad mouth. The mechanic flipped the helmet off, to reveal a tightly curled cascade of gold-bronze curls. The face slid into perspective. It was the face of the girl who had been Fraesch's guide in the corridors.

The mechanic smiled at Fraesch. "Well! Our replacement director. Welcome to the motor pool!"

"You were a harem girl, Lot's Daughter, I believe?"

"There, I was. Here I am Tschimedie Pendru, Master Mechanic of striders." She accented both names on the last syllables.

Fraesch began, "Well, Mechanic Pendru, it would seem that I have a problem. . . ."

She corrected him, "You can call me Tschimedie, or Chim'. After all, we've met socially."

"Why were you working when you have days off, you and your partner? Associate?"

"Elester Cude is no associate, but apprentice, although I fear he'll never make it; he has hands of thumbs. I had us out so we could replace the crawl sequencer on this number one. The replacement part came in the last delivery, and the repair is overdue. We have to start on the winterization schedule tomorrow, so I did not want to be bothered with this pesky part; and besides, I was bored. I wanted to fix this flaming machine so I could have an excuse to drive to town—you know—a test run."

"I approve! You have earned it. That was part of my problem: I need to go to town."

"Why didn't you say so? There are four other machines in service."

"The other part of my problem is that I don't know how to operate them, and hesitated, lest I embarrass us all by backing one through the wall of the hangar."

"Well said, Director Fraesch! Are you perhaps in a hurry?"

"No, not particularly."

"Direct me, then! Shall I drive, or shall I instruct?"

"Since we are, as you say, acquainted socially, I am Joachim, or Jake. Can you show me how?"

"Indeed. They are easy to drive. Too easy, in fact, and so the mechanisms suffer from handling by idiots. At last I can show someone how to do it right."

"I will be grateful for a second favor. I shall wind up owing you much, I think."

"Poof! The other night was what any right-minded person would do. You were on your way to a tryst, were you not? Who would not assist a fellow-romantic? We who have been here have long since exhausted the possibilities, and so explore novelties, more or less bizarre . . . and as for today, why, that is my job. Fear not! I will not dun you, nor hound your path with creditors. . . . You could arrange for a shipment of new men to replace these old ones here."

"They would probably ask for more women, and thereby would occur a complete turnover of people, who would also doubtless become bored with one another. . . . The problem possibly has no rational solution."

Tschimedie rubbed her chin thoughtfully. "Possibly you are right; there are things we could have done, but we seemed to have brought all our bad habits with us. We were used to a planetfull of people—they would never run out. But here, in this closed-in little place. . . . Who would have ever thought it would have gone on so long? Well, at any rate, follow me, up into it, and we will begin." She gestured up at the cab of the machine.

Tschimedie opened a panel and actuated a small hand lever, which caused a ladder to extend out of the machine and then pivot to the concrete floor. She went first, without looking back. Fraesch watched her ascend the ladder from behind and below and noted that she did not look especially feminine from that view, in the heavy coveralls. She was slim-hipped and fairly heavy-shouldered. When she had entered the cab, she turned around and caught Fraesch staring, and flashed him back a wicked, knowing grin. "Come on."

"Sorry. I was daydreaming." He started up the ladder, face reddening slightly.

"You have paid off some of your debt; I appreciate the attention."

Fraesch joined her in the cab, which was a little tight with both of them in it. Tschimedie continued, "When one works as something, one soon becomes accepted as being that. Everyone here knows me as a mechanic, and so no one even tries to look down the front of my coveralls; I have to dress up like a Babylonian whore to get more than cursory attention. . . . I succeed as a person, but fail as a woman."

Fraesch said thoughtfully, "You are candid. I will be as well: men have the same problem—it is a human equation, a tension between conflicting drives. If we develop the one, the other suffers. You lead me again to a solution of irrational numbers. I cannot tell you which is best, for we must give up something to gain anything. I, too, would wish to be desired by beautiful women."

"You seem to have succeeded at least once."

Fraesch said, with a mixture of truth, and a certain coyness born of the moment. "Who can say what our motives are, or how long they will last? Come now. The other night we were mysterious strangers groping in the corridor; perhaps we shall be again. But now, however it happened, we are different people. I am your student. Teach me."

Tschimedia nodded. "Just so, now. . . ." She moved aside so that Fraesch could move past her into the driver's seat, posting herself at the back of the cab so she could observe him, and yet give him room. "Now, the starting procedure is as follows. . . ." So began Fraesch's instruction in the care and handling of striders.

She did not waste words, nor elaborate on theories to excess, but she was exacting and demanding, showing Fraesch each procedure, making dry runs through each sequence with him. Fraesch estimated that, all in all, it lasted no more than perhaps half an hour. But it seemed longer, and he was somewhat relieved to hear Tschimedie say at last, "You seem to have the basics straight. Now start it; for real, this time. After you get it idled down, I will open the doors and you can back out. Set it on crawl and move to the fuel pumps, we will need some to get to town." She left the cab, climbed down the ladder, and went to the doors, pushing each one open in turn. Fraesch nervously followed the procedure he had just learned, and was much relieved to hear the engine whine into life somewhere behind him, and see the instruments begin coming to life. After the engine had warmed a bit, he managed to get the strider turned around, a little slowly, perhaps, but he did no one any discredit, and as he engaged the drive selector to "crawl" and depressed the throttle gingerly, he was quite pleased to guide the machine successfully through the opening between the bay doors, and out into the open, where Tschimedie stood waiting, a broad grin on her wide mouth, her eyes flashing.

Fraesch directed the machine to town along the road the way he remembered, displaying, if anything, an overactive sense of caution which Tschimedie approved for the beginner. She observed, "Too many succeed in getting it pointed down the hill, and then engage 'dead run' gait, neither anticipating nor contemplating what the road might bring. Full speed ahead! No, you are doing it right; there will be plenty of time to master the gait changes, the evasive maneuvers." Like Pelletier, whom he recalled, Fraesch also slowed for the sandy road on the riverbank, and let the strider find its own way.

The weather did not improve as the day progressed; the skies remained a stark iron-gray, and the wind increased, coming off the sea and ruffling the estuary into small white-caps.

Tschimedie watched the way pass in silence for awhile, and then asked, "What might you be looking for in the metropolis of On the Waves?"

Fraesch saw no need to dissemble. "I search for enlightenment concerning certain matters. . . . I was hoping to find Urbifrage. You know of him?"

"Urbifrage? Indeed so; he has been most useful to us in the maintenance division."

"Where does one find him?"

"He usually finds you. I am surprised that you require him and he's not appeared on his own. No, I am quite serious, that is the way it seems."

"He came here with me on the train. But he got off back up in the hills, at a junction."

"Urbifrage has a small place here in town, which serves as

well as any. Just dropping in, I'd say we have as good a chance as not at finding him in—even odds."

"What kind of place?"

"A small shop—machine shop, with a flat over it, very much in the local style. He does repairs, some fabrication, tinkers with inventions involving motion machinery, things like that. He also owns an ancient strider which needs constant repairs; that's how he gets around, back in the back country. Also they have meetings in there, which I don't know anything about. Apparently he is associated with some local religious thing—you are likely to meet anyone there, as both beachies and townies frequent the place."

"I know townies. What are beachies?"

"Beach people. Haven't you seen them? They live in shanties along the coast. . . . It's said they circle the continent, except in the worst of the north. They are from the old days—people who just ran away. They live by fishing, hunting, a little gardening, scavenging. They are as loose as the townies are rigorous. Oh, they all come to Urbifrage. I suppose that is what makes him so uncommonly useful—he knows everybody along the northwest coast, and they know him, which means that they have a common point through him."

"And the site as well?"

"Not so much so. . . . I had the idea more than once that he didn't like us at all, but I could never pin it down."

"Probably because when the work is done, the people at the site can pick up and leave, while the rest, whatever their motives, will stay here, on Mulcahen."

Tschimedie agreed readily. "You are probably close to it. . . . Well, here we are, crossing the suburbs. Soon we will be downtown. Slow to a crawl, so we don't miss it."

She gave Fraesch directions, following winding lanes called streets, back of the main street paralleling the waterfront, and he followed them, guiding the machine along progressively narrower ways until they came to a place with large sliding wooden doors to one side of its plain front. There was no sign. There were windows, tall and narrow, after the local style, and through them they could see the yellow glow of lamplight, mixed incongruously with a sporadic blue arcing. A thin smoke trailed in the bitter wind from a ramshackle chimney.

Tschimedie observed, "He's in. Go ahead and just walk in,

no need to knock. We'll leave the strider here—as good as any other place, and the locals don't steal."

"Where are you going?"

"Oh, around. I need to buy some things . . . and I think you don't need me."

Fraesch said, "I never said so."

"Never mind. You came looking for Urbifrage, so it's a matter of some importance, not a social call. You can tell me later, if you wish. I'm discreet."

"I'm sure you are. Fine, then—you will come back here?"

"Yes. After a bit."

"Are there places to eat in town?"

"Yes, very good, for the food; poor, for atmosphere."

"We could visit one you know, if you will."

"Yes . . . I know of a good place, we can go there."

"I will be looking for you."

They shut the strider down, and climbed out of it. Tschimedie left without a backward glance, setting out for the waterfront, or at the least so Fraesch surmised. Fraesch went to the door to Urbifrage's establishment, and, as he had been told, went in without knocking.

Inside it was somewhat like Fraesch had expected, and again, something unlike. The inside of the building was a single large room, very dark, illuminated only by a couple of badly placed oil lamps. A small iron stove provided heat, and not much of that. Fraesch could recognize many basic shop tools—a lathe, grinding machines, saws. There was a methane-powered generator, a rack of gases in pressure bottles, welding torches, and a sophisticated device which Fraesch did not immediately recognize, with heavy electrical connections as well as gas lines. It looked cluttered, but Fraesch knew this was only an impression by someone who did not know. Actually, he could sense an order to it all.

Urbifrage was indeed there, but he took no notice of Fraesch. His attention was occupied with the leg of a strider, which he was welding with short strokes of an electrode, from time to time, replacing the old one with a new one. From somewhere out in the back of the building, Fraesch could hear a generator running, which was apparently his power source. No mystery here.

Fraesch waited until Urbifrage was finished with the task at hand, finding a box to sit on. And after a time, the figure stopped, removed his face shield, went outside, and the generator stopped. Urbifrage came back in.

Fraesch stood. "You remember me?"

Urbifrage said, without looking directly at the visitor, "Yes, of course. . . . Figured you'd be along sooner or later; told you to be careful, didn't I?"

"You mean the lady on the train."

"Who else?"

"She's been here before."

Urbifrage now stopped puttering around and looked directly at Fraesch. "You figured that out on your own? Good! You may survive that place yet."

"I put it together from observations of her. She doesn't seem to care that I figure it out, although she was at no pains to tell me that she'd been here. . . . Who is she?"

Urbifrage filled a pot from a hand-pump tap, and set the pot on the stove. "Tea, for us. . . . Her. Actually, I do not know who she is. She came with a party when they were finishing construction of the site. . . . Off-worlders, you know, they're all one. I thought at the time, just another inspector, or insurance rep, or something else. I am sure she didn't take any notice of me. . . . I couldn't say so in so many words on the train, since you seemed hell-bent on arranging something."

"Well, I arranged it, as you say. I only wonder if I didn't let myself get suckered into something."

"What's she doing out there?"

"Working with the lab equipment, with the computer."

Urbifrage looked blank for a moment, staring off into space. Then he said, "Odd . . . I believe that was the area she was interested in before. She came down to town a couple of times to check in component arrivals from the train—personally. She seemed to know exactly what she was looking for, so I am told."

"Do you know who was in the party she was with?"

"No. Actually, I didn't pay much attention to them at the time; I was preoccupied with other affairs. . . . I was out there, but I only saw her at a distance—we did not meet."

"Were there any others with her, something that might give me a clue?"

Urbifrage hesitated a moment. "Well, there was something. . . . You know of Moricle and Nachitose? They came, then, with that group, not with the workers who came later. And when this woman left, Moricle and Nachitose accompanied her to the depot, as it were, to see her off. I saw that. And also. . . ."

"Yes?"

"That they seemed to treat her with a great deal of . . . regard; almost fear, although their attitudes spoke clearly of respect. I thought at the time that she might have been some kind of inspector, from the company . . . is she giving you problems?"

"Not exactly . . . except that I am curious why she should return, claiming by inference to be one thing, while she is most certainly something else, which I do not know."

"Her records are in order?"

"Of course. But they can be bought."

"What does she claim to be?"

"An analytical linguist whom Moricle sent for."

"Hm. If he had, and of course that's possible, there was no record of the request. After the fire, we reviewed the message traffic."

"She seems competent enough. However, that doesn't explain her presence earlier."

Urbifrage agreed. "No, it doesn't. What are your suspicions?"

Fraesch pondered, and then said, "I thought a commercial spy, at first, from a competitor of the company. But now, that doesn't fit so well. She could easily be a company inspector, but if so, why not just say so?"

"She's not here, if that's the case, to judge you, so she might not want you making decisions with her in mind. She's not here for you, but for something else . . . perhaps whatever came after Moricle."

"She . . . ah, seems to have agreed to an arrangement willingly. As a fact, it seems she has gone to some trouble to involve herself with me."

Urbifrage nodded. "I understand . . . I do see a pattern, there. It is obvious she has another motive for being here. By involving you with her in an arrangement, she captures your attention on her body and personality, her personal characteristics, while she pursues something else; and you are neutralized—put off at a remove. She *knows* you did not kill Moricle, so she must keep you segregated from the remaining group, any one of which might have."

"She does not appear to be interested in that issue, but in the lab, in the process."

"Maybe Moricle reported something that caught her attention."

"Did you see any of that?"

"No. All his operational reports back to the company were in the fire. Even so, if she is an inspector, then I would be even more wary of her. And if she is not . . ."

Fraesch sat in silence. "Then you do not know what she is." It was more a statement than a question.

"No. . . . I am considered a good judge of identity in these parts, but she escapes me entirely. She has a mutable quality beyond my experience; but then again, all you off-worlders on Longlife seem to have that, more than normal people. No offense."

Fraesch said, "None intended, none taken. Please explain that last."

"Identity? Simple. It's a matter of knowing people—just a sense you pick up, knowing what people think of themselves. A person with a single life to live eventually picks an identity and develops it, it shines through all concealments; but many off-worlders have a shimmering, mutable quality to their identity-sense; I have imagined that it comes from living so long; you may outlive us but you still develop at the same old rates, so you overlay the old."

"You see this in me?"

"Barely, but it is there. You are now an administrator, but you will become something else."

"And her? Tell me again."

"Completely obscured . . . she knows computers and thinking machines, that for sure, but there is much, much more. I do not doubt she is a linguist as she implies she is, or says so, however it goes."

Fraesch thought on that. He would not tell Urbifrage how many Longlife treatments he had had: one. And what had Urbifrage said, about his own identity? ". . . Barely concealed . . ." And of Tula? ". . . completely obscured. . . ." The implications were not to his liking; by Urbifrage's perceptions, Tula had been the recipient of many Longlife treatments . . . and the cost went up geometrically, so that she had to be extremely wealthy, at the least, and at worst, in a rare class, indeed. Fraesch felt duel emotions: one, fearing the unknown that he might be up against. And the other, that such an individual should choose to have an affair with him, whatever the motives. Some things he knew to be difficult to conceal, and certain of Tula's reactions had had the ring of truth. It posed a problem, however it went.

Urbifrage interrupted Fraesch's musings, "Pardon me, but I have been slack in my duties as host. Let me introduce my

other visitor, the Venerable Salud Hoja." Urbifrage gestured
to a dark corner.

At last motion separated a human figure from the cluttered
background. Fraesch felt a chill. He hadn't even suspected
that this person had been there all along. Not deliberately
hiding, it had sat so still as to have become invisible. The figure now revealed was tall and gaunt, dressed in plain black
garments, and wearing a tall, narrow hat, cone-shaped, with a
drooping wide brim. The figure nodded politely towards
Fraesch, but did not speak.

Urbifrage introduced Fraesch, and then added, to Fraesch,
"The Hoja and I were having a demonological discourse
when you arrived. . . . Perhaps you would care to join us—
you have doubtless observed manifestations on other worlds."

Fraesch suddenly felt way out of depth. He said, neutrally,
"This is a matter in which I am not knowledgable. I have
heard many things, and reserve judgment, but have no general knowledge to report from personal experience."

The Hoja now spoke, a deep, cavernous voice: "The common sort seem to perceive the demons as creatures of sur-
passing ugliness, this is a matter testified to by history and
art."

Fraesch said, "Yes, I would suppose this to be the case.
Demons would be creatures of fearsome aspect." There was a
distinct air of unreality, which Urbifrage had obviously deliberately created. The elder man accepted his remark equitably.

Then he said, "We settlers of the towns have known differently, which is why we seem somewhat grim to you . . . we
have found that the truth is that the demons are invariably
pleasant, familiar; they take on the lineaments of reasonable,
personable men and women; above all, they are persuasive
and do not threaten. It requires stern discipline to avoid their
blandishments."

Fraesch said, "Your view is a new one to me, I admit. I
would have thought of a demon as having repulsive features,
such as scaly wings, claws . . . perhaps a face where faces
should not be found." He added the last cautiously, not
knowing how far to go with this stern fanatic.

"Correct," said the Hoja. "A bowlegged runt with his arse
between his eyes! Would that it were so! We could use more
demons with their arses between their eyes—those ones you
could avoid with an honest sense of accomplishment. Such
are our hopes. But it is not to be so. They come to us like
one's best friend, a brother, a parent. Then they entice us off

the One Path, each off his own. . . . You should come to us more often; we can grant you great help. It is our life's task to enlighten others of their risks, if they will ask of us." The interview seemed to be over, as if the elder had said what he wished to, and no more need be said.

Fraesch said, politely, "The traveler meets with many views in his course, and scoffs at none. I hope to become more familiar with your perceptions during my stay here."

The Hoja turned to go and added, "He can show you the way." Then he left, with a gesture to Urbifrage.

Fraesch said, "What was that about?"

"The townsfolk are a stern people, tempered by hardships here; I listen to the theology of a native religion, for there is wisdom in all well-considered things . . . Mulcahen has not revealed all its sides to us, rationally."

"Why should that worry us? It is a pleasant enough world, save for the weather, which is not severe enough to hide from."

Urbifrage said, "There is much here to learn. *They* see it one way; others, another. Who is correct? We cannot say. But we know that this world seems to have had odd effects on people coming here. Not enough to examine with the tools of rationality, but something, none the less. They think a demon murdered Moricle . . . and that it served Moricle right, for calling to it with his machine."

Fraesch said, "But I thought Moricle's machine was only to record and analyze wave-motions, not talk back to them. How could he call it?"

Urbifrage said, as if choosing his words carefully, "You and I exist in different perceptual universes; they are farther yet. But that is what they think . . . it may be a useful concept, at least to begin something."

Fraesch said, "I am not certain I would wish to meet Moricle's demon, even if I believed in such a thing."

"I know you feel that way—which is why I offer you this little assistance, without obligation, that you may avoid it. Moricle became obsessed with his lab and his machine, and now you have this woman working with it again; take care, and have a care for her—she is tampering with part of the problem out there."

"I have detected no animosity or bad attitude out there; no vandalism."

Urbifrage agreed. "That is true. It stopped after the fire."

"What are your real suspicions?"

"My real suspicions? Someone murders another; here we have a victim, and here an assailant. We may deliver justice to the latter without improving the lot of the former, who is now dead, in any event. But that only goes to one level; and there are more, never doubt it! Why does one feel such pressure—murder is no ordinary act. No. There are subterranean rivers of causality. As constable, I wish to find the worldly answer. Who did it? Why? But as an inhabitant, I wish to understand why such a thing would come to be, what events surround it. In many cases the surround is more interesting than the poor exemplars it selects to do its dirty work. I cannot tell you what they did out there; only that something wasn't going right. And I suggest that you proceed with caution now; watch her closely. And then we might uncover a murderer, or better, comprehend the forces that would shape such a thing, for it is in controlling the forces under the crime that we control crime itself."

Fraesch said, "You mean that you think some sort of force is operating out there, to create, say, certain attitudes, in the people?"

"You could describe it that way."

"A force outside of them, hence, alien, or integral to the society and thus native?"

"We live in times very different from those times in which our sort of creature was shaped, times and environment as well. We travel to new planets, live there, create new polities, new pools; the new environment may have drastic effects or subtle ones—who can tell. We observe odd reactions and we say something caused it. But we may not know the source immediately. Then there are the different kinds of life—natural and prolonged. The realities of life for humans has not changed, the basic realities: one becomes adult, one participates in procreation—which is only part sex—one is confronted with death, and all the things in between. There seem to be as many ways to dance the life dance as there are dancers; yet you lifters seem to elude something, and in escaping it, lose something. You have the length of days, but to us who take only our own portion you are as ephemeral as mist, ghosts. I know that. I wonder that having a lot of such ghosts concentrated in one place might not cause something. And listening to the sea! Can you imagine! Hoja would put it well: he would say—what should they expect to hear but the thoughts of demons, the malevolences of the great ocean."

Fraesch knew very well Urbifrage was trying to tell him

something, but it was fading even as he said it, for he could not follow the stream of his thought. He felt an urge to leave, sure that the answer he was seeking was not here. He said, "Then we may have brought something into being that only we who made it may understand, is that it?"

"Have you thought long on the question you would ask to this place? There will be such a question, you know, for each place you pass through."

Fraesch stopped then. He almost said something, but then he realized that he did not know; yet, at any rate. He said, "I came here to ask you to confirm one of my suspicions; you confirmed it, but I really did not need the answer. As to the rest, I have not yet formed it. It now has . . . too many parts, I should say."

"Yes. It needs a simplifying. I see that you are not prepared to ask it."

Fraesch added, getting to his feet, "And not exactly certain I'm ready for the answer, either, simple or complex. Why did you go to the trouble you did, to find me, to guide me here, to this place?"

Urbifrage also rose, half-turning away, as if to return to his generator. He looked back at Fraesch, and said, "When you have asked your question and understood, then you will understand that as well." There was a finality in his tone that told Fraesch, better than any words, that the interview was over. For now.

Fraesch returned to the strider outside, feeling again the bite of the bitter winter wind, whistling around the sharp corners of the town. Tschimedie was waiting inside it, with her purchases already stowed in the baggage compartment. He said little to her about what he had learned of Urbifrage, and she asked less.

They did take supper at the place Tschimedie knew of, and it was indeed as she had described it—very good food, and a bleak atmosphere which thoroughly chilled any intimacy which either might have wanted. When they finished, the girl mechanic offered to operate the machine back to the site, and Fraesch did not object; they rode back in silence, declining even small talk, hearing only the hum and mechanical noises of the strider and the wind outside.

She returned the strider to the hangar, and they parted, pleasantly enough, but without commitment. Fraesch found his own way back to his place, across the darkened yard.

Inside the dormitory building once again, insulated from

the cold and the wind and the dampness, Fraesch felt oddly at home, alien as it was to him. He thought, *As strange as this house is, it is less strange than those who have made this world their home.* He saw that a small note had been taped to his door, and he was not surprised to see it there. Nor was he surprised at who had written it. It said:

> "At work tomorrow, please see me. There is something in the lab I need to show you.
>
> —T."

10

Fraesch went directly to his desk in the computor building and paused, waiting to see if anything turned up after the long break. Nothing did. Everything remained quiet, which led Fraesch to reflect that one of his instructors, long ago, had said, "The perfection of management is the self-elimination of managers." That was to say that one worked to eliminate one's own job, that the end of organization was not a complex layered structure of disconnected executives, but rather a line force of prime workers perfectly in tune. It was never achieved, of course; yet now and again, one could catch glimpses of that which could nearly be. He felt reassured, left his desk, and walked down the hall to the lab proper.

This was an area which was nearly as mysterious to him as Urbifrage's shop had been. Here were complex machines, more complex tasks. There was a shadowless white illumination, low noises, mostly of cooling air fans, muttering to themselves. And there was Tula, wearing one of the pale, plain tunic-and-pants outfits which seemed to come alive when she wore them. When Fraesch had come in, she had been sitting at a console at the far end of the room, but when she heard him, she got up and came to him.

"You got my note, then?"

"Yes. Something here I need to see?"

"Yes. Come with me, if you will . . . do you know what they are trying to do, here?"

She had turned to lead him toward the back of the lab, but she turned back to see as well as hear his answer.

Fraesch hesitated a moment, which he realized told her everything.

"I know the stock answer, and I also know the real answer."

Tula turned to face Fraesch squarely. "So do I, one and the other; I have worked for these people before. That is why

146

I marveled at the request of Moricle. But all that aside, you and I both know that this is an experimental tracking system, and for now neither one needs say how we know."

"Agreed."

"You are not a computer man."

"No."

"The sensor arrays pick up wave motions, a transducer converts them to an electronic signal, and we analyze them here. The analysis is the chief part. Against electronics, where we search higher and higher bands, here, in this system, the signal we seek lies on the lower ranges . . . we may talk in electronics of so many cycles per second; in this we may talk of cycles per day, or per hour, or per minute. Our computer is programmed to search for those very low frequency waves. We pick them all up as a matter of course, but the tracking system uses the lower ranges."

"I think I understand the basics; a wave generated by the solar tides would have a frequency of two cycles per day."

"Correct. And there are resonances and harmonics, reflections as well to consider. This is a blend of acoustics, electronics and astrophysics, and interferometry, since we have two sensor arrays. That I wondered long about, since the original specifications only required one sensor—for what we are doing, the planet itself can give us position. But never mind. We can pick any band and study it in great detail. In practice, it's done only at the lower levels, but the capability is there for any frequency band. We can also tune out some of the noise, to increase the clarity of the bands we are looking in. . . ."

"You haven't had it on long enough to get any meaningful signal from the lower bands, have you?"

"No. It will take some time to collect that. You catch on fast."

"I understand the basics."

"Well, in what I've been able to read, since I started it up day before yesterday, I'm getting patterns here utterly unlike what I would expect."

Fraesch looked at Tula squarely. "You told me much there, didn't you? I mean, you know what you are looking for, so you are not merely an analytical linguist, if indeed you are that."

Tula looked away for a moment, and then turned to face Fraesch. She said, carefully, "I am as much as I've said. I've not deceived you."

"But you are more."

"So are we all."

"That's not really an answer, or anything . . ."

"I do not wish to fight with you. I will tell you that I know this equipment, that I have used it in other circumstances, in tests, on other worlds. I helped design it. Therefore I know what I should see during the first part of a run: so much have I seen in every other circumstance. Do you know that on oceanic worlds, worlds with very large open bodies of water, primitive people navigate by learning star patterns for a directional reference, and then overlay knowledge of ocean wave frequencies and directions. They use fairly low-frequency wavebands, using the balance system of the body as the receiver. They can feel an island they are approaching long before it can be seen by any visual system, because of the way the waves refract around it, or reflect from it. The concept goes back to ancient man on Old Earth."

"Go on."

"We know this well; we know what we should be seeing during the initial stages of intercept. There are significant differences here, but I can't yet say what the difference is going to be. . . . The problem is that I don't know how to explain it to you."

"Try."

"Very well. At this stage, the bands we can see should be filled with random noise, a great deal of it. Or there would be narrow clear signals, narrow in bandwidth; these are caused by storm systems, movements of the atmosphere. What I am seeing here, after two days, is that the random noise is thin and weak, and that the storm source signals seem to be suppressed into even narrower bandwidths, almost pure tones, to use an acoustic analogue. Resonance with air causes the signal to be narrow. But here it is narrower than I expect it to be. The fluid of Mulcahen is fairly ordinary seawater, of no particular difference from the seawater of other water-planets; and the atmosphere is not greatly different, although it runs a bit high in noble gases, argon, neon, krypton, xenon. Those do not change significantly the properties of the fluid interface between the two."

"In other words, it has more clarity . . . ?"

"Yes, yes. It's very quiet. You can hear very well in it. I am picking up clear signals from storms I should not be receiving. I have not tried to track them, but I think they are very far away."

"Was Moricle as knowledgeable about these concepts as you?"

"About the purpose of the system, yes. In other ways, no. That was why he asked for help. Nachitose was the same. . . ."

"And you were sent out here to find out why they diverted from their assignment and began studying something else they heard, so to speak?"

"So to speak, yes."

"Why do you need me? I am off-center to these events in more ways than one. I am essentially just an administrator, just to bring some continuity and order to this place until I can get a replacement from the company in here; moreover, I am no technician—I have no knowledge to share with you about signal analysis."

Tula reflected for a time, and then said, "This is a discipline of vanishingly small and subtle studies. We may say that the previous technicians who were working here were both knowledgeable and completely trustworthy; yet under the influence of something they discovered in their reception, they changed the course of their studies here, became obsessed with something, and then died, under suspicious circumstances. Their decline was not sudden, but steady and continuous. During that period, social conditions here at the site deteriorated as well. You are practical and not given to intense disciplines. I want you, frankly, as an anchor."

"You think you are going to see something in this signal?"

"The differences I have seen so far indicate that we are going to see something. There was no reason for what happened to have happened to Moricle; yet it did. You must prevent that from happening to me."

"By being your lover?"

"Joachim, to speak truth, that is the icing, not the cake. We will have to be comrades and associates as well. . . . You must also act as head of site and tell me what to do to solve this."

"You fear what's in there that much?"

"The decline of Moricle is inexplicable; my instructions are to find out what is in those signals. The refinement of the tracking data is secondary."

"You will understand that I do not entirely trust you, now."

"I am sorry for that. . . . Believe me when I say that I

mean that nothing bad will come to you, and that in the end
I will tell you everything."

Fraesch looked at the woman, at the contours of her classic face, the finely modeled features, the pale skin, the dark
eyes. Everything in her face shouted sincerity, truth, even if it
was just a portion of it. He breathed deeply, and said slowly,
"All right. Let it be so, then. Solve it, Tula. And I will want
to be informed of your progress, constantly."

She relaxed visibly. "Good, good. I will do so. And you
will help me, as you come to know more, too." She laid her
hand on his arm softly. It was not calculated, but direct, af-
fectionate. "And the rest to continue as well. Yes, I want
that. For no reasons but the simplest ones."

Fraesch was touched, despite his suspicions. Whatever she
was, she apparently meant what she said. He recalled a pale,
slender body, kisses which were driven by strong inner forces.
He said, "Yes. That, too, Tula. . . . But we must continue to
live apart."

"Then you are wise there, too . . . now you must go make
your rounds and see to these people. I must get back to work.
What would the boss say?" She stepped forward and kissed
him lightly. Fraesch touched her face, then she stepped back,
a slow flush in her pale cheeks.

Fraesch left the lab, and visited other work centers. But he
could not erase the image from his mind that she had left
him with. He thought to himself that there was a certain risk
in what he was now doing, but that in the end, it might just be
well worth it. When he thought that, he shook his head in dis-
belief, continuing just the same.

Fraesch now busied himself in his daily work, thinking it
best that Tula be left to her own devices for a time. At any
rate, there was nothing they could do until they had intercepted some appreciable amount of signal from the waves to
work with. He understood that with very low frequency
waves, moving at the speeds ocean waves propagated, it would
require time for any data at all to build up. He thought on
that, and what she had said of cycles per hour, rather than
per second . . . that involved an expansion factor of 3600.
Actually, he did not know what kind of expansion factor was
involved, to make things equivalent, in a cps reference, so as
to understand. Then he thought—that's not right; we're not
going to listen to it. We'd most likely look at parts of it, or
see something displayed which was based on a part of the

data extracted. . . . He also thought that knowing what was being done did not always mean there was a clear picture of how it might be done.

Several days passed in this fashion, but in such a small site, sooner or later the really necessary work would begin to thin out, and Fraesch began to have more and more time on his hands. He saw Tula infrequently during the day, somewhat intermittently at night. Their relations now encompassed a wariness, a distance, but in some manner related to general human emotional perversity, he found that this quality added something; she seemed to respond similarly, and so it became a sort of game between them, while they waited.

One thing Fraesch did notice was that Tula was starting to show some signs of strain. There was nothing he could quite put his finger on; just the general symptoms of overwork, although she did not talk at all about what she was doing. Fraesch imagined that her work probably involved a lot of waiting.

They rationed their intimacies now; neither a gold rush nor a retreat from Moscow was to their liking, yet they seemed to take something from each other's company that would have been absent otherwise. Neither of them found the exhibitionist parties and gatherings to their liking, so they avoided them.

It was while this indefinite situation was continuing, without apparent change in defiance of all reason, that Fraesch one day happened upon Pelletier again.

Nirod Pelletier had once described himself as a repairer of striders. The truth was rather more than that, for Fraesch had shortly found out that Pelletier was actually chief of site maintenance. Of all the sections, his seemed to have fallen down the least, and so Fraesch had accordingly spent little time with it.

Pelletier had a small cubbyhole off one of the shops, and there spent his days. Fraesch stumbled on the place quite by accident, and equally accidentally, found Pelletier in, surrounded by an untidy litter of rumpled blueprints, parts catalogs, and volumes of equipment specifications. Pelletier cleared a space for Fraesch and invited him in.

They spent a certain time passing commonplace pleasantries, and a little more time on the subjects of programs in effect, and the concurrent difficulties of getting proper supplies at the end of all supply lines. Finally, Pelletier introduced a subject that bore neither on maintenance nor on supply.

He said, rather casually, "Scuttlebutt has it that you've activated the computer again, and that the lab's running."

Fraesch saw no reason to conceal this, and admitted that it was so.

Pelletier reflected on this without change of expression for a long moment, then said, "Suppose we'll start hearing things again, then. I'll order some soundproofing now, so we'll have it to install when the voices start."

Fraesch hadn't the faintest idea of what he was talking about, and said so.

Pelletier answered, "I know this sounds crazy . . . but there were some very strange sounds leaking out of that lab. Enough people talked about it until Moricle ordered me to soundproof the place—more so than it was already."

"There were sounds coming from the lab? What kind of sounds?"

"Well, at first, I heard the talk—you know, this place runs on rumors, and paid no attention to them. They talked about hearing odd music, and odd sounds, and then voices, coming from the lab. I says, 'hah, that's just Moricle and Nachitose in there, jugging away, couple of weird ducks what wants to do it in the lab instead of groping with the rest of us—so they chant while it's on—who knows?" And they all said, no, it's not that kind of talk, it's like discussions and arguments and chants, and sometimes a funny kind of singing, and there's more speakers than old Moricle and Nachitose themselves could account for, and it's not in any language anyone knows. . . ."

"Go on."

"Well, I went and listened myself, and it was just like they said."

"Voices?"

"Voices. Sounded like a radio program from a planet far away. It faded in and out, was broken by static bursts, but I heard several speakers. More than two. What I heard was like an animated discussion, or argument. Got pretty heated, although I couldn't understand a word of it. Then it got quiet, and there was something like music, you know, like this abstract electronic music, and then there was something like a chorus."

"Men or women?"

"Well, neither, for my money. It was voices, all right, but

they didn't sound like people, exactly. You know, you can tell a woman's voice by pitch—it's higher than a man's. These were all mixed up, and they shifted all the time, sort of like singing, but not that, either. I went to Moricle and asked him about it, and he told me to mind my own business and soundproof the place. Never said a word about what it was."

"How long ago was that?"

"Last year, about this time, although the rumors had been going on for awhile before that. I did as he said, and we heard no more."

Fraesch said, considering. "What made you associate it with the computer?"

"The first Mod 3000 they had here—I think it had been handled roughly in shipping—they were always having trouble with it. When it was down, there were no voices. Whenever we brought it on line again, right away people started hearing things."

"What could they have been doing in there?"

"Well, we suspected they were just playing with the equipment, you know, experimenting around, making tapes of each other and then replaying them with selected distortions. They never allowed anyone to see what they were doing there, so I just don't know. If you are interested, you could talk to Ciare, who did most of the repair work on the computer."

"Techist Dekedice?"

"The same, although she sometimes goes by quite another name during our little gatherings . . . you should try her, sometime. Or just come to them, and participate. We would like to show you some things . . ."

Fraesch politely demurred, then told Pelletier he would ask Dekadice about the repairs. Pelletier asked, in return, "Do you expect to hear them as well?"

Now Fraesch was guarded. "Well, not exactly. I don't know what I expect to come out of there. Vicinczin is doing the work, and all I know is that she isn't getting the kinds of response she expects. Frankly, I don't see any connection, but I also don't understand what they could have been doing playing with the equipment when they both knew what they were here for, and were working under time pressure. Did Moricle and Nachitose attend the parties?"

"Not at first. We could tell they were old associates."

"Not lovers?"

"No. That kind of thing shows . . ." This he added, with a stage leer for Fraesch's benefit, as if he viewed Fraesch's be-

havior as not yet up to the standard they expected of him.
"Maybe I'd better tell you more of it."

"I hope so. Nobody's told me much of anything."

"Well, I suppose you could say that they invented the parties. There was a time when people just sort of wandered
about; most disorderly. But after a time, they showed us the
way, and we all fell into it, and have continued. I mean, at
the dark gatherings we are not so aware of who we are in the
workaday world; only what we desire to become, although
that's a pallid transcript of a most rosy reality, may I wax po-
etic. I can't recall being conscious of actually ever meeting
Moricle or Nachitose, although I always felt that they were
either there, or nearby, just offstage, so to speak."

Fraesch thought a moment, then commented, "That's odd
you'd put it that way; it suggests a reference Pendru made to
Nachitose on the night I stumbled onto one of your parties
by mistake; you know, I talked to you there."

"You did? I did?"

"You said you were 'Lightning'. Pendru was dressed as a
belly dancer, and there was a fellow dressed up in chains
. . ." He let his words trail off when it became apparent that
Pelletier had no recollection of the events at all. Blank in-
comprehension met his explanation. "At any rate," Fraesch
continued, "Pendru spoke of Nachitose as if she were still
there; but offstage somewhere, a figure of inspiration, or
something like that."

For some reason, Pelletier seemed anxious to leave the subject. He fidgeted, and then got up and began rearranging the
assortments of odds and ends which characterized his office.
"Well, I think it was something like that. . . . Dekadice can
doubtless tell you more about the malfunctions, and the
voices as well; she was the one who told me about it. Although, if I may say so, I should tread carefully on the subject with her; she's an arty type, and the whole thing had her
a bit unstrung, as the saying goes; she's . . . ah, suggestable,
that's the word."

"I'll be discreet and polite. I shouldn't want our computer
repairman down. How do I find her?"

"She's an on-call type. When we want her, we call her. She
doesn't have to do anything except stay on the site, unless
specific arrangements are made."

"What a job! How do I sign up for it?"

Pelletier laughed. "You wouldn't have it on a bet! I mean,
she doesn't have regular hours, but when we call her up, she

works until whatever we needed her for is done—however long it takes."

"She's repairman for all the control systems . . . ?"

"All of it. Mind, she's very good. Completely thorough. I mean, things do malfunction here. Not often, and there's not that many of them, because this is, after all, a simple station. But there's a lot of sophisticated controls here that you don't see. And if it takes 72 hours to get a crucial component on-line, well, she gets it on line . . . so I don't bother her unless there's a need."

"I understand. I'll not bother her but for a moment. Where does she live?"

"Easy for you to find! Next to you. Up the corridor from your place, next one up the hall."

Fraesch excused himself, conscious that Pelletier seemed to want to be rid of him, without saying so in so many words. It was time to go home anyway, so he thought he'd stop in along the way. It shouldn't take but a moment.

When Fraesch rang at her door, Ciare Dekadice was a long time coming; in fact, he was about to give up and try again, when the door opened a crack and a pert face peered into the dim hallway.

"Yes? Yes? What is it?" The tone of her voice had an aggravated, bratty undertone, as if whoever it was, whatever they wanted, could not possibly have been more important than what she had been doing at the moment. Fraesch had already turned to go, and when he heard her, he almost kept on going. But he was here, so. . . . He said, "Sorry to interrupt, but I was on my way back, and there was a thing I needed to ask you about. Pelletier referred me to you."

"That's all?"

"No more than that."

"Very well. Come along." She opened the door for him. Then she vanished into the interior, apparently expecting Fraesch to find his own way.

Fraesch did, although he did not know exactly what to expect. As in, apparently, the case of every apartment, there was a foyer landing, a small space, which led to other parts of the quarters. In this case, the way was up; a narrow, steep stairwell started opposite the door and curved sharply to the left. There was no other way to go, so he closed the front door and climbed the stairs.

In his own case, as well as in Tula's, their apartments still had something of the character of the former inhabitants. But here, the original inhabitant was still in place, so Fraesch was attentive to the messages the place would give him about the identity of the occupant.

The stairwell emerged into a large room, round in plan, with the canted triangular windows completely encircling it. Another stairwell, opposite, led down. In the center, a large viewscreen occupied a low pedestal; around the perimeter, low couches alternating with racks of either tape reels or electronic controls finished the room. There was no skylight, no ceiling illumination. The only light, other than what came in from outside, came from small, translucent globes spotted about the room, or small spotlights. Ciare Dekadice waited for him, facing the viewscreen, dressed in a shapeless white coverall.

She was much as Fraesch recalled from their brief meeting when he had first arrived; thin, underdeveloped, with a childish face that featured a mouth long set in a permanent sulk. Fraesch suspected she would be difficult, except perhaps when she was doing her own job.

He said, "It looks like a spaceship control room."

She had been standing, but now she settled awkwardly into one of the cushions. "I can't leave the site, as this is where I entertain myself."

"There's always the parties and, ah, gatherings. . . ."

She looked even more sullen. "That's going somewhere else, just as if you rode away."

"I can understand that; they seem, well, a little disoriented."

"Disoriented!" She gave a short, harsh laugh without humor. "They don't even know what planet they're on."

"It seemed to me there's more there than simply liberated psyches would account for. A local drug?"

"The beachies. They gave something to Moricle."

"For sale? I hear they scrounge, a sort of hand-to-mouth existence."

"No. They gave it. He went to them for enlightenment, so I hear."

Fraesch felt the first twinges of alarm. Drug use didn't offend his sense of proprieties; it was that they were taking something completely unknown. Here indeed could be a problem, for he possessed little power to forbid something taking place on so wide a scale. He said, "The gatherings didn't appeal to me; they seemed bizarre, an excess."

Ciare shrugged. "They all do at first—say that—but sooner or later, they dress up and go to their first one, and what they did and with whom is a little dim when they think about it."

"You don't?"

"I can't. I mean, at first, I went with the rest, but I soon discovered that I couldn't function as I am."

"Pendru took an antidote. . . ."

Ciare laughed again. "And how sober was she, really?"

"Well . . . she could act more or less normally; she knew her way around, and was rational."

"But she wasn't sober, now?"

"No. . . ."

"So that is what happened to me. I went, I became. What do you know but that when things were getting good—I was doing something delicious, I don't recall exactly what—they call me up to the reactor, an everyday electronic problem I could do in my sleep, and I get there, and I can't do it. That's all I can say about it. I couldn't perform. I didn't care, sober or not."

"Did you?"

"Eventually, that night. Somehow. It's a blur. But I weighed things and said no to those pleasures, those becomings . . ."

"I can't see how. . . ."

"You haven't *become* yet. You don't know what it's like to let your dark side emerge. It doesn't want to go back to its kennel. Then it's the workaday world that becomes dim. Unreal."

"How many are there like you?"

"Nachitose was reputed not to go to them. But I have the feeling that she was already there, so to speak, somewhere beyond that, as a fact . . . No, I think I'm the last holdout. At least, until you and Vicinczin came."

"So you are alone, here . . ."

"More or less, although . . . never mind. I spend a lot of time, here, alone. And so I have my sensors, my traps." She gestured at the viewscreen mechanism squatting in the middle of the floor, and then at the controls set into the panels between the seat-backs. "When I can get away for the tiniest bit, or when I can bribe someone, I have them implant a remote somewhere . . . so I wait, and watch, and listen."

"For what are you listening?"

Her expression softened. "I don't know. I've felt as if there

was something I should be watching for. Come around here
and see one of my traps."

Fraesch circled around the viewer and stood beside the
girl. On the screen was a view of an ocean, from some high
place, looking to the horizons. The picture was impossible for
Fraesch to distinguish from a simple window, it was so clear. It
was just a sea. The waves tossed and heaved and marched in
ranks, undulating forever. It was, he realized, both empty,
and a picture of a scene of infinite detail.

Ciare said, "There's a frequency-shift converter circuit
designed into it. Now it's on plain daylight, and the converter
is inactive. At night, I can switch to IR, for example, so I can
still see something. If I wish."

Fraesch thought of the reason he had come, and for a moment, almost canceled his question. She was disturbed, pro-
foundly, either by some quality in her individual makeup, or
by factors from the environment. Nevertheless, he felt along
the subject, gently.

"I came to see you because I heard a very strange tale, and
the person who told me suggested you might be a better
source than he."

He sat in one of the cushions, looking at her. Her face had
kept its soft, childlike cast, and there had been something ex-
pectant, released on it. Now, that faded a little. Ciare said,
looking at the image of the waves, "Go ahead."

"I hear stories of 'voices' coming from the lab . . ."

Ciare Dekadice shuddered, a deep, shivering that passed
over her entire body. She looked off into space for a time,
and when she spoke, she did not turn to Fraesch, but spoke
softly, into space. "Yes . . . I heard voices coming from the
lab, voices which were not Moricle, were not Nachitose,
which could not be them, voices, music I have never heard
before, sounds of singing. . . ."

"What did they say?"

"It was not in speech I knew. None of it. But they spoke,
you could sense it, of dire things, secrets, those things which
are not to be named, nor known, nor spoken of, *and they listened,* night after night. It would be late, when there would
be no one about, that they listened. I heard, because I have no
schedule, and sleep as I will. . . . I felt as if I could almost
understand what they were saying, if I went just a little
more. . . . But I didn't want to. I feared what the voices
promised, even though I could not know what it was. I
feared. I still hear them in my dreams, orating, booming,

thundering their awful message. I spoke of it to Pelletier, and he soundproofed the place, so that you could hear no more, by the lab."

"When was this?"

"We were here a time before I heard them. Moricle had already started to change. After that, he became worse. He had some tapes in his apartment, and sometimes I could hear them, deep in the night, the awful voices."

"He played tapes, you think, in his room?"

"Absolutely. And it was always the same tape, too. I know it well. I can hear it now . . . the evil voices. They crackled with evil knowledge, with . . . I can't say anymore." She turned now to Fraesch, abruptly, and grasped his hands. Her thin hands were pale, and the finger-nails were gnawed off short. They were also very cold. She said, "You are not going to bring them back! Please do not! We cannot survive another Moricle obsession."

Fraesch said, "I would avoid it, if I knew what to avoid. I don't know how he received whatever it was he and Nachitose were listening to. You are a technician; do you know how they did it?"

"They did not permit me to work in the lab, at all. Moricle forbade it from the first. Access only to him and Jenserico. He became more emphatic later on, and was, after I heard the voices, violent about it. I feared him, then; many did. Believe me, what happened here was terrible. Also it was a great relief, because it released us, somehow. I feel the pressure again . . . what are you people doing in there?"

"You've not been told?"

"That we are here to study the ocean."

"Let it be that, then," he said. Yes, it was that, but somehow they had done something more. "You said Moricle played tapes in his place. Could they still be there?"

"I don't know. After the accident, people went through and looked around a lot, in everybody's places, and especially in those apartments, but I think they found little enough. Moricle was very secretive about what they were doing in the lab, so I doubt he would have left anything in his apartment. You haven't found anything?"

"I didn't know until now that there was anything worth looking for."

"I didn't tell them about the voices. No one would admit hearing them except me, and I didn't want to get shipped back. Have I said too much to you? Do you think I imagined it?"

Fraesch reassured her, clasping her cold hands firmly. "No, I don't. And what you told me fits with something else I know, which gives it a certain validity. Now. How did he get the voices?" At the last, he was thinking aloud.

11

The winter solstice came, and at the bottom of the year, this latitude of Mulcahen was dark and dreary. The sun—what could be seen of it through the overcast and storms—rose late and set early. As far as Fraesch was concerned, nothing happened to mark the event, save that he noticed the next day that few people were at work, and the ones that were seemed disconnected from reality; they went about their tasks like zombies.

Tula was still showing some strain, and so Fraesch took her down to the pool, where they spent a long, unknown time, unthinking. Between episodes of mindless lovemaking, he gently but firmly massaged some of the tenseness out of her. They did not speak of the work in the lab, nor of any other work. They, too, took a day off, and such was the measured pace of work at the site that they were not missed.

Except by the small communications center, which had left a note for Fraesch, taped to his door. The note said:

"There is a long message, in cipher, for you at the Comm Center. Please pick it up at your earliest convenience."

Fraesch read the note, and set off for the Comm Center as fast as he could, without advertising the fact that he was in a hurry. A message, in cipher! It could only be from Pergales; he had read Fraesch's request and answered in the same way. Of course, it would take time to decipher it, but then he had plenty of time.

The message was long. In the private system Fraesch and Pergales used, there was a general correspondence between letters in the original message and characters in the final cipher, so Fraesch could tell, even before he read it out, that there was considerable meat in it. He signed a receipt for the message and took it to his apartment, where he could decipher it at leisure.

Later, much later, his eyes swimming from making too many diagrams on graph paper, Fraesch began to appreciate Pergales' wry joke on him. Pergales despised cipher, and always replied in full standard language—no abbreviations. But it was worth the work.

"To J from R. Why we need cipher is a mystery to me, but I'll go along with it, for now. Will answer your questions according to the order they came, as much as we have been able to find out, which isn't very much, after all.

"1. Tula Vicinczin. I didn't relish going through the census listings of either Earth or Aegaea, even in alphabetical order, so we tried to backtrack, assuming that this person was at the site. She began her journey from Earth, making only one change, from Radial Express to Puteshestvia, at Pshenst. Thereby begins the fun: she lists residence as Aegaea, but on Aegaea there's no record of her as resident, and all residents are rigidly registered, complete with stereogram. We checked Earth listings, and there are no rpt no 'Vicinczins' listed anywhere. Russia has a number of 'Vishenskys,' but then, so do Paris and New York, and Tokyo carried four. There was also one in Ulan Bator. None of these matches the photo from passenger records. We have no idea who she is. Can you give me any more to go on?

"2. Speculations. I assume you want to know the stuff that isn't public. There is very little of that. They list certain persons as officers of the corporation, but for all we know, those names may be just that—names. We could not make a reliable match of any real person with the names listed in their reports. Similarly, they engage in a double-blind system of supervision which insures that no employee can jump over his supervisor—for the reason that in most cases, the next one up isn't known; or where known is unavailable. All public contact—I repeat all—is either through media reps or spokesmen who very obviously are not key people within the organization. As for the organizations which

have done business with them, all they have seen of
Speculations have been its commercial representatives, or factors associated with them. No one I
talked with had thought deeply on this matter, but it
is a facet of them as far back as we can go. Oh, yes—
by the way—everything is strictly legal and above
board. The supposed reason for the secrecy is that,
of course, they deal in ideas, which by their nature,
are not patentable. One of the fellows on the inves-
tigative staff, though, thinks that this facade of
strict legality, plus the anonymity, probably equates
to something extremely shady and disreputable, as a
systematic part of their operations, which also goes
back to the beginnings. All we can say is what everyone else does—that they pay their bills on time,
and they honor contacts to the letter. There is more
we found out, but it is associated with the three remaining topics.

"3. Moricle. Apparently he is a real person, although his original name was Moricand. We have
traced him all the way back. He claimed French
citizenship, but was born in Beirut, on Earth. What
little traces he has left are always associated with
Speculations. We were unable to uncover any evidence he was ever associated with anyone else. By
education, he had a hard science background heavily weighted toward electronics and related systems,
although he was not a professional engineer, and
shows no evidence of advanced degrees. We have
not been able to find out much of what he did for
Speculations, although he is known to have been associated with advisorship contracts under the military branch. In short, he was a mercenary, although
a rather modern-day one. All of this information
came from the losers in those differences of opinion. They rate him as quote effective and ruthless
unquote. Evidence suggests he had one Longlife
treatment cycle, and the available dates on his
movements agree. We cannot determine why he
was posted there, unless the task underway de-
manded his known ability to get the job done,
whatever it was.

"4. Nachitose. Another one of Speculations' vanishing employees. We drew a blank, except that she

claims to have originated on New Hokkaido, which was settled by a group which was predominantly Japanese from Earth. We have retained the S'su Min Chen Kang.[1] Security Agency to conduct a level-one search for traces of her activities. Sorry we can't afford more.

"5. Conceptualizer. This was news to me, but we did find this one. It is marketed by Unicorn Sales, which incidentally is wholly owned by Speculations. It was originally intended for the psyche wards as a diagnostic tool, and in that capacity, has been around for some time. The new version, however, is completely oriented to consumers. They are frightfully expensive, and the major surgery to implant one of the sensors is added to that. As we understand it, they can be set to pick up various subjects, which presumably would reflect the deep interests of the buyer, whatever they are. They are not marketed strongly, the prevailing opinion on them being that they are a vice, which they certainly have the potential for being. There's just one thing: they include a stimulation circuit, so that there is a constant level of activity for them to record, and for this reason, rapidly become addictive, although their effects have not been publicly brought to light. The rep for Unicorn was rather cool about the whole thing, but he did mention a choice of several models, and a lot of ancillary terminal equipment which apparently goes with their use. You can even get a holotheater for one, which includes a sequencing computer that uses known human behavioral parameters and constants to flesh out dramas. There is an apocryphal story about to the effect that Speculations once wired up a homicidal maniac with one of these and made transcripts, which were then sold off as purported products of avant-garde theater, of course, by imaginary playwrights. They were reputedly not particularly popular, but they attracted considerable attention. This is an un-

---

[1] Chinese, Mandarin: Lewd Blue Spirit of the Thunderbolt, originally the title for one of the innumerable Taoist demons.

proven allegation. Why do you ask? Do you want
one? I know you can't afford it."

And that was all there was. All in all, it was disappointing.
But he knew two things for certain that he did not know before: that not one, but two people, Tula and Nachitose, had
apparently appeared out of thin air—materialized out of
nothing, with no past—and came to Mulcahen. And that
Speculations was secretive about its key people, and while
Moricle, or Moricand, may have been important, he was not
protected with the level of anonymity provided for Nachitose.
Or . . . Tula. There was more he needed to learn, and he
could apparently do so only through her—she was the only
surviving link with Speculations. But there was a question
in that as well: what, exactly, was her link with the shadowy
think-tank company? Another thought crossed Fraesch's mind,
as he reflected on some of the things alluded to in Pergales'
communication. There was more than a suggestion that Speculations was engaged in . . . what could he call it? Manipulating
art media? Was that so criminal, at any rate, any more than
the real participants were doing? He chuckled to himself; he
would have to inquire into the name of the supposed mad
playwright—when he got back to civilization, he might even
take one in, if he could find some troupe producing it. Ha!
Might be better than some he had seen.

Fraesch had been so absorbed in the message that he had
completely ignored the passage of time. He was in the study,
which had no windows, no access to the outside. He got up, a
little unsteadily, and made his way to the kitchen, where he
dialed himself a meal. That done, he looked for a window; it
was dark. Night. He found the chromometer, and it agreed.
Indeed, it was night—and late, at that. A bell on the cooker
sounded, and Fraesch retrieved his supper, returning to the
study.
When he had heard about Moricle having a tape outside
the lab, he had returned and made a search of the suite, paying attention to all the little nooks and crannies in which
someone might have hidden something no larger than a tape,
or a cassette; but he found nothing; indeed, save in the study,
everything small and portable in the suite was his.
The study posed problems of a different sort—for here, ev-

erything was Moricle's; and yet there was nothing obviously hidden, unless one went through the racks one item at a time. Even so, he knew Urbifrage had not mentioned a tape; and a cursory search had not turned up anything for Fraesch. He thought some more. Dekadice had said she heard it more than once. The same tape . . . Fraesch thought it unlikely Moricle would carry it back and forth, when he could presumably get more. No, it was here. It was knowing what to look for, that was it. It was a tape, but it might not be so housed, or lettered. What would Moricle have called it? Strange Voices—Part One? Ridiculous.

Fraesch stood up and stretched. Then he went to a wall panel, at which he turned on more lights. He had been going through the books in the shelves, out of sheer curiosity as much as anything else. There were a lot of reference works dealing with electronics and related topics; propagation studies of all sorts of waves in every conceivable medium; antennas and related reception and emission devices, primitive and sophisticated. There were also folders of abstracts on the same subjects—apparently, Moricle had subscribed to an academic extract service. Many of these were dated, and filed in rough chronological order—and some were quite old, and were tattered from much handling. Whatever kind of mercenary work Moricle had done, he had been in the field of wave propagation for a long time. Electronic eavesdropping? Signal intelligence? All Fraesch knew of the field was hearsay, an esoteric and demanding art.

Moricle also had seemingly considered himself something of a connoisseur—at least a collector—of several forms of art. There were extensive works on several types of painting, some of which Fraesch had enjoyed looking through. One set dealt solely with the art of revolutionary movements from many places and times and was vivid and realistic throughout. Another bound set of volumes contained photographs of well-known tyrants, dictators, demagogues and conquerors, again, from many places and times. Fraesch had also found this set interesting. There was a collection of pornography, generally of a mild type, but exquisitely produced.

One entire section of the shelving had been devoted to a collection of music. This was all tapes, and there was a playback unit in the shelves, with controls which would allow the music to be sent to any part of the suite. Fraesch had not yet sampled extensively from this section, although he had put an occasional tape on. For the most part, the selections were not

works or styles with which he was familiar. Many lacked any
title except a numerical reference, which identified them as
neoclassical works of more or less formal compositional
methods. For example, the many woodwind concertos of a
Wolf Mantergeistmann were well-represented, as were the
symphonies of Ektor Dabora-Oliest. There were others.

And here was the section he had taken some tapes from—
contemporary singing, which of course had not changed for
thousands of years, except in minor matters of styles. Below
that section were what appeared to be live recordings Moricle
had made at a number of places and times—festivals, night-
clubs, concerts, the whole range was here.

The last tape was labeled, simply, "Other Voices," and had
no other reference. Fraesch hesitated a moment, then pulled
the tape case from its place. Inside, there was no program, no
explanation, which he knew to be at variance with Moricle's
preferred system. Fraesch started to put the tape back, but
halted, thinking; an eerie prickling crawled around the back
of his scalp, and he instinctively glanced over to the conceptualizer, which continued to display its infinite program of the
faces of woman. He could not quite make the face out from
his angle and distance, so he stepped closer. The face was
familiar, of course. It was Tula, beyond a doubt. It began
fading as he approached it. Fraesch at first did not feel anything, seeing Tula's face in the conceptualizer which had been
attuned to Moricle; it only confirmed what he already knew:
that she had been here before, in the company of Moricle.
He also knew that it was no surprise Moricle's program
picked her up, for she was singularly attractive. What did
give him a certain pause, and a deep stillness inside in which
he could hear himself breathing, was that the expression on
the face was one which a viewer would only see during a
very specific set of circumstances. Fraesch sighed, and turned
away from the frame, as the image died out, fading into the
silvery blankness. It shouldn't make any difference.

He glanced back at the frame as he started back to the re-
player; another image was coming in . . . and this one was
another one of the abstract patterns of generally horizontal,
gently curving sets of lines, broken by odd places where the
lines would curve together, or just fade out, and the random
little fuzzy patches. Odd. He could only imagine that the filtering program had been set too broad, and had picked up
something from Moricle which was not really part of the se-

lections it had been set for—faces whose aspect pleased or
stimulated him.

The weight of the tape he was still holding reminded him
that he had taken a tape from the shelves. Fraesch looked at
the tape and half wondered how it had gotten there. Other
Voices. Fraesch went to the player, set the tape in the recep-
tacle, and waited as the machine threaded the tape into itself.
There was no sound or any indication that anything was happening within the machine, but after a moment, the green
"ready" light illuminated. Fraesch depressed the "play" button without hesitation.

There was a moment of silence, and then an ordinary human voice began speaking. The voice was not that of a professional speaker or entertainer, but that of an everyday
person, full of all the blurs and slips and accents of ordinary
speech. The voice was slightly gravelly, throaty in a slightly
unpleasant, menacing sense—rather suggestive of an antago-
nist of the adventure dramas. The language was Standard,
but there was a gargling accent to it which suggested that it
was not the tongue of the speaker's birth. It said:

"Attention! This reproduction has been calibrated and syn-
chronized in accordance with protocol C. This is Run Five,
source numbers 114332 through 114573 inclusive. Run begins: five, four, three. . . ." The voice stopped, but at the exact time when it would have reached zero, a short tone
beeped, and the recording proper began.

Immediately, it was disappointing: there was no sound at
all, and Fraesch caught himself thinking that the tape had
been erased. Then some sounds began to be heard, as if the
person recording the tape had adjusted the volume controls to
a better setting.

It sounded like . . . something maddeningly familiar. What
was it? It came to him: like a live recording made outside, in
the open. There were no particular sounds that he could identify, but there was a certain quality. It was quiet, but not
empty. There was a moment of this, and then this quality
faded, not as if the volume were going down, but as if the
scene were becoming very still, very quiet. Fraesch thought:
now comes the singing, or the playing, or both. Or perhaps
erotica—mumbles and groans, other less describable sounds.

The quality of the . . . environment continued to change,
although it was clear the recording apparatus was not being
moved. Now the background took on still another quality, as
if it were shifting into an immense cavernous space. There

was a swishy, flowing sound, something large moving (?), and then, from far away, but very clear, came a call: "OURSHKH SSH?" It had a rising inflection on the end which made it sound exactly like a question. The swishing sound seemed to come closer, and the same voice added, in a drawn-out wail, "AUUWAAUUU" rising slowly in pitch and then leveling off as it faded. Wherever it had been, there were echoes. The hair on the back of Fraesch's neck and along the centerline of his back began a crawling motion he had not felt since he had been a very young child. This voice was deep and musical, and it was unmistakably vocal speech, but it did not sound particularly human, although what could have made it was impossible to determine.

There was a reply. The echoes died out, and a rustling, stealthy movement was made, very close. Another voice, higher in pitch, and with an unpleasant nasal twang to it, spoke: "ARREH IN. SFTHRAKAK. MREKESH." The rustling became even more stealthy. This voice was close by, and it spoke quietly, as if to itself.

The first heard, and answered, "HHOLAT!"

The distant swishing, now yet closer, could be heard more clearly. Now it seemed to have a rhythmic component.

Second voice: "HH OURAG'N KHNA MREKESH KSHTI, ELLEE . . . (pause) MU, EHHH." It ended its declamation with an evil hissing. It reminded Fraesch somewhat of trying to say "H" with the front of the mouth, although that comparison did not convey the mouthy, slobbery quality of whoever had said it.

First: "NUR! 'M -A-GHLOBAT IM." This, with a suggestion of great solemnity, deepening in tone, like some high priest in nameless rites in forgotten underground places.

Second: "OURAGN!"

First: "NEIGHN!" Pause. "HHNEIGN KK." Emphatic.

Other, less identifiable sounds could be heard on the recording, concurrent with the voices, if that was what they were. Fraesch was not entirely certain that he was hearing exactly what had been recorded, but thought it was possible that his brain was substituting something familiar in form for sounds that were entirely incomprehensible. These sounds he heard; they were like voices, but yet unlike any voices he had ever heard. They had a curious mutability, in that while each one so far retained a certain identity, a certain similarity, they varied in a manner hard to perceive accurately, a changefulness that reminded him of badly controlled robot synthesizers attempting to reproduce human voice patterns.

Fraesch stopped the tape, and ran it through on high speed to the end, where he returned to normal recording speed.

When he turned the tape back on, he heard the fading echoes of a mighty chorus, a kind of singing, or chant, although the singers kept sliding in and out of phase with one another. The choral singing faded, as if moving away, behind something which blocked their sound. Moving offstage . . . ? The recording level was still high: he could sense other sounds from farther off, none particularly pleasant; one was a very distant rhythmic pounding, as of many feet, but it was hard to tell. There was also a distant flapping sound, very pattery, nervous, but also suggestive of something strong and heavy. The tape stopped. There was no explanation given at the end by whoever had recorded it, although Fraesch felt certain that he had been hearing, at the beginning of the tape, the voice of Leonid Moricle.

Fraesch rewound the tape, removed it from the machine and placed it carefully back in its case. He now felt very uneasy, as he set the tape back in the shelf from which it had come. "Other Voices." Before this, he had been prepared to write off some of the strange tales he had been hearing as a sort of mass-funk, a by-product of whatever it was they ingested in conjunction with the odd parties they all seemed to attend: a drug which broke down some inhibitive program, some reluctance, and whose aftereffects might be hallucinations . . . yes. He had thought that. But he could not, any more, because he was certain that he had the very tape of which Dekadice had spoken. He thought of calling her down to positively identify it, except that she had seemed too unstable when she had spoken of it—after all, she had heard the whole tape several times. He thought better of the idea and decided to proceed. He needed no more proof. This was the tape. It was from the same source; this, and what she had heard outside the lab: they were the same kind of thing.

It had come from the lab . . . that was the inescapable conclusion. But what had they been doing in there, to record voices? Had this whole thing been some accidental discovery of Moricle's, something which caused him to close off the lab to access by anyone except himself and Nachitose, even barring his best repair technician from equipment she knew well, and ignoring the study he had been sent here to do? All right.

Moricle ignored his wave-motion collector, and recorded weird voices instead. But in what medium? Where had his pickups been located? This was definitely a subject he would need to take up with Tula, first thing in the morning. And as he turned out the lights in the study, he caught himself thinking that it was probably a very good thing that he and Tula had made their working arrangement, for he felt that she was, no matter what else, extraordinarily capable, and he could use her help. Fraesch thought: she said she needed me, but that was just tact and good manners: actually, I need her expertise far more, and we need to be allies, whatever glue we use to cement it with. And with that thought, he negotiated the tightly curved passages and ladders of his suite to the bedroom he had taken as his own.

12

The next morning, Fraesch awoke after his usual manner, breakfasted, showered, dressed, without much thought to the matter, or what was going on outside the apartment, out in the air. He had ceased to think about it, the weather had been so dreary in the winter of Mulcahen. He had once imagined how things must be back in Gorod: with a continental climate to contend with, it would be clearly awful: bone-chilling cold, constant wind, dry-cold snow which would whip around the corners of the buildings and sting one's face. By the site of Halcyon, the prospects were not a lot better—in place of the hard cold of the interior, they had the damp, numbing cold of the seacoast in winter, a lot of drizzly rain driven by erratic storm winds, and rarely, some wet, sticky snow which seemed good for nothing except making slushy messes. The prevailing mood among the inhabitants of the site was, ignore it, and eventually it will go away. We have our comforts. Fraesch found it easy to fall into that thinking, even though he still, along with Tula, seemed to retain something they had given up.

He has having a last cup of tea when he noticed an odd light coming from his dining room, something bright and completely out of the ordinary; mornings in this season had been, as a rule, overcast, or at best, watery and pale. This light was bright and open, almost painfully so. Fraesch got up and went into the room, which he rarely visited.

This room was similar to the one in Tula's suite, that is, it was a formal dining room, intended specifically for entertaining. But there were more differences past that point than there were similarities; where Tula's (formerly Nachitose's) was rich and warm, this one was cool and distant, severely elegant. The table occupying the center of the room was of the famous oval-square shape and made of some synthetic material whose crystallization patterns left a delicate tracery of a hexagonal grid of fine silver lines all over it. Its base

color was a pale gray, rather like the tone of bleached driftwood. The sideboards were of the same material. There was
no skylight: illumination from the ceiling was provided by a
row of geodesic hemispheres distorted into the shape of el-
lipses and flattened. Only the windows retained the shape of
the structure. Fraesch avoided the room entirely, as he never
felt at ease in it.

Now, however, he went in and made his way around the
table to the windows, three of the outward-leaning, base-
down triangular orifices, and stood in the shallow alcove they
formed with their outward curve, looking at the outside in
open wonder.

The view was to the southwest. From here, Fraesch could
look down the slope of the hill, to the mouth of the little
creek. There was a sandbar there. Beyond, the ridge and its
contorted evergreens dove sharply into the ocean in a tumble
of wet rocks. Gray and stormy, or lit at best by weak sunlight, it was now brightly lit, full of movement. The sun
shone out of the mountains to the east, and the sky was clear
and intensely blue. The ocean was indigo, almost black, and
the waves splashed and played among the rocks. Far off, on
the horizon, there were clouds, but he could not tell if they
were advancing or retreating.

On the point, the waves were breaking, but beyond, they
seemed to be regular and perfectly shaped, although he could
not see the beach proper from the angle of the room. Judging
by the spray, there was a light wind from the southeast, but it
did not seem strong. And it looked warm, or at least comfortable. He knew it had to be but a temporary freak of the
weather, but all the same he wanted very much to get out,
out of the enclosed habitat. Fraesch turned away from the
windows with reluctance, and looking back into the suite and
the severe dining room, he saw that it was both dark and
dull. He wanted to be out of it even more.

On his way out, an idea crossed his mind: Tula. Perfect;
he would go up to the lab and get her. He was sure that she
would be there—she was spending considerable time there,
more and more. He would get her at once, and at least for a
brief time, as much as they could steal from the iron-gray
skies of winter, they would walk along the beach and do
nothing more significant than gather . . . whatever was cast
up on the beaches of Mulcahen. He realized with a start that
he did not know. He had thought there would be seashells,

but he did not know. No matter. There would be driftwood, and pebbles, at the least.

When he opened the door to the outside, it was as the light had intimidated: the air was slightly cool, warm in direct sunlight and dry. There was an odor of resinous evergreens and deep forests, a fresh, living scent in direct contrast to the bitter airs off the sea. Fraesch went up the hill to the lab building in great strides.

He found Tula, as he had expected, in the lab proper, intently studying an enormous strip of paper; there were irregular markings all along its length, but he did not pause to try to see what they were; they were not writing, or symbols, at any rate. She did not look up when he came in, she was so deep into concentration.

She was not dressed in her usual working clothes, but in a tan sweater and brown, loosely flowing pants. When Fraesch approached her, she looked up at him, but she did not break her concentration on what was on the paper. A quick flicker which did not reveal any particular recognition. Her eyes were slightly bloodshot and there were faint strain lines at the outer corners. Fraesch took her arm gently.

At last he interrupted her concentration on the paper, which stretched along the central worktables from one end of the lab to the other.

Fraesch asked, "How long have you been here—all night?"

Tula said, "Not all night. But I did come early. Couldn't sleep. And so I came up here and programmed this run." She stopped, as if she were waiting for a certain set of words. "Joachim, there is something in this intercept; I wasn't sure until I had it run out in this form, but now I'm sure of it. . . ."

He said, "Never mind. Come on. You need to get out of here for awhile. The weather's broken. Get out for awhile— it's warm outside."

"No, listen, I have to work on this, I've got to tell you what I think is. . . ."

"Forget it for awhile. It will wait. That will be here when you get back, we can go over it then."

She shook her head, and glanced back at the roll of paper. Then back at Fraesch. "No, no, you don't understand, let me tell you, this is . . . if this is what I think it is, then I know why Moricle. . . ."

"Tula. Now listen to me. Please."

Fraesch did not let her finish. "No. Not now. Let it wait. It will wait for us, Tula. You know that. You have been at this much too hard, and for once you have got to stop, at least for the morning. It's beautiful outside, and it can't last, so come with me—we're going to walk along the beach, and forget this for an hour or two."

"But I need to tell you. . . ."

"Come with me and forget it for an hour or two, and I'll listen all day and all night. Tula—I am worried about you—you are pushing it too hard."

"Fraesch, you are impossible, I must tell you."

"Afterward. Not a word before then."

"Dammit, I know my own abilities, and this, this. . . ."

"You said you wanted me to take charge and direct you. I do so. Employee Vicinczin, you need to relax. You will make bad judgments if you are overstressed, which will be to no one's benefit."

"Well, that's true, but just the same. . . ."

She was wavering. "Not a word."

"But it's vital, I need to . . . I need your help, we have to. . . ."

"What you see in that, what you suspect, Tula, has waited the whole time we've been here. Can an hour make any difference?"

"No. But. . . ."

Fraesch took both her arms, held them firmly. There was a suggestion of resignation in her face, and a great tiredness he had never seen before. "Tula—please. For your own sake. When I came here, I was to ask you for my sake, but seeing you, I know you need a walk outside far more than me. Right now—you're on the edge. . . ."

"You can say that!"

". . . And rushing into it is the worst thing you can do."

Now Tula said nothing, and glanced back at the paper, as if she wondered if it were still there; then around the lab, the tape banks, the console which operated the Mod 3000, whose main frame was located deep underground, beneath them. Then at Fraesch. After a long time, she said, "All right. I'll do as you say. There is truth in what you have suggested." She hugged Fraesch quickly, touching her cheek to his, and then stood back. "Very well. I promise. Not until after we have walked."

"No shop talk on the beach!" Fraesch glowered at her, mock-stern.

"None?"

"Absolutely none!" He ventured a Russianism; *"Nichevo ob rabote."*

She answered, instantly, *"Vo istinye tak."* A weak smile fled over her face, and she gestured at the lab door, behind Fraesch. "Take me there, before the winter closes in again."

Fraesch did as she asked, and turned from her to start for the door. He did not see, turning away from her, the slow flush that added to her pale skin, for a moment, a rosy color, and faded slowly away, leaving her normal pallid ivory. She was glad that he did not see it.

And it was true that he had not. But he had heard her answer him. Instinctively, without the hesitation of translation, however short. Fraesch had spoken student Russian to her; and she had answered him not only as a native, but as a native who had been deeply steeped in culture and tradition. Only a native would use *instina* for "truth" instead of *pravda,* which was not so much truth as it was correctness. And so Fraesch glimpsed another datum about Tula. It was no answer, but another question.

Not every year, and not in precisely every place, but often enough, deep in the bowels of the coldest part of the year, there will come short breaks in the grasp of the iron jaws of winter, and for a day, for an hour, for a little space, a warmth steals in from an odd quarter of the compass. Men noted this phenomenon on every planet they discovered which had seasons at all to speak of, and for all their knowledge, could not completely explain it; but they responded to it well enough.

Walking down the hill to the beach, a light and playful wind ruffling their hair, Fraesch and Tula alike felt, it seemed, years peeling off them, years of difficult and steady work, although it had been nowhere near that long. The sun remained low, floating across the south as it should in the season, but it was clear and bright and golden.

At first, Tula had gone somewhat reluctantly, as if someone else had averred this was good for her. But by the time they had reached the sand bars where the creek flowed into the ocean, much of this reluctance had vanished as if it had never been, and she was moving more loosely, more relaxedly. Fraesch could see the lines around her eyes fading, and her face becoming less set, less tense.

They were blocked from going farther south by the creek

and its clear water, washing innocently over brown pebbles. Fraesch said, "Seems this is as far as we can go, this way. But there's always the north. I don't know what the next creek, there, is."

Tula looked around for a moment, and then began removing her shoes, low, soft boots. "We've already been up that way."

"You're not going wading, you goose!"

"How else? We came for an adventure, so let us have one!" And without a backward glance, she skipped across the bar, across the shallow creek mouth. Fraesch hesitated, but only for a moment, and then he removed his shoes as well, rolled up his pants and followed her. The water was icy.

Fraesch reached Tula. She was sitting on a rock, digging her feet into a sunlit patch of warm sand. Fraesch sat beside her and did likewise. He winked at her, and said, "Cold?"

"Glacial, for sure. I've never felt anything so cold."

"No glacier. Water's too clear."

"You're no consolation."

"You're the one who went wading."

They smiled slyly at one another, and then looked outward, from where they were. It was, in a way, as if they had entered another world. Behind them, now partially blocked by a screen of native growth, was the site, and the even beach it fell down to in a smooth slope. But here, this was just the world as it had been since its creation—rocks, spray, the indigo sea, the resinous fragrance of the conifers behind them up the hill.

Fraesch looked out to sea, farther, past the rows of incoming perfect waves, each one coving underneath as it rose to greet the shore in long, immaculate rolls, trailing feathers of silver as the light easterly breeze would catch the spill of the breaking waves and lift it back in a smooth veil. They marched in ranks to the horizon. There, at the edge of the world, massed banks of thunderclouds hung motionless, frozen, so it seemed at a single focus. But if he looked away, and then back, he could see change. They were a mighty wall around the world, ever so slightly yellowish, their tops domed, and the steamers of hail, rain and snow moved slowly about them like the filmy veils of the dancer. But more slowly; much more slowly. Fraesch looked at the cloud wall for a long time; it was, no mistaking it, violent weather. But he could not tell if it were approaching or not, or even being blown back by whatever change in the weather patterns of Mulcahen had provoked this unseasonable warm spell.

He caught Tula's glance, and indicated the cloud bank. "That out there says this won't last."

Tula nodded, reluctantly. "I know. It's not spring. Behind those it's just the same as it's been . . . maybe worse. How far off do you think that bank is?"

Fraesch squinted at the distant clouds through the clear atmosphere again. He said, "25-30 kilometers, easily, maybe more."

"So even if the pattern changes, we still have a little time."

"Probably the greater part of the day . . . but I don't trust it."

She stood up, brushed the sand off her feet and put her shoes back on. "Come on, then! If we're going to do any exploring down this way, we should get on with it."

Fraesch put his shoes back on as well, and followed her.

Soon, almost immediately, they reached a part of the ridge where the rocks seemed to run straight out of the slope and into the ocean. But among the rocks, there was a way— whether path or accidental arrangement of sand and rocks, they could not tell, but Tula, in the lead, followed it as the trail, or open way, climbed upward as it curved around the point. Soon they were out of sight of Halcyon Station entirely, and the only sounds they could hear were the waves below them, which met the point with prolonged blows they could feel in the ground. Tula reached a point where, apparently, the way turned abruptly downward, for she sank from view. And when Fraesch caught up with her, she was waiting for him, motioning him to stop and be still.

Around the corner, there was a steep little secluded cove, all rocky, cut sharply into the ridge rocks almost like some rude amphitheater or some ancient race. Fraesch saw why Tula had stopped: a human, or something human in appearance, was climbing up the rocks from the sea. After a moment, Fraesch thought, from motions the person made negotiating the rocks, that it was most likely a woman, or girl.

She had an untidy mop of gold-brown hair, and wore a shapeless garment that looked rather like a large poncho, and little else. Fraesch could see her legs and feet under the poncho as she climbed. From this distance, he could not make out any details of her features, but some cues suggested that she was shorter than Tula, broad at shoulder and hip, agile and strong as an animal. Fraesch had a momentary surge of alarm: was it dangerous? He looked around, upward, over the cove. Where did she live? In a cave? He noticed an odor in the air, very faint, almost undetectable. Woodsmoke. He leaned forward, almost touching Tula, and asked, "Did she see us?"

"I don't know; she seems alert enough."

The girl continued climbing the rocks, moving sure-footedly, without using her hands for holds or her arms for balance. Fraesch had spent an extended lifetime among people who only shared one constant—that they were all un-sure of themselves. The only difference had been in degree. Everything in the human universe occurred within the con-fines of a metalanguage which possessed only one mood; the subjunctive—as if it were. He watched the girl, and he *saw* this, concurrently, because of what he realized she was—a creature who had moved into an indicative universe. Not necessarily retreating back to the eternal present of animal models. No. Her motions were too sure, too right, too cor-rect. Too true. She looked up at them, from under the mop of hair, intelligent, aware, almost totally unconcerned. It was not to see them that she looked, but to communicate to them that she knew they were there. *You cannot surprise me, therefore fear not.* Yes. He understood. He also understood that very probably everything she did would surprise them, on the other side of it. Fraesch stood up in plain sight.

Tula, feeling the motion, looked across her shoulder, with some alarm. "Joachim. . . . ?"

"No matter. Come on. We'll go meet her. This is one of the beach people I've heard about. This will distract you from your work for sure."

Below, the girl continued her unhurried pace up the slope. Fraesch helped Tula to her feet and motioned to her that they should proceed, more or less across the slope so as to meet the girl coming up. Tula went ahead, but slowly and uncertainly.

They met on a level spot, the girl having reached the spot marginally ahead of them. She paused, with the perfect tim-ing of a musician, to wait for them, an arrested motion, not a stopped one. She said, quietly, "I am Collot; you may come with me, if you wish." The voice was throaty and deep, and it carried clearly over the noisy splashings of the waves on the rocks.

Tula told her name, and Fraesch spoke his—first names

only. The girl nodded, and continued her way upward, without a backward glance to see if they were coming. Fraesch and Tula turned and followed.

The place where Collot lived was neither a cave nor a rude lean-to of faggots and roots, but a substantial low cabin built of adzed logs and caulked with a gray-blue clay; this was the cabin they had once seen from the beach. There were few windows, and those were small and high up on the walls, just under the eaves. By contrast, the single door facing the ocean was large, taking up easily a third of that wall, and mounted so that it slid to the side to open. Presumably in fine weather it would be opened all the way. Inside the large door was a smaller one, barely large enough to crawl through, and it was through this one that the girl entered, holding it open for them after she had gone through it.

The inside was a single room, with shelves around the walls. The floor was covered with heavy rugs, and felt slightly springy underfoot. The south wall held a stone fireplace, in which there was a small fire. The air was warm and dry, and smelled only of wood-smoke.

Collot, apparently ignoring Fraesch and Tula, brightened the fire with some small, oily roots, and then added another kind of wood from neat piles close by the fireplace. She took an iron pot full of water, and added things from crocks—dried leaves, wrinkled berries—and set the pot in the fireplace close to the fire. Only then did she turn to her visitors, settling on the floor in one integrated motion, all the time looking at them without the slightest expectation. She said, "Sit, join me. While you are here, it is yours."

Tula and Fraesch sat, Fraesch easily, Tula with a nervous little flutter. Collot said, "Now, we three. Three is not so good, do you know? It should be two, or four. There is a lack with odd numbers, there is no flow. Perhaps Umparo will be here, or Twilo, and then the circuit may be completed. Can you dance?"

Fraesch said carefully, "I can, but I am much out of practice . . . Also, we have no music." He glanced around the room.

Collot said, matter-of-factly, "No matter. We can make that, if we need it . . . Why are you here?"

Fraesch answered, "We were walking and saw you."

"Then you do not know . . . so. Yes, I see; I do not know you, so you must be the new ones, who came to fill the places

of the two who left. They told me, but I knew that it would
be so, anyway."

"Who told you?"

The girl answered, "The rest, who come and visit, and . . .
trade things. Glass, pots, metal for the slots the door rides in,
the little wheels."

Fraesch said, "Trade is an equivalence: something changes
hands. What do they take from you?"

"Myself, and others like me." She corrected Fraesch, but
not reprovingly. Or was it an answer? Hallucinating am-
biguity.

Fraesch, following an impulse, said, "You knew Moricle
and Nachitose, then? They came here?"

"Moricle? Ah . . . yes, that one. He came, bursting with
waking dreams of stride, a head full of all that you hold
worthy; but he came again and asked me to teach him, and
so I did. The woman, the slender one, she came, but she did
not stay. Most of them from your station, for although we on
the shore have given away almost everything, still we have
something that the people of your universe want."

Fraesch said, "I see that. I do not know if I want what you
have bad enough to cut myself off from the worlds I left behind."

Collot shrugged, gently. "All you have to do is let go of;
there is nothing so much to take, although for those who can
see no other way, there is a thing we can do for them."

"What is that?" Fraesch asked gently.

She shrugged. "We say that the first ones of us came here,
away, seeking wholeness and peace; this is, in its way, a
beautiful world. Or, at least, so I am told, so I hear. I have
not been more than a day's walk from this place in my life.
But with lessening amounts of those things they brought with
them—what they could carry—it grew hard, because this is
not really our world, a human world. We are invaders. They
did not know what they could eat, and there are some things
that do not sit well. Tlemcen found the Doors. . . . We call
them that, because they can be opened, in you, and
closed. . . ."

Fraesch said quietly, "A drug—more properly, a set of
drugs."

"Perhaps. For us it has become a way to understand something of the strangeness and glory of the world; through the
Doors we hear and understand. . . . Moricle was bad in his
heart, but he knew this, and desired to be made whole, so I

thought to help him, but it didn't work right with him, I think. It didn't help, that I know. But he knew how to get it, and so illuminated the rest, who seemed to share his visions."

Fraesch said, "I see. How do you make it?"

"No way—it is found. A sea creature makes within itself a series of stones connected by strands. We call the creature 'the sock.' It has little shape of its own. The stone opens, and a flake of the dried hide of the creatures closes. You can find them along the water line."

Tula said, "We know the effect this has on our people. What does it do to you?"

"I lie in my house, and the sun dances across the sky, and the ocean speaks of secrets, and I listen and know, but I cannot tell you these things, because we have not the words between us."

Fraesch asked, "Is this why your people always live near the ocean?"

"I don't know . . . we all live on the sea coast, that is true. Back inland, there were people just like us, but they are not so now. They are different. They are neither of your worlds, nor of this one, and so they are harsh and stern."

"And yours?"

"They never left your worlds, and so in time they will return to them . . . or become them again, for they still carry its promises in their hearts. But we have escaped, and the years pass, and we will always be here and hear the voices of the world."

"You hear voices?"

She looked sly, like a child. "Sometimes."

"Could I hear them?"

Collot thought a moment. "I thought Moricle might; yet he did not, nor does anyone else there, so I understand. So I do not know if you would . . . it takes a lot of understanding, much work. But of this we know peace and freedom from strife."

The pot Collot had placed by the fire was now bubbling; this she removed, and with the aid of a shell of curious shape, she dipped portions of it into simple bowls, which she proffered.

Tula looked at Fraesch. "Is it safe?"

Collot answered, "Only an herbal infusion."

Fraesch nodded, and took his, and after blowing on it for a bit, sipped some; it was aromatic and had a pleasant tart bite to it. For the moment, he saw nothing alarming about it.

Tula, hesitating, sipped at hers as well, seeing that Fraesch
had taken his without ill effects.

Collot leaned back against the hearthstone and stretched
her legs out. They were covered with fine gold hairs. Underneath, smooth skin tanned a tawny golden color by exposure.
Her poncho was nothing more than a blanket with a hole in
the middle of it. Fraesch found himself being attracted to the
girl, despite the fact—undeniable—that she had none of the
attributes he thought he looked for. But she did have a lazy,
unassuming grace and a blazing animal vitality.

He said, "Tell me about your people, how they live. What
are their rites, their ceremonies?"

Collot said, after a moment, "We are casual people who
live things out in their turn; life is short—too much so to
waste on mannerism. We take the joys and pains as they
come."

"You live alone. Will you always?"

"Probably . . . most of the time. For now, there is Twilo,
and Umparo . . . I am not alone; I have a boy-child, Damerand, who has left to learn mansway with Umparo, and a
younger girl, Irie, whom I instruct as I was instructed by my
mother. We live alone, and come together as the need is."

Tula asked, "Do the men wander, or live in houses like
this?"

"We are mostly all the same. We go to one another according to the way we feel, what we need. But we do not
stay; each has its place."

Fraesch began to understand something of the beach
people, listening to the girl. Hidden in her words was a story,
a highly structured one. On the surface, it sounded like Poly-
nesian free love, live for the moment and raise the conse-
quences. But there was much more to it than that—he could
glimpse the order. Each one had a place, and natural attrition
probably kept their numbers low, so that they did not crowd
each other. Everyone had a place. A territory. Their society
did not have families as such because the whole thing was a
family. He asked, "Is Damerand the child of Umparo also?"

She said, "Umparo had no boy; Damerand sought a guide.
That is all that need be."

Fraesch, for a moment, found himself envying these people
as he had done seldom in his life. After all, it was haunting, a
dream of freedom as old as man: to live by the sea and be
casual. But he also saw the thorns in it—eventually, this idyl-
lic life, with its intermittent hardships and hazards, would be

crowded more and more by the more organized, committed people of the interior—company types, the stern villagers, the nomads. He was sure that the people of the beach would outlast the site; but what else, however much one longed for the life they led. It was sad.

He said, "You are not, after all, so different from us; a generation or so back, you *were* us."

Collot looked back expressionlessly. She answered, "So I have heard; and after the new owners came—owners, hah—they sent emissaries all up and down the coast, offering to take us all as guides. Now we had become the natives, you know. But none of us went. We came for escape, the ones who heard and harkened to the voices of this world."

"Voices?"

"There is a voice, there are voices within every world if you will but listen to them. *They* will tell you what to do, more reliably than those who pay you. What are they, and what can you buy?"

Tula said, "We can prolong our living. Surely that is worth something."

"Thus spoke both Moricle and Nachitose. Yet they came to me; I did not go to them. Would you return as well—for in giving up everything, we have gained something you have lost."

Fraesch asked softly, "What is this?"

"We are talking of ultimates and unanswerable questions. You avoid them; we live in them. It is difficult to cross gulf. We, now; if we come back, what are we but the lowest of the low, menials? Yet here, I am wise, a survivor, one whose counsel is sought. And what do I counsel? That there is nothing more than love."

Tula shook her head, and started to protest, but Collot held up her hand. "No. Do not deny it. Especially since you and he, who came here strangers, protect each other from the unknowns you face with that very thing. But would you give up everything for it?"

Tula said, "Everything encompasses a lot of alternatives."

"There is much to protect against, and most of that is inside yourselves."

Fraesch said, "And you thought you were helping Moricle . . . ?"

She nodded slowly. "And Nachitose. I did not know that there is something inside you that must fade before you can use the Doors. It was my error, and for it I must atone."

Fraesch said, "They take something . . . then they gather in the most bizarre costumes, and do strange deeds of which they remember little. No one seems to get hurt, or damaged in any way, but I have seen them and do not trust them entirely in that state. Something dark is stirring in them; I know there are other darknesses in us besides the far side of sex."

Collot answered, "Our holy man, Tlemcen, told us that long ago, on the origin world, long lives back, men secretly worshipped a god who dealt with all those matters. Dionysus was his name, although they called him other names, too: Zagreus, Iacchos. I have heard Tlemcen call to them in his odes. They feared him, and forgot him for a god of the light. . . . The Doors for us open to the light, but for you they open to the darkness. You see that it is nothing but a matter of which way you face yourself."

"And what of Tlemcen? What does he face? And does he still walk on this world?"

"He often goes among the men of the old way, but he brings few to us now. Still he searches."

"What is his name?"

"To us, he is Tlemcen. He was one of the first. Then he had another name, a last name. Kapicioglu. When he is among you now he calls himself Malo Pomalu. Have you met him?"

Fraesch felt the stillness and the quiet of the room becoming a tangible thing, a crystalline rigidity; the mood faded. He said, ". . . Yes. He sought me out when I arrived. But I did not know what he wanted; I do not know, entirely, now."

"He came for you? Then all is known! You will be of us, live here by the sea. Perhaps you will father children with a woman of the people, and instruct other boys."

Fraesch shook his head. "No children. When you pass through the treatments that prolong life, that is one price you must pay. It is a side effect of the process. No children."

Collot was not dissuaded. She said, "No matter. You will be taught, and then you will teach; it is all one. And you can use the Doors to help you."

Fraesch said, "No."

"Do you hold on so hard?"

"It is that I do not wish to know whether I face the light or the darkness."

Collot smiled. "Spoken like one of the people, truly. Who else would wish unknowing. All the better. You are halfway there."

Tula now said, "All to the good is this, but Ser Fraesch came here to do a job, until replaced by the people who hired his services. He cannot just run off in the wild. . . ."

Fraesch interrupted, "But I have no mind to go wandering off. Of course I have things to do at the station. So do we all. And I will do them."

The first he said to Collot, but it was for Tula's benefit. Now he spoke for Collot: "But when all is done, I do not reject your interpretation of things. It is that it isn't the time, and as you say, I haven't let go. I don't know if I want to."

Collot nodded. "Well said; you are straight with me. I could wish no more. Promise me nothing! And now." She glanced at the high windows, where the light had undergone a subtle change of which Fraesch and Tula had been unaware, "I do not take back my hospitality, but I do advise you that unless you wish to spend the night, it is time for you to return. Winter returns."

Fraesch got up from the crosslegged position in which he had been sitting and found that his legs were a little stiff. But he went to the door, opened it, and looked outside. Then, after a moment, he stepped through the door and stood, overlooking the sea. After a moment, Tula joined him on the rocks.

The waves were still coming in with the regularity and perfection they had seen earlier, but now everything else was changed. The sky was filmed over with a veil of high cirrus, which diffused and yellowed the light of the sun. The sea was no longer ultramarine dark blue, but a greenish-black, and farther out there were whitecaps. The cloud bank was much closer; Fraesch found himself looking up at an angle to see the soaring tops of the thunderheads.

Collot joined them, and for a time she stood still, not saying anything. Then: "Notice the air is still. Soon the winds from them will come, and the sandbar will be gone; there is no need for haste, yet you must decide and act now."

Fraesch felt the stillness of the air; it was unnatural, after months of wind. Surely the girl was right. He nodded to Collot, took Tula's hand. "We will go. Thank you."

They started back down the rocks. Collot said, "Come when you will: you are always welcome—both of you, if it be so."

They waved in return, and then turned to the rocks, and to the way they picked out back down around the corner of the hill, to the sandbar, which they crossed after removing their

shoes. This time, though, the water was higher, and there was
an undercurrent. After they had scuffed the sand off their feet
as best they could, and put their shoes back on, starting back
up the hill to the station, they looked back, and saw waves
beginning to break over the bar. When they looked up, they
saw that the cloud tops were now almost overhead, and the
light of day was darkening rapidly, although it was, by any
reasonable esfimation, still day for hours yet.

Still, they did not speak along the way back, for there was
much that had happened that had troubled them both—or
better said, unsettled them, and so they did not speak of it.
Then, when they had reentered the building, Fraesch started
for his apartments, but Tula laid a hand on his arm, and said,
"Now. Come with me. I have something to show you, in the
lab. This you did promise, and now I hold you to it."

13

When they entered the lab, Tula waited until Fraesch had entered, and then locked the door behind them. Fraesch asked, "Why did you do that?"

"It is now late in the day, but I want no chances with what I am going to show you. No overhearing, no eavesdropping, no chances. You must keep it to yourself as well."

Fraesch said, a little uneasily, "Have no fears on that score. I am discreet by nature, and furthermore, am paid to be so."

Tula nodded, grimly. "Good. Because what I suspect is here contradicts everything I know to be reasonable and proper about the nature of things, and I do not wish to be thought deranged. I have worked too long for what I have to have to risk that. Come over here." She walked to the central table and indicated the long chart Fraesch had seen spread out earlier. She said, peremptorily, "Do you know what this is?"

Fraesch said, "No."

"I will explain; basically, it is simple. Here we have our intercept collated and displayed. Since we turned the equipment on. The horizontal dimension represents time, the vertical, frequency. Everything was stored on a master set, so we could get this run. This is the record of all the waves which have passed the collection sensors."

Fraesch picked a point on the chart at random and looked at it. What he saw was a tracing of tiny dots, which assembled themselves into patterns . . . he could see there was order, some kind of order, but it made no sense to him, although something in the back of his mind kept flickering on the edge of consciousness, almost like the sensation of déjà vu.

She said, "What do you see?"

"Patterns of dots on heat-sensitive paper, which seem to be organized in irregular groups—sometimes in very irregular areas, sometimes in groups of streaks."

Tula approached the table, searched the chart from side to side for a moment, as if searching for something. She found a grouping which seemed to satisfy her requirements, and this she marked off with a pen, bordering the area to the left and right. "See that? Now I want to show you this." She left the table and retrieved, from a filing cabinet, a large textbook, illustrated with many diagrams. She thumbed through the book, until she found a particular page. This she placed on the work table to the side of the area she had marked off.

Obviously, she wanted him to compare the two; and to Fraesch's untrained eye, the two were almost identical. Almost. There were some differences, but the basic pattern was the same. In both, there was a generally horizontal pattern of parallel lines running from left to right, starting somewhat upward, but leveling off. The lines toward the bottom seemed to droop a little below the horizontal, opening up a small, eye-shaped area which was free of marks entirely. At the top, there was a similar, smaller opening, created by a divergence of the upper lines. At the end, all the lines seemed to tend together in a kind of pinching, above which, higher up, there was a smudge which faded to the right. The main difference Fraesch could see was that on the unrolled chart, there were more of the lines, and they seemed to be better-defined. More crisp, as it were. The areas around the pattern were completely clear of tracings, where in the book, there were light streaks and small spots. He looked at Tula.

"These are, more or less, the same, or so they seem to me. What are they?"

Tula indicated the book. "This is a basic text about phonetics. Those pictures are sound spectrograms of human speech, pronouncing various sounds and combinations. Voiceprint analysis. The lines are harmonies, and their pattern is distinctive; you can identify a sound with this, a person's linguistic group, and in addition, in most cases, you can identify individuals. It is difficult, but not impossible. In the book are words, spoken. On the chart is a pattern created by ocean waves. Yet they seem identical."

Fraesch said, "If anything, the wave-chart recordings seem more clear, and slightly more complex."

"Exactly my thought. In the book, the speaker displays so many harmonic bands; on the chart, there are a third more, approximately within the same frequency band. I see some other differentiations, but they are relatively unimportant.

What you see in the area I marked on the chart is the sound '-ar,' with a soft, untrilled 'r.' "

"Is the whole thing like that?"

"Most of it. There are other patterns on it I don't know, but almost all we have seems to be like that. I haven't gone into it deeply enough yet, only so much as to verify a suspicion I had about what it might look like."

"Then this is speech?"

"Impossible as it may sound, that is exactly what this looks like."

Fraesch sighed. "All the while I had been thinking I'd seen this before, but I couldn't remember where . . . now I do. It was on Moricle's conceptualizer; interspersed among the women's faces, there were pictures that looked like these . . . patterns. Moricle saw the same thing we are seeing here." Fraesch felt shivery as he said this. A premonition? Or perhaps just coincidence. He added, "At least we know Moricle saw this; that was his motivation for calling for you." He almost mentioned the tape, but for the moment, thought better of it. Why, he could not say. Something about this was running also to a pattern, and he did not like the exactitude with which he and Tula were following the track laid down by Nachitose and Moricle. Next would come tapes, he was sure. It seemed the only thing to do. Tula would want to hear the speakers as well as see their patterns of speech. . . .

"Tula, this is absurd. Waves don't talk! There must be some malfunction, some wire crossed somewhere, some interference. . . ."

She shook her head. "I don't think so. The wave-sensor array records physical motions, and then converts that into an electronic signal. The line is shielded, and its laser guideline all the way into the computer—land line." She shrugged. "It's the waves, all right."

"But there's nothing out there!"

"Nothing we've seen, or know we've seen."

"I wouldn't think that this would be a good band for communicating; after all, ocean waves travel slowly, and there's bound to be a lot of interference, a lot of random noise."

"There is some noise in this . . . I have it filtered out in this program that you see. Still, there is less than I expect. Much less. But you have to think rates of time as well. I once read a theory which postulated that every kind of creature perceived subjectively the same amount of time along its life line—that to a fly, the fly lived as long a life as a man's, and that men were terribly slow creatures, ponderous and gross. Birds, too, the same. Perhaps we are dealing with something that lives at a slower rate than us, to whom the waves of the sea are fast. . . ."

"Then they would live longer and be larger."

"Exactly."

"But there's nothing like that on this world."

She corrected him. "Nothing we've *seen*."

Fraesch left that unanswered area, for the time. Speakers they had, he thought; they could figure out where they were later. He sat, looking blankly at the chart for a long time. Then he spoke, and he thought his voice sounded too loud in the quiet of the lab. "Can you break it?"

"Break it? Oh, as in decrypt?"

"Yes. Can you make sense of it?"

"I'm not one-hundred percent certain that it's speech, or better said, language. It may just be natural sounds. I find the whole thing a little . . . improbable."

Fraesch said, carefully, "It's equally improbable that we'd go out into space, and the first extraterres we meet turn out to be primate humanoids—upright posture, two arms, two legs, two sexes, live birth. Klatzanans even look roughly human. But their planet has DNA that uses one amino acid we don't have, and so the two of us turn out to be protein-incompatible—poisonous in various subtle ways to each other. Methane-breathers might have been more interesting."

Tula's face did not change at his mention of Klatzana, but her soft brown chocolate eyes did manage to look slightly more flinty, or opaque. She said, after a moment, "True. As a fact, despite all the claptrap about natural sequences of events, the universe itself is of low probability."

Fraesch said, "Besides being a school game, what that illustrates is not that we understand probability, but rather that we don't."

Tula agreed. "Just so: surprises are everywhere. It is good there is something left to discover."

"You will go ahead with it, then?"

"Yes. I am obligated, of course; second, I am personally curious. Third, if we need it, there is the fact that there is so much of this . . . speech cluttering up the band we work with that the tracking data does not seem to get through it. In a sense I have to find out what is causing this effect before we can proceed further."

Fraesch said, "Then I should not expect replacement soon."

Tula said, quite animatedly, "By no means. As a fact, you have become essential to the success of the project. I see you do little or nothing, you expect few, if any privileges . . ."

"You are one of them."

"Just so; you deserve it, do you not? But whatever you do, the site runs without crisis."

Fraesch said modestly, "Administration should be invisible. Leader-cults have no place in serious affairs—they are counterproductive. The ego prevents accomplishment, and they provoke responses. I get paid to be invisible."

Tula said, "Yours is an exacting and subtle art; few seem to have mastered it."

"That is why they pay us, instead of their own people, in most cases. But to the present instead of the universal—come have supper with me?"

Tula shook her head reluctantly. "No. My mind is full of this. I have too many questions now. Let me at it in my way."

"I'll have something sent up."

"That would be nice, Joachim. You are thoughtful . . . please do that."

"Good night, Tula."

"I'll take care."

He left the lab and went outside, where a furious snow-storm was in progress and the air was full of spinning snow-flakes as big as thumbprints, all being stirred and whirled by high, gusty winds, and lit not only by the lights of the station, but by high-altitude lightning that was almost continuous. Odd as it seemed to Fraesch, and although the snow was piling up in the windshadows of buildings, the air was not especially cold, although now and then he'd get hit by a truly frigid gust. He knew that he was not dressed for this; yet he did not hurry. He felt a kind of elation, an energy, a wakeful alertness.

At the door of his own place, shaking off the fast-melting snow, Fraesch found another note taped to his door—another message had arrived at the communications center, from an R. Pergales. Of course, in cipher. Putting off dinner for a while, Fraesch hurried back outside and went to collect his message; while he was on the way, ordered some supper for Tula.

Fraesch absentmindedly fixed something simple for himself, and retired to the study, to run Pergales' message through many sheets of square-grid graph paper, alternating nibbling at supper, and also half-listening to some of Moricle's music tapes, which seemed to help his concentration. It was a long message, and the night was well advanced when he finally had a complete copy, but it was worth the effort.

"Dear Fraesch: The SMCKSA has run to ground some most interesting things about the issues you asked about earlier, so I thought I'd forward what we know as it gets developed. Coordination has enough questions about this that had we known this at the beginning we probably would not have taken the contract. So, attend.

"1. Speculations: This company uses a curious practice, curious because of the degree to which it is carried. The classic management problem is whether to build it yourself, or have it done outside. They contract everything, including employees. Tracing back through shipping and passenger records, as well as through several cooperative clearing houses, we found that as far as individual projects are concerned, virtually all the workers on the project are contract temporaries. We were able to trace Halcyon: all the support types came from a company called The Body Shop, Ltd. More significantly, they seem to own no property, but lease or rent. Not even through front subsidiaries do they hold title to anything we have yet been able to uncover. Their scale is large and their operating costs great, therefore they have to be making enormous incomes in order to continue to operate. SMCKSA has found the project so interesting that they are donating some time to it, along with a computer and a very good accountant—they think they will uncover enough to sue Speculations over some offense, or negotiate with them over an ethical-practices litigation. This, at the least! They now estimate 'that the Company itself may consist of fewer than a dozen people, all on multiple Longlife and highly protected by anonymity.

"More: Speculations produces certain goods and services, and of course must have suppliers and vendors of the more basic components of these things. They have a practice of letting supply contracts out to relatively small outfits, preferably limited and local in scope, using more or less standard parameters. The catch is, of course, that the small companies are more eager for the business, and through a very smooth and practiced sequence of events, they become 'captured' by Speculations, totally dependent on their orders for continued existence. When they have served their purpose, Speculations buys them out and liquidates them. If you can believe this, a certain class of operations of this type is managed by a—correct—contract factoring service, which was captured by Speculations early in its history. Our source is a junior partner who was bought out. This practice alone is estimated by the source to account for as much as forty percent of total income.

"2. They have a well-known address, which is a post box in Times Square Station, New York. The mail is picked up daily, the rent is paid without fail, the forms are impeccable: but there's nothing there except the post box. The corporation is properly registered everywhere, and its original incorporation is—are you ready?—in Vatican City. Again, a mail address.

"3. To summarize, they are well-known, but when you probe, there is almost nothing there. Small amounts of the stock are traded publicly, but that may be a dodge. Considering the scope of its operations, and the soundness of its finances judged by performance, the personal fortunes available to its few real members must be planetary in scale, and although unknowable, unseen, and invisible, they must possess abilities to influence events on a scale which even conventionally wealthy people could not begin to imagine. We are now quite concerned about this, and at the least will terminate relations with them upon conclusion of your contract.

"4. Moricle, alias Moricand. Confirm that he was not a member of S., although he has had a lifelong association with them. He incorporated himself as Crataegus, SA, and worked for them under contract. He has the easiest trail to follow, and has a history of trying repeatedly to get into S. Considering that it is suspected that the members are probably the original founders, or the majority of them, this would seem difficult, at the least.

"5. Nachitose. I will not explain the details, but SMCKSA has derived information linking Nachitose with Speculations. Inner circle—has to be. Always innocent and obscure titles and position, where listed at all. Most recent history shows no traces whatsoever—the concept is that she was a relatively junior member, and didn't attain the full privacy treatment until (relatively) recently.

"6. According to the report of a contractor, they have the nasty habit of putting a spy in the heart of one's contract operations, and the spy is always one of the most senior members, with full powers to do as they wish. This is not confirmed, but in events where we can see this at all, the sequences of events are undeniable. This has direct bearing on you and us: SMCKSA assigns a probability of your having a plant in Halcyon at 89.6 percent, which we consider virtual certainty. Do not expect the usual industrial espionage types—this one will not have to report to anybody, and probably won't have any outside contacts. Be careful and correct.

"7. Tula Vicinczin. No trace. For all we know, she materialized at Plesetsk out of thin air. The implications, in view of the foregoing, are obvious and need not be reiterated to the person of common sense that I know you to be.

"Conclusion: We are exploring the possiblity of voiding the contract and getting you out of there as soon as practicable. The 'Fun-and-Games' option has not been ruled out. We are not concerned with any moral or ethical issue so much as we are with questions of survival. Economic—ours—and personal—yours. SMCKSA already has one investigator not reporting, a condition they rarely encounter. Yours—RP."

Fraesch read what he had decrypted through once. And then again. And a third time. He put the worksheet down, and stared up into the darkened ceiling, not even bothering to ask who the probable plant might be. He knew, without

asking. He felt lightheaded. Still, he thought, although Tula
had to be the one, he felt certain that her primary problem,
as he saw it, was not him, nor was it manipulating Intercord
into a captive relationship, but was getting to the root of
whatever Moricle had seen. Think of it: Speculations had put
a plant here before—Nachitose—and had hired their most
dependable tough, by all standards an alert and sophisticated
electronic mercenary, to complete his part of an elaborate
scheme. And not only had the whole thing gone to hell in a
pushcart, but their two best people had gotten themselves
killed by persons unknown in the process. So now, they send
Tula. She must be under a terrific strain. Judging from what
Aalet had told him, they must be pressing for results hard.
Yet now Tula had also seen certain patterns and was going
after them, to determine what they were—assuming that she
had told him the truth, more or less, and somehow, he thought
that she had. Certainly not all of it, but as much as she had
said—that was true.

The question was, now that some of his suspicions were
confirmed, what action would he take, as ostensible director.
Fraesch did not console himself with illusions. He didn't
know what Tula was within Speculations, but whatever she
was, he had no doubts that she could counter anything he
might attempt; and what change would he make? He was
convinced that Speculations did not kill Moricle and
Nachitose. He was no Investigator, nor an Enforcer, yet he
could see no reason; doubtless Speculations had much more
sophisticated methods of pressing for results, and punishing
failures. No—that whole idea rang wrongly. No. He was in
no danger from Tula; to her, he was a side issue. Presumably,
as an administrator, he was doing his job well. As her lover
. . . the relationship was casual, after the manners of the
times, and she seemed pleased enough with things as they were.
He caught himself thinking wryly that he would suppose that
he could feel a certain sense of accomplishment there, as
well.

No. Not that; it wasn't true. There was something there—
her reactions had been too genuine. Still, even if genuine,
then what would come of it? Whatever Tula was, he and she
were from vastly different universes, and he could see no reason for them to remain associated, after Halcyon. It would
end, and they'd part, and the words would be sad farewells,
but farewells they would be. And as for himself? Fraesch
would admit with regrets that his reactions were genuine as

well. So what? The results were the same, whether real or
posed fake.

He threw up both hands in frustration, and got up, to
gather the papers and turn the tape player off. But as he left
the room, an idea occurred to him, something to suggest to
Tula the very next day. Something which would conceal
where he got the idea. Who could tell—it might answer some
questions. Yes. That would be the way it should go. He had
never doubted that Tula was at least what she claimed to be,
however much more she was. By stressing that, that admitted
true part, perhaps even more would surface. Yes, Fraesch
went to bed and slept easily.

At these latitudes, Winter was not so cold because Halcyon
was disposed on a seacoast with a western exposure, but it
was seemingly endless, a succession of gray, windy days;
Fraesch wished to escape them as fervently as did the rest of
the inhabitants of Halcyon. He looked for Tula, but she
seemed to be either working or sleeping, and before he could
look further into it, his attention was diverted by the require-
ment to send off the annual reports, if "annual" was the
proper term. They did not fall at the same time in the Mulcahen year, but at shorter intervals, which suggested that the
"annual" was probably the period of revolution on a planet
of a small star, something very close in, perhaps even an artificial world.

So it was that Fraesch became preoccupied for an extended period lasting over a week, and saw little or nothing of
Tula during that time.

The annual reports were an event of the site which occupied everyone, more or less, and at the conclusion of the
process there seemed to be an extended holiday unofficially
practiced, which Fraesch did not disturb, although he planned
to stay close to his place, as rumor had it that most of the
time would be devoted to an expanded version of the party
he had inadvertently walked into while searching for Tula's
suite. Fraesch still recalled the scenes he had seen with aston-
ishment, and refused to imagine what an expanded version
might look like, to the sober. Fraesch dutifully reviewed the
medical logs of the dispensary for the previous similar period,
as well as some duty logs, and to his relief, at the last such
occurrence, no one had turned up missing, and no one had
had to be treated for injuries more serious than psychic ones,
and those recovered quickly. Except that, of course, the in-

cident which had made such a permanent change in the state
of Nachitose and Moricle had occurred just after everything
had returned to normal.

Was there any connection? Fraesch knew something of
myth and symbol—the subject was required in his training
syllabus—and he knew enough about the dark gods of the
past to be fearful of indulging in a drug which released those
atavistic urges. As he had told Collot, he didn't know whether
he faced the light or the darkness, and did not wish to find
out. All he had seen of the action of the Doors had in fact
been nothing more alarming than sex—bizarre and exhibi-
tionistic—but when all was said and done, sex was still sex. It
was that he thought that it represented not itself, but the tip
of something deeper that disturbed him. And there was, of
course, much that went deeper in the still-unpenetrated
shadows of the heart.

Tula was still another problem. She was now working almost constantly in the lab, performing extremely detailed
hand work on segments which she had the computer present
in various forms and serve up to her. When he saw her, she
was totally absorbed in her work and distracted; at the times
when he could expect to see her outside the lab, she simply
wasn't. He estimated she was probably spending two-thirds of
the Mulcahen day-cycle on the problem, and the other third
in rest which could not be doing very much for her except
some form of minimal recharging. He had stopped by her
place several times, and each time had found her not in. At
first, he had then gone by the lab, but she was so deeply en-
grossed in the work that the encounters had had little savor
of anything.

Fraesch at first would have said—had he been asked—that
he was mildly curious about Tula; as things had developed,
he had become more interested. Now, even more so. Except
through the tenuous link he had with Pergales and through
him, and S'su Men Chien Kang Security Agency, he seemed
to have little ability to satisfy his curiosity. There was Tula
herself, but it seemed that she would only confirm as much as
he could unravel by himself, and since she'd seen those patterns, they had had, effectively, no real communication.

It occurred to Fraesch that perhaps he could put this to advantage. Privacy was highly valued, of course, and uninvited
intrusions were not welcomed. But being acting station director did have some powers . . . one was that he could manu-
ally override, with a small printed-circuit card, the locking

system of any door in the complex. The device was kept secured in a safe, and Fraesch had never done anything with it,
except verify that it was there. He could only use it once on
any given door; the second time would cause the door to
dump its settings and lock in the open position. Considering
these items, Fraesch wondered if there could possibly be anything in her suite which would clarify Tula's position.

After making sure that Tula was indeed in the lab and absorbed in her work, Fraesch removed the opener-circuit from
the safe, and made his way unobstrusively to Tula's suite.
Feeling like a burglar, he opened an access panel beside the
door, inserted the card and depressed a red button. There was
no indication anything had happened, but when he touched
the door, it opened. Fraesch removed the card and closed the
panel, and then entered Tula's suite.

Fraesch felt even more like a burglar, a profession for
which he had neither aptitude nor luck. He let the door close,
listening tautly. The apartment was empty and silent. There
was no presence, no living thing there.

The entry room was as he remembered it; the parlor beyond, at the foot of the stair, the same as well. . . . No.
There was a difference: the walls were bare. The photographs
were gone.

Fraesch looked about the parlor, now seeing it only by a
weak daylight which filtered in through a star-shaped skylight. The light was gray, and the burlap and dark woods of
the room did not reflect much of what light came in. But he
could see that the parlor had no storage areas built in. Everything looked solid.

Evidently this was not a room Tula used much, if at all.
That was not unusual, he didn't use his, either. Fraesch left
the parlor, and began exploring the suite. Here, he was somewhat at sea, for he did not know the labyrinthine ways of
Tula's apartment well. He found the kitchen and dining room
easily enough, as well as the entry to the underground pool.
But after that, he was more on his own. These were rooms
she used; he could tell by an undefinable sense of subtle
disorder, a faint scent in the air of the perfume she used.

Tula's own bedroom was plain and simple, and contained
nothing except a small tray of cosmetics, hardly anything,
and her clothes. Fraesch did not ransack the place, but
looked carefully and as quickly as he could. There was nothing here.

The other bedrooms were empty, both of Tula's presence, and of traces of any inhabitants or visitors. If she did any work here at all, she did not perform it in the bedrooms or kitchen. He continued. He found a library study, similar in function to his, but much lighter in tone: the entire west wall, if he had his directions correct, was a mural in stained glass of a bucolic country scene, complete with vines, wheat fields, shepherds and milkmaids, all done in an elaborate art-nouveau style. Fraesch privately thought it a little too much for his tastes, but did admit that it was different and somewhat refreshing, after the almost academic austerity of his own quarters. The walls were lined with shelves, filled with books, tape spools, recording tapes. This all had a well-used look to it, and he imagined that most of it was probably Nachitose's. He picked out a couple of things at random and confirmed his suspicion.

There were drawers and closed cabinets below the shelves, and a large desk in the center of the room. These would bear the most scrutiny. Fraesch first looked in the cabinets. There, in neat stacks, were the pictures from all over the apartment. There were a fair number of them. Fraesch went through them quickly, and soon enough found something of what he thought he was looking for: a photograph of Nachitose and Tula together, this one apparently having been taken in the foyer of some building. It looked like some kind of presentation; Tula was handing something to Nachitose, and grasping her hand. There was another, showing them sitting at their ease at a sidewalk cafe, sipping drinks, and dressed in an odd style: long light-colored dresses of severe cut, the broad-brimmed hats whose brims drooped languidly. In the background were plants which resembled palms. This picture seemed candid, and in addition showed that it had been greatly enlarged from a picture of a much larger area; nevertheless, the two women were Tula and Jenserico. There was another picture—a posed group photograph of eight women and seven men, all looking either very self-conscious or somewhat drunk, he could not be sure which it was. Fifteen people . . . this was Speculations, he felt certain. They were essentially unremarkable people, although all appeared to be somewhat more . . . finished (was that the word?), more fit and more attentive. There was no clue as to who was senior to whom, if indeed such relationships existed. Fraesch carefully put the pictures back. This was not the great leap forward he had hoped to find, but merely the simple confirmation of what he already had almost as a certainty. So, then—Tula and Nachitose were both high-level Speculations people. Confirmed.

Fraesch left the cabinets and began going through the desk. In the side and lower drawers he found nothing of interest, but in the center compartment, he found a small leather folder, limp and soft, small enough to fit easily in a purse, a pouch, a pocket. Inside the folder was a small white card of some unknown material, unmarked on one side. On the reverse side was a simple legend:

> "MASTER AUTHENTICATOR. THIS INSTRUMENT IS KEYED TO THE ENCEPHALOGRAPHIC PATTERNS OF ITS PROPER OWNER. USE BY UNAUTHORIZED PERSONS, ORGANISMS OR MACHINES WILL RESULT IN ACTIVATION OF DESTRUCTION SEQUENCE. THIS IS NOT A CREDIT CARD."

Fraesch read the legend, and finished. As he looked at the card, faint blue letters appeared slowly below the black ones. These said, in the same typeface as the rest, "WARNING. IF YOU HAVE READ THIS FAR, YOU ARE NOT THE OWNER. REPLACE THIS CARD IN ITS CASE AND WITHDRAW ONE HUNDRED METERS IMMEDIATELY. WARNING. CONTINUED UNAUTHORIZED POSSESSION WILL RESULT IN BODILY INJURY."

Fraesch complied, inserting the card back in its case, and replacing it in the desk. For a moment, he debated staying, to look for something else, but upon second thought, decided he really did not wish to serve as a test subject, and so left Tula's suite as fast as he could without disturbing anything. He wasn't sure about the hundred-meter warning, but he thought that somewhere near his place would be far enough. He left, without thinking overmuch about it.

It was after he had reached his own place, gone inside, and secured the door, that he suddenly realized that he was very frightened, and that he had just done something he would not care to repeat.

What was the card? Master Authenticator? Not a credit card? Whatever it was, it was certain to have a computer in it—or perhaps it was itself a computer, fantastically miniaturized, complex enough to scan the brain-wave pattern of a person holding it, recognize that the holder was not the owner, which was presumably Tula, and issue a warning. Reading it had probably activated it, as that was an activity of the conscious mind and would create recognizable encephalic patterns. What could it have done? It looked too small to have contained any dangerous amounts of any substance with which he was familiar, but then again, he did not know what it could do, or what "destruction" referred to, the card itself, or the surroundings, or the holder. Whatever it was, it was technology far beyond anything he had seen, and he would hereby grant that Tula undoubtedly had means by which to protect not only herself, but as well the keys which would allow her access . . . to what? As with everything he had done concerning Tula, the answer raised more questions than it answered. But it had answered one question, at least in part.

Fraesch was not uncomfortable around computers that talked back—they were common enough to be as ignorable as a brand of furniture. It was the size of it, and its reaction, which were the keys to it. Such an instrument represented two things: power and money. Here was proof indeed that Tula was definitely high in the councils of Speculations, although as he thought it, he was certain that he had missed something, but he couldn't quite recall it. Well—no matter. He knew something.

And again, he asked himself—what did he know? Fraesch decided that tonight, or better, now, might be the best time to speak directly with Tula. He was not impressed with the results he had gotten from sneaking and investigating, but dealing directly had at the least gained him working solutions and arrangements.

He went to the lab to find Tula, more or less expecting her to make her usual excuses, but when he asked her to at least take the night off and relax, she agreed, brightening visibly, and after cursorily straightening some papers absentmindedly, suggested that they leave immediately. She suited word to action and began turning equipment off, turning lights out. Fraesch asked, "Aren't you coming back?"

"Absolutely not!" She continued shutting the lab down. "I may not come back for several days. I have been up to my ears in it, and I'm tired of it. Besides, I'm not getting anywhere; the problem is that I don't believe what I'm seeing!"

He said, "I will be sorry to tell you what I arranged to; you will doubtless come running back here as soon as you hear it."

"To here? Not on a bet! I mean it! Speak as you will—I will not work for a day or so . . . or maybe more."

Fraesch extended his hand to Tula, and she took it, turning off the last of the switches, and together they left. At the door, she paused, and locked up. The lab was dark and empty. Tula smiled and said, "Why are we waiting? Come along."

Fraesch had known Tula to be one who was careful of the art of properly setting moods, but this time, by contrast, she had become abandoned and spontaneous; this time, there was no careful dressing, no artful arranging of the lights. He started off toward his suite, and Tula came along. He thought it a bit out of character, knowing how meticulous she was about her appearance, however subtle were the changes she cycled through; for now she came just as he had found her, wearing a loose, baggy sweater and a most nondescript pair of well-worn pants. He thought he could see lines in her face he had not noticed before; the ethereal perfection was gone. Yet he felt at ease with this Tula. Something had changed, and he caught an irrational thought—that he liked this Tula much better.

Their talk along the way was inconsequential and neutral in content: idle chatter, about the weather, which hadn't visibly improved, and about the happenings of the site, that there was to be a marathon party.

Fraesch programmed the kitchen and served up a light dinner, hardly more than a snack, while Tula busied herself around the kitchen, rummaging in the cabinets for just the right ingredients for some special drink she wanted to mix. Fraesch was happy with this state of affairs, but also slightly ill at ease. His earlier resolve, to tell what he knew and get to the bottom of things, seemed shaky now. They obviously fit together well; why upset the arrangement? Or had she anticipated this, and shifted a behavioral pattern, exactly so as to disarm him? He did not doubt that she probably would be able to do so, should she wish.

After supper, Fraesch suggested that they retire to the study, and they went, darkening the lights. When they came to the study, of course the conceptualizer was still on, and it was still shifting through its endless cycle of faces, some hardened by experience, others soft and blurred and innocent, some animated by the coquetry of young children experimenting, others driven by the most astonishing lusts and furious desires, cupidity naked in every line, shadow and plane. Tula stopped by the frame, and as if the machine had read her mind, instead of remembering Moricle's, the conceptualizer faded out of the face it had been displaying, and evolved to yet another presentation of Tula herself. She looked at it curiously, and then at Fraesch, with engaging, pleasant expression. She said, "I know you have seen my face before in that; if not, you should have, for I am there. This much I know."

Fraesch did not answer. Now, her candor had indeed disarmed him.

Tula looked at the face, herself, for a lingering moment, and then turned to go, a graceful maneuver almost like dancing. She stopped and leaned on an overstuffed settee. "Yes. I knew Moricle. I knew Moricle for a long time. And so my face is in there. It means nothing, and something, all in one. Nothing, because there are the faces of absolute strangers in there—people Moricle saw for an instant. And something, because Moricle fancied himself my lover, even though he was not my type, nor could he be made that way." She turned and pinioned Fraesch with a direct, hard look which Fraesch met. "But not the less to him for that. Moricle was ferocious, tenacious, asking no quarter, giving none. He was of an original type. And yet he failed, here, in what he was sent to do, and failed to capture me, which was his major work, in life. And then was killed—a wary, animal man who never took chances, who was always ready, who literally could not be caught by surprise. He was admirable and fearsome, and you now say that with those choices why should I . . . come to you?"

"My thought. Unfair. It was to be my line."

"You have something to tell me now, about myself. If it's true, I already know it. I have seen it coming. So tell me."

"You're in Speculations. . . ."

"Correct."

". . . They sent you here to finish Moricle's undone work, and to keep an eye on me. You're high in the company, higher than Moricle . . . what are you—a kind of troubleshooter?"

"Nobody sent me, Joachim. And Moricle wasn't in the Company. I wouldn't let him in. I decide. The rest work for me."

Fraesch said, slowly, "Then you are. . . ."

"We don't use titles any more; we all know who we are.

We knew long ago, and we only deal through those we know. But through so many dodges, only a computer can follow, I am the owner, or chairman, or president, or chief. Titles don't matter when you own two-thirds of it, or the circulating funds that compose it. Does that clear the air between us?"

"Why do you tell me now?"

"Why do you think I would tell an outsider anything? You know more about me right now than Moricle did, and he spent untold sums trying to uncover who I really was. And he failed at that, too. But I have told you something I have told no one as long as I have been in it."

"Why me?"

"You would like to think, 'Here is the richest woman in the universe, who could have a planet of athletes to serve her slightest whim.' But can you imagine, just for a moment, how boring and empty such a life would be? How destructive? Do you understand that wealth is only a means to get things done, a facilitator, and when you try to take it, it engulfs you? Think of it? I could not ever share it, never admit anything, lest I create a toady. It is the measure of faith I have in . . . what we are, that I dare to tell you this. And because it may not make much difference. No doubt you have heard of the tale of the princess and her suitor, who swore undying love even if the princess was an urchin of the streets; and the princess lost everything, and became an urchin, and her suitor left her. I was no more born a princess than I was born Tula Vicinczin, but like the name, it is an identity I have grown to. And the loss of everything is possible."

"How much was true?"

"Some. I was born on Old Earth, in Russia, but I know little more than what chemanalysis tells me: I am not Slavic by genes or internal chemistry. At any rate, I was a beggar in Syzran beside a vast river. It is a dreary story I will not willingly retell; suffice it to say that one fine day I decided I was tired of hunger and fear, and that there would be no more of it. I have had many adventures, but this was the biggest gamble of all, and I am losing it."

"Your project is not entirely secret. Aalet told me of the essentials of it . . . how far you were stretched out."

"It is much worse that Aalet's sources know. I came here to see if there was anything we could salvage, and your place was exactly as advertised—to run things so that routine would not get in my way. We are liquidating assets to stay afloat at a rate which will devour everything within a year.

And as we were anonymous, so when we fall, we vanish without a trace."

"Then the gamble on the accuracy of the tracking system and Klatzana was true?"

"Yes. That is what we were after. If you heard it from Aalet, then there are no surprises for you there."

"Why did you stay?"

Only now did Tula allow herself to settle into the sofa. She stretched out along its length, looking up at the darkened ceiling. She reflected, "When you involve yourself in risk adventures, timing becomes important, and a kind of abandon . . . at its realities, despite the rationalist trappings we put on it, it's as irrational as anything in the universe: loyalty, honor, love. That is how we went so far: Longlife and the art that we saw it was irrational. We *knew* we could pull it off . . . and we sent our best soldier to polish off the last decimal place for us. After which we would at last let him in."

Fraesch interrupted her, "What was Nachitose's place?"

"She was his monitor. But Moricle was not supposed to be aware that this was the condition. Then there were delays, and some odd behavior, and then we started getting these requests from Moricle. . . . I was already on my way here when the accident happened. We lost time during Moricle's end-game; we knew then the rhythm had been broken, that it would no longer be smooth, even if it worked. Every moment past a certain point we were decapitalizing ourselves. You know that only a very small part of our total operations was involved in the think-tank business; in fact, we used the rest to subsidize it from the beginning. That was how we came to have all these things going. R and D is the best work in the world, but it's expensive, and it doesn't yield return most of the time. We figured out a way to pay for it, and then we discovered that we liked the other paying end even more as a game, and it went from there. During all that time we were careful, so careful, so guarded. After a certain point, there could be no slips, no mistakes, no time off, no romance, if I may use the word loosely. And so I came here and met you. Do not ask me for reasons; I neither know them nor want to find them."

"You could perhaps have gone off somewhere and made yourself an empress."

Tula laughed aloud, the first time Fraesch had heard her laugh. "Yes, that, too. The last shame: politics. When all the rest of our vices are under control, that is the one that masters us. Yes. And with Longlife, I wouldn't have to worry about a successor, but could live forever. Forever!" Again she turned her penetrating stare upon Fraesch, who had come around to sit on the edge of the sofa. "How many extensions have you gone through?"

"One."

"Not pleasant, was it? You say, worth it, once, perhaps twice. But it gets steadily worse, longer and more drastic each time." She sighed, deeply. "You know I've gone through it many times; why confuse the issue. But if I were an empress, I'd lose the thing I value most: my freedom and my privacy."

"What are you going to do here? Just fold it up and let them go home?"

"They are contracted for a period of time. It's already paid for. We'll let it run until that runs out." She was almost casual about it.

"I had more to tell you than what I suspected you were. . . . Moricle made a tape, and I found it. I've also done some digging around in some of his reference works, and you gave me the last clue. There was something I wanted you to do with the stuff you've recorded so far."

Tula sat up, attentive. "Tell me."

"Moricle had a tape of what sounded like voices, speaking an outlandish language. For a long time I couldn't understand the connection. Then I found a place he'd studied a lot. There is an entire section in the bookcase, all new material, about wave-propagated sensory systems, information-exchange systems, such as exist in wild creatures. You are from Earth. Do you know of whales?"

"Yes, yes, whales. What have whales to do with it?"

"Whales have sound communication. Through the water."

"Yes, I know that. They are famous for it."

"If you speed whale sound up fifteen times, it sounds like birdsong. Exactly. And if you slow down birdsong, it sounds like whales."

Tula looked thoughtful. "Go on."

"You showed me that the time-frequency displays of the signals you were receiving through the surface-wave sensor array looked like the formants of speech. I believe that Moricle discovered that, and made recordings of the signal, vastly speeded up. I have that tape."

"You have heard it?"

"Yes."

"What does it sound like?"

"I will play it for you. But it sounds a bit like speech, although I suspect that I'm interpreting it that way. Nevertheless it does sound like language. And if you are what you
claim to be. . . .'"

"Do you know what you are suggesting—no, proving to
me?"

Fraesch chuckled. "Yes, yes. That something on this planet
speaks through surface waves."

"Do you have any idea how slow such a system might be,
what its carrying rate would be?"

"I believe that all creatures live the same amount of sub-
jective time in their natural lives; all these things have to do
is have lives which are slower than the waves, and by all in-
tents they seem to."

Tula said, "To speak, not just cry out, or bray, or hoot, implies a calculating mind at work: intelligence. To them, we
must race about like mad insects, buzzing down the summer
of our days."

"Looking at it is one thing, but I thought you might want
to manipulate the system in the lab to . . . see if you could
get anything meaningful out of it."

"Yes. . . . We could do that. But difficult, difficult. Worst
possible case."

"How so?"

"So there are things, and they speak. Of what do they
speak? If we have an alien folk, we observe carefully, we
make visual and aural recordings, and we watch for referen-
tial objects. Rituals we can recognize. We work inward from
the specific and concrete to the abstract. Recordings of com-
merce are the best, because we can get the number system
out of it. It is a cryptanalytic process. But in this case . . .
totally alien. We can't see them, and we don't know what
they do. . . . There's no bridge."

"I thought you might know of some way into it."

"There's no easy way."

"Perhaps Moricle got into it, somehow. The tape I have
was not made at the end, but early on, judging by the tales
I've heard about others hearing him play it in the suite, loud,
so that even the soundproofing was defeated. He had long
enough to think on it."

"He had Nachitose's help, too; if he got as far as a tape,
then she would have attacked it, making the assumption that
however absurd it might be, it could be treated as speech
. . . and then?"

"And then we don't know. . . . I'm almost afraid to have us go into this, this way."

"You think that the tape has something to do with their accident?"

"I don't know: it's ludicrous. But I do know that no one has found a killer, and Aalet doesn't believe in accidents."

"Neither do I." She stopped a moment and suddenly smiled. "And once more you have made me glad I have acted toward you as I have."

Fraesch smiled shyly. "Why?"

Tula answered, "You guided me to act in the area I know best, and have added considerable spark to the time we have remaining to us; you. . . . Never mind, Joachim. Play the tape, and then you and I, we will plot some. The game is not over!"

"Nor for us, either?"

"Have I spoken of endings?"

"No; and it seems that I have forgotten to."

"It is a slip, but I will forgive you for it. And now we must be partners, allies, work together, we have little time left to solve this. Will you?"

It was plain enough, but Fraesch thought that she had another meaning to the question, something asked shyly. He said, "Yes. Let us get on to it."

14

Fraesch played Moricle's tape for Tula. during the play-through, Tula listened, but made no gestures, indeed, did not show any expression on her face whatsoever. When the tape ended, she only said, "Play it again, please." The second time produced no more reaction from her than the first. Before it was finished, Fraesch had retreated to the kitchen to brew some tea. When he returned, the tape was over, and Tula was slouched back into the sofa, staring blankly at the ceiling.

Fraesch handed her a steaming cup and said, "What do you think of it?"

Tula replied, "The suggestion is very strong, of course, that what is on that tape is, indeed, speech, much as we know it. There are clues, however, that there was a lot of processing done, and that quite a bit has been edited out of it to reinforce that impression. It is by no means as simple and direct as I believe you think it is." Tula held up her graceful hand and counted on her fingers. "First, the truly random noise elements must be suppressed; this, alone, is a great difficulty, especially in such a case as this, in which we do not really know what elements are truly operative. Secondly, how much of the bandwidth do we include? Human speech, for example, as speech alone, generally operates within a bandwidth of, say, 6,000 hertz, oriented to the lower end of the scale . . . but singing expands the range greatly, and—more significantly, speech can still be intelligible even within a compressed band of 3,000 hertz, although some people have difficulty following such communication. Third, there is the time parameter, the constant of transformation which changes the actual data, as it was received, into something that we think sounds like speech. Those are the first of the major questions; there are minor ones to go with them."

She continued, "This tape has value only in that it suggests. . . . It is worthless as far as something to attack, because so much has been suppressed out of it, and the original is lost. We will have to attack what we have at hand, and be very careful about it. It may sound very different from this when I am done with it."

Fraesch said, "It is relatively easy for us—we had our suspicions, and the example you just heard—predecessors, as it were. But how would Moricle have thought to try this?"

Tula shrugged. "Without going into the details, many of which I do not know, I can assure you that Moricle was an expert on cryptography, cryptophonology, and scramble systems. This would not have required great thought, but would have occurred to him immediately. He was famous for seeing and hearing meaningful patterns in collections of data which you or I would regard as mere noise. That, as a fact, was one of the reasons why we held off on letting him join us. He was not a balanced, whole person; his interests approached obsession at times, and it was difficult to extricate him from his assigned jobs when his role was completed. I understand that that behavior is a hazard of the trade."

"What, exactly, was Moricle's job?"

Tula replied matter-of-factly, "Electronic espionage, both political and commercial, intercept and penetration of any and all types of communications systems and networks, insertion of bogus information in same, disruption of infrastructures, creation of breakdowns in systems. . . ." She made a gesture as if pulling something from a pocket, offering an imaginary sheaf of things to Fraesch. She added, candidly, "Mind, he was good at it. I mean, *good.* In part, we gained control of him early to prevent his use against us. He was a dangerous tool, indeed. We had been giving him somewhat broader assignments, so as to move him out of that area—he was well-known for the ability to get a job done."

She continued, "And so the anticipation was that things would proceed with the usual dispatch we were accustomed to from Moricle. Nachitose was, of course, a check on him. That Moricle turned from his assignment was not what brought me, by the way; it was that Nachitose ceased reporting. She was my own candidate, and was reporting directly to me. I expected problems with Moricle, and had ways of dealing with those; but Nachitose's silence was truly alarming."

Fraesch said, "It doesn't take genius to see through that, that Jenserico had the means to control Moricle, and that when you lost contact with her, you had no control over Moricle."

Tula nodded briskly. "Correct. On my way here, I stopped

by Earth and heard that there had been an accident here. I
could hardly go any faster than the way I was already coming. The rest I made up. Moricle had no need of an analytical linguist—he was one, and in addition had Nachitose, who
was an expert on the use of a Mod 3000."

Fraesch said, "But you saw patterns like speech-formants
yourself."

"True, I saw them, but they can be seen, somewhat like
that, in many contexts, if the discrimination of the process is
finely tuned enough. Those patterns are just something you
have to work through, dig below, so to speak. When we did
the basic research work on this kind of analysis, we found
similar patterns in every case; we ignored the data, because
we were looking for something below that level. . . ."

"You mean that you see those harmonic patterns wherever
you do this kind of thing with ocean waves?"

"Yes. Perhaps we should have investigated those. . . .
Well, it's always the things you decide to overlook that sneak
up on you and bite down hard. You and I, we will attack
this."

"I know nothing about it."

"I will show you. There is much you can do, and I also
wish to have the benefit of your perceptions; there has occurred something here which I do not feel right about."

Fraesch chuckled, and said, "Aye, that, Tula. Much,
indeed. I can only hope that I am not the one who gets assigned to reorient these people back to whatever place they
came from."

Tula glanced sharply at him. There was good-natured ban-
ter in her tone, but beneath it there was also firmness. "They
used to say, 'never laugh at a woman's intuition.' I might add,
especially not at the intuition of one who has been through as
many Longlife treatments as I have. Something here is very
false, very wrong, deliberately so; I sense it. I *know* it. But I
do not know where this sensation is coming from."

"Danger?"

"No . . . not so much danger. Odd, that, but it doesn't feel
that way. Just something not right." She stood up, stretching.
"But whatever it is. . . ." She let the remark trail off. An arch
look passed across her face. "Feel like a dip?"

"Pleasure before work?"

"What else do we work for but an occasional respite from
striving?"

"All else aside, you are candid. I accept. Shall we slink, or stride proudly?"

"We shall go plainly, perhaps holding hands, as if it were the most normal thing in the world, which of course it is."

"You do not worry that I might be intimidated?"

"How could you be? Shortly, we will be the same."

Fraesch shook his head, smiling. "Whatever you have lost as a result of this gamble, whatever changes your income has gone through, there is nothing ordinary about you."

Tula took Fraesch's hand. "On worlds where a game called poker is played, there is a saying: 'To the good player, there are no bad cards.' . . . I have no regrets, and I do not look back. I will play again; it is the game that is all . . . and some permanent things which we who play extract from it from rare time to rare time."

"Perhaps we can take the long view, now."

"As it is; follow the wave. Come." And they left, without preparation, or ceremony, for none seemed called for. Leaving the study, they had to pass by the conceptualizer, and Tula stopped to look at it before they left. Fraesch looked too. It was still, of course, presenting its endless array of faces within the silvery substance held within the frame, but now it seemed as if the changes were coming faster; an image would form, or start to form, and then it would abruptly shift to another, or perhaps a formless, shifting inchoate nothingness which Fraesch could not identify. It was almost as if something were interfering with the sequencer, interrupting it.

Fraesch asked, "A malfunction?"

Tula looked thoughtfully at the frame. "Shouldn't be. They are designed to be nearly error-free, free of maintenance difficulties. This particular model is a very advanced one; the circuits are sealed. It's possible, I suppose—nothing is perfect. This just started?"

"I think so. I hadn't noticed it before tonight." They looked again. The images were again forming in their usual fashion, one after another, in measured, relaxed progression. Tula said, "Perhaps a transient fault." She turned away from it, and they left Fraesch's suite.

The night was advanced as they walked together up the corridor toward Tula's suite, and they expected to see no one at this late hour; the parties should already be well underway, and all who were prepared to attend and behave more or less bizarrely should have been in place, posturing and projecting whatever internal demons had elected to issue forth this night. There were no sounds of people in the corridors: but then, there never were. Fraesch often reflected on this, the oddity of the habitat of Halcyon: a self-contained urban totality set down in the midst of essentially untamed country. Moreover, it was a *perfected* urbanism of soundproofed suites, silent, labyrinthine walkways in which there was little disturbance or the noise of people. He supposed that the parties which most of the inhabitants periodically attended served as some sort of counterweight, psychically, to the extreme sense of selfness which such an environment seemed to enhance. For people who were self-motivated, with plenty to occupy them, it seemed to have little effect; Tula didn't seem to notice it at all. As for himself, he had noted an occasional passing restlessness, but that was nothing.

It therefore surprised him when he heard, faintly, the sounds of voices behind them, somewhere in the interconnecting corridors. Voices, speaking quietly among themselves, indistinguishable and incomprehensible. A sense of urgency? He looked around, but in the dim lighting and curving distances, could see nothing.

Tula said, "What's wrong?"

"Nothing. I heard people, behind us. I've never heard anyone in the corridors before, that's all."

"Nothing now." Tula had stopped, listening. "Nobody's there."

Fraesch listened, now standing still. There was nothing, except a slight sound of wind from the outside, muffled and distorted by vents and ducts. "No, I did hear some people, but not now."

"Perhaps they turned off, or you heard the ventilators. They make a random kind of noise, which we who study such things call $1/f$ noise[1] . . . it has a powerful effect on the mind, sometimes, suggesting many things. You might have heard that and . . . Joachim, you look a little wild! Are you reverting to a primitive before my very eyes?"

---

[1] $1/f$ noise: systemic variations between the extremes of totally disorganized random (white noise), and brownian variation, which is recursive in function, that is, what is has been determined by what has gone before. Most variations in nature are $1/f$, and certain forms of music and speech approach it closely. For a more technical and factual presentation of this phenomenon, please refer to *Fractals: Form, Chance and Dimension*, Benoit Mandelbrot, Freeman and Co., 1977.

Fraesch listened again, and then turned to Tula. "And if I were? Would you then cry out, 'Oh, crush me, I'm a grape'?"

Tula's face flickered with several responses, ranging the full span from open humor to surprise and even indignation. She breathed deeply, and answered, "It is uncharacteristic of you to be so attentive to a mere background."

"I once worked on a planet on which the cities were so wild with street gangs that the offices and plants were armed fortresses and strongpoints, and one traveled with a body-guard, and one's apartments were cells of steel with airlock doors. I grew accustomed to it, and have never felt ill at ease in any place since. I have never thought of danger, here, of any kind. We were immune to everything. But there was something in what I heard which I distinctly do not like. Let us go, now."

They continued along the corridor, now listening carefully; they heard nothing except the faint rushing sounds of the ventilators. After several moments of this, they relaxed a little, and resumed their normal pace.

Disembodied voices floated through the emptiness of the corridors, at the threshold of audibility. They seemed to start up from somewhere behind them, but this time, Fraesch was not sure; they had a mutable quality, a mobile aspect that made them seem to come from the side, from behind. At first just snatches and spatters, fragments, they began to assemble into an eerie mosaic of whispers, incomplete chants, sudden hurried, stifled exclamations, purposeless, tuneless singing or moaning. Fraesch looked sharply at Tula, and saw her now listening intently, trying to suppress the sympathetic motions of her eyes, but nonetheless looking about wildly.

Fraesch stopped. "You hear it now?"

She whispered shakily, "Yes."

"What is this?"

"I don't know. I have never heard anything like it. And I do not like it at all."

Fraesch whispered, "In front of us, too."

"Suggestive. . . ."

During their whispered conversation the sounds had seemed to come from all around them, ahead as well as behind, still low in tone, dynamically almost nonexistent. Fraesch was still unable to identify the source of the sounds, although certain qualities they had seemed to bring to mind some of the sounds which had been in the taped section Moricle had made. The connection was weak, though.

And then the sounds stopped.

Fraesch and Tula stood in a five-way junction, looking now this way, now that. Motion caught their sensitized attentions: a light was bobbing in one of the corridors, coming toward them, a light surrounded by a moving darkness. . . . The apparition materialized into a silent figure, clothed from head to toe in a long robe with a heavy cowl, like a medieval monk's, walking with a curious gait that was measured carefully, but also paused at each step, an unsettling hiatus. Stride, hesitate. The figure was carrying a candle whose light was almost completely blotted out by the black garments of its bearer.

They watched the approaching figure, trying to see who it might be; Tula stood close by Fraesch. Fraesch, watching, felt as if he were in the midst of a multitude, a queasy feeling. When he thought to look around him, he saw that similarly clothed figures were all around them, standing silently, their hands folded within voluminous sleeves.

Their faces were deeply shadowed under the heavy, over-hanging cowls, and neither identity nor expression was revealed. All he could see were the reflections in their eyes of the light of the single candle. The people carried no weapons, made no remarks or gestures—they might well have been statues which had been wheeled in for some stage set dramatizing a ghost story; yet this was the stuff of primal fear, the essence of nightmare. Here, undoubtedly, were the voices they heard.

Fraesch spoke with an artificial firmness in his tone he did not truly feel. "What do you want?"

The one holding the candle spoke in a low, throbbing tone, a husky half-whisper, half-sung incantatory style which made identification impossible. "This is the occasion of the great gathering; all come, and release themselves to revel. We all know one another, but we do not know you, and you. You Fraesch-man and Vicinczin-woman have not joined with us; we wish to invite you, that we all may be of one mind. Come and know the incomparable joy of release, that which may not be spoken of."

Fraesch had seen part of one of their gatherings; he knew by the words that this was, despite its odd delivery, apparently an invitation to an orgy . . . or perhaps something more. He waited, uncertain.

A voice from the rear said, ritually, "The Moricle brought

us the gift from the mother ocean, but he would not be of us."

Another voice said, "And Nachitose brooded, secret and alone, within her castle at the top of the house of the people, and betimes their daysouls would enter, and emerge enlightened, but their revelation was of the things of the light."

Still another, "But we have unchained the eternal darkness."

Another, "From the gulfs of night to the deeps of space."

Another, "You have done much, but it is daystuff, and your current does not flow in the corpora; come with us."

Fraesch now felt an acute fear. What was it? "Moricle would not be of us." Had these inhabitants, concerted somehow by the action of a drug of unknown effects, killed Moricle and Nachitose? His skin prickled. Now there was real danger. There was a living unity here—an irrational mob. They had followed them to this place, to speak of these things.

He said, "I respect and honor the things you do; may I only ask that you grant me the same privilege. Harsh words I have had with none of you."

The light bearer, so Fraesch identified him/her, thinking of the ancient name *Lucifer*, the light bearer, intoned, "That is why we come now to this place. Honor! And to do is to be."

The congregation responded, "To be is to do."

Fraesch said, "Allow us to pass our way, and perhaps in time we will come to your way."

The light bearer said to Tula, "Not to be, is this your will as well?"

Tula said, a little shakily, "We have worked to have the pleasure of each other's warmth."

The bearer then said, "Then let be what will be, o my brothers!" And without sound or apparent effort, Fraesch felt himself grasped firmly, by hands that seemed to possess immense strength beyond human norms; they held them lightly, without straining, but he could not break the hold. He saw Tula similarly held. She moved a little, but subsided, coming to the same realization as Fraesch had. He smelled a hot pungency in someone's breath, a scent he had smelled before ... Tschimedie, the night he had seen her as Lot's Daughter.

The bearer then said, "Bring forth the other exile."

From a side corridor, two more came, escorting a third, dressed in a soft, loose robe, whom Fraesch recognized as Ciare Dekadice, the technician who had been overly sensitive.

She had a look in her eyes like that of a trapped animal, a rabbit captured, yet unhurt, in the embrace of a leopard, a lizard in the maw of the serpent.

The bearer now intoned, "We wish you to be with us in our release, and that this is kindness and fellowship that we bring, not pain or terror. But there is something we must do and we ask that you not be difficult; these restraints will soon be unnecessary, in any event."

Despite the reassuring words, Fraesch knew what was shortly forthcoming: the Doors. He tried not to give his intent away, but he jerked free of his holders, and shouted, "Tula! Ciare! Run!"

At this moment, then, action. The uncertainties dissolved and fell away and there was a ringing in his ears, as of the aftersound of the crash of mighty cymbals: the silence after. Everyone seemed to be moving in slow motion, but he did note that they were all moving, reaching. Tula slumped, as if relaxing, going passive, and made a shivering motion, and was also free, moving with a curious set of movements that seemed half-swimming, half-dance. Whatever discipline she was using, she seemed untouchable, uncatchable. Hands reached, grasped, touched, she shrugged or flowed, and the hands were elsewhere, clutching at empty air. Ciare remained where she was, mouth slightly open, as if in a trance.

Fraesch did not attempt to attack any of them, but only tried to break free of the group, which he thought was about twenty or so. Tula seemed to occupy their attention most; she was so close, and yet so untouchable. Within the flowing movements of her dance, he saw her lightly touch someone, caressingly, along the side of the neck, and that cowled would-be captor fell to the corridor floor as if he or she had been poleaxed. Another clasped her from behind, and she made a casual motion with one arm, as a swimmer lazily making a backstroke, and that person fell away from behind Tula, now tightly grasping its stomach and retching, spinning away into one of the side corridors.

He also saw, as he made his own efforts, that Tula was making no real attempt to get away, but was trying to work her way to the group holding Dekadice. They sensed this, and drew closer together, and moved fractionally away from Tula.

Fraesch's efforts were in finding the openings, and following them, turning those who came at him into each other; he was almost out of it, now, as the robes swirled around them.

He called out, "Tula! Leave her! Get yourself out!" He felt himself jarred by the impact of a body, a kind of body-block which deflected his course, and, he saw, made his escape somewhat less probable. He whirled and ducked, trying to re-capture his former momentum, but someone bumped him again, a heavy, solid, mass that deflected him further into the seemingly uncoordinated motions of the group. The bumps came more frequently, now, and he thought he was losing some advantage. There was a series of collisions, none partic-ularly painful, but he was hemmed in, and the group linked arms with each other and bore him down with their lurching mass alone, a confused tangle of torsos and limbs. Fraesch was spun impossibly and ended up on the floor, on his back, and someone straddled his chest, expertly pried his mouth open before he realized what was happening, and thrust something hard and smooth and slick deep into his throat; he swallowed, reflex, and stopped fighting his captors. Through a narrow opening in the mass of bodies around him, he caught a last glimpse of Tula; someone had caught hold of her pants. She moved in a manner Fraesch did not entirely com-prehend, and tumbled out of the pants. She was free, and he saw her slender legs flashing in the soft, flat light of the cor-ridor as she sprinted away.

Fraesch had two thoughts simultaneously. The first was that he was very sorry that Tula had not tried to get him free; the second was that he would not wish to be one of the revelers when she came back, as she most certainly would. And could. She probably knew her way around this maze better than anyone else, and it was virtual certainty that she had either designed the place herself or had been aware of the plans during construction. This thought cheered him somewhat, even though he felt apprehensive at what was even now rushing through his digestive system, into the blood-stream, to the brain.

His captors seemed to realize that this struggle was over. This quarry was no longer resisting, and they relaxed their holds upon him a little. What matter that he escape them again? They had done their work. The person who had straddled him leaned closer, over him, so that Fraesch could see the brown-gold ringlets fall out of the cowl that over-shadowed her face, tightly curled: Tschimedie.

She leaned closer, and said softly, "The roughness we re-gret, used on you; great regrets. But required, that you be-come us. Relax and let it happen to you. Perhaps now in the flux which will ensue you and I will perform some amazing rite."

Fraesch tried to say something, but somehow his voice wouldn't work properly. He made the effort, but some connection was broken, somewhere. The mode of speech would not operate. Tschimedie nodded, as if she understood. She said, a husky whisper, "Don't try to talk, just now; that is one of the transient first effects. Yes, it's already working—it's very quick, so you can't get rid of it by throwing it up, either."

By supreme effort (he was astounded how much effort it took), he managed to mumble out, "Let me up. I know it's too late to run."

Tschimedie smiled, looked up, throwing her head back with a motion which tensed her lower body against Fraesch's. She laughed, a low chuckle, throaty and ripe, and said, "I could, just so, but perhaps I would prefer to remain where I am." She made a suggestive motion with her hips. "How much would you struggle then?"

Fraesch rolled his eyes, again deserted by speech. But it crossed his mind that in more normal circumstances it would not be totally unpleasurable to have a tussle with this strong-featured, sturdy woman. Of course, there would be no ancillary emotion attached to such an adventure. . . . It was something else that was missing. Odd, that. He would have known it in a minute, but it seemed to slip away from him effortlessly, like wisps of fog.

Tschimedie looked over her shoulder, then back. "Little Ciare, she of the boyish figure, has also been given something good for her, and will soon come around. And you? What is it you will become? A high priest of some temple of darkness? A barbarian, who will take his women by force and crush them panting in violent embrace? A silken courtier of some ancient court, clad in silks, mind burning with realizations of desire unknown to the common ruck? A romantic poet? A revolutionary? It does not always emerge as we might imagine, or hope, but something comes forth, full of the vigor of the uttermost psyche. . . ."

Fraesch forced out, "Did the group kill Moricle? Nachitose? Because they would not participate?"

"Life? Death? These are somewhat imprecise terms, which suspend upon much else to give them their own truth. To kill someone, now there's a thought; but a limited one, no doubt, for there's no more of them then. No, and no, those are the

answers. Besides, I have always wished to think of them as
. . . somewhere else. Gone visiting, as it were. But they were
not unattractive, however they had their secrets from us.
Hah! We had some, too! But Moricle—he had the air of a
wild bull of the empty places about him, dark and stormy
and full of the dark power which all might know, the men by
contesting and the women by . . . what's the word? Sex and
combat, they're the same, down at the root of it that we
plumb. But all we are trying to do is tear a rent in a curtain
that separates us all. Here, we can arrange that it be withdrawn for a little. And Jenserico! There is much about that
one which the pale woman you took up with shares. I see
now that Nachitose was a younger version of Tula, a less
perfected form, something like, there."

One by one, now, they were releasing their holds on him
and drawing away silently, although in a way he did not entirely understand; Fraesch could sense that they were relaxed
and pleased with their work. Tschimedie remained where she
was, but Fraesch did not try to shake her off. He felt odd and
disconnected, as if his physical body had somehow become
larger, a roomier house, as it were, and it didn't matter any
more what happened to that house. But at the same time he
felt that, he also felt an enlargement of spirit, of soul, of
psyche. Something was changing.

Tschimedie leaned over, lifting her weight from his torso,
and asked, "You are feeling it now?"

Fraesch shook his head, as if trying to clear his vision. He
nodded weakly, then said, "Yes . . . large and small, all at
once."

She got to her feet and extended her hand to help him up.
"Come on, then. Now you'll need some time . . . you have
to feel your way into it. There are also some time effects to
it."

Fraesch stood, a little unsteady. He saw that two of the figures were still standing with Dekadice, although they were
not holding or restraining her in any way. He said, "Tell me
something; why do you wear the costumes, or the decorations?"

Tschimedie tossed her head, letting the hood fall away
from her hair, so that her face was completely exposed. She
blinked, a long, slow delayed motion, and Fraesch saw that
she had painted eyes, exactly like her own, on her eyelids, so
that blinking seemed to have no effect—something flickered
over the eyes, all of which stared glassily. Fraesch looked, but

he could not determine which were real, although he knew
very well that her real eyes would move and track objects,
and the painted ones wouldn't. . . . It didn't seem to make
any difference. When she looked at him, it seemed as if she
could see him either way.

She said, "For the reflection you get back from others . . .
you can pretend any time you wish, but no one will believe
you; but now they believe . . . choose carefully the picture,
for you will become it, it will become you. With this, we now
understand all that we send to one another, where without we
receive, but we do not understand. I am not so good with the
words."

He was consicous of many things now, but each one stayed
in its proper place, neither confounding nor swamping any
other. He heard the sounds of wind in the ventilators, the rain
on the roof, the overall flowness of the living ocean of air; he
felt the waves as they came up on the beach, or engaged the
rocks of the point, or spattered over the shingled shallows,
there, in the darkness, a hundred meters or so distant. He
knew Tschimedie, and her projection was becoming less absurd and self-gratifying with every moment of time, and more
right and more truly her. He understood that where before he
had seen as an outsider a preposterous sexual masquerade, he
was now seeing that the masque was like a door itself into a
wider world, and that without moving he had already passed
through it. He was different, yet the same; and on the other
side. And they, the others, too were receding, drawing away
from the girl Ciare Dekadice, who was terrified. Fraesch felt
a great compassion for her, a great sadness because she feared
this experience, which made any view she could take a bad
one. She stood where they had left her, and he wanted to go
to her and help, but he knew that the motions he would make
to communicate with her would be filtered, abstracted,
changed. Yes. That was why they dressed up—to project
through it, like a positive image made through the projection
of the tonereversed negative. He thought one thing: it was
executed differently—and somehow, the same.

Fraesch went to the girl, touched her arm. He said, "There
is no need to fear it. I will get them to help. Why do you
fear?"

Ciare responded in a monotone, very low in dynamics, but
not a whisper, "These things we become, in this . . . they
should be hard to reach, diffuse, symbolized in gestures and
words and things we might buy with much money, and only

then glimpse them. Here, now, we become just by wishing, and we do not want to return to the shells of illusion, pulled this way and that by the compromises that the world makes on us. I see and understand, now: in the old days this was controlled by the visions of the tribe, and by the shaman who minded those visions, that the higher world match the lower. You have not been here before—I have: I can see many things in this state I *know*, but can see no way to fit them to the world we must perforce inhabit. So then, was it of old—perhaps savages saw things like our present, but only pieces of it, and so it was of no use to them, and so it is of no use to us, save to devil us with ideas we cannot attain! The whole is so damned slow! But our thoughts move faster than light. And we have only one common dream, and so it is through these bodies that we must act . . ."

Fraesch said, "Each sees according to what they are, what their interests and passions are." He stopped, head cocked, as if listening to something just beyond identification. "Does one hear music?"

Ciare focused on his face for the first time. "Yes, but I've never had the opportunity to pursue it . . ."

Fraesch said, "I thought I heard . . ." He looked around, and the nexus of the five corridors had a familiar air of duality: near and very small, far and enormous. He had no idea of scale whatsoever, and even though his selfness seemed to match whatever view he arbitrarily chose, the idea of mutable scale still terrified him. They were alone, and they were not alone; they were within reach of the others, even though none were in sight.

Fraesch looked at Ciare again. He saw the same, plain girl he had seen before, once when he arrived, and in a short conversation in her suite. Her face was not attractive, as a female face, in the sense of Tula's smooth delicacy, or in Tschimedie's harsh, earthy strength; it was a face which could belong to girl or boy without effort; thin, tense, a little angular and troubled by hidden knots of muscles gathered below the skin. An urchin's face. And a thin, flatchested body to go with it. She moved, uncertainly, and Fraesch felt, in a manner analogous to the scale shift he was experiencing, a change in the way he perceived Ciare—she became, instantly, an object of intense desire. The shift, once made, was unbalanced, and accelerated itself. His whole field shifted, to accommodate this view.

He said, shakily, "How do you know what you will be? How do you . . . find what to put on?"

"I already know mine . . . you will have to look a little for yours, and then find something suitable to express it. I can help. Indeed I must, for that is my unchangeable nature: to help, to guide. Come." She set out before Fraesch with a resolute motion which caused the random and unarranged curls of her colorless hair to shake. Fraesch followed. He did not see, but he was certain that others followed them, too, just out of sight.

They traversed the corridors to Ciare's suite, entered and climbed the stairs to her aerie, her spaceship, her watchful environment. It was night, and the windows were dark, now being pelted with cold, fat raindrops, assaulted by gusts of wind or flecked with momentary bursts of wet, sticky snow which would cling for a moment and then slide down. She commanded Fraesch to wait, and then hurried down the other stairwell, off to another part of the suite. Her sounds on the stairs faded, and the suite was silent, save for the wind fretting at the windows, and a distant, barely audible hum from the equipment with which she had filled the room. Fraesch selected a seat, and sank into it, gratefully.

He wanted to set his thoughts straight, but they whirled around madly, uncatchable; even as he saw that he had them at all, in any configuration, they vanished. There was nothing stable, nothing fixed. There was only motion, flux, change. Something was coming of the pattern of chaos, but he could not understand or act on it yet. Only that something was there.

Where he sat faced the vision screens Ciare had set up, and the one he was most directly facing was the one which showed the high view of the sea. Now it was dark outside, but something interpolated in the circuits continued to make visible the waves as they traversed their medium; if any change was apparent, it was perhaps that the image was clearer, more distinct, sharper. Fraesch found himself watching the image, fascinated. It helped focus his mind, clarify his perceptions. He could almost sense meaning in those tossing, restless motions, never still, patterns for which he was still too fast, try as he would to slow down for them. What made the waves? Wind, the flow and flux of two fluids, air and water, and the interface between them. Winds . . . and there was nothing there, yet Ciare had thought something

was, and had planted sensors to watch for it . . . Fraesch
had an idea that, absurd as it was, something was indeed out
there, something so alien they could never understand it, and
that they would never see it or them as such, until it was
much too late to do anything about it. It was not malevolent,
and it did not wish to rule the universe, but it did not care
very much, either, for if those who spoke on the waves were
slow, then what were men to them but the flitting of mayflies,
summer gnats, alive for the day perhaps, and with the night
they'd go . . . wherever those temporary little striving lives
went. Was that it? He looked at the waves some more.

Fraesch tried to reason it out, for he felt as if he were on
the very edge of it, but it failed him and his thoughts spiraled
into nothingness. Waves. He had heard them, speeded up
greatly, filtered, their frequencies and wavelengths translated
into sound patterns, and what he heard sounded like speech,
and now he was seeing the waves, as they rolled and tossed
their foaming heads to the black, howling sky. What was it
that made waves in the sea? What was it shaped them, refract-
ed them, enhanced some frequencies and suppressed others?
Was this just not another media problem? And of what would
such sonorous, long voices speak? Of firefly lives? He was trying, but now all he could do was question, for that part of
him was sinking, and another was rising from some black
depth, something he had to do, something he had to be.

A host of personages, personae, roles, ritual identities, symbols began to be real to him, things he had known from
books, from histories, from entertainments, stories, fictions,
speculations, investigations, evolutions, revolutions; they were
all together, a multicellular crowd, an organism, and they
would shimmer into one, whose aspect was strange and won-
drous, desirable to *be*, he could be that, he was that. He
remembered (that was not really what was happening to him,
but it seemed that way, and so it was so) kings and em-
porers, conquerors and concubines: shadows that flickered
for an instant and were gone. Now he saw truth. He saw behind the apparent reality of the great—that few indeed *had*
been great in truth, but were animated dummies propped up
by those who reaped their rewards offstage, but bore none of
the crushing weight. Tales as old as man itself, perhaps older,
something rooted in the chaos that was the mother of
creation. He was Bagoas the eunuch in ancient Achaemenid
Persia, poisoning emperor after emperor until at last caught
at his deeds by Darius III, and terminated after the same

manner. He was Iago, whispering to the Moor. He was
Lavrenty Beria, and a host more on the side of Ahriman the
Dark God. Equally detailed, he was also a host of offstage
manipulators who pursued light after the manner of
Ahuramazda. He was Machiavelli, Disraeli, Henry Kissinger,
Metternich. He was the unseen power behind the visible powers, the one who really had what control there was to have.
He was invisible, and his subtle acts changed lives without
their knowing. He was also a thousand more, who had never
been seen; now he could see them through the shadows of
those who had carried the banners, and whom no record had
ever known, good and evil alike. He saw it with everything
that had been, everything he had done. He had been choosing
them all his life, and they had been waiting for him. It was a
relief to admit it, and to feel their collective identity settle on
his shoulders, fade into him, become him, and he, them. Now
he knew what he had to do: to orchestrate this unruly, random, searching, disorganized crowd into something beyond
themselves, something greater than they could imagine, could
know, even after they had done it . . . and even then, they
would not realize it was he who led them to it, but would
imagine they thought of it themselves. Yes. Let it be so.

Fraesch stood up suddenly. There was no time to lose,
now. Ciare. . . . Where was Ciare the Technician? She
would have to provide some things for him, for he would
have to dress the part—yes, those seemed to be the rules.
And even though it would be obvious, it would be hidden. He
liked that: double deception. He went to the stairs, down
which the girl had gone, and looked down: a spiral went
down out of sight: there was darkness at the root of the spiral, broken only by the hint of a watchlight somewhere down
there. He knew he did not know the way, but it did not matter. He stepped forward and followed the spiral down. Down.
It was a long way, and when he reached the bottom at last, he
found himself in a tiny, cramped foyer. Constricted tunnels
led off to left and right, both equally dark in themselves, both
illuminated somewhere distant, indirectly, as from the side.
While he hesitated, he sensed motion in one, motion which
suggested a sinuous, slender figure coming toward him, walking with measured pace, steadily. . . . It resolved itself into
a person he knew, and yet did not know.

Ciare appeared and stood, a little abstracted, by the tunnel
mouth. The curious ambosexual air she had once had now
was gone entirely, along with the hoydenish clothing she ha-

bitually wore—mechanic's coveralls. Now she wore a pale translucent clinging gown made of something delicate and woven, so that it both clung to her and flowed around her, accenting, suggesting, enhancing, concealing. Through it, the shadows played, contours and outlines shifted, appearing and vanishing with every motion. The body beneath the gown was as slim and boyish as it ever had been, but now the accent was different, and with it the message. Completing the costume was a conical cap with a shirt behind and a veil before, so that only the eyes showed clearly. She had become a princess of the house of unendurable pleasure indefinitely prolonged, something unattainable and unspeakable at the same time: forbidden fruit, and all the sweeter for it, the more so: poisonous and pernicious. Time was shifting, mutating, and she did something, and something slipped entirely, was lost.

Time, skipping and looping, returned to show an image in the confines of a mirror, which resembled no person Fraesch could be said to know, to have known, to wish to know, to know enough to know. No, no, no. Unlike many of the party-goers, this one was dressed from head to toe; a soft cap, something like an overgrown beret. A shirt-jacket, something like a bush jacket, and also something like a collarless military tunic, in which the front opening was not a simple slit, to be closed by joining edges, but a flap which buttoned across the throat and down both sides of the chest. It ended in a little decorative ruffle which reminded Fraesch of a character in an opera about Renaissance princes. The bottom was a set of tights, and there was a leather codpiece which looked peculiar, no doubt, but which felt even more peculiar. Dark, dark, but not black. Black would call attention; this was shadows, unnoticing, not-seeing. Elegant, but fog, nothing, an afterimage. Ciare bowed formally to the figure, in the mirror, said softly, "My lord, you have remained in the shadows overlong; will you attend?"

"I will come there, but what I must do, I could do from here."

"You could, aye, but you must not."

"Perhaps you are right; so I will attend."

"Follow me by the ways I know; let a princess guide the hunter to the fields of night. I will be the staked goat, though I carry my chain with me, and therefrom you must prey upon us."

"It will be as you say; do you claim precedence?"

"Nay! Strike as you will! My eyes are not green, and I wear no horns."

"Take you no offense, then, that in what I orchestrate it may not come to pass between me and thee."

She said, "It will not matter; now we live forever, and in time all must know all, even unto the last man and the last woman. Now!"

And she then guided Fraesch into a corridor and through a set of passages whose existence he had not suspected, eventually into a passage which looked like one of the public passages of the building, and then to a large room, decorated solely with cushions and sideboards, in which others were gathering. As they entered, no one noticed them, and yet he sensed that unconsciously the group aligned itself to them. Something changed, shifted, lines of forces altered themselves.

He saw no one he could assign to a person of the workaday world whose identity he knew. Here were jongleurs, mountebanks, dwarves and thieves; courtesans, muscle dancers, their flesh crawling and rippling, mimes and acrobats, hoodwinked sybils. Slaves and overseers, carrying whips and electric prods, enigmatic, heraldic figures of an unknown patent of nobility, bizarre sexual athletes. It looked as if someone had taken the Waite/Pamela Smith Tarot as a starting point, and then extrapolated a maniacal Hugoesque-Tolstoyan multiplanetary universe out of that seed material, transforming and multiplying and variating the mix according to a canon which might be laid to Aleister Crowley. A harlot with eyes tattooed on her eyelids approached and glared.

Fraesch exclaimed, "Lot's Daughter!"

The woman answered, "No! Kethuzalem, the harlot of Jerusalem!"

"Workman, ply thy trade!"

"I hear!" She cried, and turned away, favoring Fraesch with a lewd leer as she turned, moving her hips in an exaggerated manner.

Fraesch breathed deeply and sighed, "Buns!"

He turned his head, to make a remark to Ciare, but the princess was gone. Nearby, a satyr embraced a chaste ballet dancer dressed in a pale tutu, while a troupe of mimes created changing reflections of their gestures in a kaleidoscopic panorama within which all possibilities were examined

dispassionately. He gestured suavely to them all, and the diorama began to drift apart, each one still acting out the motions it had been performing, but broken and disconnected, as
if seeking a new anchor, a new referend.

He wandered on. He met a cossack leading a muzzled she-
bear by a leash of flowers, the cossack doing an odd little
half-mincing dance, the bear lumbering and growling. (It was
not a real bear, something told him, but a costume.) He
called to the cossack, "Hark! What will you with the bear?"

"Lord, I am held too homely and too shy for real women
to pleasure, and so I go to bed my she-bear, who is in heat,
and will not object to my lack of beauty."

He said, "What? This is a wild animal, dangerous of tooth
and claw! Shall we not clip her claws, muzzle her ferocious
mouth? You might be injured!"

"Nay, neither! The claws are blunt, and moreover, I will
surely wish to kiss the beast; let her be unmuzzled!"

"You are a son of truth. Do as thy wilt shall be the whole
of the law."

The pair passed on, orbiting wihin the confines of the
crowd.

He met another animal act, this one being, apparently, a
sacred cow, two people sharing a costume, one being the
front legs, head and shoulders, while the other occupied the
hind quarters. He looked into sad brown glass eyes and said,
solemnly, "You are a cow, is this so?"

Two voices replied, distantly, muffled, "This is so. We seek
peace and bucolic vision, identification with the mother spirit
of the world."

Fraesch favored the cow with a squint. "All of this is com-
mendable, and your identity is exact. This is indeed something bovine that I see before me, the udder toward my hand.
Exactly so! You are to be commended for your effort. But—
here I ask a question which is frankly speculative in
nature—what would you assay to do should you meet—a real
bull?"

There was a hurried consultation from within the cow,
conducted in whispers and murmurs. At last came the answer, "We are, in a word, at a loss. This is a contingency
we had not considered. Will you advise us?"

Fraesch answered, "Indeed I will do so: for the front quarters, you must maintain your dignity in case my contingency
becomes real. Stir not! And for the hindquarters person—you

must brace yourself!" He turned away before they had decided upon a reply.

As he circulated among the guests, he spoke now to one,
now to another, here engaging in ribald repartee, there offering advice of a dubious nature, and yet there making serious
comments when pressed as if the weight of the entire universe
were waiting upon every word. Yes, they wore outrageous
costumes, yes, they suggested a nightmare beyond all conceiv-
ing, but he saw them with the vision he had cultivated for untold years in the field, he saw into them as if they were glass,
and even with the aid if the drug they took, he saw most
clearly that they did little, however much they showed, or
gestured, or implied. It was all a potential situation, but what
actually happened was ordinary enough. Tonight, however,
things would be different; he would see to that. Skillfully, just
as he managed an operation in the dayworld by subtlety and
unseen direction and egolessness, so here, he prodded, suggested, implied, nudged, and in the end, slowly, recursively
served as a catalyst, which edged the group, as a whole, one
millimeter past the balance point. He erased the distinction in
them between dreams and possibilities, and thus unhinged and
overbalanced, they began to drift now into a new awareness.
He could feel it growing, under his feet, in the murmur in the
air, in the solar plexus, in the seat of his pants, and all
around him, slowly at first, but the rate would soon increase.
He would be at the center of it all when it came, the unutter-
able culmination of all their unleashed fantasies, yet they
would not know he was there, nor, only dimly if at all, would
they know he had initiated this. A small voice reminded him
that real bodies in the real world might perceive events differently, that they might regard this whole sequence as dangerous at the least, but he did not consider it much, for now he
did not trouble himself about those matters. This was the reality. He heard, and he knew. No more need be said.

He could not say how, by what means, this happened. It
was not a process he understood; but however it formed itself, by what transition rules it transexisted, he sensed that
one by one they were tuning themselves to him, although
there was nothing he could identify as proving this. Just a
terrible certainty, and an equally terrible sense of purpose
whose end product he could not have said in words; they had
left that behind. By the sideboard, now, Fraesch paused to

feel the yearnings of the demoniac orchestra. Now he raised an arm casually, and through the crowd there rippled a motion which in each was insignificant, but which in the whole told all. It was time. He raised it again, and now they turned now openly, waiting.

He paused in the middle of the gesture: what was it they were to do? Even at the moment of initiation, the answer was unfathomable, unknowable. As he waited, just that moment, some approached him, to urge him onward, in ordinary words whose tones carried the accents of something utterly unspeakable.

Tschimedie came, Lot's Daughter, Kethuzalem, whatever she was, with palms turned outward, showing the staring ophidian eyes painted on them. She hissed, "Speak in the loud voice, o messenger! Pour out the vial on the surface of the sun."

A princess of the ancient days, of slight figure, came near, and whispered, throatily, "And now the last mystery; bring us to it!"

Another figure, apparently a woman, dressed as a ghost, whom he had not seen before, glided across to him, purposeful and filled with will and power. For a moment, he felt hesitation; what if this one should challenge his right to lead . . . ? Now he could perceive little else about this figure, save the force of her. She wore a white hooded garment that covered her from head to toe, and within the hood, concealed her face with a veil. Only the eyes showed, dark empty openings into infinity. He said, "And your last request?"

She was immediately before him: he could feel the warmth of her body. She stopped and said calmly, absolutely neutrally, "Take this, o seer of visions and guide across the sill between the known and the unknown." With no preparation, or anticipatory motions, she deftly thrust something in his mouth, another quick, practiced motion, and he swallowed involuntarily.

He stuttered, "You. . . ."

She stepped beside him, whispered harshly in his ear, "Don't fight it, you fool! It's the antidote!"

She stood beside him, as if co-presiding, smiling and the faces which were now turned to them, avid and waiting. Fraesch struggled with the conflict of two colliding chemical messages in him, the one still trying to drive him onward, the other striving to extract the first and counter its effects. He swayed, giddily, and involuntarily made a gesture which

could have indicated denial, abdication. The faces lost some
of their unholy unison and began to move randomly, again
obeying self-generated impulses. In another moment, their attention was withdrawn, and drifting, and still another, and
they were beginning to move, no longer interested in the focus
they had created. There was a sense of deflation, of disap-
pointment, which could be assuaged by methods basic and
well-known. Cossack reached for bear, satyr for ballerina,
and Fraesch, head spinning, sank down on one knee, bracing
himself with one arm to keep from falling. The ghost sank
down on her knees beside him, and said, "Do you know me
now?"

A state of perception faded away and he lost it, the exulta-
tion, the power, the will. He was just Joachim Fraesch again.
There was a sadness and a weariness the like of which he had
never known. He stared at the visage of the ghost, and now
saw what he could not see before. Tula. He had only the
strength to nod agreement.

She said, "Come with me, now. I will lead you. They are
now too far into it to put up any organized resistance, although only a moment ago you could have commanded them
to give it to me."

He said, slowly, "That would not have been the end of it,
you know. You took a great chance. . . ." He had a lucid
moment, and then conflicting chemistry blanked his ability to
speak or feel or move, and he stopped. Tula helped him to
his feet, and together they began to drift out of the hall, into
the empty corridor, whose silence was now a blessing, and
whose coolness helped. He was still dazed, however, and only
barely noticed that Tula led him back to his own place,
rather than hers.

15

Fraesch and Tula were back in his study, and Tula was handing him a cup of hot tea. By the time they had made their way there, he had regained control of himself, stripped off the costume he had been wearing and was now wrapped up in an old bathrobe. Tula had taken his new one, being no fonder of what she had worn than Fraesch had been of his costume.

He mused, "How did you know it would go that way?"

"Actually, I didn't; but I suspected that what that drug does is to enhance a basic component of identity which is normally carefully concealed. In the case of most of these people, what comes out is rampant sexuality, more or less bizarre, because they are content to be followers, let someone else make the decisions—that type. In such an assemblage, a leader figure is necessary. They always lacked one, and so were thwarted, as from what I understand, neither Moricle nor Nachitose would participate. Moricle was by nature heavy handed, but that was compensatory behavior: he was actually a weak leader. On the other hand, you . . . I knew they would try for us sooner or later. . . . By the way, I had a time picking you out; I had no idea exactly what you'd appear as."

"What do you imagine I would have had them do?"

"I think kill Dekadice. She's a sacrificial type, no? No doubt about it—as a fact, they may patch up a procedure and kill her anyway."

"Are we safe? I thought there were extra passages connecting with her suite, because we went to the gathering another way."

"No problem there; certain sections of this complex can be sealed, if you know how to activate the mechanisms. That was the first thing I did when I got you out of there. Have no apprehensions: we are secure. Remember, I designed this place."

"Could you have done anything for her?"

"Dekadice?" Here she stopped, looking at the darkened ceiling. "Probably not. You are not one to sit still for much control, whereas she required it. For certainty, she would have resisted me, and that was a situation in which grace and style was everything. . . . Besides, what would I have gained by that?"

"You weighed it. . . ."

"Hearts or currencies, indeed do I weigh it all to a microgram. If I could return for one, who would it be? For once in my life, there wasn't much choice, although I am saddened that we were not able to do much for her. After all, what we should have done should have been done long ago. But Ciare? She would identify me as a strong woman, and make herself a pet, when what I wished to do is run with the wolves and fly with the eagles. No, there really wasn't much choosing to do."

"What shall we do with these people now? I ask your advice, as you have an interest in the proceedings here."

"I took the action. I used my authenticator, the one you saw when you investigated my apartment. . . ."

". . . You know that?"

"Yes. There's a larger unit which is part of that, remoted from it. No matter. . . . I am only surprised you waited as long as you did. But what I did was issue orders that this place be terminated—in an orderly manner. Some of them will get their notices next week, and of course they revert back to The Body Shop, Ltd. to finish out their contracts. There's a penalty for closing the lease early, of course. I specified that they are to be posted to the four winds, and paid for that, too, out of our dwindling treasury. . . ."

"What are you going to do, yourself?"

"I hadn't thought much about it . . . I thought it would be forever."

"You mean it's really over? Speculations is finished?"

"Just that," she said quietly, very subdued. "Over. Done with. We reached . . . and we didn't make it. They don't tell many stories about those kinds of adventures, do they, even though that is the most of our lives, all of us?"

"What about you yourself?"

"Naturally, I've got my own, put away for a rainy day . . . don't you?"

"Well, yes. It's not much, though. . . ."

"Mine isn't either, proportionately . . . but it will do. I live

modestly, you know . . . I've done a lot, but I came back.
Money's only good for so much, and some problems it can't
touch, and as I never lost any sleep over it—let the fools
spend it on luxuries. I mean, what could I do with, say, a
personal spacecraft, except draw attention, thieves, parasites
and terrorists to myself? I think I'll be very modest for
awhile."

"I know you well enough to know that won't last long."

"Well said! Come do it with me."

"Tula, you are a madwoman! How long do you think that
would last?"

She smiled, softly warming the space that separated them.
There was no doubt whatsoever that it was sincere. "Does
time matter to you and me any more?" As he heard it, he
knew it to be the most multiplex question he had ever heard.
She knew there could be no answer, and followed this with,
"You are good enough at what you do to free-lance at it. You
can, hence, go where you will."

"I've a contract to finish, as do most of us."

"They run out, don't they? And . . . what matter that? I
can go anywhere I want for awhile, if you will . . . take the
leap, damn it, and use the wings you've grown."

"Decisions are discounted today . . . they are four to the
den'ga, I believe, in the currency of Mulcahen. A twenty-five
grosh-worth says yes, easily enough."

She leaned forward and squeezed his hand. "Good! That's
settled at least for awhile."

Fraesch said, "Shall we continue to work on the content of
the waves? I would think you would wish to attack it, out of
curiosity, if nothing else."

Tula leaned back, and said, "Yes. Tomorrow we begin. We
won't be interrupted for awhile—this present orgy will take
several days to unwind, and they'll leave us alone. . . . Of
course, we could spend the time in bed, if you like. They
won't bother us there, either." At the last, she had a mischie-
vous smile and had settled back in her chair into a languor-
ous posture which was extremely elegant and sensual and
inviting.

Fraesch screwed up his face into what he imagined a har-
ridan might resemble, and said, in a cracked voice, "Not
tonight, dearie, I've got a headache and me hair's up in the
curlers!"

"I can well imagine . . . well, come to bed with me anyway. I am going to sleep here tonight and since I'm here, and

since I came and got you, at the least I insist on having you near me. It's been nice, you know, just that much, sometimes."

Fraesch got up, still a little unsteady, and took Tula's slender hand. They paused to glance at the conceptualizer, out of habit more than anything else. It was now failing entirely to show faces; and apparently what it was displaying was a type of visual image for which its imaging systems were not well suited. This image was a series of intersecting lines and bands of varying widths, more or less vertical and horizontal, although the bands seemed to vary somewhat from that, together, as if the view were moving rhythmically. The conceptualizer was not suited to conveying the sense of motion within time, so that the image seemed to be blurred by its motions, sliding from one state to another. And they noticed that this scene stayed on longer than the faces had, and despite its incomprehensibility and motion in time (which the faces had lacked utterly—they were static images), it seemed to possess an internal sense of correctness, of rightness. Whatever it was, it was less a dream than the faces had been.

Fraesch said so, and Tula answered, "Yes. That is what bothers me the most about this interference. But when you first came here, you did not see this kind of thing . . ."

"No. There were only the faces: more rarely, busts. And they changed with a regular rhythm. This is erratic, but it is strong, definite."

"Yes, as if something is overriding the program that cycles through the patterns stored in the memory and forcing it. All this time, we have worked on Signal and Noise, there in the lab, yet here in an ordinary machine we seem to be seeing what must be signal, not noise, and I know of no way, absolutely no way, such a thing could happen."

Fraesch nodded. "According to what I know about artifacts such as this, a malfunction would tend to increase the random noise factor."

Tula said, "Depends on which section it occurred in. What you are talking about would be true for the projection section, but you could have a breakdown in prememory or structure, and the images would still arrive whole . . . a little inappropriate, but whole. Then instead of pretty women, you could get ugly ones, or grotesques, or even nonhuman configurations."

"Those devices are preset to search out a special type of image, so I understand. . . ."

"Yes, but it's not exactly like flipping through an album of pictures at random and selecting images at random because they meet visual criteria. I mean, how do you teach a dumb machine to select women? You or I would know instantly, but the procedure by which we know is not limited to the visual, even if it is only presented that way; there are other clues, and an enormous body of comparison data stored in the human memory, all of which is used in a very short time. No, the collection sensor is not wholly visual, so one has to be very careful when one programs the search patterns, so that the input will be limited, if we intend to produce patterns of a specific type, as here. The only explanation I can think of—if the machine is operating properly—is that somewhere Moricle stored these images in his mind, and the other criteria were so strong that they override visual presentations . . . whatever this is, it represents something which was extremely meaningful to him, even more so than the faces of women, and Moricle was known to be a great lecher."

"Just so—but why now?"

"Perhaps they've been there all along—remember, it's never turned off."

"Ignore it, and it'll go away?"

"Only if you whistle to show that you don't care!"

Fraesch whistled a lame little tune, part of a bawdy song he had overheard in a tavern, and said, "Very well! We'll whistle whenever we pass the damn thing, from now onwards. Deadly things! I would no more have one of those things fitted to me than I would volunteer for a cancer transplant."

Tula was unperturbed. "They have been useful in psychiatry, and intense luxuries only the egotistical could know the full pleasure of; still, they are valuable, no matter how set; they are not reserved for lechers."

Fraesch did not answer her, and they made their way to his bedchamber, turning out lights as they went. Now the events of the last few hours began to tell on him, and his eyes became heavy, and his steps slow; Tula understood, and guided him to his place, pulling the covers over him after he had stretched out, and settling beside him herself—she, too, had been overextended. Dark sleep called to him, but just before everything faded out into that furry all-embracing darkness, he had one clear thought that shone like the sun, and then yet another! The two thoughts flowed together and became one: that Tula knew her own machine device well

enough, but all the easy explanations concealed the undeniable fact that she didn't know what was causing the problem
with the conceptualizer. And Fraesch did. It was so simple it
was stupid. And having solved that riddle, and many more
besides that were connected with it, he slept, and forgot. But
it would come to him again.

Sometime they awoke, breakfasted, and went to the lab. It
was late in the day, but it did not seem to matter; time now
was losing its meaning. Everything was unfolding, lying
down, coming unfastened. What matter hours? Sleep until
you wake, and work until you're tired. The rest might not
know it yet, but they no longer needed Fraesch. Events had
been set in motion . . . No. They had been in motion all
along.

Tula first set up a series of tests on the material they had
collected, were still collecting. These were of the nature of
rechecks on assumptions she had made earlier. And while the
computer was running these tests, they began organizing the
sounds they heard into phonetic groupings, so as to isolate
them. Tula showed him how to do part of this from a visual
display on a screen, arranging the signals from the waves by
frequency and time, vertical and horizontal, respectively.
Fraesch's task was to isolate the broad, harmonic sections and
identify them by type, using Tula's reference material as a
guide. These would be the "vowels." The remainder of the
stream was left to Tula, to isolate "consonants," inflections
and other possible signals. At first, Fraesch had a lot of questions, but he was soon proceeding on his own, and ignored
Tula and the computer entirely.

After a time, Tula stopped her work, examined the printout which the computer had provided, and came to where
Fraesch was still working.

"How many have you found so far?"

Fraesch looked up. "Twenty-nine, so far . . . The last
groups I've looked at are not producing new sounds at all.
There may be more in there, but they will be rare ones. We
may be able to reduce this list a bit; some of the sounds seem
to be repeating multiple units."

"Diphthongs?"

"Twos, maybe threes. I'm not sure."

"Have you been able to assign values to them?"

"Some. 'Ah' was fairly easy to spot, but there are variations I don't understand very well—you may be able to make more sense of them. . . ."

"I have had the same problem with the part I worked on; I think part of the problem here is that we are imagining 'speakers' for this, complete with a lung-powered oscillator. Of course, it isn't so. We apparently edit what we have heard of this so that it sounds like speech, but in reality, there are sounds in this stream which cannot be formed by any vocal apparatus I know of. You can classify consonants according to which part of the mouth they occur in, and how they are formed, but these sounds. . . ."

"What does the Mod 3000 say?"

"It says that this is coherent language, according to every test I have directed it to run. It's not an accident, or random noise we manipulate, or random, or even the signaling of animals, but directed speech. I should say, it is conversational speech, between a varying number of participants."

"Varying?"

"Yes. And they change, so that assigning identity is difficult. No 'speaker,' if I may call it that, seems to last very long. One goes, and another takes its place. Also it seems that there is some sort of internal change going on in the speaker, as well, and that the apparent sources of the emissions are mobile. All this needs looking into. So far what we have is a simple précis, a summary from the computer, based on certain assumptions I gave it. . . ." She shrugged, as if she didn't believe what her own computer was telling her. "It says we are intercepting conversations of a passing crowd."

Fraesch pondered a moment, staring at the screen. Then he said, "Then it's not 'a speaker' that we heard, even in Moricle's tape?"

"Apparently not."

"Does it bother you what might be making these sounds?"

"Yes, and no . . . In that we seem to have no manifestation of any sort of creature or being, then the sounds are just a puzzle . . . We have equipment which now hears voices in the night, from the waves, may I add, and yet we see and feel nothing."

"It worries me that we have no idea what we are dealing with. . . . Can you have the computer identify the speakers? I mean, assign them an arbitrary identity as they become heard, and track them, in reference to the physical world, to the surface of the planet?"

"Yes. The equipment, as added on by Moricle, is easily suited to that."

"Let's do that, then. . . . Feed it what we've got here and see if we can't have it print up some kind of transcript; are we to that stage yet?"

". . . Yes. Perhaps we need to classify things a little more, but we can do that."

"Let's go now with what we have. . . . the sections that won't resolve we can treat separately."

"Oh, now I see what you're getting at!"

"I want to find out what they are; we can't see them or sense them, apparently, but speakers they are, and at least I want to know what they are doing, and where they were, relative to us. It may tell us something . . . and you need this, too."

Tula looked surprised. "How so?"

"We've got an intercept, apparently of language, by a number of changing different speakers who are mobile . . . How can you break into this language totally without reference points? We have no Rosetta Stone here, you know. We can't even see them, so we can't know what they're talking about. I don't see how you are going to translate any of it, even with a computer, unless we can make some assumptions about what the speakers might be. It is a shame you issued the order to commence shutdown of the site, for there might be enough here to occupy you for years."

"Yes. You are right. I missed that, looking too hard for something else. It is a notable problem. I will set it up and have a presentation run for us now."

The first thing Fraesch suggested was that Tula instruct the computer to assign numerical identities to such individual speakers as could be identified by positional continuity, and then prepare a map, showing the paths taken by the speakers, and the points along the paths at which speechlike emissions had occurred. This would be the product of the whole section they had recorded, and would give them an idea of how many there were, and where the most activities were. Fraesch referred to it, from the beginning, as a "ghost-map."

The program was entered, registered and commenced. For one standard minute, nothing outwardly happened. This was when the Mod 3000 actually ran the program. Then it set the Tracking Register, a large automated mapping table, into operation, carrying out the program. Completing the map took almost an hour. Fraesch and Tula stood over the Tracking Register, whose original purpose was to record the test tracks received by the experimental tracking system, their faces illuminated by the light from the table's surface. First were drawn in lines of latitude and longitude, carefully drawn by a fussy little car which roamed freely over the surface, guided by lines of magnetic flux set up in the table's top. Then came an irregular, random, wandering line which passed from, more or less, north to south. Fraesch assumed that the line represented the west coast of Pangaea.

"Why wouldn't it put the station in the center of the map? It's drawing the coastline too far to the right."

"I instructed it to center according to the tracks it had; this would be right. The system, operated this way, can't follow things over land for any distance."

The printer car finished its coastline, and then hurried northwest across the map diagonally. In the far upper corner, it began drawing another north-south line, another coastline, or drawn the same.

"What's that? There's nothing out there . . ."

Tula bent closer, looking sharply. "Perhaps islands . . . there are a few . . . no, the line's continuous." She stopped and followed the line. "Wait, I see . . . that's the east coast of Pangaea it's drawing now; this map is going to show the entire Empyrean . . . at least the northern hemisphere."

Fraesch said nothing. The little car finished the east coast, and wandered around the map, putting in small islands here and there. Then it selected a point at random, and began printing a small legend, identifying the track as "Object One," and adding a date/time group. Then it began printing in the path taken by the object, changing the character of the line at places in which emission was taking place, adding time hacks at selected places.

Tula said, "This emitter would be the one which was active when I turned the equipment on. Since this is a gross overview of the whole intercept period. It will finish the track out before going to the next one. This will take some time—let's go get a bite to eat."

"Think we'll find anybody up and around?"

"Should be some stragglers about; perhaps enough that the cafeteria might even be open."

"I've lost track of time."

"It's night now. No matter, that. Are you feeling any better?"

"Mostly . . . I still get some twinges now and then. Shouldn't we start looking for Dekadice?"

"Not yet. Quite a few will still be deep in it and I don't want to chance them, just yet . . . things should be settled enough in the morning, although I fear what we may find. I want to cut them off from this drug, but I can't see any better way than removing them from the source of it."

"True . . . we don't have large-scale police, here, only Urbifrage and whoever he rounds up as deputies, if any."

"This was a problem we didn't anticipate. *I* didn't anticipate. There! So much for blame! Now if we opt for force, we get sued by The Body Shop, and have to pay rental honorariums to whoever has troops on the planet. . . ."

Fraesch contributed, "Aalet probably has some troops available."

Tula shrugged, "He'd charge us double the going rate. . . . It's funny, that: before we started this project, we could have bought KOSTORG outright, and posted Aalet off to a cesium mine at the edge of the universe. Too late for regrets, now!"

"You mean you can't afford force any more."

"Speculations will do well to pay off what debts it already has; I doubt there's a grosh left for anything else . . . well! Come on!"

The cafeteria was open, although it was barely populated, and had something of an end-of-the-world atmosphere. Fraesch and Tula ate a sandwich and left without ceremonies. No one there seemed to take any notice of them, but sat down to their orders cheerlessly and mechanically, like people with massive hangovers and no firm recollections where they had been the night before.

When they returned to the lab, the Tracking Register had just completed its mapping of the emission tracks, and was stowing the printer-car away in its compartment. Even across the room, they could see that something had been printed on the map, for its surface was covered with a network of lines; they hurried to the table to see what was there.

Neither Fraesch nor Tula had a clear idea of what they would see. Fraesch expected something more random. What was actually on the map was a massive overlay of lines which curved and swept across the surface from west to east. Far to the west, they tended to a northerly bias, only gradually leaving the east coast of Pangaea; near the west coast of the continent, they tended to move southerly, curving back to a dead-east course as they neared the shore. At the northern border of the chart, there were many beginnings, while toward the southern edge there was some eddying and backmotion, and some of the lines apparently followed the equator back to the west. Far from being disorderly, the pattern thus revealed suggested a deep and strong order.

Fraesch stared at the chart for a time, and then turned away from it. He spoke, as if to the air, "I thought this would tell us something; it asks more questions than it answers."

Tula still studied the map, saying over her shoulder, "It is not what I expected, either. This . . . this is too orderly. It looks like weather tracks."

"Computer error?"

"I don't think so; I was careful, and everything seems to be in order. And look here! The movement is always from west to east—the date/time groups of speech emissions follow the lines. . . ."

Fraesch interrupted her, "Do any of the lines come near us?"

"Yes! Many of them. They seem to curve over this way a little."

"Then whatever these emitters are, many of them have passed within sight of us?"

"I should think so. . . . Also, they are particularly active near here, say, within a thousand kilometers. Yes. And according to the coding printed on this, there is more repetition of individual sounds close to us; farther away, repetition occurs, but at a lower rate."

"I want to know what these things are, almost more than I want to know what they are saying. Can you turn that computer to real-time working, instead of using the recorded intercept?"

Tula looked at Fraesch. ". . . Yes. Yes, I can. Now that it has the basic patterns, it should be no difficulty."

"How does it follow them when they are not emitting?"

"There is some noise associated with the emitter whose content carries no language-coded information; that has been edited out of the tapes you have heard, and I imagine Moricle found that, too—his tape was clear of that."

"Tula, I have another idea, too: ask it to describe the emitter."

"Describe?"

"Whatever it can determine about the nature of the source; how big is it, how does it emit, that kind of thing."

Tula nodded, and went to the operator's console, where she touched fingerprints on a surface, which from Fraesch's point of view showed no markings whatsoever. She did this for a long moment, and stepped back. "You embarrass me; I should have thought of it months ago. A moment, there will be a printout on the screen." She watched the screen a moment, and then said, "The sources do not exhibit hard surfaces and radiate omnidirectionally, although they seem able to move the direction of the major part of the signal. That is how the tracking system is able to associate multiple emitters into coordinating groups. The source is vague in exact dimensions, but will typically be between one and three kilometers in diameter. Mind, that's on the ocean surface. If the source declines in size below that point, it stops emitting and later dissipates. If it gets larger than four kilometers, it breaks up into a major and several minor parts, which may emit later. Another thing is that in distant groups, coordinated emissions occur: they 'say' the same things together, I mean the sounds are the same patterns, but each one seems to maintain a different basic tone level."

"A natural resonance effect?"

"No. One seems to elicit responses, but once set up, they emit before the wavefronts from the others reach them."

"There is something like singing, like a chorus, on Moricle's tape."

"Yes, and what you call 'singing' is in this, too."

"Set it to real-time and ask it if an emitter is near us, or will approach us within the next few days."

"Done." Again, Tula's pale fingers traced a pattern over the smooth surface. She said, after she finished, "It will have to search out recent tracks. . . . Wait a moment." She stopped, and waited for the screen to reply. Then she read aloud, "A medium-sized emitter is approaching, course now 085 degrees, speed 30 Kilometers an hour, which will cross the coast in a few hours, say, around sunrise."

"Very good! Is it doing anything? I mean, emitting?"

"Not at the moment."

"Have the sound it makes that's not the stuff that sounds like speech piped in here over the speakers. I want to hear that, too."

Tula again manipulated the touch keyboard to the computer. "You will hear it—this is a recording of this emitter's last day prior to its present position."

It was a moment before Fraesch was conscious that he was hearing anything, the sound was so natural. In fact, it was only because it was so out of place within the lab that he heard it at all. It was a rhythmic, surging, lapping sound, somewhat like something very large moving through tall grass, steadily, without effort. Part of it sounded a little like breathing, although he wasn't so sure of that. The suggestions the sounds brought to mind were eerie and contradictory. His ears told him he heard a large, bulky animal moving through grass, *toward him,* with an onrushing pace that did not vary. His instincts shouted, *"Run!"* Very high up in frequency, there was, barely audible, a static-like crackling.

"That static . . . is it part of the emitter?"

Tula answered, "Yes. Unlike the passage sound and the speech, that crackling varies a great deal, and appears to carry no information."

"Is the passage-body larger than the emission body?"

"Yes, again. . . . The passage sound is emitted by an area about twice as large as the one which makes the speechlike sounds."

"Three choices, Tula: They are underwater, in the air, or are two-dimensional surface bodies."

"No. And no. Not underwater—they don't detour around islands, and they continue to emit after crossing the coast—the signal fades out rapidly, but not because they stop there. And the same arguments for flatland creatures. Whatever it is, it's in the air."

Fraesch nodded, and smiled to himself. Then, to Tula. "Come on—shut the place down and let's go for a walk."

"Joachim—are you still feeling that awful drug they gave you? We have to stay at it. . . ."

"If what I think is true, it won't matter much; you'll not be able to get into that 'speech' before time runs out for the site. Come on—I want to show you something . . . I think."

"You think you can see one, now, when they've passed right through us for six months and we haven't seen a thing?"

Fraesch said, enigmatically, "Seeing . . . is knowing what to look for—otherwise, the visual field is a lot of uncoordinated noise. We select what we sense. To answer your question. . . . Yes, I think we can see one. You'll understand why you'll not be able to break the speech; it's more alien than anything you can imagine, and therefore, you can't make the key assumptions that would allow you to break it."

Fraesch paused a minute. "And Tula?"

"Yes?"

"I'd almost rather that you left, as soon as you can. I can close things up here."

"Danger? How gallant to send me away. I mean it both ways, dear, true and sarcastic. Send me away? When this is my site? *Absolyut'no Nyet! Ni v kakom-nibud' sluchaye!*"

Fraesch chuckled at her exasperation which had caused an outburst in Russian. He translated to himself, "No way!"

Tula added, shaking her head, "Fraesch, we must meet this together." And she added, "Besides, were there danger, it should be I who sends you away—I know where to find you."

"Come on. See."

Tula, without notable enthusiasm, did as he asked, turning things off or switching them to a standby condition; and they left the lab building.

Fraesch took Tula's hand and led her toward the living structure, but instead of entering it by the near entrance, he detoured around it below the place where he lived, and led them out toward the beach. Some distance from the beach proper, he stopped.

After a moment, they could sense the state of time around them. The air was still, and they could smell wet sand, dry grass, the odor of the sea. To the west, the surf muttered on the shore. The air was chill, predawn, prespiring. Overhead, the sky was crystalline, and the strange stars glittered brightly, points in the heavens which had no names save numbers in a catalogue somewhere.

Fraesch said, "Course, 085. The reciprocal of that course is two-sixty-five degrees. West-southwest, to the left. Look that way, now."

Tula turned to the west and looked, with Fraesch; at first, they saw nothing: stars speckled the velvet night sky almost to the horizon. But as their eyes adjusted to the darkness, and they averted their vision a little, soon they could see, from time to time, a distant flicker beyond the horizon. It wasn't much, because the clear air gave it nothing to reflect against. But it was there, nevertheless, and unmistakable. Lightning. Weak, and far away, but that was what it was.

Tula said, "Lightning, there."

Fraesch nodded. "Exactly. We'll see more in the morning." And he turned to go back.

Tula remained where she was, staring at the west. When Fraesch stopped to wait for her to catch up, she turned to him, but did not come. He said, "It's cool, you know."

She said, softly, so softly he could barely hear her, "I know. Warm me, here. And wait with me. I understand, now. We will meet it together."

And when Fraesch went back to her, and touched her, she clasped herself to him with a fierceness he had never known, and by the time their senses had cleared again, the first stirrings of pale predawn light were shading the eastern horizon. They sat on a sand dune in a huddle, and faced the west, waiting. And the lightning on the horizon grew.

16

———————— ❖ ————————

There was a soft light behind the evergreen-clad mountains behind them, not yet driving the night away; but overhead and to the west, they had ceased to be able to see stars. Something was blotting them out, one by one.

The air, breezy as always, had calmed, and the waving, grasslike plants along the dunes had stopped rustling. All they could hear were the waves, rolling up onto the shore. In the heart of the darkness that was towering over them, lightning flickered and played in the heights, inside the cloud, illuminating it from within. There was thunder, but it was muted and distant. For the remainder of the night, they had sat in the hollow of a dune, their arms around each other, without words, without excuses, without explanations. There was no need to speak. But now that day was coming and it was near, they began stirring, moving. Speaking again.

Tula said, barely audible over the rustle of the waves, "How did you suspect this? The idea is more alien than one could imagine."

"I wasn't thinking of forms, but looking for an answer. The only alternative explanation I could have followed was ghosts—we couldn't see what was making the voices, so it had to be something we saw but didn't see as a possible source. It was the map that did it, I think: I don't remember at what point I knew. That was why I said you would not get into the speech . . . if it's even speech as we know it."

"But then these things are life-forms! They may have an intelligence!"

Fraesch added, "They could be friendly, or hostile, or indifferent. My own feeling is that it's the latter. All creatures live in different progressions of time, according to a point outside them all, but inside each one, time is the same. Each creature lives the same amount of its own time, to itself. And these things? Who knows how long they persist as individual entities, how they reproduce, what they feed on, what they excrete. No one knows these things; the weathermen track them as far as their interest goes, and they are forgotten. Judging by their speech, which we have to speed up almost six thousand times to hear as sound audible to us . . ." Think of it—if they have an intelligence, their world must whirl madly, and the sun of Mulcahen is a blur in the sky. And who knows how they perceive, what their senses are . . . what they came from. They are more alien than anything we can imagine."

Tula said, "Thunderstorms occur on most worlds. . . ."

"Surely a case of natural law. Perhaps here conditions have favored them. . . ."

She added, "Or circumstances arranged things so that we could perceive them at all . . . Joachim, there must be a way."

"I think one could be found in time . . . but there's no hurry, is there? They will be here tomorrow, as the saying goes. And what would happen if we did make contact, somehow? Could we invite one to come with us? What kind of life-support system would the ship have to have? What is the real life, the essential germ? No. Lose no sleep over it."

"What are you going to do?"

"Stay until everyone has been posted off, and then collect my check and go to find you."

"We have left much undone here; I am sad over that. Too much unaccomplished, too much undone, too much undiscovered . . . And we will never know who killed Moricle and Nachitose, either."

"Is that still bothering you? Why?"

"This whole thing here. The drug, the parties . . . it is all so foolish and so uncharacteristic of either of them, to get caught up in something like that . . ."

"What were they, really, to you?"

"Moricle was our best operative; I imagine you were able to pick up some of his traces."

". . . I know, more or less, who Moricle is. But who is Nachitose?"

Now he could see Tula's face by the light, but she turned away from him and stared out to sea, looking at infinity.

Fraesch asked her again, "Who is Nachitose?"

Tula looked at Fraesch with a hard glint in her expression, an expression of calculation. She said, softly, "You ask, 'who is' . . . when it's really 'was'."

"No was to it, but is, I think . . . At the least I suspect."

"You think they are alive? But what about the reports, what about Urbifrage the constable? What about all those oversexed maniacs?"

Fraesch laughed, "You took me skinny-dipping in a pool of warm oil and call them oversexed? We are no innocents!"

Tula shook her head in exasperation. "No, no, no! It's not what you do, but what you think you do! We became lovers, they became . . . what? Monsters, bizarre caricatures? I admit that we have probably had more of the real thing than they—it's a possibility. And why alive? How do you know? What have you seen that I didn't?"

Fraesch paused, and said, "The conceptualizer, Tula. The interference we saw in it."

"What about it?"

"Moricle had a pickup implanted in him, and presumably it's electronic, and the transmitter has limited range. It was turned off, but I turned it back on. And he was out of range. Now he's back in range. I know Moricle's alive. I kept trying to figure out what that pattern was we kept seeing, the lines and the motion. It was familiar, somehow, but I couldn't place it—it kept eluding me. But it just came to me the other night, just as I went to sleep. Ask yourself, where could they go on this planet where no one would know of them?"

"There isn't any place. Urbifrage would hear it from someone, wherever they went; or if not him, than Aalet. I know the planet's half wild, but all the same, they would be reported somewhere, except unless they . . . Fraesch! The ocean!"

"The one part of the planet that's ignored. And now answer me one last part, that only you would know: What did Moricle do for recreation? What was his hobby? I know what it has to be. . . ."

"He sailed boats on the oceans during his leaves."

"Sail-powered, not internal power?"

"Yes, yes, he was a fanatic on the subject. Only sail. Jenserico was also fond of it. . . ."

"How well do you know Jenserico?"

She answered him directly, without hesitating, "As well as one could know one's own daughter."

Fraesch asked, "How so, that? You are on Longlife . . ."

"I was not always. She was the child of my youth. That is a story I will tell you someday, for it is a long one and one I have never shared. That is your measure. But I wanted her to have the things I had gained, but also to attain them herself. It was a long and painful process."

"That was why we could not find out anything about her."

"Exactly. I left no tracks for any investigator to follow, for I wanted her to come into Speculations on her own merit. She did, finally. . . . Why has Moricle come back, now?"

"Perhaps to pick us up—or at least you. They don't know me."

Tula looked back at the ocean, and turned back to Fraesch, rapidly. "There's a ship, there, behind the point, to the left!"

Fraesch stood up and moved to the right, so as to see better around the point; he said, after peering through the grey dawn light touched with rose and violet along the edges, "Sure enough, a ship!"

Tula asked, "And why did they come back?"

"Perhaps to see what happened . . . perhaps to collect us. I know some of the old ships, too—that one there is a type called *Sacoleva,* I believe."

"It's so small!"

They could now make out the outlines of a curious little sailing ship, two masted, wooden, broad through the beam, from whose prow bow protruded a long sprit. The foremast was square-rigged, but with a large gaff sail added to it. The sprit also carried a yard for a small spritsail. The aftermast, the same height as the foremast, carried only a large lateen sail, truncated at the forward point, and served, apparently, as a support for a series of staysails supported by rigging between the two of them. It seemed to be no more than thirty, thirty-five, meters in length, but the masts were tall: the foremast carried yards for mainsail, topsail, and top-gallant courses.

Fraesch said, "The type is roomy, and good in variable winds, although no great shakes for speed . . . They probably trade between opposite coasts, coasting up and down along the coasts until they have enough for the ocean crossing. They wouldn't leave any emission tracks, and the beach people wouldn't have to worry about power sources, either—they could make them up out of what they knew, for sail power needs only native materials—wood, vegetable fiber to weave into sails and cordage."

"Why?"

"My guess is that in operating the equipment, he and Nachitose saw the first indications, just as we did, and pursued them just about the way we did, until they also heard the voices on the medium of the waves . . . and as we arrived at the conclusion that not only could we not make that 'last-decimal-point' leap to perfect the tracking system you people had designed, so equally they saw, as we did, that they couldn't get into the voices, either. Moricle simply could not fail Speculations! So they arranged this way out. So much I imagine is the way it has gone. But they could not accept the failure, as you did, nor could they make the decision and execute it."

"We reached so far, here."

"Not far enough. And yet perhaps their answer is not entirely a bad one, either. The images which were interfering with the memory being displayed in the conceptualizer surely represented something powerful and moving to Moricle, something that could even, in real life, override his imagined lusts. And though we never saw Nachitose, I would imagine that there was enough for her to go along with it. It would be easy to pull it off—all they had to do was wait until the people at the site were either blown to the winds, or recovering, and arrange a mechanical accident. And no one would think to look out to the ocean, for a wooden ship fading over the horizon."

"Why wouldn't Urbifrage suspect it?"

"He didn't have good contact with the beach people; he was oriented to the land, and to our civilization, however much a wild man he might have become. Urbifrage was an exile, forever looking back; but the beach people, poor and primitive, were looking forward. I know that KOSTORG will run their operation here and eventually pull out and go on to another world, and all these miners and settlers and others will follow them after a time—that's the way our universe is, yours and mine and Aalet's and Urbifrage's, too. But not those people who showed Moricle how to escape the round he was on."

Now Fraesch stood up, absentmindedly brushing sand off himself. He extended his hand to Tula.

She took it, getting to her feet, and saying, "Where are we going?"

"Down there; let's go talk to them. Perhaps they'll invite us along."

"You wouldn't go?"

"Why not?"

Tula looked away, and then back. "I don't want to."

"Wait for me, here, then. I'll be but a minute." And as Fraesch began trudging down the sandy slopes of the dunes toward the left, to the little creek that flowed into the sea, now greenish-purple under the eaves of the storm. Overhead the thunder muttered to itself, sounding farther away than ever, but the overhang of the cloud covered most of the sky, and even the east was beginning to film over.

Fraesch negotiated the sandbar and climbed over the rocks to the cove, above which the house of Collot still sat quietly, facing the sea—from which the voices came. The house was dark and still; he sensed that she was not there. Perhaps on the ship. And at last he reached the bottom of the cove and stood on the wet rocks opposite the ship while lazy waves sloshed onto them without energy, lazily. Here, the ship looked larger and more seaworthy than it had from the beach, although its size had not changed. At anchor, the sails carefully furled, it did not lose its sense of belonging to things which flowed and moved in time.

There was motion, activity on the ship; people were moving about, and sounds drifted across the water. The activity seemed purposeful and directed, as if they were getting ready to do something. Were they preparing to leave?

A small boat, tied to the stern, was untied and brought along the side, where it was held while someone climbed down to it; a figure seemingly dressed in a brown blanket, Collot, surely. She settled into the tiny rowboat and set out for the rocks alone. As she rowed across the small distance that separated the ship from the shore, Fraesch saw that aboard the ship, several people were cranking the anchor up with a windlass, which began to turn the ship toward the open sea. Another climbed out on the bowsprit and began untying the spritsail. Still turning slowly, the ship began to feel a weak breeze drifting down from the rocks. Two of the indistinct figures came to stand by the rail, to watch the progress of the rower. They seemed aware that he was there, but took no special notice of him.

One was slender, a woman, he thought, with sharp features, wearing a complicated turban, while the other was a heavyset man whose black, curly hair hung loosely from under a headband. Moricle and Nachitose? Another figure joined them at the rail, this one slender and slight, boyish of figure. The distance was frustrating, for it was close enough to make out some features, but not close enough to be sure. Dekadice?

The rowboat slid up to the rocks, and Collot climbed out, and pulled the boat up onto the shore. It was light, just a shell

of some marine creature turned upside down. When she had
secured the shell, she came to stand beside Fraesch.

He said, "Moricle and Nachitose."

"Yes. And the girl, too. We were there, and took her without anyone being the wiser."

"They came back for her?"

"For anyone who would leave . . . they came here more
or less in the course of their travels."

The figures standing by the rail of the ship raised their
hands in greeting—or farewell. Fraesch waved back. Collot
said, "There is still time, if you would adventure with
them. . . ."

Fraesch looked back up the shore to the site, then to the
ship, which was now almost stern to them. He said, "I couldn't
get Tula in time."

Collot said, "She wouldn't go anyway. It was you that they
invited, if you wish."

Fraesch looked at the ship, at the dark sky, at the sea. And
once more at Collot, standing barefoot in the wash of the cold
waves. There were no words he could say. But after a moment, he began climbing back up the rocks, never looking
back. As he climbed, he felt a chill wind start up, erratic, but
generally out of the northeast. And when he had crossed the
bar at the mouth of the creek and returned to the spot where
he and Tula had sat, and found Tula waiting for him, then
he looked back at the ocean, at the Empyrean Sea, where a
sailing ship was moving out from the shore, gathering way
with every moment as more and more sails were unfurled
and sheeted into position. Lightning descended from the upper reaches of the cloud and played all around them, and
they felt waves of prickling pass over them.

Tula said, "Was it so?"

"Yes. Just as I imagined. Dekadice was with them. They
came into the party in disguise, and carried her off."

"And us?"

"Collot said I could go . . . and that you wouldn't."

"Both are true . . . I see you remained behind, for some
reason. May it be that you not regret your choice."

Fraesch laid a gentle hand on her shoulder and turned her
back toward the site. He said, softly, "There are adventures,
and there are . . . other adventures. I will make no judgments, but be true to what I have been. Come along, now—
we have much to do, and schemes to plot."

Tula added, "and other seas to sail on, I think. But I will

take as much as I can of the records we made. I intend to get
to the bottom of this and someday, come back here."

"You're not serious."

"I want to know what those things were saying—perhaps
they were speaking to us."

"And," he chuckled, "perhaps they were not."

During the next few weeks, as the warm season returned to
the North Coast, one by one, the people who had been assigned to Halcyon station drifted off as their reassignments
came in. Some found immediate placement with another job,
others were returned to a holding area maintained by The
Body Shop. A few were released, with payoffs, and they
drifted off to find their own way. Tula arranged with Aalet
for Urbifrage to act as her agent in disposing of everything
portable, and last of all, she and Fraesch also left. All that
remained of the massive effort they had mounted here was
contained in a small package, which contained transcripts
and tapes.

The train approached them as they waited for it in the village. Smoke pouring out the stack, steam blowing off at the
four cylinders driving its articulated underframe, the boiler
swinging far to left and right as the front part negotiated
curves before the main frame had entered them, it was an
antique terror out of the far past of man's machines, hissing,
puffing and emitting a piercing high whistle that made
Fraesch's teeth vibrate. Now they saw details of it they could
not have seen before: three headlights illuminated by tung-
sten arcs which cast a blinding bluish light, and on the front
pilot beam, enormous hydraulic buffers used to help set tension between locomotive and cars. The boiler itself was
sheathed in brass plate, and polished to a high shine. They
felt the heat on their faces as it passed them.

Tula looked at the machine and sighed, shaking her head.
"If I had seen that at the beginning, I might not have
come."

Fraesch nodded agreement. "True; but if we knew, would
we do anything?"

And Tula said, "This is the way back . . . I hope the bandits have been pacified, at least for this trip."

Fraesch helped her lift her bags to the floor of the car
they picked, and together, they climbed aboard and found a
compartment. And after a moment, for On The Waves was

but a small stop, the train jerked, and moved, and began laboring up the grade into the hills. The air was limpid and transparent, and the conifers were streaming clouds of yellow pollen in the afternoon light, and far out to the west over the water, a thunderstorm lay in massed banks on the horizon, and grew ice flowers into the aqua skies of Mulcahen.